HARLEQUIN IS DEAD

Richard Brinsley Sheridan Mysteries

Book One

R M Cullen

SAPERE
BOOKS

HARLEQUIN IS DEAD

Published by Sapere Books.

24 Trafalgar Road, Ilkley, LS29 8HH

saperebooks.com

ISBN: 978-0-85495-639-5

For Mum

ACKNOWLEDGMENTS

First and foremost, I would like to thank my family for all their support over the years. In particular I owe a debt of gratitude to my late mother who loved me to read to her, preferably over a cup of coffee and a chocolate éclair. Her enthusiasm spurred me on and when she made a comment it was always insightful. My sister, Patricia Jones, likewise has brought the instincts of a voracious reader to bear on my efforts.

Old friends and former colleagues read early drafts or patiently listened to me wittering on about the story, for which they have my heartfelt thanks. Carole Thomson, always the toughest of critics. Jan Weddup with a beady eye, sharp as a tack. Ellen Fox and Olly James, forever kind and supportive. A thank you also to E. M. Powell for her professional eye.

I have been truly blessed to belong to the South Manchester Writers group. The feedback in the group sessions and from beta readers who tackled the whole manuscript kept me on track and determined to improve the novel with each draft. My thanks in particular go to Patricia Cunningham, Peter Barnes, Jane Byrne and Seamus Daly.

My interest in Sheridan's political career began as a student; in large part thanks are due to the direction from my tutor, Frank O'Gorman, now Professor Emeritus of History at Manchester University.

Lastly, a huge debt of gratitude to Sapere Books for taking on my Sheridan series and in particular I am grateful to my editor, Amy Durant, who has wielded the red pen with great flair and licked the final manuscript into a shape which I can feel proud of.

CHAPTER ONE

London, 1791

Richard Brinsley Sheridan had come to witness her death. It had been a long and harrowing process. The interior stripped quite bare, the work of demolition on Old Dame Drury might now begin in earnest.

Sheridan stood on the pavement, gazing up at the ageing façade of his theatre. He nodded as the foreman of his works, Mr Knatchbull, made his report. Workmen were already on the roof, setting about its destruction. Their shouts drifted down over the noise of the traffic on Drury Lane, hawkers crying their wares, carts trundling over cobbles, the clip-clop of horses' hooves. Sheridan stepped aside to allow a lady and her maid to pass, before again fixing his gaze on his theatre to stamp the image in his mind forever.

Designed by Sir Christopher Wren — in whose times Nell Gwyn had trod those very boards to great acclaim — it had seen the first productions of Sheridan's *The School for Scandal*, and of his teasing satire *The Critic*. Occasions for pride and glory. In those heady days the ownership and management of the Theatre Royal and the writing of plays had been the great sum of his ambitions.

That was before the clarion call to another stage had swept him into Westminster as the Member of Parliament for Stafford and diverted so much of his energies. Still, he could not entirely neglect his theatrical interest. He had not been born to wealth or privilege. This theatre was his estate, his means. Here came all the world, from the lowest to the very highest, to pay court to him. He could have sworn that there had not been a dry eye in the house when the final curtain fell; certainly his own eyes had been wet.

Old Drury was all packed up. Sets, props, and costumes, and a precious library of scripts and music scores, had all been temporarily rehoused. Having long waited to be filed and sorted, sundry ledgers would now be in even greater disarray. The image afforded Sheridan some satisfaction. He withdrew a flask from his coat pocket and took a swig of brandy. For once he had a plausible excuse to keep his creditors at bay; how should he know what he might owe them without the proofs?

A sharp yell came from above and he was yanked backwards by his foreman as a piece of masonry hurtled over the edge of the roof. Plaster exploded into a thousand fragments at his feet in a cloud of billowing dust.

'God's teeth!' Knatchbull exclaimed. 'I'll have their hides, sir.'

Sheridan flicked debris from his sleeve. 'Perhaps a cordon, Mr Knatchbull, might be advisable.'

'Straight away, sir.'

Sheridan retreated to the other side of the street. He snorted. Really, who would miss Dame Drury? She had lost the last vestiges of charm, with her shabby draperies and her parlous state of repair, her stinking warren of dressing rooms and her rancid offices. It would have bankrupted him to keep her alive any longer. The order to demolish was a blessing in disguise. He was free to envisage the grand palace of entertainment which would rise in her place, with only the trifling matter of raising the necessary funds through debentures to keep him awake at night.

'Mr Sheridan! Good day to you, sir!'

Timothy Legge waved an arm as he hastened across the busy thoroughfare, awkwardly sidestepping an old woman with bundles of kindling heaped on her bent shoulders. She let loose a stream of ripe curses and the young man backed away apologising, narrowly avoiding a coal cart, before he arrived breathless at Sheridan's side.

'Timothy, you look as browbeat as my theatre.' Sheridan gestured to the bruises on the man's face.

'Oh, it is nothing, sir. I am returned from Birmingham.'

'Ah.' Sheridan nodded in comprehension. 'You have faced down the rioters single-handed?'

'As near as, dammit!' Timothy's eyes flashed with fury. 'Those rioters deliberately set upon us; and I am certain they were paid!'

Sheridan put a hand on the young man's shoulder. 'Come, here is the Cock and Magpie. Take a jug with me and tell me all.'

Timothy took a deep breath to calm himself. 'I apologise, sir. I interrupt your business?'

'I am done. I have delivered her eulogy. Old Dame Drury is quite dead to me now.'

'She shall rise again, Mr Sheridan.'

'Like a phoenix — but without the flames, I am assured! All manner of safety curtains and waterworks are planned to avert any conceivable threat of fire; she shall be a new theatre for the modern age.'

Sheridan and his companion found a snug corner and were soon tucking into platters of steaming pigeon pie with a good mountain of potato. For all the fright of the unrest in Birmingham, Sheridan's young friend had not lost his usual hearty appetite. Sheridan regarded him paternally. Timothy was the second son of a constituent, Josiah Legge, a kindly, honest man of trade. Whilst the elder son had joined his father's business, Timothy had chosen to study law, serving in chambers at the Inns of Temple. He had also immersed himself in the reformist movements of the day.

Dark auburn hair tumbled about his ears in unruly curls, whilst warm hazel eyes held both sincerity and steadfast purpose. There was always some petition he was canvassing. The working conditions for Staffordshire miners in Botteslow or Cannock. The abolition of the slave trade. The scourge of rotten boroughs over which he would fairly thump on the table. The Revolution in France had only served to increase his zeal for the ideals of democracy and fraternity.

'The riots began in consequence of a dinner arranged by Mr Priestley?' Sheridan prompted.

'To celebrate the anniversary of the Bastille.' Timothy nodded, raising his voice above the general hubbub of the tavern. 'The rioters then marched to Mr Priestley's house at Fair Hill, shouting for Church and King, but there was no jot of Christian feeling amongst them, nor honour to King George — they were set only on looting and burning! The apparatus of his experimental work laid waste — at what cost to humanity, Mr Sheridan?' Timothy's jaw tightened as he stabbed his fork into a piece of pie.

Sheridan sighed. 'A great loss.'

'Several of the rioters made free with John Ryland's wine cellar at Baskerville House and then were too drunk to save themselves in the conflagration which they had started! And where were the militia? Three days of wanton destruction before the dragoons arrived.' Timothy thumped the table, rattling the plates. 'These rioters think to demonstrate their patriotism, but tell me, Mr Sheridan, what is patriotic about burning down the house of a man who would do more of benefit and worth than the king and his government ever would?'

'Timothy —' Sheridan waved his hand to indicate that young Mr Legge should lower his voice. 'Have a care when you talk of the king and Mr Pitt; there are spies and informants everywhere these days.' Timothy was right, of course — what had His Majesty King George III ever done for the poorer sort? But the too loud expression of this view in a crowded tavern courted danger.

'The authorities mean to quell our radical voice, Mr Sheridan, but we shall not be silenced.'

'Do not lose heart, Timothy. You may find the voice for reform raised still in Manchester or Edinburgh. And in parliament.'

'Of course, sir, you are ever at the forefront in matters of reform.' Timothy's eyes gleamed with fervour. 'Have you read Mr Paine? His *Rights of Man*, just published? I hear him speak at the end of the month.'

Sheridan was saved from confessing to that omission when he caught sight of Mr Knatchbull, heading in his direction. He groaned inwardly; this was no doubt a signal that the workmen were again threatening to lay down their tools unless some dispute of payment were settled.

Knatchbull snatched his hat from his head and made a curt bow. 'Pardon the interruption, Mr Sheridan, but I need you to come at once.'

'Let me go, yer stinkin' bunghole! I told yer I ain't took nuthin'!'

Sheridan peered with bemusement at the small boy in the pool of light afforded by the foreman's lantern. In the gloom of the backstage area he looked to be no more than six years of age, but then he might well be stunted if he had crawled out of the fetid squalor of the nearby rookeries.

A thickset workman held the ragged creature by the scruff of the neck as the scrap squirmed and protested. He let out a volley of ripe oaths, which were more a show of bravado than any serious attempt to put up a resistance.

'You ain't had the chance, yer little chit, that's why.' The workman gave the boy a tweak of his earlobe.

Mr Knatchbull turned to Sheridan. 'We can take him down to Bow Street if you like, sir. Or Jedidiah here can give him a good thrashing for his trespass.'

'Oh, surely not,' Timothy Legge interjected, looking alarmed. He turned to Sheridan. 'The child is clearly malnourished and perhaps thought only to find some small item of salvage. After all, the theatre is empty.' Timothy smiled kindly on the boy. 'What may we call you?'

The urchin glared from beneath furrowed brows. 'None of yer beaky business.'

'Oi, you little scut.' Jedidiah tweaked the boy's ear again. 'That's a gentleman yer speakin' with, so mind yer manners.'

'Do you have a parent?' Timothy continued, crouching down to the boy's level.

The child shook his head sullenly, watching Jedidiah all the while from the corner of his eye.

'An orphan?' Timothy straightened and sighed. 'Do you know, I consider he may have been misused, Mr Sheridan. There is much ill-treatment of children in our society.'

Sheridan could see that the filthy little rascal presented the young lawyer with the subject of yet another favourite hobbyhorse.

'Some rogue has seen an opening to the building and squeezed the boy through to search out anything of value. I have heard of such villainous coves.'

Sheridan appraised the boy keenly. 'I should have thought that a boy like you knows how to keep hidden in dark corners... I wonder that you have been caught at all.' Sheridan shook his head to underline his amazement.

The workman let out a deep, guttural laugh. 'He claims to have seen a devil, sir! Came streaking up them cellar stairs, yelling fit to wake the dead, right into my arms!'

'A devil? In my cellars? Did he wield a pitchfork? All ready to toss you into hell's fires? I should like to see that fellow.'

Mr Knatchbull interposed and gestured below. 'Nothing that I could see, sir. The last of the barrels were shifted only this morning. There was a lantern set at the bottom of the stairs. The lad as like snuck down and then took fright when it burnt out and all went dark.'

The boy shook his head, staring wide-eyed up at Sheridan. 'I saw him, mister, honest I did! He's beneath the floor — the very devil — I thought he was gonna grab me and pull me down — then the little bit o' light went out and I — I thought I was done for!'

'Indeed?' Sheridan nodded. 'Have you ever thought of becoming an actor? Your performance is so lively — I am quite tempted to believe you.'

'On me honour.'

Jedidiah snorted and tugged the boy up by the scruff of his neck. 'Honour, me lad? Only the sort to be found amongst thieves and cutthroats.'

'I believe the boy, Mr Sheridan.' Timothy asserted. 'He has had some genuine fright.'

'Mr Knatchbull,' Sheridan said, turning to the foreman, 'I should like to take a look below, if you please. My curiosity has quite overwhelmed me. If there is a demon down there, I should have to inform him that we are currently closed to auditions but he shall find many a devil taken on at the Covent Garden Theatre.'

'As you wish, sir.'

'Tom, you must lead the way, and I think Jedidiah may safely release you for the present.'

The workman let go of the boy with a grunt and shoved him towards the entrance to the cellars.

'Please, sir, don't make me go down them stairs again!'

'Sadly, it is either that or the magistrates' court in Bow Street. Which is it to be, Tom?'

The boy scowled in defeat. 'Why'd you call me Tom? My name's Billy.' He rubbed at his earlobe.

Sheridan clapped his hands. 'Ah, Billy! I knew you for either a Tom or a Billy. My son is called Tom, you see, and you remind me of him, though he is now fifteen years old and taller than you, of course. Lead the way, Billy. We are right behind you; you need have no fear when we have Mr Legge with us. As you can see from his battle scars, he is a fighting man and the devil should be made to think twice.'

They began their descent down the uneven stone steps into the theatre's cellars, the foreman following the boy with his lantern and Jedidiah bringing up the rear. The darkness was profound. Sheridan groped his way down the stairs with one hand on the dank walls to steady himself. It was many years since he had ventured down into these particular cellars. It was deeper than the area under the stage, where one might find the mechanisms for trapdoors and where parts of scenery might be stored — that area had been in constant use. But these cellars were seldom entered. A fusty, chilly miasma seemed to rise up from below. A stench of decay. One could well imagine this to be the lair of some sinister and malevolent creature.

Mr Knatchbull arced his lantern about the desolate space. 'I see nothing, as I said. Show us your devil then, boy — and do not try to give us the slip; you will not get past Jedidiah.'

Billy pointed into the darkness. ''T'were over there.'

Reluctantly the boy allowed himself to be nudged forward. Timothy moved ahead and gave the child's shoulder a reassuring squeeze.

'Perhaps it was a rat you saw, Billy. Their beady eyes might glitter in the lantern's glow and give anyone a fright. I myself have always had a horror of rats.' The young man shivered to emphasise his abhorrence.

Billy shrugged the hand from his shoulder. 'I know rats well enough, mister — 't'weren't no rat.' He stopped and gestured. 'There. Under that stone.'

Sheridan squinted and could make out a runnel of slab stones set in the floor.

The foreman grunted in recognition. 'There's an old drain underneath. Streams run underground all about the city, and this may feed in.' He swung his lantern along the course of the channel and stopped to illuminate a loose slab. He approached and then strained to peer into the gap below.

Mr Knatchbull suddenly recoiled. 'Egad! I think there is something!'

Sheridan felt his heart quicken with an irrational fear.

No demon with forked tongue leapt forth to greet them, however, and Knatchbull quickly regained his composure. 'Jedidiah, give us a hand to shift this stone.'

The brawny workman grunted and laid his lantern down by the side of the runnel. He bent and slid the long length of stone up onto the neighbouring slab with ease.

Billy flinched and took a step back. Any intention to use the distraction to slip away was forestalled by Timothy, who seized the boy's arm as he leaned in for a closer look. 'God help us — what is that?'

A masked skull stared up at them. The mask covered the nose and eye sockets, below which a jawbone hung open in a wide scream. It was picked clean of flesh, an array of teeth stark in the lamplight. The frayed remnants of a cockaded hat framed the skull.

'It is Harlequin!' Sheridan pointed to a short wooden paddle that lay alongside what remained of the corpse. 'See, there is his slapstick.'

Timothy yelped as a rat scurried across the diamond-patterned costume which shrouded the skeleton. 'What is he doing here?' he exclaimed.

'I rather suspect he has met with foul play, Timothy,' Sheridan offered. 'This Harlequin has been murdered.'

CHAPTER TWO

A workman was dispatched at once to the Bow Street Public Office. In due course a young officer arrived and introduced himself as Petty Constable Nicholls.

He bowed to Sheridan and Mr Knatchbull. 'I apologise, gentlemen, that only I can be spared at this present juncture.'

'This looks like murder, Constable — not some theft of a bag of nails.' Mr Knatchbull puffed out his chest.

The tall, dark-haired constable sighed his regret. 'The magistrates have set all available constables and watchmen on patrols about the city this evening, sir, ordered to be alert to any threat of violence in the wake of the rioting in Birmingham. The fear is of contagion.'

'I do not doubt the magistrates are right to be prepared, Constable Nicholls,' Sheridan said. 'These are unsettling times. I trust the Public Office will protect all good citizens, whatever their political persuasion.'

Nicholls nodded curtly. 'I would hope so, sir.'

'But you cannot be certain.'

Nicholls grimaced and changed the subject. 'Is the victim known to you, Mr Sheridan?'

Sheridan pursed his lips. 'I don't doubt I will have had a passing acquaintance with the fellow, perhaps paid his salary.'

'One of your theatre company, then?'

Sheridan nodded. 'But I have no name for him as yet, other than Harlequin.'

Nicholls looked puzzled.

'You shall understand when we take you below to see the remains.'

'Who found the body?'

'A boy named Billy. Very small and very grubby.'

Nicholls nodded in understanding. 'I imagine the theatre has been beset by scavengers from the day the company moved out.'

'You'd not be wrong there, Constable,' Mr Knatchbull muttered. 'My men must have their tools about them all the time, for if they turn their back for just one moment, they will have been stolen.'

'Where is this boy now?'

'A young friend of mine, Mr Legge, has insisted on taking Billy to the pie and eel shop on the corner. He felt the boy was in need of sustenance after so dreadful an encounter. A good, hearty meal is Mr Legge's preferred answer to any upset.' Sheridan withdrew his brandy flask from his pocket. 'We are all in need of a restorative, I can assure you, Constable. It is not a sight for the faint-hearted.' He took a swig.

'I shall need to speak with him after.'

'Naturally.'

Mr Knatchbull ushered them down the stone stairs so that the constable might view the remains in the cellar. A ring of lanterns had been set in place and Jedediah had stayed on guard.

'I've kept jollier company,' he said in greeting as they approached.

Sheridan shuddered to imagine such murderous goings-on in his theatre. He tried to imagine who this Harlequin might be. Actors were transient by nature, particularly the performers in pantomimes and interludes. Posturers, jugglers, singers and dancers, they all came and went. Many were foreigners — French, Italian, Dutch — or hailed from Scotland or Ireland, or some other far-flung corner of the British Isles. These were the low entertainers, looked down upon by the Shakespearean tragediennes who displayed a sneering contempt. A number of these performers, the more skilled who could command the fee, ran between shows at different theatres on the same evening, sometimes as far afield as Sadler's Wells or Astley's Royal Grove. The task of identifying this Harlequin would be no easy matter.

From what Sheridan had glimpsed by the lantern light, the victim was little more than a skeleton. None of them had cared to examine it more closely. Who knew when the man had died? The poor unfortunate might have come to his end years before in these dank cellars, rotting in his unmarked grave. Sheridan shivered at the thought. It had been natural to assume that he had been murdered, for who would willingly place themselves in a stinking drain? The victim was still in costume, which implied that his death must have happened on the premises. The killer had been intent on keeping the body from discovery and had brought the corpse down to this lonely place. Or, perhaps Harlequin had been lured to the cellars and the murder had been committed beyond all prying eyes. Yes, that made sense.

Nicholls knelt by the side of the runnel and was studying the remains intently.

'When did the theatre close, sir?'

'On His Majesty the King's birthday, the 4th of June.'

'Five weeks ago...' The constable reached in to move the Harlequin's hat. Some strands of dark hair remained.

'Do you have any suggestion as to how long this sad corpse may have lain here, Constable?' Sheridan asked.

'That is guesswork, sir, but —' Nicholls carefully slid the mask up over the skull, which gleamed in the lamplight — 'I should say these bones are not so long exposed. Within the year; perhaps no more than three or four months.'

Sheridan frowned. 'Might decay be so very rapid?'

'Not decay, sir.' The constable looked up. 'This man has been picked clean by rats. I should think there are any number of the creatures down here, and they will have made short work of him.'

Sheridan felt his stomach churn; he reached again for his flask.

'See his costume,' the constable continued, fingering the diamond-patterned cloth. 'The ruff and jerkin are stained, but the colour is not faded. His hat is still in shape.'

'Within the year, you say?' Sheridan swigged at his brandy. To his disappointment, the flask was now empty.

'I might even hazard the murderer chose this spot quite deliberately, reckoning the rats would leave little to signify who his victim might be.' Nicholls nodded to himself. 'If the killer knew that the theatre was to close and demolition follow soon after, then feeding the corpse to the rats might be an excellent strategy.'

'And yet,' Sheridan pondered, 'the victim wears his costume still — and all the accoutrements of that part, the mask and the slapstick. Odd, if the murderer did not intend for the man to be identified.' He gave a puzzled laugh. 'But who should know how the mind of a killer works?'

Nicholls leaned further in and reached for the skeletal throat. After some moments, he re-emerged holding aloft a small fragment of bone, which he examined. 'I believe your actor has been strangled. Perhaps garrotted. This small bone — the hyoid, I believe it is named — is fractured. I have seen similar in such instances; I sometimes attend the anatomies, sir,' he added by way of explanation.

Sheridan eyed the young constable with fresh interest. He was tall and well built. His hair, pitch-black and tied back, framed a well-chiselled face with a slight hook to his nose. It would seem the young constable's interest in this murder was piqued by curiosity alone, as there had been no talk as yet of rewards or financial inducement to investigate the matter.

'I should like to see his killer brought to justice,' said Sheridan. 'But how might that be done?'

Nicholls shook his head. 'I do not know, sir. Until we know who the victim might be, we cannot discover who had cause to see him dead.'

'Nor who might pay for his funeral and say a prayer over his grave,' Mr Knatchbull murmured. 'Poor soul.'

'I shall see that he receives the proper rites, Mr Knatchbull,' Sheridan assured the foreman. It was the least that he could do for one who had been of his company, even if he might never know what name to have engraved on the headstone. A thought occurred to him. 'Constable, might you reach down for the slapstick?' He pointed. 'That paddle beside the body.'

Nicholls retrieved the stick and handed it up to Sheridan. It was in fact two thin pieces of wood strapped together at the base. The design allowed for a loud whacking noise whenever the Harlequin hit another character on the posterior during the comic chase sequences. With perfect timing, the business never failed to bring gales of laughter from the audience. Sheridan tapped his own thigh and heard a pleasing resemblance to a whack. He searched the implement for any decoration.

In recent decades, the Harlequin, as much magician as trickster, would also use the stick to transform the stage scenery. By knocking down a series of hinged flaps on the scenery flats, he would appear to flee from one location to another during the chase scenes. Sheridan wished that he could tap this 'magic wand' and transport them all to another scene entirely, one that did not include murder.

He sighed with frustration. He could see no initials carved into the stick, no distinguishing marks to identify the owner.

'Something glitters.' Nicholls was still looking down at the skeleton. He glanced at the workman, who was holding a lantern. 'A little closer, if you would, Jedidiah.'

In reaching for the slapstick, the costume had been caught, revealing something shining beneath. Nicholls reached down and withdrew a metal object from within the Harlequin's jerkin. He held it up to the light.

Sheridan saw something resembling a brooch. Finely decorated and filigreed, it was shaped into an equal cross, with four triangular arms fanning out from a central circle, each of the eight tips marked with a small ball. Between the arms of the cross were four fleur-de-lys. Sheridan had seen nothing like it before.

'A fine piece of jewellery for a member of the pantomime,' he commented.

Nicholls rubbed at the metal and it gleamed silver. 'Not jewellery; it is a religious cross, sir.'

'It looks more like a medal than a cross.'

Nicholls nodded in agreement. 'The design is based on the Order of the Holy Spirit.'

The constable rose to his feet and presented the pendant for Sheridan's inspection. 'There is often, in addition, a small representation of a dove hanging from the cross — the symbol for the Holy Spirit. A spirit of resistance in the face of persecution. It is missing here, but you may note this broken link. This is a Huguenot Cross, sir. The four arms are the Gospels. See these eight points at the extremities of the cross; they represent the eight Beatitudes. Between, there is the four fleur-de-lys, each with three petals — that is for the twelve apostles. And this open space where the arms of the cross and flower join, that is in the form of a heart. To signify loyalty.'

Sheridan squinted at the cross. 'How come you to know all this, Nicholls?'

'My mother is Huguenot, sir.'

'You are French then?'

Nicholls laughed and shook his head. 'In only a small degree might I be called French, despite my name being Louis-Pierre. My mother's ancestors came to London over two hundred years ago. My father, however, is a mason whose family came down from Bedford. He is English.'

'A Huguenot Cross... Well, that must provide some indication as to who this Harlequin might be.'

'You have records and ledgers of payment to your company that will suggest a name?'

Sheridan spread his arms wide. 'Two months ago that might have been an easy matter. But as you can see, Constable, we are all packed up.'

Nicholls looked disappointed.

'The treasurer may have lists of the company accounts, but everything is in disorder. No, it will be quicker by far to seek out the man who habitually plays the part of Clown. They are something of a tandem, Harlequin and Clown, as you might be aware if you have ever seen the *commedia dell'arte* or the harlequinade, Constable?'

'I have had little time for the theatre, sir.'

'That omission must be corrected. I shall invite you to our next season, Mr Nicholls.'

'Do you know where this Clown is to be found?'

Sheridan nodded. 'He is presently at Sadler's Wells. And rather promisingly, the man we must ask for is a Frenchman to boot: Monsieur Dubois.'

Nicholls brightened. 'Then we may soon know this unfortunate victim's name.'

'Yes, I rather hope we shall.' Sheridan gazed down at the remains, which had been stripped of their horror and become instead a spectacle of pathos. No one seemed to have raised an alarm at this man's disappearance. Would there be any who would mourn him? Sheridan would make enquiry about a Huguenot church. The man might at least be buried among his fellows. Mr Knatchbull could arrange to have the remains removed to Mr Lowe, an undertaker who had once been a carpenter at the theatre.

'Shall Monsieur Dubois be at Sadler's Wells this evening, sir?' asked Nicholls.

'I don't doubt.'

'Once I have spoken with the boy, I shall go straight there.'

'I shall accompany you, Constable. We may go in my carriage.'

'That will not be necessary, Mr Sheridan.'

'You have not met Monsieur Dubois,' Sheridan said, ominously.

'As you wish, sir.' Nicholls held out the cross. 'Will you take this for safekeeping, Mr Sheridan? Once the identity of your actor is known, you might find a relative.'

Sheridan weighed the cross in his palm. It was a striking piece and must have had some value aside from the sentimental. He slipped it into his waistcoat pocket.

CHAPTER THREE

Sheridan and Constable Nicholls had found Billy at the pie and eel shop, where he was enthusiastically tucking in to a second helping. The appearance of the Bow Street Runner caused instant alarm, and the boy looked about desperately for an avenue of escape.

'Billy, is it not?' Constable Nicholls asked.

The boy bit his lip and shrank behind Timothy.

Timothy rose from the table and bowed curtly. 'Constable, allow me to introduce myself: I am Mr Timothy Legge, student of law, and —' he glanced at Billy — 'Billy's legal representative.'

Sheridan raised an eyebrow; it seemed young Mr Legge had found another cause worthy of his best efforts.

Nicholls' eyes narrowed. 'What possible case may you present, Mr Legge, when this urchin was caught on the premises? He may rightfully be charged with trespassing, breaking and entering —'

Timothy interrupted. 'But Mr Sheridan will surely not press any charges — nothing was taken!'

Nicholls raised his chin. 'It is the duty of the Public Office to tackle the scourge of thieves in this great city.'

'Sir, you cannot mean to arrest this boy?' Timothy laid a hand on Billy's shoulder as if to pre-empt any such action.

'We cannot return him to whence he came, where he may re-join the Blackguard Youth and grow and prosper in villainy.'

Sheridan shrugged. 'I do believe the constable makes a fair point, Timothy.'

Timothy was defiant. 'And at Newgate he will certainly mix with true villains of the very worst sort!'

'What else do you propose, Mr Legge? As Billy's legal representative,' Sheridan added.

'Why, he ... he...' Timothy brightened at a sudden thought. 'Billy is an orphan! He might be found a place at Dr Coram's. There the boy may receive an education and be taught to become a useful member of society.'

Sheridan inclined his head. 'What would you say to that outcome, Constable Nicholls?'

'I should say...' The constable scratched his chin. 'I should say that is a capital idea.' The young constable grinned.

Sheridan laughed. 'We are sorry to have teased you, my dear Legge. A Foundling Home has already been the constable's suggestion.' He wagged a finger at Billy. 'But Billy should know how fortunate he is.'

Timothy sighed with relief. 'He does, I am sure. Don't you, Billy?'

The boy looked cautiously between the three men. 'I am not to go to Newgate then?'

'No, my dear boy.'

'I am not to dance a jig then?'

'No. You will not hang.'

'But I am not to go back to Battlin' —' The boy stopped suddenly.

Nicholls interjected. 'Battling Poll? She is your keeper?'

Billy kept his lips sealed.

'Who is this Battling Poll?' Timothy asked.

'A villainess of the most wicked sort,' Nicholls explained. 'Keeps a house of guttersnipes and teaches them to snaffle and pickpocket.'

'Poll'll not like it if I don't go back. She'll think I've done a runner. Turned King's Evidence. You tell that traps —' he pointed at the constable — 'I ain't no squealer!'

'You will never have to see this woman again, Billy.'

Billy shook his head. 'She'll find me — then I'm as good as dead!'

Timothy sighed with exasperation. 'You will be quite safe, my boy.' He turned abruptly to the Runner. 'Constable Nicholls, if you know of this woman, why do you not arrest her?'

'I wish it were that simple, sir. Her lair is deep in the rookeries. My fellow officers may only enter such territories at risk to their own lives. Locating Battling Poll would be one issue; having the proofs against her would be quite another matter. Who should take the word of a ragamuffin boy like Billy against a poor, "honest" washerwoman?'

'Battling Poll,' Sheridan mused, 'that is quite the soubriquet.'

'She was once a pugilist, sir, as fierce in the ring as any man you will find at Marylebone Fields.'

Timothy turned to Billy with a reassuring smile. 'Billy, you shall be well looked after at Coram's. And I shall take a particular interest in your welfare.'

Billy still looked doubtful.

Sheridan clapped his hands. 'Then it is settled. I shall take you to Coram's myself. Mr Legge can accompany us. If you are free, Timothy?'

The young man nodded.

'But first, Billy, you shall turn out your pockets.'

Billy started in a panic.

The constable eyed the boy afresh and Timothy looked momentarily disconcerted.

'Yes, you have been hiding something, have you not? I have noticed that your hand goes frequently to your right pocket — to be sure that the object is safe, I presume?'

The boy instinctively placed a hand over the said pocket.

Sheridan assumed a serious posture. 'I am in your debt, Billy. You have discovered my unfortunate Harlequin, most dreadfully murdered. But at least he may now be buried in a Christian grave, and that is thanks to you. Murder is a bad business, is it not?'

The boy nodded.

'And any little thing, however small and seemingly insignificant, may help to find who has done this terrible deed. There will be a very fine uniform for you at Coram's Foundling Hospital; you shall be divested of your rags and your pockets turned out in any case. Better now to show the constable what you have found.'

Billy gulped and retrieved something from his pocket. 'I was gonna tell yer. It was just dropped on the floor.'

'I have no doubt you would have told us. You had simply forgotten in your fright, as anyone might. But we had better see it.'

The boy opened his fist. In the palm of his small, grubby hand was a phial. A silver loop on the lid suggested that it had once hung from a chain.

Sheridan drew out the Huguenot Cross from his own waistcoat pocket. 'It is a match, I believe,' he observed.

Nicholls took the proffered object and examined it more closely. 'The dove is a more typical addition on these crosses, but I have heard tell that a maker in Lyon substituted a phial — to hold a drop of anointed oil.'

'That it is unusual may help to identify the owner of this cross.'

Nicholls unscrewed the top of the phial. 'Yes, see — it will open.' He dipped his nose to sniff the contents and recoiled immediately. 'It is no perfume, that is for sure!' The constable quickly replaced the lid.

Sheridan turned to the boy. 'Now, Billy, have you ever been to the pantomime?'

Sheridan stifled a yawn. It was all the usual business. A sly Harlequin crept up behind Clown. He gestured for the audience at Sadler's Wells to keep their peace, so that the foolish bumpkin should not be warned of his approach. Pretty Columbine was meanwhile hiding behind a pillar from which she peered out, her mouth a wide 'o' and her hands to her head in an attitude of terror, fearful that her father's servant should discover her. In that moment Clown spotted the girl and pounced, grinning with triumphant glee. He began to chase the distressed maiden around the stage. Harlequin made his move, tripped the clumsy buffoon and as he fell to the ground, soundly whacked his posterior with his slapstick.

Billy laughed with unrestrained delight. He clutched at the rail in front of the box and leant out, straining over the pit below to gain a better view of the play.

'Tha's got him — the great booby!'

'Have a care, Billy!' Timothy said, making a grab for the boy to hold him back.

Harlequin snatched the hand of his beloved Columbine and the two were fleeing upstage, right under the balcony where old Pantalone was waving a fist in outraged fury. Harlequin paused to cock a snook. Members of the audience followed suit, in turn gesturing derisively at old Pantalone and calling out ribald insults. Billy joined in with alarmingly rude gestures of his own.

When they had arrived at Sadler's Wells midway through the evening's entertainment, one of the proprietors, Mr Wroughton, had ushered them to his own box to sit out the show until Monsieur Dubois should be available. He had regarded the motley group with some amusement.

'You always did have some choice friends, Sheridan.'

'I am a man of the people, my good Wroughton, from the Highest to the Lowest.'

The harlequinade ended to thunderous applause and enthusiastic whoops from Billy. A troop of posturers tumbled onto the lip of the stage in front of the descending curtain to next enthral the audience with their feats of acrobatics.

'Now is the time to make our enquiries of Monsieur Dubois,' Sheridan announced as he got to his feet.

Reluctantly Billy was drawn away from the performance and the party made their way backstage. The young boy's eyes widened to see so many of the performers in their bright costumes, some wearing masks or paint on their faces. In the Green Room, a young woman practised a song and winked as they glanced through the door. Behind her, another young woman in the costume of Columbine suckled her baby. A lad mimicked a lecherous old man to peals of raucous laughter from the rest of the room, but on catching sight of Sheridan he somersaulted to the open doorway.

'Mr Sheridan, you have come to the Wells!' The youth had a strange accent, a mix of the East End and something else. He was a stocky, strong-looking boy of about twelve or thirteen.

'Ah, Joey. How is your mother?' Sheridan asked.

'She's all right. Is it true you move to The Kings?'

'All being well, the Drury Lane Theatre Company shall take up residence in Haymarket for the season — if terms can be agreed. And yes, there shall be a part for a Grimaldi in my company.'

Joey grinned widely.

'I'm looking for Monsieur Dubois — can you direct me?'

Joey's grin evaporated. 'That cutting gloak!' He jerked his head towards the corridor. 'At the end. No one will share a room with 'im!'

'Much obliged, Joey.'

A group of young dancers in flimsy costume, none much above the age of ten, squeezed passed them as they proceeded up the corridor. They arrived outside the furthest dressing room and Sheridan rapped loudly on Dubois' door.

'*Entrée!*'

Constable Nicholls made to enter first, but Sheridan held out a restraining arm and nudged the door open cautiously. As the door swung to its full extent, a knife whistled past the opening and twanged into a corkboard on the wall.

'Monsieur Dubois!' Sheridan called out gaily before stepping into the room, noting that the knife had struck the outer edge of a figure drawn on to the board.

The Frenchman groaned. '*Sacré bleu!* The very Devil! You 'ave my terms, Monsieur Sherrie. You will not 'ave me for a farthing less — in advance!'

Monsieur Dubois was lounging in a rickety chair with his boots up on the counter. He had changed into another costume, a woodsman by the looks of it. The chair seemed altogether too small to hold his height and bulk as he flexed the muscles straining beneath his shirt. Sheridan was reminded that aside from his prodigious acrobatic skills, Monsieur Dubois was also a noted strongman.

Sheridan bowed politely. 'Oh, I am sure we will reach a satisfactory agreement on your contract, monsieur, but it is on another matter that I wish to speak, if you will.'

'Indeed. What is it?'

'An enquiry that Constable Nicholls wishes to make.' Sheridan gestured for the Bow Street Runner and the rest of the party to follow him into the cramped dressing room.

The Frenchman scowled at the constable. 'Why do you bring the police to me?' He picked up another knife from the counter and examined the sharpness of the point.

'Murder, Monsieur Dubois,' Constable Nicholls stated baldly.

Dubois jerked his boots from the counter and sat up straight. 'Who speaks of murder?'

Sheridan raised a placating hand. 'A body has been found in the cellars of Old Drury. By this boy.'

Dubois raised an eyebrow and appraised Billy. 'Why come to me?'

'The man was in the costume of a Harlequin, sir,' Nicholls informed him. 'Mr Sheridan here informs me that you may be able to help us identify the player.'

Dubois relaxed and nodded. 'Arlecchino is dead.'

'Yes,' Sheridan concurred. 'Harlequin is dead. He met his end sometime this year, it is believed. The question is — which Harlequin might he be?'

Dubois shrugged. 'Actors come and actors go.'

'Precisely.'

'An item was found which may give some suggestion,' Nicholls continued. 'A Huguenot Cross.'

Dubois tapped the point of his knife on the counter.

They waited.

Dubois sighed deeply. 'Gaspard Bernon, perhaps.'

'Ah yes, Gaspard… I had assumed that he had been poached by Covent Garden.'

Dubois shook his head and frowned. 'I did not know Bernon was a Huguenot — I did know he was *un bâtard*!'

'Why do you say that, sir?' Nicholls prompted.

'Because he owes me money — Bernon owes *everyone* money. He is a man that gambles on how high the flea will jump!'

'You are saying he is heavily in debt?'

Dubois rolled his eyes. 'And some of these men he wagers with, like Mr Drewe, they do not like to be kept waiting.'

'He was in hock to Zachary Drewe?' Nicholls was suddenly alert.

Dubois laughed coldly. 'At the time he disappeared, I thought Bernon has done a flit. But now I think…' He raised the knife and made a cutting gesture across his throat.

Sheridan looked unconvinced. 'In my experience, a creditor might be more likely to make threats of violence against a man in the hope of extracting some recompense, rather than actually cutting the source of payment.'

Dubois stared at Sheridan. 'And there are those who would set an example so that others might pay without hesitation.'

'When did he disappear?' Nicholls asked.

The Frenchman shrugged. 'February, March — then at Drury Lane we had that scoundrel, Handsome Jack.' Dubois snorted. 'He is no true comic. Bernon may have been *un bâtard*, but he was a good Arlecchino. A real trickster.'

'Do you know where Gaspard Bernon might be found?' pressed Nicholls.

Dubois thought for a moment. 'Paris, perhaps — to be safe from the hungry sharks.'

'Anyone who might know for certain?'

'Columbine. Her child, it is Bernon's.'

Sheridan exchanged a quick glance with Constable Nicholls.

'We shall speak with her presently. But first, do you know of any other Harlequin who might have been a Huguenot?'

'There is Carlo Goldoni, he is Italian … and Jack Champion, from London —'

'Champion?' Nicholls cut in.

Dubois flicked a hand in the air. 'Jack — he go too. Whish!'

The constable's face lit up. 'Champion — that is a name to be found amongst Huguenots, Mr Sheridan. Originally the name was Champenois.' He turned back to Dubois. 'Sir, you say this man has also disappeared?'

Dubois snapped his fingers. '*Vite*! *Double rapide*! The husband is coming for him!'

'Handsome Jack … ah yes, I remember him now.' Sheridan smiled wryly. 'There was talk that he had seduced the wife of a grenadier. They do say one should not cross a grenadier if one values one's life.'

'You have heard nothing of him since he left?' asked Nicholls.

Dubois shook his head. He was appraising young Billy keenly.

'Bernon. Champion. It may be that one or the other is our Harlequin, Constable,' Sheridan surmised with a shake of the head.

Dubois addressed Billy. '*Garçon*, you are a brave boy?'

Billy flushed. 'Brave as any other cove!'

Dubois nodded. 'And you can keep still, very still?'

Billy shrugged. 'Still as yer like.'

'I would like.'

Billy stiffened and straightened. In that second, the knife cut through the air and landed in the cork on the wall a whisker above the boy's head. Billy gasped.

Timothy, who had thus far quietly observed the interview, now leapt forward towards Dubois. 'Sir! What mean you by this outrage?' He turned to the Bow Street Runner. 'Constable, you must apprehend this madman at once!'

'That will not be necessary.' Sheridan stepped in. 'I rather think Monsieur Dubois was auditioning young Billy.'

'Auditioning!' Timothy exclaimed.

'For his William Tell act, the story of a Switzer rebel who shot an apple from his son's head. Monsieur Dubois has difficulty persuading some of the younger performers into the part of the son.' Sheridan turned to the boy, who was still open-mouthed. 'What say you, Billy? Are you drawn to a career on the stage?'

CHAPTER FOUR

After quitting Monsieur Dubois' dressing room, Sheridan and Constable Nicholls had questioned everyone they could find who had acquaintance with either Bernon or Champion, or both. None of that company had seen or heard from either man since their sudden departures from the theatre at Drury Lane. None seemed overly surprised, either. Here was a mystery indeed.

Margaret Bedwell, the young actress playing the part of Columbine, confirmed that Gaspard Bernon was indeed the father of the six-month-old boy she cradled in her lap. Bernon had promised marriage all the way up to the infant's birth and beyond, she claimed. Then, in March, she had discovered the truth. There was a wife and daughter already, abandoned in Paris. And no, she had received no word from him, nor help towards her child, nor did she know where he might be. She had been to his lodgings but they were empty, and the landlord in high dudgeon about the rent that was still outstanding. If Margaret Bedwell never saw Gaspard Bernon again, it would be too soon — though she should like to see him placed in the stocks where she might fling a cabbage at his head.

'Was Monsieur Bernon a Huguenot, by any chance?' Nicholls ventured.

'Religious? Gaspard? Hah! Don't make me laugh! His only religion was money and cards.' Her face suddenly twitched in a flash of memory. 'Now, that is something I recall. Gaspard came into some money. When was that? Just after the nipper was born. January ... February ... he even bought Antoine here a silver spoon.' She jiggled the baby and laughed bitterly.

'Said there was more to come, that he could pay off all his debts and then some. Promised me we'd get married. Then I found out about the first Madame Bernon back in Paris.'

'Where did the money come from? Do you know?' Sheridan asked. He knew for a fact that the bounty had not come from his coffers.

Margaret shrugged. 'Someone French, I think. There's a load of 'em come over here since the Revolution — scared of getting their heads chopped off.'

'What were the payments for?'

'Gaspard said it was easy money. He'd only to keep his eyes and ears open, he said.'

'A spy?'

Margaret laughed again. 'I think that's what he fancied. Gaspard was always puffing himself up, liked to think he was clever. Thought he really was a Harlequin.' Her face suddenly crumpled. 'You reckon this dead fella might really be Gaspard?' She pulled baby Antoine into her shoulder and stroked his bobbing head.

'Sadly, that is a possibility, my dear.'

'He's a rogue and a devil, but he don't deserve that.'

Margaret cradled Antoine closer to her as she looked askance at young Billy. The boy was perched on a stool, swinging his scrawny legs and scratching at the lice in his hair.

'There is also the possibility that the deceased may be a Mr Champion,' said Nicholls. 'The man who succeeded Monsieur Bernon in the part of Harlequin. He too seems to have gone missing.'

'Handsome Jack?'

'You know of him?'

'Well, he's a Londoner. Me, I was brought up in the theatre. A travelling troupe. Dancing on the stage when I was three.

But Jack, he was apprenticed in some trade. Don't know what. He never wanted to talk about them days; there was some break with his family. Wanted adventure, I reckon. He weren't the greatest performer, truth be told, but he was a proper chancer. He liked the costumes. Liked playing at being different characters. He were always borrowing gentleman's outfits from the wardrobe — Lord! Mrs Petty was always having conniptions!'

'Our Wardrobe Mistress, Constable, the formidable Mrs Petty,' Sheridan explained.

'Oh, she'd fume all right, but then Jack had such a devilish charm…'

'We wonder if Jack may have come from a French Huguenot family. The surname is also known in that community.'

'He did speak the language, as it happens.'

'Really?'

'I know a word or two myself from Gaspard. Not long before he disappeared a woman come backstage at Old Drury, talking French. Not a doxy, more like a real lady. I thought to myself, blind me, Jack, you're aiming high!'

'A Frenchwoman?'

'A proper fine lady.'

'We have heard that there was a grenadier who might have had cause to confront Mr Champion — this was his lady wife, perhaps?'

'Oh no, that was another dalliance altogether! I warned him about Mrs Jeffreys; *that'll be trouble*, I said, her husband being a cheesemonger.'

Timothy frowned. 'Cheesemonger? I thought he was a military man?'

Margaret grinned. 'Life Guards — better known as the Cheeses! Gives himself airs does Captain Jeffreys, but he weren't more than a common trooper in the Grenadier Guards to start with. I think it was his uncle that bought the commission — I hear he is a cheesemonger an' all!'

'I see.'

'Jack, he'd never listen, had the very devil in him. And so had she, that Mrs Jeffreys. She ain't all she seems either, for all her pretence of respectability.'

'How so?' asked Sheridan.

'I'm not one to gossip, but the mice did play, that's for sure. Still, Jack was scared enough when the cat returned — he's a mean brute, that Captain Jeffreys!'

The baby, Antoine, began to mewl.

'There, there, hush now. If you'll excuse me, gentlemen, I must get back to my lodgings.' Margaret rose and then skirted around Billy, who was now picking his nose. 'If you should find Gaspard ... well, you can let him know that Antoine thrives.'

'Naturally, Ms Bedwell. We thank you for your time.'

As the group walked back towards Sheridan's waiting carriage, he began to summarise what they had learnt.

'So, it seems we have not one Harlequin but two! And we do not know which one might be our victim.'

Nicholls concurred. 'Both men had enemies, it would appear, sir. And both may have been Huguenot, although that is not yet certain in either case. I shall make enquiries amongst the local community. Someone may know. If we can identify our deceased Harlequin, then at least we'll have some avenues to pursue.'

Sheridan nodded. 'An enraged creditor on the one hand, or Captain Jeffreys of the Life Guards on the other.'

'If you were to ask me, you need look no further than that devilish Dubois for your killer.' Timothy laid a protective hand on Billy's shoulder as he spoke. 'I should think him perfectly capable of any and all such evil and murderous acts — and at very little provocation!'

Nicholls nodded. 'That thought did occur to me, Mr Legge. Monsieur Dubois clearly had no love for Gaspard Bernon — nor for Mr Champion.'

'And he was well placed to dispatch either man — or both!'

'Come, Timothy, you are not often given to flights of fancy — that is my domain. Do you imagine that our Monsieur Dubois is a habitual cut-throat and that our second Harlequin may also be murdered? That his corpse lies yet to be discovered in the nether regions of Dame Drury? No one can doubt Monsieur Dubois has a sinister manner, but would he have spoken so freely of his dislikes were he really the perpetrator?'

Timothy flushed under the glow of the streetlight. 'You are right, of course, Mr Sheridan. It is an irrational conjecture and I have developed a prejudice against this fellow Dubois. I am a lawyer and should only consider the facts.'

Billy shook his head in awe. 'He's very flash with them knives! Isn't he, Mister Sheridan? I should like to see that act, I truly would!'

Sheridan rather suspected that given a choice of heroes, Billy might unfairly opt for Monsieur Dubois over Timothy.

CHAPTER FIVE

The sun was beginning to drop behind the trees and the heat of the day was subsiding. Were it not for the overpowering stench of manure and other unmentionable effluences, one could say this late summer's evening was become very pleasant. The Strand was busy with pedestrians and vehicles of every kind — carriages, wagons, drays and horses; Sheridan even caught sight of Mr Hunter driving his buffalo-drawn cart, the creatures specially trained for the Scottish anatomist. There was an air of jollity and holiday. Labouring men, market traders, domestic servants scurrying home from errands and shop workers closing their doors were all anticipating a few hours of leisure and entertainment at the tavern or theatre.

It was two days since the gruesome find in the theatre cellars. The remains had been removed and arrangements made for a burial. Constable Nicholls had promised to report back to Sheridan if anything further came of his enquiries. He was circumspect; so many weeks had lapsed since the murderous deed that the prospect of an easy resolution seemed forlorn. Sheridan allowed the horrors of the discovery to recede from his mind. The prospect of an enjoyable evening lay ahead at Carlton House, where he would join His Royal Highness the Prince of Wales and guests. They would drink champagne, delight in the various entertainments, exchange witticisms and indulge in risqué flirtations. Sheridan would be expected to act the role of court jester. What a comedy was his life when he thought on it. A veritable *commedia dell'arte*. But who was he to be? Clown or Pantalone, or the trickster, Harlequin?

Sheridan's carriage passed alongside the leafy arbours of St James's Park. Well-dressed families were strolling beneath the trees. A boy with a hoop. A couple of dragoons loitering in the shade. His heart leapt; up ahead he fancied that he glimpsed the Duchess of Devonshire in her landau with her sister, Harriet, Lady Duncannon. But no, it was the eminently respectable Duchess of Richmond with a companion. He experienced a lurch of disappointment. Of course, Harriet was still in Bath, taking the waters; she was quite seriously ill, he had been informed. How he had longed to rush to her side, but that was no longer a possibility. Lady Duncannon must avoid him at all costs. Their liaison had brought them both dangerously close to catastrophe. They had been caught in flagrante. The furious Lord Duncannon, who cared little for his wife but everything for his reputation, had been livid enough to countenance divorce. Sheridan would be, as his wife Eliza had exclaimed with horror, 'an object of ridicule and abuse to all the world.'

Yet more cause for Eliza to feel the pain of neglect. Sheridan's ill-disguised passion for Harriet had driven his wife to despair. The scandal of a suit would have caused further distress. Thankfully, the Duke of Devonshire had intervened to avert such a disaster. Sweet, dear Harriet. His Harriet. She would always be his Harriet, although she was wont to tease that she 'could never love anyone but a little'. Sheridan sighed and endeavoured to turn his thoughts elsewhere.

When Sheridan entered Carlton House, the first indication that something was amiss came with his greeting from Fino the Pomeranian and the terrier, Tiny. Usually as placid as their master, both dogs began yapping at Sheridan's heels from the moment he arrived in the magnificent rotunda foyer, as though to alert him to some distress in their sovereign lord.

'What is it, Fino?' Sheridan reached down and patted the black and white dog's head. Tiny butted against his stockings and growled. 'And you, you little fiend? What has you both in such a flap?'

Fino let out a bark.

'Ah, I see! In that case…' Sheridan adjusted the ruffles of his jabot. 'We must be on our guard.' He turned to the smaller dog. 'Here, Tiny, you must protect me.' The little dog leapt into his outstretched arms.

When Sheridan was announced, Prince George wheeled around and caught him in the full glare of his eye. 'Ah, Sherry — good of you to turn up!' he snapped.

Sheridan bowed low. 'Your Royal Highness, I trust you do not wait on me. 'Tis most assuredly the other way, I promise you; I await your command, as ever.' He scratched the dog under its chin. 'Myself and Tiny here are at your service, and I'll wear whatever livery would so please you — only let it not be the livid green with rose buttons; the colours ill favour my complexion.'

The prince guffawed and spoke to Lady Lade at his side. 'Ever since I allowed this rogue a chamber of his own here at Carlton House, the blasted fellow thinks he can come and go as he damn well pleases!'

'That's to be expected of a tinker, sir, especially the Irish variety — was your name not originally O'Sheridan?' Lady Lade placed an emphasis on the 'O'.

'And who may have a greater right to the "O" than we have, Laetitia? For we owe to everybody.'

'Never a truer word spoken.' Major George Hanger, recently appointed equerry, appeared at the Prince of Wales' shoulder. He was a handsome man with a prominent nose and was made all the more dashing by his military uniform and bearing.

'Tinkers would be the least of your acquaintance, I imagine, Lady Lade,' Sheridan countered, with playful emphasis on the surname of the woman reputed to have once served in a brothel and been mistress to a highwayman who had danced the fatal jig on the Tyburn Tree.

Lady Lade rapped him with her fan. 'You are a whorry dog, Sherry, who should be whipped and sent to the kennels forthwith! Is that not right, sir?' she said, turning to the prince.

'I have a better notion, Your Royal Highness.' Hanger sniffed at the rose he habitually wore in his lapel. 'A mongrel, methinks, who does not know his manners —' the equerry eyed Sheridan with wicked intent — 'should be kept under the table and fed on scraps.'

'Capital!' the prince tittered. 'You are to sit under the dinner table, Sherry, and Laetitia here will feed you little titbits if you are good.'

'Why, that is no punishment at all, sir! Is it, Tiny?' Sheridan pulled at the dog's ears. 'For we shall have a grand view of all the ladies' ankles!'

He swung his gaze about the glittering reception room and alighted on a coterie of ladies dressed in the French style. They were in the entourage of the Duc d'Orléans. Sheridan's mouth fell open and his heart fluttered. There at the centre was one of the most ravishing creatures he had ever set eyes on.

Lady Lade poked him with her fan. 'And we can all see whose skirts you shall be sniffing about, sir.'

Prince George tapped his foot. 'I admit, I am dashed impatient to be introduced to Madame LeClaire myself. Hanger, be a good fellow and nudge His Serene Highness the Duc in this direction.'

Hanger nodded and wove a discreet path across the reception room.

The prince waved his glass impatiently and a manservant hastened forward to replenish it. Prince Augustus took the opportunity to scurry over in an attempt to capture his older brother's attention.

'Who is she?' Sheridan whispered to Lady Lade.

'Her husband, Baron LeClaire, is a follower of the duc but is conveniently and frequently absent, it seems. Madame is a companion to the Comtesse de Buffon.'

Sheridan noted the presence of the Duc d'Orléans' long-time mistress. He raised an eyebrow. Was Madame LeClaire preparing to become the comtesse's successor?

'Soon to replace her, I shouldn't wonder,' Lady Lade snorted, giving voice to his thoughts.

Orléans was well known to have an insatiable appetite for women. His visits to London had frequently been characterised by tours of the taverns along the Strand, and he was known to relish doxies of the commonest sort, quipping that it was testimony to his taste for democracy. From what Sheridan had observed, this did little to dent the duc's haughty nature. The prince looked on him as an older brother and mentor, sharing a taste not only for women but also for gambling and horseracing, much to the displeasure of his father, King George III.

Sheridan regarded this cousin of the French King thoughtfully. For all his libertine nature, His Serene Highness had long promoted a reformist agenda. Many of the noble French émigrés gathering in London already regarded Orléans as dangerously treasonous. It was noticeable that none of that select assemblage had been invited to this soiree; that should have soured the atmosphere very swiftly.

The situation in France had become increasingly volatile since Louis XVI and his family had attempted to escape Paris disguised as servants. Louis was now a prisoner in all but name. A puppet leader. The National Assembly allowed that he would retain the throne under a constitutional monarchy. Plans to draw up that constitution were currently underway. The question remained, however: would the French people continue to accept Louis as their king? To many, the French King's cousin, the Duc d'Orléans presented an attractive alternative should Louis be persuaded to abdicate. Orléans had placed himself on the side of reform from the first. But events were moving fast. The mood of republicanism was running high. Only days before, protestors had gathered at the Champ de Mars to demand an immediate end to the monarchy. The crowd had been dispersed with gunfire. It was being described as a massacre. All of France now stood dangerously on the brink.

'Madame LeClaire has every man in London panting at her feet, including our dear Prince George.'

Lady Lade drew Sheridan to one side as Orléans approached with the Comtesse de Buffon on one arm and the baroness on the other. As the young woman neared, Sheridan was able to fully appreciate her daring ensemble. Madame LeClaire was attired in the very latest French fashion, a simple chemise gown of white muslin, with plain sleeves and a drawstring neck with no ruffles. It was high-waisted under her pert bosom, and the skirt hung straight down over her lithe figure. There was no padding that Sheridan could see. Her beauty was unadorned, for she required no decoration. Her skin was a fine alabaster and her eyes had an almost violet hue. Most daring of all, her hair had been cut into a tight crop of dark curls, lending her a bold look of childish mischief. Sheridan was utterly entranced.

'Your Royal Highness, allow me to introduce to you the companion of my dearest Comtesse de Buffon, her cousin, Madame LeClaire.'

The ladies curtsied and His Royal Highness bowed in return.

'Delighted, madame, most delighted. I should be honoured if you would sit by me at dinner, Madame LeClaire. I should so very much like to become better acquainted.'

'Sire, it is I who am most honoured. And do, I beg you, call me Marceline — for I feel sure we are to be great friends.'

Sheridan felt that he too should like nothing more than the chance to become the greatest of friends with this most captivating young woman.

Orléans smiled indulgently and addressed himself to the prince. 'You should know, my dearest friend, that today is our charming Marceline's birthday. With your permission, sir, I have ordered fireworks in celebration.'

Prince George clapped his hands. 'A birthday and fireworks, how splendid!'

Try as he might, Sheridan found all routes to Madame LeClaire were blocked that evening. Two other men, he noticed, were jockeying for a position within her orbit. The Chevalier de Saint-Gelais, he deduced from the young man's peeved looks, was a spurned or former lover. Sir Roderick Howgill, a young baronet who had lately inherited his father's title and estates, was a dandified popinjay and Sheridan rather suspected that he was Marceline's current beau, for he caught a number of sly looks and smiles that passed between the pair when they thought themselves unobserved.

A sumptuous dinner of glazed guinea fowls, green goose, lobster mousse and a pineapple cluster was followed by musical entertainment and tables of faro and brusquembille.

Both the Prince of Wales and the Duc d'Orléans were avid gamblers, and their play attracted a boisterous crowd of supporting followers. Luck did not favour the prince, and his forced smiles and laughter did not convince Sheridan that his mood was about to improve as the evening progressed. Sheridan refrained from joining the gaming tables. There were many vices which he would own, but thankfully gambling was not one of them. He had creditors enough.

Major Hanger appeared at his elbow. 'Sheridan, you are to stay at Carlton House tonight. His Royal Highness wishes to have a tête-à-tête with you. He had rather hoped to do so earlier, but you are always so devilish late. So, for your penance I am to drag you from your bed whenever he wakes and you are to wait on him in his bedchamber.'

'Can you say on what subject he wishes to confer?' Sheridan asked.

'Afraid not. His Royal Highness received a note this afternoon and has been out of sorts ever since. Been at the claret with a vengeance.'

Sheridan was left to stew on what this might signify. Some trouble or scandal to be smoothed over. Since the recent crisis regarding the king's madness, when he had been the one to act as intermediary between the Prince of Wales and the Whig Party regarding King George III's malady, the prince had increasingly turned to him. Sheridan's thoughts were so distracted that he scarcely noticed the figure gliding gracefully towards him across the salon.

'Monsieur Sheridan, forgive my imposition but I have so longed to meet the man who has penned *The School for Scandal* that I must presume the introduction myself! Ah, Lady Teazle, if I were to be an actress, that should be my part!'

Sheridan found himself gazing into violet eyes bright with interest and humour. He feared that he blushed.

The young woman laughed, a light, tinkling sound. 'Ah! But you see I am so in thrall to your genius, Monsieur Sheridan, I forget to introduce myself. I am Madame —'

'LeClaire,' he finished for her and bowed. '*Enchanté*, madame.'

Her eyes widened. 'Oh, that you should take notice of me, monsieur! I am, how do you say —' she clapped her hands in delight — 'overwhelmed! For so long I am your admirer! The *premiere fanatic*! Listen to me, monsieur, I am like an excited schoolgirl and you must find me a terrible bore!'

'That should never be possible, madame.'

'You are all kindness, monsieur, but you are from Ireland, and they are a kind people, so I have heard.'

'Very merry, madame.'

'Marceline, you must call me Marceline — I insist.'

'Then I am Richard, or Dick, if it please you, madame — Marceline.'

'Your theatre it is closed, demolished.' She struck an attitude of pouting sorrow. 'I am *très désolé*.'

'No need to be sorry — we shall rise again,' he reassured.

Sir Roderick interrupted. 'My dear Baronne, His Serene Highness asks for you.' The young man presented his arm and continued, 'The fireworks display is about to commence, and I am told it will be truly spectacular.'

'Ah, yes — I do believe the fireworks, they will begin.'

As Madame LeClaire gave her hand to Sir Roderick, Sheridan could have sworn that she turned and winked at him.

CHAPTER SIX

Prince George had clearly had a restless night, for it was scarcely beyond dawn when Sheridan was rudely awoken from his slumbers. The manservant drew the curtains apart so that there could be no doubt that Sheridan was summoned. He was still rubbing the sleep from his eyes as he staggered down the corridors towards the State Apartments. John Townsend approached, a solid man in his early thirties, the Bow Street officer who had occasional charge of the security for the Royal Family.

'You are abroad early, Mr Sheridan,' Townsend observed. 'Or is it that you have not yet retired, sir?'

Sheridan yawned in reply. 'I am called at the Prince of Wales' pleasure.'

'Have a care you do not lead His Royal Highness astray with any more of your foolish pranks, sir.'

'What the deuce can you mean?' Sheridan replied in mock offence.

Townsend raised an eyebrow. 'Last month — impersonating an officer of the law.'

'Ah, should we not have arrested Her Ladyship? The dear old dowager was in the grip of a criminal frenzy.' Sheridan grinned at the recollection.

'Her Ladyship was on the verge of apoplexy.'

'Then we are fortunate that you were to hand with the smelling salts, my good Townsend.'

Sheridan rapped on the chamber door and entered on command. Prince George was swathed in a silken robe, his hair dishevelled as he paced the room, scowling. The valet was dismissed and ordered to let no one disturb them. They were quite alone. Sheridan felt a prickle of anxiety. He lingered by the door, trying to consider how he should present himself. The usual fool? Cheerful and blithe? Or should he be serious and statesmanlike?

The prince stamped his foot. 'Am I not a patriot, Sherry?'

Sheridan nodded quickly. 'Who could doubt it, sir?'

'Then why will the king not allow me a commission?' he thundered. 'I should be as devilish a fighting man as any of my brothers who are drawing swords in Prussia and Hanover!'

Sheridan nodded again in sympathy. 'The very devil, sir.'

He had a notion now of what may have distressed the prince. Some buffoon had unwittingly impugned his courage. Alone amongst his brothers, the Prince of Wales had been denied a military career. Where the younger princes had received the opportunity to garner accolades on the field and to serve with purpose, the heir to the throne must kick his heels at home and simmer in his father's displeasure. Sheridan awaited the familiar rant against His Majesty from the king's eldest son.

'And pray tell, how does His Majesty expect that I can run a household fit for the heir to the throne on so paltry an allowance? Does it surprise anyone that we should be mired in debt?' The prince glared at Sheridan.

Sheridan swallowed. The prince had moved swiftly on to the subject of his enormous debts. That perennial old carp. How Sheridan longed for that stew pond to dry up. The previous year, a group of leading grandees had sought to raise the tremendous sum of three hundred thousand pounds from bankers in Antwerp. But there seemed to be no end to the debts incurred by the royal brothers.

Recently, Sheridan had been placed on a parliamentary committee to investigate the Prince of Wales' financial problems, a poison chalice if ever there was one. The Prime Minister must be laughing up his sleeve. His Royal Highness' debts were in every sense a monstrous challenge. It was true that His Majesty King George III was miserly in the extreme, being of an abstemious disposition himself, but it was also true that his sons were extravagant and spendthrift, with a weakness for women and gambling. And none more so than the Prince of Wales and his brother the Duke of York.

'My brother York has been swayed to marry our Prussian cousin, the Princess Frederica.'

Sheridan had heard the rumours; now they were confirmed.

'A Treaty of Marriage waits on the table at Berlin — well, and notwithstanding this sacrifice from my dear brother, His Majesty quibbles over the marriage portion, offering only half the sum to York that would pay his debts. So, still my brother must come begging to me. And what am I to do, by God?' Prince George beat his fist against his palm.

Where were all these histrionics leading? For as sure as eggs are eggs the prince must want Sheridan to do something. What, though? His mind raced. Was he expected to sabotage the work of the parliamentary investigation? Or to persuade the government that His Royal Highness' debts must all be honoured — yet again? That was beyond the wit of any man. Why on earth had the prince called on him? Now that he was on the committee, the less he knew about the prince's financial affairs the better.

Sheridan felt aggrieved. He prided himself that he was no 'place man'. He had never accepted bribes or positions for his own advancement. He held one of the most democratic seats in the whole country at Stafford; no safe seat in a rotten borough for him, unlike Mr Pitt! Was the prince about to compromise his integrity? For a moment he saw the heir to the throne as his critics were wont to see him — as a selfish, reckless, profligate young man — and he felt a sudden anger.

'And now this!' The prince picked up a note from an occasional table and thrust it towards Sheridan.

Sheridan opened the sheet of paper and perused the contents.

Sir,

Is the son of Albion become a TRAITOR? One that would pension our great country to a foreign pirate? Shall he have the blackguard's rings put through his nose by N_ P_ F_ and be led to perform like a DANCING BEAR? Take heed!

A TRUE FRIEND of Albion

Sheridan paled. This True Friend of Albion, whoever he may be, did not mince his words. What dangerous pickle had his princely friend found himself in? Surely something that involved the Duc d'Orléans, for he must be the 'foreign pirate', with the rings which he habitually wore in his ears. And N_P_F_ must be Mr Nathaniel Parker Forth, the duc's agent, a very smooth character by all accounts. Sheridan was suddenly worried, for Prince George was being accused of high treason.

This was an accusation more serious than profligacy. The charge appeared to be that the Prince of Wales had been prepared to *pension our great country*. He must have turned to Orléans for some financial assistance, a loan. After all, the duc was amongst the wealthiest of men in the whole of Europe. The two men were friends and had been for some time. To be beholden to a friend was one thing, but a future King of England indebted to a potential King of France — well, that was quite another.

'Sir, this letter is most incendiary. A calumny from beginning to end. The writer should be found and thoroughly thrashed for his impudence.'

'And so he shall be, egad!'

'You have perhaps borrowed some trifling amount from the Duc d'Orléans, a friend of long standing…'

Sheridan noted a slight twitch at His Royal Highness' left cheek.

'…and some fellow seeks to threaten you with —' he struggled for a moment to find the right expression — 'what should be a very minor scandal.'

The prince grunted.

'The miserable fellow seeks to inveigle monies or favour from you, sir,' Sheridan continued. 'He is a villain and dashed impolite. I should pay no heed.'

'Sherry…' The Prince of Wales placed a hand to his brow. 'I must sit down; I feel a little faint.'

And indeed, His Royal Highness had turned suddenly very pale with a thin line of sweat beading his brow. Sheridan rushed to his side and helped him to the bed.

'Shall I call for your man, sir? He might bring a tonic.'

'No … no … that won't be necessary.' With a shaking hand, the prince picked up a glass that had been placed on his bedside table. 'I have just such a cure in readiness. I fear I may have imbibed rather too much of the claret and the maraschino last night.'

The prince gulped back the remedy. He sniffed and then began to sob. His plump shoulders heaved as tears coursed down his cheeks.

Sheridan hesitated before he laid a hand on the younger man's shoulder. Then George was clutching at him and weeping into his breast. Tentatively, Sheridan began to pat his back and murmur reassuring words. The young prince was in so many ways a fine fellow, warm and witty, of surprising erudition, artistic leanings and enlightened sympathies. Yet he was at heart an unloved child, constantly at odds with his distant father. To whom should he turn in his distress? What else could Sheridan do but offer his solicitude? More, how could he turn away from this cry for help?

Sheridan sighed. 'You must tell me everything, sir.'

Sheridan then teased out as much of the business as he could. There had been a number of attempts to raise bonds with the assistance of Mr Nathaniel Parker Forth and the Duc d'Orléans. The royal brothers had then panicked; Lord Loughborough had mentioned in passing that it was treasonable to refer to the king's death in a document. Realising their blunder in the wording of the bonds, Prince George and the Duke of York had instructed Mr Parker Forth to retrieve all of them at once. The agent had accomplished this after much tribulation, including being stabbed with a clasp knife by one of the bond holders.

'Mr Parker Forth brought the bonds to us. York and I then burnt them, every one!'

Sheridan pulled out a handkerchief and handed it to George, who dabbed at his eyes.

'We thought that to be the end of the matter.'

Sheridan felt his stomach lurch. Had the anonymous writer managed to get hold of some piece of incriminating evidence? In the wrong hands, how might that be used against His Royal Highness?

'You mentioned that was the first attempt to raise bonds — there has been another?'

The prince nodded. 'But it has not yet come to anything, Sherry.'

'And the collateral?'

The prince stuttered. 'Corn … Corn…'

'Cornwall?' Sheridan shuddered. The revenues of the Duchy of Cornwall.

The Prince of Wales sobbed anew.

To sign an agreement of this nature without His Majesty the King's cognisance could all too easily be classed as high treason; had the prince learnt nothing?

Sheridan knew not what to say in response.

The prince pulled back and wiped his tears. His expression flashed from remorse to peevishness. 'But if my father the king and parliament will not aid me, then where else must I turn? I have been forced to this, Sherry!'

That should be a moot point. How far had these negotiations progressed? There was every advantage to Orléans in the arrangement. The Prince of Wales might thus be prevailed upon to openly support his friend's ambitions in France. With support from the Prince of Wales, even some of the counter-revolutionary émigré factions might be won over to accept Orléans as King of France, particularly if their properties and interests were guaranteed.

'Who knows of this, sir?'

George shrugged. 'Orléans, Parker Forth, my brother — he was to benefit also. Who else, I am not sure … various bondholders, I suppose…'

Sheridan's eyes narrowed. 'Mr Parker Forth may play a double game, but there is some unknown who has knowledge of the affair and writes this anonymous letter. Why? That is the question. Is this missive a warning or a threat?'

'Quite. Let the blackguard lay his cards on the table.' His Royal Highness sniffed. 'His Majesty must on no account hear of this contract — Sherry, you must find out who this is.'

'I, sir?'

'I count on you, Sherry. I know that in you I can place my trust.' He pointed to the letter still clutched in Sheridan's hand. 'No one else but you should know of this poisonous bile. I cannot risk it. You have the wit to find this fellow out.'

Sheridan felt his heart sink.

The prince nodded with determined cheeriness. 'And then he and I may come to some terms of understanding.' He grabbed the letter and with undisguised feeling tore it into tiny strips.

CHAPTER SEVEN

When Sheridan returned to his house in Grosvenor Street later that day, his butler handed him a note which had been delivered from Bow Street. Constable Nicholls informed Sheridan that some of his enquiries had borne fruit. First, the actor Jack Champion had quit his last known lodgings before his final performance at Drury Lane and left no forwarding address; no one seemed to know where he had gone. Second, one of Nicholls' relatives knew of a family of silk weavers in Spitalfields by the name of Champion. Furthermore, it was said that the eldest son had abandoned the family. The constable's investigations had located the house where the Champions resided and he planned to visit them early on the morrow.

Sheridan deliberated. He was due to meet with the lessees at the King's Theatre to settle the terms for his company's temporary residence. The negotiations had been tricky. But the truth was that the company was now homeless. It meant that he must rent another space. The terms for the King's Theatre were criminally extortionate in Sheridan's view. But he was thoroughly jammed. What choices presented themselves? Better terms? But a smaller theatre? He was at the mercy of scoundrels. Well, they would all rue this day when he had his new theatre at Drury Lane — audiences flocking to the spectacles he should present.

He felt his gall rise. He would take pleasure in keeping the management waiting before he allowed them to fleece him. He would instead join Constable Nicholls in the visit to Spitalfields. After all, if this were Jack Champion's family, they might recognise the cross which lay snug in his waistcoat pocket. His Harlequin would be identified; he could offer condolences and stand a reward of twenty guineas for information leading to the capture of the villain who had slain the young actor. There, he had decided. He scribbled a note to that effect and proposed to join the constable at Bow Street at nine o'clock the following morning.

Sheridan then retired to his armchair to think over the extraordinary revelations which the prince had felt impelled to share with him. The whole country knew something of the parlous state of His Royal Highness' finances; it was constant fodder for the cartoonists. But quite how astonishing a figure those debts had amounted to was not so well known. King George would be incandescent. His Majesty might very well be tempted to find ways to bypass the Prince of Wales in the line of succession; there were plenty of younger sons to choose from. The king might even consider the Duke of York when that reprobate married the Princess Frederica and, given the celebrated Prussian fecundity, was likely to produce a next generation of royal heirs.

If the prince had acted treasonably, then it might take very little for King George to disinherit his eldest son altogether. Then where should Sheridan stand? His friendly relations with the prince were a cornerstone of his political influence within the Whig party.

He wished that His Royal Highness had not destroyed the note so that he might examine the handwriting more closely. Although from what he had seen, the characters were written in a very plain block hand, the intent to disguise. A list of potential suspects must be his first task, along with thoughts on their motives. He very much hoped that whoever this True Friend of Albion might be, he should prove to be friend rather than foe.

At some time approaching eleven o'clock the following morning, Sheridan's carriage drew up outside number 4 Bow Street. He entered the building which had once been home to the esteemed author and magistrate Henry Fielding. Looking about to enquire after Constable Nicholls, he found himself hailed by the current Chief Magistrate, Sir Sampson Wright.

'Ah, Mr Sheridan, good day to you, sir.'

The two men bowed politely to each other.

'What brings you hither? Are you to stand before me?' Sir Sampson chuckled. 'I should like to hear your defence; it should be lively and entertaining, unlike the usual caterwauling to which I am habitually subjected.'

'On what charge would you arraign me, Sir Sampson?'

'Why, I should say desertion, sir!'

'Desertion, yes, that is a capital charge, something I might get my teeth into. And of what in particular am I accused of deserting?'

'Your duty to write another *School for Scandal*, Mr Sheridan.'

'Ah, but I am conscripted by the electorate of Stafford to write for another stage, Sir Sampson, the one at Westminster. So, you must find another charge.'

'Of being late, sir.'

Sheridan turned to find Constable Nicholls glowering at him.

'Ah, am I so very unpunctual?' Sheridan smiled disarmingly.

Sir Sampson grinned. 'This earnest young officer does not know your reputation, Sheridan. Constable Nicholls, here, is one of my best at Bow Street and is all industry! But Nicholls, you must always allow an hour or two for any appointment with Mr Sheridan, and then one may never be disappointed. Good day, sir.'

Sir Sampson was ushered towards his chambers by a waiting clerk of the court.

'I do hope you will pardon my tardiness, Mr Nicholls. On this occasion I offer no excuse; there is none other than my aversion to rising in the morning.'

The Bow Street Runner continued to glower. 'We are men of action here, you understand, sir.'

'I am suitably admonished. Now, let's to our business. My carriage waits outside.'

Spitalfields had long been home to an industry of silk weaving amongst the Huguenot community, skills which the French refugees had brought with them in their flight from persecution, Nicholls explained. As he warmed to his subject, the young policeman's chagrin began to ebb, or rather to redirect towards the ills which had been suffered in France. The Runner fumed about the practice of dragonnades, a policy whereby soldiers were billeted in Huguenot households, their unruly behaviour then forcing the occupants to either flee or convert to Catholicism.

As they passed St Paul's Cathedral, Sheridan was momentarily distracted. He strained for a view through the carriage window; yes, he was certain he caught sight of Marceline, her dress and attitude so distinctive. She was pointing up towards the great dome, no doubt on a sightseeing expedition, and accompanied by a gentleman whose countenance Sheridan could not quite glimpse. Too tall to be the spry Chevalier de Saint-Gelais. Sir Roderick Howgill, then? The fellow seemed of a slightly broader build than the elegant fop. With dismay Sheridan wondered if Marceline's companion might be the lady's own husband. How very inconvenient that should be. The couple disappeared from view and Sheridan sank back into his seat.

'…schools, churches, all destroyed. Children wrenched from their parents.' Nicholls clenched his fist. 'My ancestor, Henri Mesnard, was imprisoned and tortured. To leave the country without a permit was a crime. But what choice did he have? His family must seek refuge across borders, be smuggled on to ships, with nothing.'

'A sad plight; it speaks much of Bourbon tyranny.'

'At least here in England, Huguenots have found sanctuary.'

'I am glad of it, Nicholls.'

The constable smiled at last as the carriage rumbled into Brick Lane.

'Is there a reason that Huguenots have settled here in Spitalfields?'

'It is outside the City of London, sir. They avoid the control of the Guilds.'

'They have prospered then?'

'The master weavers. But most are journeymen, living on piecemeal, and they suffer the vagaries of the market. Times can be hard, sir. When there is peace with France, silk may be imported cheaply. And in recent decades the silks from India and China have become fashionable.'

'Ah yes, chinoiserie, that is all the rage.'

'There were riots some twenty years ago, protests at low wages and the use of new machinery. I was a small boy, but I remember my grand-mère came to stay with us in Marylebone in fear of the violence. The situation little improves, but for the most part these are God-fearing, hardworking people.'

'The Champions, what do you know of them?'

'They have met with much misfortune. The father was knocked over by a wagon when a horse bolted. Injured his head. It left him a lunatic who sits and gabbles nonsense all day long. They live in a house with three or four other families; all must work at the loom for as many hours of the day as they can manage. Jack was the eldest, but he had no taste for weaving and so ran off. Some years ago, he made a return visit but his mother refused to speak with him.'

'A black sheep, then?'

'It would seem so, sir. Our welcome is not assured, but at least we may know whether he might be our Harlequin.'

The carriage had drawn up into a side street and come to a halt outside a mean dwelling in a row of semi-derelict terraced houses.

A young girl lugging a basket heavy with potatoes slowed to stare at the fine conveyance.

Sheridan caught her eye as he descended to the pavement. 'My dear child, do you know where we may find Mistress Champion?'

The girl's eyes widened even more when a Bow Street Runner followed, clutching his stick.

'Are we to be turned out?' the girl asked tremulously.

'No, my dear,' Sheridan reassured. 'We are come to make enquiry —' he looked at her closely — 'of your brother.'

'Henry? Oh, what has he done?'

'Is he like to have done something he should not?' Nicholls asked with interest.

The girl flushed.

'Well, that is not the business of our investigations. It is Jack that is our concern.'

'Jack?' The girl started with surprise.

Sheridan nodded. 'Yes, he would be your eldest brother, would he not?'

'He does not live with us, sir.'

'But you know him?'

'Scarce, sir. I was born after he left.'

Sheridan smiled. 'And how old are you now?'

'I am ten years since March.'

'But he has been here?' Nicholls pressed.

A woman, who might be described as young were she not so careworn, appeared on the step of the house and laid an arm about the girl's shoulder. She glared with suspicion between Sheridan and the constable.

'Who are you gentlemen, that question my sister?'

Sheridan bowed. 'I am Mr Sheridan of Drury Lane, and this is Constable Nicholls of the Bow Street Magistrates' Court. We make enquiry of your brother Jack.'

The woman bridled. 'You will not find him here.'

A small crowd of onlookers, mostly urchins, had begun to gather.

'Mother will not speak to him,' the young girl piped up.

Sheridan gestured towards the curious neighbours. 'I pray you, madam, may we converse within?'

The woman thought for a moment and then nodded. 'Come to my lodgings first, sir, before you trouble my mother. I am with my husband on the second floor.' She turned to the girl. 'Cecile, get inside and do not say anything of this to Mother — not a word, mind.'

The girl nodded and hurried inside.

'Gentlemen, if you will.'

'Obliged, Madame —?'

'Forrestier, or Forster, if you like.'

They followed her up dark and creaking stairs until they reached a landing with two doors. The young woman opened the furthest door and called out above the clacking sound of a loom.

'Simon, we have visitors.'

After a moment the loom stopped and Sheridan and Nicholls found themselves squeezed into an accommodation which must serve as both workplace and home. The handloom, which was set up by the window to catch the daylight, dominated the space and stole the light from the rest of the room. At its frame stood a young man. He was stooped, with thin, dark features and spectacles perched on the end of his nose. The sudden silence of the machinery allowed for another surprising sound. There was a trill of birdsong and Sheridan's eye was caught by a cage that hung behind Simon Forster. Within were three songbirds, a goldfinch and two greenfinches.

'These gentlemen enquire after my brother Jack.'

'Then your visit shall be a short one, sirs,' Simon responded brusquely.

Mrs Forster turned to them. 'We are in private now, gentlemen. You may speak. What business have you with my brother?'

Sheridan stepped forward. 'Jack Champion is an actor of my company, some twenty-five years of age, I should say. First, I must ask, do you have such a brother of that age who has taken employment on the stage?'

The young woman nodded. 'My father met with an accident some ten years ago which left him unable. Jack took charge of the loom but he had never liked the work. One morning we found that he was gone. It was a bitter time, I will not deny. Then, two years ago, Jack returned.' Her face lit up. 'He was dressed in a fine suit and said he was a great success upon the stage. He wished to share his good fortune —'

'He desired to lord it over you all, in truth!' Simon sneered.

'My mother told him to be gone.' Mrs Forster wrung her hands in distress. 'That as he had shown no family feeling when we were most in need, he should find no family here. She was harsh, sir, but she has suffered much.'

'I am sorry to hear of it,' Sheridan said. 'It would seem that my Harlequin was indeed your brother. A very fine-looking young man.'

'Looks may deceive,' Simon muttered.

Mrs Forster laid a hand on the weaver's arm. 'Jack was ever handsome. He meant to make amends, sir, truly he did. Maman would take nothing from him.' The young woman hesitated. 'We were at that time betrothed, Simon and I, but wondered how we should have the funds to make our own home together. Jack helped us.'

Simon slapped his hand on the frame. 'I should not have allowed it, but for the sake of Louise I did, you understand, sir.'

Sheridan nodded. 'I do indeed, Mr Forster. It is never desirable for a man to be indebted to his in-laws, but you felt compelled to please your beloved.'

'You have not told us what your business is with Jack.' Louise Forster glanced at the constable. 'And you bring an officer from Bow Street. What is amiss?'

'Mr Champion has vanished without notice, my dear, and quit his lodgings. Would you perhaps know where he might be found?'

Louise looked anxious. 'He is missing?'

Simon shook his head. 'He has met some trouble, I'll be bound. We have not seen him for many months.'

Nicholls straightened. 'The remains of a body have been found at Drury Lane. Sadly, we wonder if this may be Jack Champion.'

Louise Forster looked startled. 'A body?'

Simon leapt forward and placed a comforting hand on her back. 'But you are not certain, sir, that it is Jack?'

'This man was in the tattered remnants of a Harlequin costume, and we believe that the dead man was a Huguenot.'

Louise put a hand to her mouth, her face drained of colour.

'How so?' her husband pressed and drew his wife close.

Sheridan withdrew the Huguenot Cross from his waistcoat and presented it. 'This was found beneath the costume.'

Louise's hand fluttered towards the cross.

'My mother being Huguenot, I recognised the design,' Nicholls explained. 'Have you seen this particular cross before?'

'Many in our community might own such a cross,' said Simon.

'This one is particularly fine. Please, if you can examine the piece.'

Louise looked hesitant.

Her husband leaned over. 'Jack showed us a similar one. This may be the very one. I wondered at the time, for he had never been strong in his faith. There is something missing…'

'A phial, perhaps? Hanging from the cross?'

'Yes. That is what I recall. There is usually a dove.'

Louise seemed all at once overcome. 'Jack…!' She swayed until her husband caught her and led her to a seat.

Simon shot a glance at the officer. 'You have come to tell us that Jack is dead?'

'I have come to tell you that Jack Champion has been murdered.'

Louise let out a sob and it was her husband's turn to pale.

Sheridan bowed solicitously towards the young woman. 'Please accept our heartfelt condolences. And convey them to your mother — you will best know how to break such news to her. Your father, I believe, is unwell.'

The weaver responded on his wife's behalf. 'Monsieur Champion will not comprehend this report. Which may be a blessing.'

'I should be pleased to assist with the funeral arrangements,' Sheridan continued. 'A reward shall be offered in hopes that we may apprehend the villain that has done this to a member of my company.'

'Who do you suspect this villain might be?' Simon asked.

'There are suggestions of a jealous husband —'

'Might *you* have any suspicions, sir?' Nicholls cut in. 'Any person that would wish Mr Champion harm?'

Simon Forster shook his head. 'None I know of. In truth, I scarcely knew Jack.' He glanced over to his loom. 'Our worlds were very different.'

Sheridan stepped forward. 'Mrs Forster, rest assured I shall not be easy until the killer is caught.'

They said their goodbyes and Simon escorted them to the front door of the dilapidated dwelling. It was then apparent that he had something further to offer to their enquiries.

'A word, sirs.' He spoke in a whisper.

'Mr Forster?'

'I did not wish to say anything in front of my good wife. She is much distressed. Of all her family it was Louise that had the greatest attachment to Jack, naturally, for they were twins and very close as children. I think he was a kind of hero to her, despite his shame in abandoning his parents.'

'He chose to follow his dreams and make his fortune, and in some measure, he succeeded,' Sheridan countered.

'Just so.' The weaver did not look pleased at this summation.

'What is it you would impart, sir?' Nicholls asked.

Simon looked about furtively. 'The walls have too many ears here, Constable.'

'You may come to Bow Street.'

'That may not be safe either.' Simon lowered his voice again. 'There is agitation growing again in Spitalfields. I might be thought an informant if I were spied at the magistrates' court.'

'Then you must come to my house at Grosvenor Street, Mr Forster, and you may bring a sample of your silk, to signal your legitimate business, for I noted it was very fine indeed.'

The young weaver twitched a smile at the compliment.

'I am minded to commission a shawl for my wife. Shall we say ten on the morrow?'

Nicholls glanced at Sheridan and then back to the weaver. 'I should make that noon, sir.'

CHAPTER EIGHT

That evening, whilst on his way to a supper with Mr Johnson the publisher, Sheridan reflected on the encounter in Spitalfields. Nicholls had informed him that the Huguenots of Spitalfields tended to the strict Calvinist tradition. By choosing a theatrical career Jack abandoned not just his family, but their religion. Calvinists were well known to deride the theatre as encouraging idle pursuits and, worst of all, undermining civic morality. That had surely added to his mother's disappointment. And yet, at the end, Jack Champion had worn a Huguenot Cross close to his heart. What did that signal?

Sheridan wondered what it was that Simon Forster wished to tell them. Something of import which Jack had confided to his brother-in-law? And yet there seemed to have been no great love lost between the two men.

The carriage had come to a halt outside Timothy's lodgings in Clerkenwell. Sheridan peered out. A drizzle of rain had begun to fall. He spied an urchin and called him over, instructing him to go within and fetch the young lawyer. Five minutes later, the boy returned with a note.

'Gentleman says he is detained and must send his apologies.' The boy sniffed, wiping his hand across his nose and accepting his farthing.

Sheridan frowned. What might be so important that Timothy would give up this first opportunity to attend one of Joseph Johnson's famous dinners? Sheridan had arranged the invitation as a special favour, knowing how much young Timothy would relish the chance to sit and converse with some of the liveliest and most radical thinkers of the day. He was about to order his coachman onward when he thought better. It was odd that Timothy had not even descended the stairs to acquaint Sheridan personally with whatever the difficulty was. Something was amiss. Well, if his young friend needed help, then he should be the one to offer it up.

Moments later, he was rapping loudly on the door of Timothy's lodging.

After some interval, the young lawyer opened his door an inch or two and peered out.

'Mr Sheridan?' He looked startled. 'You did not receive the note?'

'Yes, I received the note. But I did not receive a satisfactory explanation as to why you would forego such a long-desired occasion. Timothy, are you quite all right?'

'Sir, I…' Timothy trailed off and flushed.

'Must we speak through a crack in the door?' Sheridan raised an eyebrow and lowered his voice confidentially. 'Do you have a woman within, Timothy? Is that the case?'

'Why, no sir!'

The two men regarded each other through the sliver of doorway, one creased with concern, the other awkward and hesitant.

Timothy gave way. 'Oh well, come in, sir. I daresay…'

Sheridan entered the untidy room, which was littered with books and papers on the desk and unmade bed. Nothing appeared to be untoward.

'The ragamuffin said that you were detained?'

'Yes, an unforeseeable event…' Timothy turned and called out, 'You may show yourself now. There is nothing to fear.'

To Sheridan's amazement, a small figure emerged from underneath the trestle bed. He recognised the uniform — the coarse brown drugget suit with its scarlet trim at the shoulders and breeches. A Coram boy. He scarcely recognised Billy, however; his greasy, ragged locks had been shorn off entirely and his face scrubbed pink.

'Billy!'

'Mister Sheridan.'

Sheridan looked to Timothy for explanation.

'I did plan to inform you, sir. You went to so much trouble to have Billy taken in at the Foundling Hospital.'

Sheridan addressed himself sternly to the boy. 'You have run away, Billy?'

'I 'ad to, sir — I was in fear o' my life, I was!'

'At Coram's?' Sheridan shook his head in disbelief.

'Allow me to explain.' Timothy stepped forward. 'Billy was spotted when a delivery cart came to the hospital. The lad on the cart recognised him and must have reported back to Battling Poll. This morning, Billy found this beneath his pillow.'

The young lawyer picked up a scrap of paper, part of a playbill, Sheridan noted, on the blank side of which was a simple X marked in charcoal.

'It's the cross bones!' Billy exclaimed. 'I'm marked. Poll will think 'cause I'm seen at Coram that I've turned snitch. But I ain't no squealer! I got to let her know — or I'm dead.'

'So, you see, Billy has sneaked his way out of the institution and found me here — he must have overheard me as I gave my address to the Warden. I wished to be kept abreast of Billy's progress at Coram's. He fears his life may be forfeit and he shall be hunted down and dispatched.'

Sheridan waved the paper with the mark of the cross bones. 'If Poll wanted you dead, Billy, then whoever put this scrap under your pillow might have done the deed last night.'

'It's a warning, Mister Sheridan.'

'She wishes you to return to her, is that it?'

Billy nodded awkwardly. 'Reckon.'

'But you came here instead, to Mr Legge?'

'He comes to me for protection, sir,' said Timothy.

'Is that right, Billy?'

The boy shrugged.

'And what do you mean to do, Mr Legge?'

'Why, protect him, sir. He may stay here until I know where he may be safe.'

Sheridan raised a bemused eyebrow. 'I suppose we might find him a berth as a ship's boy on an East Indiaman.'

Timothy looked horrified. 'I do not think him quite old enough for that kind of life, Mr Sheridan.' He turned to the boy. 'Do not be concerned, Billy. We will find a suitable place.'

Sheridan sighed. 'You will both be hungry, I daresay. There is a decent chophouse on Gray's Inn Road. I suggest we take ourselves there. And Billy, you had best remove that jacket. It is a distinctive uniform.'

Neither Timothy nor Billy had suffered any loss of appetite after their various frights. The boy had been togged in an old shirt, hitched up at the waist and with the sleeves rolled up, but not sufficient that they did not dip in the gravy. He would need a new outfit. And they should have to think what to do with him.

Sheridan had enough experience of the street urchins about Drury Lane to be sceptical. The child was a sneakthief and unlikely to mend his ways. The boy was merely in dread of a beating from Battling Poll, and with her sobriquet, that should be something to be rightly feared. Were he to return with something of value, he might stand a chance of averting that thrashing. A gentleman like Timothy should have a fine watch and chain or silk handkerchiefs or even monies to be filched that might then ease Billy's way back into his rookery nest.

Sheridan smiled to himself. It may be a timely lesson for young Timothy. However endearing his impulse to trust all and sundry, it might not serve him well in either life or career. In the meantime, let Timothy see how being *in loco parentis* suited him.

Sheridan's thoughts drifted back to the other puzzles on his mind as he refilled their tankards of small beer.

'Timothy, what think you of coincidences?'

'I have never given the matter much thought.'

'They are a well-worn device in drama. I have utilised them myself. In comedies coincidences are an essential ingredient, offering great scope for humour; indeed, there is nothing an audience enjoys so thoroughly as a well-staged coincidence. Tragedies, too — but there they are never a happy accident.'

'Why, I think you are right, sir. They do appear frequently on the stage.'

Sheridan nodded. 'But in the real world, true coincidences are rare as hen's teeth. So, think on … here we have not one but two Harlequins who have disappeared. At least one of them fatally, it would seem. Both men have some French association. Jack Champion has a Huguenot history. Gaspard Bernon, nothing as yet to say that he has not. Both men have quit their lodgings, one in a flit and the other on fair terms with the landlord. But we do not know where either man went next, as neither left a forwarding address. And in consequence we have seen neither man's effects. I find all this to be too coincidental, Timothy. Were it a drama, it might even strain my suspension of disbelief.'

'I see what you mean, sir. It is striking odd.'

'What are we to make of it? That is the question.'

'Well … as a lawyer, I might suggest there is connection.'

'Precisely.' Sheridan drummed his fingers on the table. 'Gaspard Bernon and Jack Champion, so many connections. Could it be that one of these connections might point towards the killer?'

Timothy frowned. 'I thought, sir, that you already have a suspect? The officer of the Life Guards.'

'Ah yes, Captain Jeffreys. His regiment is on manoeuvres, Constable Nicholls informs me, but returns presently. That possibility shall be pursued. You are right; he may be our answer, plain and simple, and yet…'

'And yet what, sir?'

'And yet, would the brave captain not have called Champion out rather than strangle him in a cellar?'

'I should think twice about duelling with a military man!' Timothy exclaimed.

'Sound advice. And what honour is to be saved if a man has none to start with?'

'If Champion did decline the challenge, the captain may have become enraged, confronted Champion at the theatre and —'

'— in his fury, he throttled him.' Sheridan finished the sentence for him. It was a plausible enough scenario. And yet there was still the problem of coincidence.

By the time Sheridan arrived at the house of the publisher, the hour was approaching ten. He offered profuse apologies, which were accepted with benign good humour by his host.

'Mr Sheridan, I should think something truly amiss were you to appear any earlier! And see —' Johnson indicated a couple of empty chairs at the far end of the dining table — 'there are guests yet to arrive. You have missed the boiled cod, but the rice pudding shall be served at once.'

A great chatter circulated at the table. Sheridan caught snatches of conversation on either side: the talk was of Rousseau's ideas on education, of the role of the latest scientific advances and, of course, the recent disturbances in Birmingham and Paris. Sheridan settled himself into his seat and looked about the gathering. Timothy Legge would have been struck with awe.

The Reverend John Newton sat across from him; the abolitionist was giving a vivid description of the slave ships in that inhuman and horrid trade to his neighbour, Horne Tooke. On his right Sheridan found Mary Wollstonecraft, lately made infamous by the rebuttal to Mr Burke in her *Vindication of the Rights of Men*, for which Sheridan held the lady in great admiration, though he could not help but find the former governess altogether too serious and intense in her passions. One of which was evident at that moment to both Sheridan and the Swiss artist, Mr Fuseli, to whom she was expressing her intention to write a piece on the rights of women. Well, that should set the cat amongst the pigeons.

As Sheridan's eyes scanned the room, he was arrested by Fuseli's painting, which hung above the diners. The rice pudding had arrived and he wondered that Mr Johnson could on the one hand serve such bland dinners whilst on the other hand subject his guests to the most disturbing artwork Sheridan had ever laid eyes on: *The Nightmare*. It was well named, that much was certain. A woman lay splayed across a bed, more dead than asleep, while a red-eyed incubus, hunched and squat on her middle, glared accusingly at the spectator, as though the imp had been unpardonably disturbed in his bestial activities. But ghouls and devils were common enough characters on the stage. No, it was the wild black horse with its flaring nostrils, gaping maw and opaque eyes which really made Sheridan shudder.

A commotion at the doorway alerted all to the arrival of the final guests of the evening. There was a ripple of excitement around the table, the anticipation palpable; some of the diners were clearly in the know. Sheridan wondered who might be the cause.

Thomas Christie entered and greeted his friend Johnson in familiar fashion. They were co-founders of the *Analytical Review*, in which young Dr Christie was making his name as a writer on matters of political reform. Yet it was Christie's companion that drew every eye in the room and a gasp from Miss Wollstonecraft.

He was a tall, bulky man in his early thirties. Ill-favoured to the point of extreme ugliness, his face sported a broken nose, pox scars and a gash across his lips, which Sheridan had heard had been sustained in an encounter with a bull. This was the Jacobin, Monsieur Georges Danton — the man many pointed to as the leading force now driving the Revolution in France.

Sheridan was suitably impressed and rose as one with the table whilst addressing his neighbour *sotto voce*, 'What on earth is Monsieur Danton doing in London?'

CHAPTER NINE

'Mr Forster.'

Sheridan bowed as the weaver was shown into the reception room of his Grosvenor Street home.

'Mr Sheridan.' Simon Forster returned the gesture and turned towards the Bow Street Runner who had risen to his feet. 'Constable Nicholls.'

'It is good of you to come, sir. And I see you have brought your samples.'

The weaver nodded and unhitched the satchel from his shoulder.

'You will take a glass of claret, gentlemen?' Sheridan asked.

'I am on duty, sir,' Nicholls responded.

Sheridan raised an eyebrow. 'That has never stopped your fellows. What about you, Mr Forster, are you also on duty?'

'I should welcome the refreshment, sir. Thank you.'

Sheridan twitched a nod towards his serving man. 'And you may lay your silk pieces on this table, Mr Forster.'

Simon laid out the examples of his workmanship with reverent care.

'Fine, very fine,' Sheridan enthused. He spent some moments examining and admiring the workmanship before he pointed to one sample. 'It should be this light green with the darker trim. That should suit Mrs Sheridan very well.' Business concluded, Sheridan turned with a look of concern to the weaver. 'How does your good wife fare today?'

'Louise is a little more composed, sir, but this news has come as a great shock to all of the family. It has quite devastated her mother. That Jack should die so violently…' Simon shook his head. 'It is another burden for the poor woman to bear.'

'Mrs Champion has my utmost sympathy.'

Nicholls looked closely at the weaver. 'You wished to speak to us. Your manner yesterday seemed urgent. You have some opinion on what has happened to your brother-in-law?'

A glass of claret was presented to Mr Forster. He clutched it in both hands nervously. 'Perhaps it is of no significance at all, sirs, and if so, I must apologise; I do not mean to waste your time.'

'Anything which furthers our knowledge of Jack Champion cannot be a waste,' Sheridan encouraged. 'Pray continue, Mr Forster.'

'It is the Huguenot Cross with the phial instead of the dove. This particular make of cross, in silver, is an emblem worn by a group which has been recently formed. A secret group,' he added.

Sheridan ears pricked: a secret society — that was always something of interest.

'Can you name this group?' Nicholls pressed.

The weaver hesitated and Sheridan caught a sudden trace of fear.

'They call themselves the Huguenot Brotherhood.'

The constable frowned. 'Brotherhood, eh? What is their object, Mr Forster?'

'I am not entirely sure. I have no interest in schemes or societies. That is what I told Jack when he showed the cross to me.'

'He wanted you to join this society?'

'I believe so.'

'He did not divulge their purpose? To tempt you into membership?'

'From what I could glean, the Brotherhood wish to see Huguenots restored to prominence in France. Jack kept saying that now, with the revolution, we should return, that Huguenots would be safe. There should never be another Revocation of Nantes, another Bourbon betrayal. He spoke of the family journeying back to France. It was our duty to support the revolution, he said.'

'But the London Huguenots have been settled here for so long, I cannot imagine a great appeal in such notions.'

'The revolutionaries would make reparation to the Huguenots, Jack said.'

'Ah, a monetary incentive.'

'Reparation?' Nicholls narrowed his eyes. 'Who talks of this? I have heard nothing amongst my relatives.'

Forster nodded. 'It's what Jack claimed: rights, possessions, even land might be restored or allocated in compensation. Many of the French nobles are fleeing the country, you see, and some of their property has been confiscated. Jack was really quite animated on the subject.'

'I daresay Mr Champion had hopes of making his fortune — that might be enough to tempt any man. But you were not swayed?'

Forster swallowed back a draught of claret. 'I told him he was being fanciful; it was our great-grandparents and earlier ancestors who came over to London; France has been long forgotten. England is our home now. But he persisted. There should be a new age, he said, a kind of Utopia. There was a fire burning in him. Someone had persuaded him in this cause and Jack had given himself over to it.'

'I am sure you are right to be sceptical, Mr Forster,' Nicholls concurred.

Sheridan rubbed his chin in thought. 'The Brotherhood is a secret society, you have said, but why should it be secret? Why not simply a group that advocates, indeed advertises, such a return to France amongst the Huguenot community?'

Simon looked grim. 'I got the impression that the Brotherhood might look to take action in support of the revolution.' He paused. 'The upheaval in France, sir, has not been without bloodshed. Jack might have continued with his persuasion, but Louise entered the room and that is when she also saw the cross. Her only thought, naturally, was that Jack had returned to his religion; she was all enthusiasm, and he and I scarce had a chance for another word on the Brotherhood.'

Nicholls nodded gravely. 'You have done right to tell us of this, Mr Forster. Membership of this Brotherhood may have no bearing on the murder, but then again it may be the very reason for it. You must know that I now have a duty to inform the authorities of the existence of this group.'

The weaver bit his lip.

'They may pose some threat.'

Simon nodded curtly but could not disguise his anxiety. 'I understand, sir.'

'I shall try to avoid naming you as the informant.'

'Thank you, sir. I am a Huguenot and proud of that, but I am English too. This country took us in in our hour of need, and I would not see any violence done here against any man in my name.'

Forster and Nicholls departed together, leaving Sheridan to muse over this new information.

'Action to support the revolutionaries?' he murmured out loud as he paced the room, glass of claret in hand. 'Espionage would be likely... Huguenots should be well embedded in many parts of this country — a ready network.' Sheridan paused. 'Assassinations?' That thought filled him with horror. If the Huguenot Brotherhood contemplated assassination, then there would be many targets. The French émigrés, for one. London had become a magnet for French nobles fleeing the upheaval, all of them set upon plotting and planning a counter-revolution.

Many of the leading Tories were arguing that the chaos could spread like an infection to England. The Huguenot Brotherhood presented a real possibility that opposing French factions might battle out their differences on British soil. Sheridan sighed. In consequence, legitimate calls for reform in England were being tainted, opening wide the door to a government of repression.

For years the Prime Minister had been using his own network of spies. That was nothing new, of course. Knowledge was power and Mr Pitt a man keen to keep a tight rein on the country. The volatile situation across the Channel in France created an ever more fertile ground for espionage. This Huguenot Brotherhood might stir up a veritable hornets' nest of intrigue. Whether or not membership of the Brotherhood had any bearing on the murder of Jack Champion, its existence could not be ignored.

Once Constable Nicholls had made his report to Sir Sampson Wright, the Chief Magistrate would no doubt speak with Henry Dundas, Secretary of State for the Home Department. Sheridan hoped that Dundas could refrain from being heavy-handed in the matter. It would not do to stir up anxiety amongst the London Huguenots. Nor would it be sensible to scaremonger, and turn the existing anti-French sentiments of the King and Church rioters against this long-established and largely law-abiding community. After what had passed in Birmingham, Sheridan shuddered to think what destruction might be caused by those gangs of ruffians if they were to rampage in Spitalfields and other Huguenot localities.

There was a knock at the door and Sheridan's butler brought in a note on a salver.

'Sir, a response is required.'

Sheridan quickly broke the seal. The message was from Thomas Christie. His houseguest, Monsieur Danton, would very much like to meet with Mr Sheridan at his earliest convenience. Sheridan felt a frisson of excitement. At the dinner on the previous evening there had been little opportunity for more than a brief introduction. Monsieur Danton's attention had been wanted on all sides. But now here was the very Man of the Age wishing to meet with him. What might that presage? It was all too intriguing to play at polite delay or prevarication. Let him be impetuous or he should explode with curiosity. He would call on Thomas Christie and Monsieur Danton that very afternoon, and he scribbled a reply to that effect, expressing his delight at the opportunity to enjoy the Frenchman's company again so soon. And further, that it should be no inconvenience to be at Soho within the next hour — or two, he added, to ensure he did not cause offence by arriving any later.

He decided to walk to Dr Christie's house. It would give him time to calm his agitated state and to ponder this request. Something was wanted of him, that much was certain.

A blue sky greeted him as he stepped onto the pavement, the bright summer sun high overhead. The streets were busy with traffic at this hour of the day, and hawkers of every kind were shouting their wares. Sheridan realised, as his stomach rumbled, that he was a little peckish and stopped by a barrow at the end of the street for a hunk of bread, cooked ham and pease pudding. It was well seasoned and he expressed his fulsome appreciation to the vendor.

Sheridan tried to recall what he knew of Georges Danton. Maybe six or seven years Sheridan's junior, it was said that he was a parvenu, an opportunist. Well, that should go hand in hand with being a lawyer. It was a profession which Sheridan himself had taken up as a young man. His father approved mightily — anything other than to follow Thomas Sheridan into a theatrical career. What a disappointment he had proved when he quit the Inns of Temple.

Danton was a man of the people, a politician known for his fiery speeches. That was another point of similarity between them; both had been hailed as being amongst the greatest orators of the age. Sheridan wondered if they should now find even more in common.

Sheridan had overheard the Duc d'Orléans speak of Danton as a man with whom one might parlay and who had avowedly admired Britain's constitutional monarchy. Reassuring, no doubt, to the duc. The two had met at a Freemason's Lodge. At the Palais-Royale, presumably. Orléans had converted part of his Parisian residence into a complex of shops, cafes and casinos. Brothels, too, it was rumoured. The cafes of the Palais-Royale were a reputed hothouse of freemasonry, as well as a frequent meeting place for the radicals of the city. In this way, the duc could keep his finger to the very pulse of the revolution.

Sheridan paused mid-stride. Brotherhoods and Freemasons. How men liked to move amongst these secret societies. They had never held any great appeal for Sheridan. Perhaps he had always been too much of an outsider, taunted from his schooldays at Harrow for being 'a player's son'. Sheridan resumed his stride, crossing into the narrow streets of Soho.

More immediately, why had Danton arrived in London? To some very particular purpose? Or was he in flight? His name had been linked with the protests at the Champ de Mars. Paris was now under martial law. There may even be an order for the Jacobin's arrest. At dinner he had heard Danton vociferously deny that he was present at the Champ de Mars. Was he telling the truth? To openly admit that he had played a key role in stirring up the mobs would have suggested that he was throwing his hand in with the republicans.

But perhaps Danton would prefer Louis XVI to abdicate in favour of his cousin? He was in London to meet with Orléans. Had Orléans whispered promises of preferment to him in some private niche of the Freemason's Lodge? Was that the object of Danton's visit — to persuade the duc that this was the time to act, before the clamour for a republic became too loud? Louis' remaining son was a mere child and captive like his father. Louis' younger brothers were both in exile and aligned with the counter-revolutionaries clamouring for intervention to restore the *ancien régime*. Had the moment come for Orléans to declare his hand and seize the throne before the tide of history might cause the monarchy to be swept away entirely?

Sheridan felt his mind buzz with the possibility that he might play some small part in the unfolding events. He was reminded of the recent crisis regarding King George III, when he had had the ear of both the prince and the Whig politician Charles James Fox. Had His Majesty not recovered from his bout of insanity, the Foxites might even now be at the helm of government through these interesting times in Europe.

Could it be that Monsieur Danton wished Sheridan to play a part in the dialogue between the two countries? Restore friendship between England and France? Silence the warmongers? The prospects were thrilling. He wiped the crumbs from his frock coat as he approached the entrance to Dr Christie's house.

CHAPTER TEN

Sheridan stared up at the sundial above the entrance of La Neuve Église on Brick Lane, the words *Umbra Sumus* engraved in Latin above the dial itself. We are shadow. The full quote from Horace he remembered from his schooldays at Harrow, *Pulvis et umbra sumus*: we are dust and shadow. Well, Jack Champion was very nearly dust already. His bones had been placed in a silk sack, made from a cloth woven by his brother Henry, and then laid in a simple casket.

A small congregation was gathered at the chapel, the family keen to keep their grief as private as possible. The pestering attentions of a journalist from Grub Street in search of a sensational story had unsettled Mrs Champion. She had let it be known to Sheridan that any advertisement of a reward for the apprehension of her son's killer was not welcome. As far as Jack Champion's mother was concerned, so much time had elapsed since the deed that the likelihood of any arrest was remote. A hue and cry should only draw attention to the family and disturb their peace within the community. She wished to bury her son and then to quietly forget him. Sheridan had bowed demurely in the face of her stern demeanour.

Perhaps Mrs Champion was right. What was the point in raking over the business? Without solid proof, how would they ever arrest anyone? It had been established that the last known sighting of Jack had been on a Friday, the first day of April. Monsieur Dubois had sworn to having seen him leave the theatre. All Fools' Day. That seemed appropriate enough. How or when the murder had taken place was a mystery and would likely remain a mystery. Jack Champion was already a shadow.

Sheridan had scarcely known the fellow, in truth. He too should forget the matter. It was enough that he had paid for the burial.

Amongst the assembled congregation were a few representatives of the Drury Lane company. Mrs Petty, the wardrobe mistress, held a handkerchief to her capacious bosom and dabbed at her eyes. Margaret Bedwell also attended with young Joey Grimaldi in tow. To Sheridan's surprise, Monsieur Dubois stood at the rear and appeared to be cleaning his fingernails with a small clasp knife. Given the scant regard he had expressed for Jack Champion at their last interview, Sheridan wondered why Dubois had bothered to come to the funeral at all.

Sheridan slipped into a pew beside Timothy Legge, who, having been present at the discovery of the body, felt duty-bound to attend this funeral service. Fidgeting between them was young Billy, who looked uncomfortable in a new suit. Sheridan marvelled that the child had not yet scarpered back to his rookery. Perhaps he had underestimated him. He should be pleased, he thought, to have been wrong. When they had deposited him at Coram's, the boy had claimed not to know his original surname, nor to have been allotted one by Battling Poll. Timothy had at once volunteered his own and expressed himself very honoured if Billy would accept it. The boy had shrugged with indifference at the time, but perhaps now he had begun to see advantage in becoming young Master Legge.

As the service began, Sheridan's thoughts turned to his meeting with Monsieur Danton the previous afternoon. The Frenchman had expressed a desire for a closer communion. He wished to be introduced to Mr Charles James Fox but appreciated that any meeting with the Government opposition must be discreet. He wondered if Sheridan might be able to arrange a private conference?

'It would not be my wish to embarrass Monsieur Fox. The situation in France, it is most delicate.'

'I wonder you are not in Paris yourself, monsieur?' Sheridan probed as disingenuously as he could.

'You are correct, Monsieur Sheridan. I should very much like to be in Paris.'

'Never have they had more need for the voice of Monsieur Danton!' Thomas Christie contributed. 'We understand that in recent days the authorities in Paris have made hundreds of arrests, meetings have been suppressed, and newspapers closed. Everything that has been gained thus far may be in jeopardy!'

Danton looked apologetic. 'Unfortunately, there was family business I must attend to in Arcis.' The big man shrugged. 'And then my stepfather requested my company here to England; he wishes to purchase a — what do you call it — spinning jenny.'

Sheridan raised an eyebrow. Well, here was a novel excuse for the visit to London.

Danton smiled. 'My stepfather, Monsieur Recordain, is a cloth maker. He is most interested in this machine. Only this afternoon he is gone to observe the jenny spinning.'

'Jenny spins most delightfully, so I am informed,' Sheridan offered. 'But Monsieur Recordain must also view more recent developments — the spinning mule, I understand, is a beast with a remarkable kick.'

Christie nodded. 'Mr Sheridan is quite right. The new inventions are truly startling in their efficiency, but of course they then threaten the livelihood of our many journeyman weavers, and that is to be regretted.'

Danton's eyes flashed. 'There is always a price to be paid for progress, is there not?'

Christie shifted uneasily. 'I daresay.'

'The time has come to sweep away the old traditions. The English, they are an inventive people. We have much to learn in France.'

There was a knock at the door and they were interrupted by a manservant. Dr Christie's attention was needed with a tradesman.

'You will excuse me a moment, gentlemen.' He bowed and followed the servant from the room.

Danton moved over to the decanter and offered further replenishment to Sheridan. The man was a heavy drinker, Sheridan observed, but with the constitution of an ox he could certainly hold his liquor.

As he held out the glass of claret to Sheridan, the Frenchman fixed him with a stare. 'You are, I think, a shrewd man, monsieur. More than you allow. I do not wish to alarm the good Dr Christie; he is most kind and generous towards myself and my stepfather. But perhaps with you, monsieur, I can confide a little?'

Sheridan accepted the glass of claret. 'I may not offer the sanctity of a confessional, Monsieur Danton; I am in no manner a priest, but unless you intend harm, I am honoured to be a confidant.'

'Just so.' The revolutionary raised his glass. 'To confidence.'

They clinked glasses and downed a toast. Then Danton heaved a sigh and withdrew a pistol from his pocket.

Sheridan was momentarily nonplussed.

'There is a price on my head, Sheridan.'

Sheridan regained his composure. 'What is the going rate for a Jacobin, if I may be so bold?'

'Fifty thousand livres.'

Sheridan shook his head in dismay. 'I should have fancied it to be a higher price for your head, sir.'

Danton hooted. 'How right you are! I should be insulted!' The Frenchman weighed the weapon in his large hand. 'Before I left Arcis, I received a warning. The note said there is one in the Cordeliers Club, the butcher Louis Legendre, that has been offered this sum to assassinate me. It is preposterous.'

Danton pointed the pistol towards Sheridan. 'Nevertheless —' he mimed taking a shot — 'I am *en garde*.'

'You say this, monsieur, that I too may know the importance of discretion in this matter.'

Danton grunted. 'I say this, monsieur, so that you too may know how cheap the life of any man may be in these tumultuous times.'

Sheridan's thoughts were interrupted by an outbreak of sobbing coming from the pew behind him. He strained to peer over his shoulder and caught sight of a well-dressed and elaborately wigged woman in a light hood and cape accompanied by a young maid. The closing words of the funeral service had reminded the woman of the finality of the occasion. Sheridan did not recognise her. She was not of the theatre company that he could recall. What connection had brought her here to La Neuve Église? And then the answer came to him. This could be Mrs Jeffreys. The married woman with whom handsome Jack Champion had cavorted.

The Champion family were leaving the chapel. The old man, led by his son Henry, smiled beneficently on all those he passed.

'Lovely day, isn't it?' Mr Champion murmured. 'Such a blue, blue sky!'

On the arm of her daughter Louise, Mrs Champion paused to nod at Sheridan. 'Thank you, Mr Sheridan. We are indebted.'

Sheridan bowed. '*Au contraire*, madam. It is the least I could do.'

'Blue sky!' Mr Champion chuckled.

Henry, a wiry young man with a scar on his left cheek, nudged his father gently down the aisle.

Sheridan appraised the young silk weaver. What had the relationship between the two brothers been like? Jack had run off at fifteen, leaving thirteen-year-old Henry to take his place — to effectively become head of the family, the main breadwinner. Had Henry resented his older brother for condemning him to long days at the loom? How had he felt when Jack had returned in his fine suits? *He desired to lord it over you all*, Simon Forster had remarked with some sourness. Had Henry refused the handouts which his brother-in-law had reluctantly accepted? Like his mother, had Henry refused to countenance Jack's return into the family fold? Was there anger and resentment enough for murder? There was a thought. He should discuss it with Constable Nicholls.

One thing puzzled Sheridan. Why should a man with no religion suddenly become a zealot? Jack had purportedly cared little for his faith and yet he had died with the Huguenot Cross about his neck and had joined a secret brotherhood. Brotherhood. There it was. Sheridan nodded to himself. Was Henry a member, sealing the bond between the fraternal siblings? Sheridan mind raced with the differing possibilities. They should speak with Henry. No, perhaps he should be observed. Nicholls might set a watch on him.

The sound of raised voices came suddenly from outside the building and Sheridan found himself hurrying to the chapel entrance alongside Timothy to see what might be the cause of the commotion. Their exit was blocked as the well-groomed woman and her maid pushed back inside the building. The woman held a hand to her mouth in terror.

'Madame, pray tell, what is happening?'

The maid hastened both women further within. 'It is Captain Jeffreys, sir! He is in a mighty rage!' She turned then to the verger. 'You must help make us escape!'

The verger nodded curtly towards the rear of the chapel.

Sheridan and Timothy exchanged worried glances and hurried to the street outside. As they edged their way through the parishioners, they were confronted by the sight of a tall, thickset man in the distinctive red uniform of the 2nd Life Guards wielding his officer's sword.

'Stand aside, you dim-witted oafs! I would see my wife! My *wife*, damn it!' The officer punched the air with his weapon and staggered back a little. His face was red with rage but he was also clearly drunk.

Before Sheridan could stop him, Timothy had pushed forward. 'Sir, Captain, show some respect! This is a funeral service we attend!'

Captain Jeffreys sneered. 'Good riddance to that snivelling, scheming cur!'

The young lawyer clenched his fists. 'Captain, you must desist and quit this place at once!'

The soldier teetered towards Timothy. 'Not without my wife! Sophia! Sophia! Show yourself! Your husband commands it!'

'You will leave now, sir,' Timothy persisted.

Captain Jeffreys raised his sword. 'You dare to stand in my way? I have a right to see her! And punish her too — she has disobeyed her husband!' he snarled.

'You will not enter.'

'Then you will feel the edge of my blade, sir!'

'Timothy!' Sheridan called out in warning as he pulled the young lawyer aside.

The officer slashed forward and narrowly missed, his sword sparking off the pavement. Captain Jeffreys lurched forward, almost losing his balance.

In that moment Monsieur Dubois leapt behind the Guards officer, twisted the man's left arm behind his back and thrust his clasp knife up to the soldier's throat.

'Drop it, monsieur!'

Jeffreys attempted to shake the Frenchman off, swinging the sword wildly. The small crowd gasped and took a step back as Jeffreys continued to flail about.

'Devil take you!'

'*Maintenant!*'

Dubois pushed the knife under the officer's neck so that a few drops of blood spilt onto the white cravat of his uniform.

Admitting defeat, the Guardsman furiously flung his weapon aside. It rattled to the ground at the feet of Master Billy Legge, who regarded the shining blade with wide, excited eyes.

Henry Champion broke away from the crowd and stood in front of the officer. His eyes narrowed. 'Are you the man that killed my brother Jack?'

Some of Henry's fellow weavers and neighbours looked amongst themselves and then with murmurs of support inched forward.

With a sinking heart, Sheridan feared there might soon be a lynching. Then London should see a corpse hanging from a lamppost as Paris had of late. He took a deep breath and raised his hands in a placatory fashion as he moved alongside Henry.

'You must answer for yourself, Captain Jeffreys. There are many here present who believe you had cause to wish Mr Champion ill.'

The officer grunted disdainfully.

'You have an unfortunate temper, sir. You accused your wife of adultery, I believe? Are we to surmise that you may have been responsible for Jack Champion's death? Shall I call for the police and have you arrested?'

'You may all go to hell,' growled Jeffreys.

Dubois nudged his deadly blade against the officer's skin.

'I should have left the rogue for dead — it was what he deserved! But I am an officer, sir!'

'An officer, that is plain to see — you wear the uniform of the 2nd Life Guards. But are you a gentleman, Captain Jeffreys? Or do you bring that proud regiment into disrepute?'

'Have a care, Mr Sheridan, or I shall call you out too!'

'You don't deny then that you challenged my performer?'

'Oh, I challenged the blackguard all right,' Jeffreys snorted. 'He showed his true colours then — he was yellow through and through!'

Sheridan could sense Henry bridling at his side and edged himself between the two men.

'When he refused to duel, you naturally sought satisfaction?'

'As any gentleman would.'

'And did you? Receive satisfaction?'

'I gave the scoundrel a good drubbing, sir. Warned him to quit the city if he knew what was good for him!'

'When was this, Captain?' Sheridan asked.

'First day of April. I waylaid the rogue when he left at the stage door.'

'And you gave him a thrashing? You did not intend to kill him; I am sure that was an unfortunate —'

'That's a damnable lie! And I have a witness to the event!'

'Sir?'

'Captain Naylor.'

'Of the Life Guards?'

Jeffreys nodded. 'We left the wretch snivelling in the dirt. Do you imagine that I should lurk in shadows and conceal bodies?'

'Captain Naylor will swear to it?'

'And this fellow!' Jeffreys looked straight at Henry with narrowed eyes. 'He saw it too, if I am not mistaken!'

'You are mistaken!' Henry flared quickly.

Jeffreys snorted and shook his head. 'Now unhand me, sirs.'

'There is the safety of your wife to consider, Captain,' Sheridan reasoned.

'I shall deal with her later. There will be no trouble here. You have my word, Mr Sheridan. Unhand me, if you please.'

Sheridan nodded to Monsieur Dubois.

Dubois hesitated and then released the officer with a shove. He wiped the short blade on his black breeches and spat on the ground before he strode off down Brick Lane.

Henry Champion reluctantly retreated to his father's side.

'Come, Father, it is time for the interment.'

'Jack is a fine fellow, is he not? Does he not join us?'

'Why no, Father, it is him we bury,' Louise reminded her parent.

'I never saw him look so well.'

Louise shook her head and exchanged a look of sadness with her brother.

'Such a blue sky...'

Captain Jeffreys stood to his full height and straightened his uniform. 'My sword, if you will.'

Billy leapt forward to retrieve the sword and held it out in front of him, feeling its pleasing weight, as he approached the officer. 'Do it run a man right through, sir?'

Jeffreys laughed. 'Why, yes — a little twig like you would be sliced clean in half!'

Timothy placed a hand on Billy's shoulder. 'There has been quite enough blood shed today. Hand the sword back to Captain Jeffreys, there's a good boy, Billy.'

Billy heaved a sigh and held out the sword.

The captain placed his hand around the basket hilt. 'Your pa's right there. Wouldn't want to cut yourself now, would you, son?'

The boy sniffed. 'He ain't me pa. I should like to be a soldier, I reckon.'

Jeffreys laughed again. 'No doubt you will be then, boy — we're never long without a war, and there's another one brewing against the French, mark my words!'

The officer replaced his weapon in its scabbard and marched away, having recovered some of his sobriety.

Sheridan watched him go with a mixture of relief and unease. If Jeffreys had not murdered Jack Champion, then who had?

CHAPTER ELEVEN

Sheridan found that he could not sleep. This business with his Harlequin kept turning over in his mind in the most irritating fashion. He got up from his bed, lit a candle and crossed to his table where a bottle of brandy had been left should he feel indisposed. He poured himself a generous bumper and went over to the window, drawing the curtains back so that he could look out over the lawns and down to the river. The night sky was cloudless, a canopy of stars with a near half-moon which glittered on the Thames below. His ears pricked at the sounds of a summer's night in the countryside. A dog barked in the distance. An owl hooted, and there was the cry of a fox. Really, the country was hardly less quiet than Mayfair or Westminster.

He had rented the villa in Isleworth to please Eliza and their son Tom, who had just yesterday returned home for a summer recess from his school in Warwickshire. And of course, it was expected that a gentleman should have a country residence for entertainment and country pursuits. Although he was a born city-dweller who relished the buzz of London, that *great and monstrous thing*, as Mr Defoe had described it, there were yet times when he conceded that a week in the country could be welcome. His wife had always been inclined towards the quieter life, and her visits to the town house in Grosvenor Street had become less frequent as the years passed. Eliza was of a shy and retiring nature, despite the celebrity of her youth. He owned that this inclination towards retirement on her part might also be due to his own disreputable behaviour and various amorous liaisons.

After the funeral in Spitalfields, he had directed his carriage on to Isleworth. He should not continue to avoid his wife. There were too many conversations left unspoken. But although it had been early in the evening when he arrived, she had already taken to her bed. The housekeeper, Mrs Tucker, expressed her fear that Mrs Sheridan might have caught a chill, she was of so delicate a constitution.

'She looked quite pale, sir, more so than normal.'

'I am sorry to hear this, Mrs Tucker. Cook has made her one of her delicious broths, I trust? They are always a tonic.' He felt suddenly alarmed. 'Or do you think we must call for the doctor?'

'She won't have it, sir. She says it is only rest and a good night's sleep that she requires.'

'We must keep ourselves quiet, then.' Sheridan looked pointedly at his son, who was of a noisy and lively disposition.

'I hear tell in the village they are warning of summer fevers in the area, sir. Yourself and Master Tom must keep yourselves well wrapped up when you go abroad.'

'That we will, Mrs Tucker.' Sheridan placed an arm around Tom's shoulder.

The housekeeper was about to leave when she swung about and addressed Sheridan again. 'And you must carry an umbrella, sir, in case you should be caught in a sudden downpour, you and Master Tom.' She nodded the injunction at the boy. 'The summer showers are the worst. You must have an umbrella about you at all times.' She shuddered, as though feeling the chill herself.

At this sound advice Tom rushed out into the hallway. He returned a moment later wielding a large, oiled umbrella.

'At all times, do you hear, Pa?' Tom twirled about the room. 'And lest we be thought not quite manly enough, as some are wont to sneer at a fellow with an umbrella, why, I have had a stupendous notion, Pa! We should attach a blade to the tip and then the whole may double as a weapon.' He thrust about and parried. 'It shall become the very height of fashion.' Tom jumped up on a chair.

'That is certainly a novel idea, Tom.'

Tom's eyes widened with sudden inspiration. 'A patent — I should take out a patent, Father, and then we might all be rich!' He turned to the housekeeper. 'And Mrs Tucker, it should be thanks to you! It shall be our slogan — *a man should have an umbrella about him at all times. With a Sheridan Umbrella, a man shall be safe not only from the rain but from any villain that assails him*!' Tom leapt to another chair and jabbed with the umbrella. 'Take that, you rogue!'

Sheridan grinned and clapped his hands. 'Splendid, Tom!'

Mrs Tucker shook her head. 'Supper shall be ready in half an hour, sirs.' And the harried housekeeper left the room, tutting under her breath.

Sheridan sipped at his brandy. He would visit Eliza tomorrow in her bedchamber if she did not rise, and he would send out for any fruits and sweet things she may desire. He and Tom should make a great fuss of her and entertain her with comic duets.

Sheridan heaved a sigh. His thoughts ran back to Captain Jeffreys. He had believed Jeffreys. The soldier was a brute, but he had not been responsible for Champion's death. Jeffreys had been right; there was something underhand about the business. *Do you imagine that I should lurk in shadows and conceal bodies?* he had said. Indeed, the manner of death was suggestive of an ambush.

Nicholls had surmised that the cause was strangulation. If Jack had been taken unawares and garrotted, then the list of suspects might be extended to include a woman's hand. Might Mrs Jeffreys have had cause to turn on her lover? Margaret Bedwell had mentioned another lady. A Frenchwoman. Margaret had thought him *aiming high*. Perhaps Mrs Jeffreys had discovered that she had been replaced by another in Jack's affections. Was she capable of exacting revenge? He must discover more about the officer's wife.

Then there was the brother, Henry. Captain Jeffreys seemed certain that Henry had been a witness to Jack's drubbing. Henry had quickly denied that he had been there — but then he would lie if he too had arrived to deal with his brother in some way. Perhaps he had carried the weak and injured Jack back into the theatre. There, the brothers had argued, Henry had been provoked to the murderous deed and then sought a place to hide the corpse. Conveniently, he had discovered the drainage runnel in the cellars. But would he have gone so far as to dress Jack in the Harlequin costume? That was a sticking point.

Perhaps Jack had not been murdered on the first day of April? Instead, he had returned to the theatre on the second day of the month, changed into his costume but never lived to perform. On the Saturday evening, Champion had not appeared for his cue and Goldoni had stepped into the role of Harlequin at short notice. That fact was confirmed by members of the company. Who would now recall after this passage of time whether Jack had nevertheless arrived earlier in the day? Sheridan must write to Nicholls and ask that a watch be kept on the young silk weaver, if for no other reason than to determine whether there might be some link between Henry Champion and this Huguenot Brotherhood.

Then there was Dubois. Had he really attended the funeral to pay his last respects, or was he there to ensure that Jack was buried for good? Oh, Monsieur Dubois, there was no denying he was a tremendous performer — but he had always made Sheridan feel a little nervous. Was he truly of a sinister character, or was that also an act?

A light rap at the door startled Sheridan. He frowned. Had something happened that a servant would disturb him at this hour? Then a thought assailed him. Eliza! She was not well — her condition had grown worse! He rushed over to the bedroom door and flung it open.

It was Eliza herself who stood before him, holding a candle and with a woollen shawl wrapped around her shoulders.

'Eliza!' He regarded her pale features with alarm. 'Are you ill? Shall I call for Mrs Tucker? Or the local doctor — Bassett, I think is his name.' He reached towards her. 'You must go back to your bed, Eliza!'

Eliza smiled wanly. 'Shush, Dick,' she said, using her pet name for him. 'You shall wake the house. I need no attention. I heard you pacing and then saw the light beneath the door, and I wish to speak with you.'

'Of course, my dearest, come in. Sit by the fire; it is laid and I shall have it lit in but a trice.'

'Really, there is no need.'

'I insist.' Sheridan bounded over to the small fireplace and looked about for the tinderbox. 'There is a chill in the night. Myself and Tom have had a great lecture from Mrs Tucker on the hazards of a summer chill; she fears we shall all be down with the fever at the slightest breeze and drip of rain.'

Sheridan poked at the kindling as the flames began to catch. All the while he was wondering what it was that Eliza felt so urgent a need to discuss that she would come to his room at such an hour.

'It is some while since we have spoken, Dick.'

He looked up at her and nodded. 'Too long, my dear.'

She smiled in the glow of the flames as the fire took and flared. Sheridan felt a surge of affection towards his beautiful wife. She really was quite entrancing. No wonder Eliza had been pursued so relentlessly by the Duke of Clarence until the prince had demanded that his younger brother desist.

Unlike so many of Sheridan's acquaintances within the world of the *bon ton*, his marriage had not been arranged or pursued for wealth and advancement. Sheridan's marriage to Eliza Linley had been that rare thing, a love match. He had fought not one but two duels with a Captain Matthews for sake of her honour; he had been near fatally wounded in the second. He had assisted Eliza's flight to France, ostensibly to escort her to the safety of a convent, and on that mission, he had been emboldened to express his true feelings. Eliza had reciprocated. On their return to England, they had fervently hoped for a blessing from both parents. That had not been forthcoming from his furious father. Resolutely his younger self had defied Thomas Sheridan and continued his courtship. When Thomas Linley had finally dropped his objection to the match, Sheridan had married Eliza at Marylebone Church.

That had been eighteen years ago, and those early years of marriage had been ones of domestic bliss. Then, his star had soared high in the firmament, first as a celebrated playwright and latterly as an upcoming Member of Parliament. Thrust onto a public stage, he had embraced his fame. They had been a golden couple in youth, but differences in temperament and shared sorrows had undermined the bedrock of the marriage. Eliza's health had never been robust. They had one precious son, Tom, but miscarriages, one after another, and then the pain of a son lost at birth had been cause for continuous grief. The words of Thomas Linley often rang in Sheridan's ears:

'You must absolutely keep from her, for every time you touch her, you drive a nail in her coffin.' And so, that physical passion had been allowed to slip away.

If he were a man of greater worth, he could have accepted that lack. He acknowledged his weakness for the carnal and was surrounded by men who thought nothing of taking a mistress or two. Sheridan had mustered little resistance to the temptations offered by the flirtatious Mrs Crewe and had not in the least curtailed his penchant for an attractive governess. Eliza had seemed to tolerate these affairs and he had adored her no less than before, just as she continued to idolise him. It was his genuine passion for Harriet Duncannon which had shifted the axis. Throughout this knavery he could not be surprised that his dear wife had lost all patience and considered pressing for their formal separation.

Eliza may have eschewed society, but society continued to seek her out. And now? How could Sheridan censure her for at last succumbing to declarations of love? For it was a love that she returned. That attention had come from the handsome Irish lord, Edward Fitzgerald.

'I know that Tom will demand all our attention tomorrow. And no doubt you do not tarry long.'

Sheridan looked apologetic. 'Prince George demands my presence in Brighton. I am charged with a delicate matter on his behalf.'

Eliza raised an eyebrow. 'He uses you, Dick. You are become his lackey.'

Sheridan murmured his demurral.

'I worry the Prince of Wales shall ruin you, for his own selfish ends.'

'His Royal Highness has need of a friend.'

'You have always been prey to flattery, Dick.'

'Flattery or praise? I rather thought all praise to be merited?' He gazed at her with wide, disingenuous eyes.

Eliza shook her head and smiled indulgently.

'There is something you wish to speak of?' he prompted gently.

Eliza hesitated and then nodded with determination. 'I believe I am expectant. I recognise the signs. My indisposition.'

It took a moment for Sheridan to digest this information. Eliza was pregnant — and he was not the father.

'Given my history, I may lose it, of course…'

'Does Fitzgerald know?'

Eliza shook her head. 'I should not like to tell him until I am certain and past the first dangers of miscarrying. But I felt that you should know. I do not want to have any secrets from you, Dick. I want only to know how you might proceed.'

How might he proceed? Did she doubt him? He knew that many a lord had, if not divorced, then cast off his wife in similar circumstances, and forbidden access to legitimate children. Sheridan should be publicly recognised as a cuckold. And yet, how could he ever hurt Eliza more than he already had with his own string of infidelities? She had tolerated and forgiven. How could he now turn about and berate her? Deprive her of the joy which her son Tom brought to her? Banish her into the wilderness? He knew full well the hypocrisy of a world where no such equality of consequence lay between men and women. And, he blushed to consider, only the year before he had fathered a child with a governess at Crewe Hall. The matter had been fairly hushed up. The Duchess of Devonshire had assisted Sheridan with the arrangements; Miss Townsend was sent abroad for her confinement. A healthy girl was delivered and fostered. He had a daughter, Fanny Mortimer. That thought sometimes caught him unawares and brought a lump to his throat. The child might never know Sheridan for her father.

'I should like to be a parent again,' he said, simply.

Eliza sighed. 'You are a good man, Dick. There are few who appreciate your true worth.'

Tears pricked his eyes and before he knew it, he was sobbing. He knew not quite why. For himself. For Eliza. For the sudden fear he had that the coming child might be that final nail in her coffin and then he should lose his wife entirely.

Eliza reached out to touch his shoulder and he let his head collapse into her lap. She murmured soft words and stroked his brow, just as she had used to in days long gone when he had been beset by doubts and woes.

After Eliza had returned to her own chamber, Sheridan reflected on this new and unexpected development. The tender feeling between Fitzgerald and his wife was palpable. He had experienced painful stabs of jealousy, as any hot-blooded male might naturally feel. And envy. There had been days when he had become crazed and spent himself in dissipation. He had been the sun to Eliza, and now he was eclipsed.

He felt himself in conflict, but also contradiction. He loved and honoured Eliza no less. He admired Fitzgerald tremendously; first cousin of Charles James Fox, the young lord was heroic and principled. They shared a number of similar reformist enthusiasms. Fitzgerald was a man of action and purpose, entirely free of deceit and dissembling. Sheridan could understand full well Eliza's unfettered love for the man. But what now? Here was irrefutable confirmation that the romantic pleasantries between Fitzgerald and his wife had been wholly consummated. What should a child bring to their strange equation?

Sheridan was not often given to self-reflection. Not because he was incapable of holding up the mirror, but because if he paused to consider himself too profoundly, then a deep melancholy rose up within him and threatened to engulf. He strived to keep that darkness at bay. If Sheridan were honest, the enforced separation from Harriet and now the happiness of Eliza and Fitzgerald made him realise just how keenly he himself was alone.

CHAPTER TWELVE

The Prince of Wales had removed to the Marine Pavilion in Brighthelmstone, or Brighton, as it was now fashionable to shorten it. It was a seaside retreat away from the prying eyes of his father's court and London society.

Although they did not reside in the same accommodation, Brighton was also where Prince George might indulge his relationship with Mrs Fitzherbert. As though they were indeed man and wife — a state of matrimony the proud Roman Catholic widow had insisted upon before she would succumb to seduction. It was a secret marriage which could never be publicly acknowledged, their union in contravention of the Royal Marriages Act, which made it illegal to marry without the monarch's consent. This both parties understood, if somewhat reluctantly on Mrs Fitzherbert's part. It meant no children could be allowed. Sheridan wondered at the pain this must cause. Mrs Fitzherbert was a naturally good-natured woman, and he read her absences and bouts of low spirits as evidence of the loss of a newborn child that had had to be spirited away.

Sheridan had received an invitation to join His Royal Highness, which could not be refused. Prince George would want him to tackle the mystery of the anonymous letter sooner rather than later. In this endeavour he had made little headway beyond a speculative list. Chief amongst his suspects were Mr Nathaniel Parker Forth, the go-between for his master the Duc d'Orléans. Parker Forth knew full well that the earlier bonds were dangerously treasonable and that if the Prince of Wales committed and signed up to the present agreements, they might be interpreted in the same way; threats to inform His

Majesty King George III might prove lucrative. Sheridan must seek an encounter with the agent and try to ascertain just how trustworthy Parker Forth was in the matter.

The second suspect was Major Hanger. He was a clever adventurer and had brought himself very close to the prince through many an eccentric escapade. Sheridan, however, had never entirely forgiven Hanger for shooting him dead in a duel.

It had been a prank engineered by the prince. Sheridan had used some flimsy excuse to challenge the major. His Royal Highness had then substituted blanks in the duelling pistols and when the shots were fired, Sheridan dropped down dead. Amidst panic and shock, all acted as if the incident should be covered up with great haste and Sheridan was speedily stretchered away. That evening, over a private dinner, he emerged ghostlike into the dimly lit room, covered in white powder. Poor Hanger quite jumped out of his skin. The prince slapped his thighs and roared with laughter. Sheridan joined in with the hilarity — but he could not easily forget that Hanger had not known it was a blank that he fired and that his aim had been to kill.

Major Hanger might have caught a whiff of these negotiations with Orléans. Sheridan would not put it past the fellow to eavesdrop or pay a servant to do so. He might see an opportunity for further advancement or monies to pay off his own considerable gambling debts.

The other possibility was that the writer might be someone of the duc's entourage, who likewise had overheard discussions. The letter, however, did not strike Sheridan as having been written by a Frenchman, though that was presumptive.

So far, Sheridan had largely considered greed as the motive, the purpose of the letter being blackmail. In which case the sender was a villain, plain and simple, but one who might be bought off. The other possibility was that the missive had been sent as a shot across the bows, a warning to His Royal Highness to refrain from a dangerous and foolish course of action. If that were so, then the fellow was acting as a patriot, just as he claimed, and was intent on saving the Prince of Wales from his own poor judgement. In which case, Sheridan would very much like to shake his hand.

A third prospect was that the True Friend of Albion was an enraged patriot hell-bent on exposing and destroying the prince and merely had the courtesy to warn him. Sheridan trembled to consider that possibility.

On the journey down through Sussex, Sheridan decided that fire must be met with fire. It was risky, he knew, but this was not a business that one should hedge around. Better to know the lay of the land as quickly as possible. The hour was late when he arrived at the Marine Pavilion, but as soon as he was settled in his room, he sent for pen and ink.

True Friend of Albion!

There is no greater love a man may have than to love his country! All good men are called to fight any foe that should threaten her sacred shores. We must protect her sovereign state and slay the dragons of treachery and perfidy.

Let us raise a glass at the Crown and Anchor tomorrow at noon and share our interest. It will be to your material benefit.

Your Brother

He sealed the note and addressed it to Major Hanger. The moon allowed a sliver of light to guide his way as Sheridan crept down to the vestibule to place the missive on a salver. He could only wait to see if the louche equerry would show and declare his hand. The prince was due to take his morning swim in the sea waters and they could both fairly absent themselves from that activity.

He was tiptoeing back up the stairs when a figure suddenly loomed over him out of the darkness. He let out a startled cry.

'Did I frighten you, Sherry?' The man chuckled slyly. 'I should have thought you were used to scuttling about in the dark!'

Sheridan recognised the voice but could not for a moment place it.

'All those backstage passages, all those behind-the-scenes machinations, rather your forte, I believe? And not only at Drury Lane.'

It was Sir Roderick Howgill. What the devil was he doing, lurking about in the early hours, Sheridan might just as well ask of him?

The young fop answered without being questioned. 'I myself am in search of a tonic for chronic indigestion, which seems always to follow one of His Royal Highness' dinners — all those mousses and stuffed quails. So you must excuse me, sir, if I am hurried away by my indisposition.'

Sir Roderick staggered down the stairs towards a light which emerged below. A night servant appeared, roused by the noise on the stairs.

'Fried pigeon dung is rather good, I hear,' Sheridan muttered after him.

As Sheridan turned at the top of the stairway, he thought he saw Sir Roderick linger for a moment by the salver and touch the note, as though reading the address. A simple curiosity, no doubt. Sheridan continued to his bed and reminded himself that he must refrain from imagining that there were spies and agents at every corner.

Sheridan was rudely awoken by a manservant. The curtains were pulled open and a stream of light flooded into the small chamber. Sheridan yawned as the raucous screech of seagulls reminded him of where he was.

'His Royal Highness wishes to see you right away, sir, in his apartment.'

Sheridan was rushed through his toilette, the powder still wafting from his hair as he scurried along the corridor towards the prince's room.

A footman gave him entry at once. 'Sir, you are expected.'

Prince George was in a state of dishabille. When Sheridan saw the piece of paper which His Royal Highness waved in his direction, he groaned inwardly.

'This will not do, Sherry!'

'Another anonymous letter, sir?'

'Hark at this!' The prince read aloud from the missive: '*Should a Royal Father know what TREACHERY lies in the bosom of a first-born SON?* Calumny! Base calumny! Do I not know my sacred duty to the Crown?'

Sheridan inclined his head. The duty of a prince might not always be equal to that of a son.

'And then this, Sherry, listen to this! *Take heed — a PRINCE may find himself in a BLOODY TOWER as in days of yore!* These are threats not to be countenanced! They speak of violence against my royal person! The Tower, egad!'

'Insolent, sir, in the extreme.'

'This is no ordinary blaggard, Sherry. What does the fellow want from me?' The prince raised a hand to forestall any response from Sheridan. 'He would have power over my royal personage, would he? Well, just let him show himself and we shall see then where the true power might lie!' The prince raised his chin and puffed out his chest. 'This is a sneaking, snivelling fellow, and this is what I think of his impudence.'

With that, George tore at the note and wafted the confetti about the room. Sheridan winced with dismay; the evidence was again destroyed.

'Do you know what galls me the most, Sherry?'

'Sir?'

'This was not delivered by messenger. It has come from within. From someone who has sat at my table and partaken of my bounty.' His Royal Highness' lower lip trembled. 'Someone I have called a friend.'

If the prince prided himself on anything, it was his gift for friendship, something his Royal Father had rarely, if ever, mastered. And to have that friendliness abused was indeed heinous.

'I shall find the villain, sir.' And at that moment, Sheridan felt determined to do so.

The Crown and Anchor was tucked away in a narrow, cobbled side street near the fish market, its weathered beams and listing walls a mark of its age. A local haunt of salty types and the odd smuggler, Sheridan speculated. The rheumy eyes of an old fisherman greeted him with ill-disguised hostility. A pall of tobacco smoke hung in the air of the dim interior and added to the general gloom. He had arrived well before the appointed time, wearing his plainest coat and a tricorn pulled low over his brow. He found a booth from which to view entrances and exits without calling too much attention to himself.

The innkeeper eyed him warily as he swept a rag across the filthy table.

'What may I get you, sir? We have a dish of freshly caught whitebait that is very good.'

Sheridan ordered himself a jug of strong stout and the proffered plate. The landlord gave him a sidelong glance as he returned to his counter. Did the fellow take him for an Excise Man?

Sheridan was relishing the simple but tasty fare when a familiar figure sat down on the bench opposite him.

'What the devil are you up to, Sherry?'

'I can recommend the whitebait, Hanger.' Sheridan took a swig of the Pharaoh. 'And the stout.'

Hanger nodded over to the loitering innkeeper, indicating that he should have the same menu. The landlord shouted out the orders, anxious, no doubt, to ingratiate himself with the military man. Sheridan noticed that the old salts in the establishment had either pressed themselves into the shadows or slunk away altogether.

'So, you whorry old Hibernian, what's the game? You are no brother of Albion, that's a certainty.'

You had to hand it to the major, he had the bluffness of a fighting man.

'Game? Is there sport to be had? I hear we are to try our hand at archery this afternoon.'

'I rather fancy you are already adept at archness, Sherry. Is this mischief all your own, or do I sniff some prank of His Royal Highness?'

The jug of stout had been replenished and a large plate of the fried whitebait arrived, delivered by a comely girl with large, swinging hips.

'Will that be all, Major?' She directed a saucy look at Hanger and his badges.

The equerry sighed with undisguised longing. 'On any other occasion, good —?'

'Sukie, sir.'

'Sukie.' Hanger nodded with satisfaction as he watched the retreating rear sway from sight. He raised his tankard and turned back to Sheridan. 'To what do we toast?'

'Our prince.'

Hanger nodded slowly. 'Our prince.' His eyes narrowed. 'He wants protection in some business?'

Sheridan mopped his plate with a hunk of bread.

'You don't trust me, is that it, Sherry?'

'In a skirmish, I should put all my faith in you, Major. But to win the war?'

The equerry laughed. 'You are a contrary fellow, Sheridan — I do believe you are set to ambush me, just as I was by those damned American Patriots at Charlotte.'

Hanger dug a hand into his pocket and pulled out Sheridan's note, which he slapped in front of Sheridan.

'This speaks of treachery.'

Sheridan raised an eyebrow as he cast an eye over the note. 'Why, so it does. Interesting choice of expression.'

'Not in your usual style.'

'Not my style at all, sir — I very much hope you would agree!' Sheridan feigned offence.

'Whose, then?'

'I cannot say, but I should like to meet the fellow and offer tuition.'

'You are charged to find out.' Hanger leaned across the table and spoke with sudden urgency. 'Someone means harm to our mutual friend?'

'Perhaps. And you, Major? You are a true friend, are you not?'

'In that we are Brothers, Sherry, even though you are a scheming bogtrotter.'

'Coleraine has more bog than Dublin, I believe.'

Hanger grunted; his father had inherited the Irish peerage. 'His Royal Highness has always had a peculiar fondness for the Irish; he appreciates our sense of humour.' Hanger spied Sukie serving at another table and called to her, 'Sukie, my dear girl.'

She approached with a knowing smile.

'Sukie, my dear, I find I am thankfully at liberty — is that not so, Sheridan?'

Sheridan pursed his lips and then nodded. 'Yes, I find I must trust you on this occasion, Major. And I suppose you would wish me to write the script of your apologies for this afternoon?'

Hanger smiled winningly. 'At which you are a dab hand, my dear fellow.'

Well, the man was undoubtedly a rogue, but Sheridan's instincts told him that he was not the blackmailer.

CHAPTER THIRTEEN

An arrow twanged into the target, hitting within the circle of the bullseye and joining two of its fellows. A round of polite applause followed from the audience ranged at the back of the field.

Sir Roderick bowed elegantly in acceptance of the accolades.

The Prince of Wales stepped forward, attired in the becoming green uniform and blue sash of the Royal Kentish Bowmen, of which society he was president.

'A fine round to finish, Sir Roderick! We salute you! A worthy champion in the great tradition of English archery!'

'Thank you, sir.'

The prince turned towards the Duc d'Orléans. 'Would you not agree, Philippe? We have you bested at this sport.'

The duc spread his hands and shrugged in his peculiarly gallic fashion. 'It is undeniable, Your Highness, Sir Roderick is an exceptional archer. His scorecard speaks to that. But would you allow he has yet to hit the dead centre?'

'That is neither here nor there; he has won today's contest fair and square.'

The duc inclined his head. 'A worthy winner, as you say. But what if I were to lay a wager, Georgy?'

'A wager?'

'A trifle, say one hundred guineas?'

'On what, Philippe?'

'That there is one of my party that can still better Sir Roderick.'

The Prince of Wales clapped his hands. 'I should like to see your fellow try! You have some secret champion, do you, sir?'

The Chevalier de Saint-Gelais stepped forward with a bow and set three arrows in preparation.

Standing in the dappled shade of a leafy beech tree, Sheridan frowned with confusion. The chevalier had not shown any great skill in the afternoon's contest. He had hit the inner circles a few times and then the outer edge of the bullseye on one occasion — nothing to match Howgill's efforts. Had the young French aristocrat been deliberately holding back? Perhaps prompted by his master the duc in preparation for a wager of this kind?

'Fancy a side bet, Sherry?' It was Sir John Lade, in his usual rig of riding boots and breeches. He smacked his crop against his boot as though urging the matter forward.

'You know I am not a gambling man, Sir John, but if His Serene Highness makes such a wager, I do not doubt that he does have some trick up his sleeve — he has a sly look in the matter. So, I will hazard ten.'

Indeed the duc was grinning from ear to ear.

'Egad, Philippe, my dear fellow, no trickery, I pray,' the prince called over in a jovial manner.

'No trickery, Georgy, on my honour.' The duc laid his hand to his heart in mock offence.

A servant came forward and unstrapped the guard on the chevalier's outstretched arm. What was this? Sheridan and Sir John exchanged puzzled glances.

De Saint-Gelais then turned about and nodded towards the women grouped in the shade under the awning of a tent. From their midst Marceline LeClaire stepped forward. Her eyes twinkled with mischief and delight as she approached the duc.

Marceline curtsied and eyed Orléans coyly. 'You honour me, sire. I hope I shall not disappoint.'

A murmur of surprise rippled around the assembly.

'That is not possible, my dearest baronne — whatever the outcome of this little contest.'

The Prince of Wales' eyes widened in amazement. 'Egad, Philippe, you do not mean to present Madame LeClaire as your archer?'

The Duc d'Orléans laughed. 'We said nothing as to the sex.'

Sheridan smiled with admiration and wonder. To enter a lady into the contest and to back her so handsomely to outdo Sir Roderick's efforts, well, this should be either an ace card or a joker.

Sir John raised an eyebrow. 'I daresay His Royal Highness won't have seen that one coming, nor anyone else for that matter!'

Marceline joined the chevalier and allowed the arm guard to be strapped to her left arm. In her right hand she revealed an apple from which she took a bite before handing it to the chevalier in exchange for the bow. The young man smirked and nodded. 'Your servant, Baronne.'

Sir Roderick, in the meantime, had stepped forward and now addressed the Prince of Wales. 'Sir, I would not wish any unfair advantage. The range has been fixed for the male archer in this afternoon's contest. If the baroness wishes to take her shot at a closer range, I have no objection.'

Marceline interjected. 'Sir Roderick, I thank you for your gallantry.' She playfully affected offence. 'Of course I am but a weak woman, but I can assure you the distance is of no consequence to me.'

As the young Frenchwoman proceeded to examine the fletches of the three arrows, Sheridan sidled along the line of spectators until he nonchalantly placed himself next to the tall Nathaniel Parker Forth.

'Which side do you take, Mr Parker Forth? I rather fancy your master the duc is leading His Royal Highness a merry dance, don't you?'

Parker Forth sneered. 'It is foolishness, sir, a mere side show.'

'You do not like a side show, sir? But that is the whole pleasure to be had in Brighton. A dancing bear, say, with a ring through its nose made to get up a jig.' Sheridan aped a jig of his own.

Parker Forth's sharp blue eyes regarded him with disdain. 'Mr Sheridan, we are not well acquainted, but I have heard that you are a ready clown and it seems I have not been misinformed.'

'You do not engage in foolery, Mr Parker Forth?'

Nathaniel raised an eyebrow but remained silent.

'It is a pleasant pastime. And may be profitable, even for a serious man of business. I believe you appreciate profit, would that not be so, Mr Parker Forth?'

'It is the first object of any man of business.'

'You are as assiduous in the Duc d'Orléans' interests? In his profit?'

'Without question; he has done rather well on my advice.'

'Of course, of course. You would have no thought to your own profit, when engaged in his investments,' Sheridan suggested blithely.

'I keep my affairs in good order, sir. Whereas I gather your situation is habitually chaotic, Mr Sheridan.'

'Sadly, that is too often the case, though I have a better head for figures than most.' Sheridan thumped his fist into his palm for emphasis. 'It is the precarious state of cash flow that undoes a man in the theatrical realm. But cast an eye about you, sir; there are few here present who do not have a creditor banging on the door. Some —' he glanced discreetly in the direction of the Prince of Wales — 'might have a queue that stretches around the block and meets itself back at the front door, as the serpent greets its own tail.'

Nathaniel Parker Forth grunted in agreement.

'The Baron LeClaire has not accompanied his wife to Brighton, I see. He remains in London?'

'LeClaire?' Parker Forth looked bemused. 'That gentleman is in France. His estates, I believe, demand his attention.'

'Ah.' Sheridan spread his hands to underline his mistake. 'I espied a gentleman escorting Madame LeClaire to St Paul's Cathedral and took it to be her husband. My error.'

'The baroness has many admirers.' Parker Forth looked askance at Marceline. 'She should have a care for her reputation.'

Sheridan wondered, fleetingly, who the gentleman at St Paul's might have been. Yet another rival for the favours of the young French beauty? His attention was then taken by the lady herself. Marceline had chosen an arrow and notched it to her bow. She placed herself side-on to the target, straightened her shoulders and raised the missile to her eyeline, stretching her right arm back as she did so, the string taut between her fingers. In the next moment the arrow flew towards the target and thwacked into the bullseye.

Murmurs of astonishment rippled around the sward. The Duc d'Orléans looked inordinately satisfied whilst Prince George shook his head in disbelief. The referee moved forward to examine the shot. He turned and shook his head, holding his fingers apart to indicate the fraction by which madame had missed the dead centre.

'Bravo, my dear!' the duc cried out, clapping his hands. 'The baronne has set her mark — the next arrow shall be true, on my honour!'

Marceline LeClaire laughed gaily and went to retrieve another arrow.

'Devil take it!' Sheridan exclaimed. 'She is stupendous, is she not, Mr Parker Forth? Diana the Huntress stepped down from Olympian heights. Or rather she is the female Eros, and with love's arrow I fear my heart is quite pierced!'

'Then that should be another lengthy queue we speak of, Mr Sheridan.'

Sheridan eyed Parker Forth. 'Very drole, sir. Your master, I would hazard, might beat all to the front rank.'

The man winced at this assertion. Was it that the agent did not approve of the Duc d'Orléans' interest in the beautiful Marceline? Perhaps she distracted the duc from weightier matters. Sheridan could imagine that to be the case. Should the admirable baronne cast her eyes in his direction again, why, he should be thoroughly distracted. Distracted to the point of lunacy, he conceded to himself with a grin.

That grin turned to perplexed uncertainty as Marceline swung about with her bow primed and took aim not at the target on the field, but straight at the heart of the Duc d'Orléans.

CHAPTER FOURTEEN

There was a collective holding of breath. A stunned silence. The Duc d'Orléans himself stood stock-still with a look of bemusement flitting across his features. And then in the next moment Marceline LeClaire shifted her aim. All eyes in the field strained to the tip of that deadly arrow and then to the direction in which it was now pointed. The Chevalier de Saint-Gelais was standing before the trunk of an old oak tree. On his head was perched a green apple. An apple from which one bite had been taken.

'The devil!' Sheridan mouthed, his pulse racing. 'She means to do it!'

The missile flew in an instant to its target. The apple split and the arrowhead lodged with a resounding *thunk* into the thick trunk above the chevalier's head. With a sweeping gesture, low and courtly, the chevalier swooped the remains of the apple from the ground and took a hearty bite. Thunderous applause greeted this action with the rush of exhilarating relief.

The chevalier smirked, withdrew another apple from his pocket and walked nonchalantly towards Sir Roderick Howgill, extending the fruit before him. 'Monsieur?'

Sir Roderick accepted the proffered fruit and held it aloft. 'A volunteer? Anyone?'

A ripple of nervous laughter greeted his request.

Sir Roderick turned to the Prince of Wales and bowed. 'My deepest apologies, sir, but I am bettered and must accept defeat, though at so fair and accomplished a hand, it cannot grieve me.'

After his initial astonishment, His Royal Highness had regained his *sangfroid*. 'Quite so. Quite so. Madame LeClaire is without parallel. Let her be crowned with laurels.'

Marceline lowered her eyes and curtsied in acknowledgement.

'Quite without equal,' the prince continued wistfully until a tug at his arm reminded him that Mrs Fitzherbert, his beloved, was also present.

'Well, that will be a hundred guineas His Royal Highness shall consider worth losing,' Sheridan observed.

Parker Forth grunted. 'If it were to come from his own pocket.'

Sheridan glanced at his neighbour; did he detect a note of disapproval?

A sudden squall had come in off the sea. Dark clouds tumbled and roiled over grey waves, which lashed the frothing shoreline. Sheridan was reminded of Mrs Tucker's injunction to carry an umbrella abroad and rather wished that he had taken heed of her advice. A combination of sea spray and rain began to beat a tattoo on the narrow path alongside the pebbled beach. He hunched his shoulders against the assailing gusts and looked about for the nearest shelter. Local fishing boats, known as hog boats, with their shallow draught and flat bottoms designed for the shingle beach, were pulled up above the tideline alongside smaller rowing craft. Their shelter would be scant in this swirling spray.

He had ventured some distance from the Steyne past net shops and rope houses. Here, under the eroding cliffs and behind the fishermen's boats, was to be found a jumbled collection of hovels above the hightide line. They were constructed, he fancied, from the flotsam and jetsam that might find itself washed up on these shores: old ship's timbers, driftwood and canvas, tarred against the worst of the weather, the more substantial dwellings built from the hog boats. These 'hoggies' now provided homes for the poorer sort of fisherfolk. Pieces of ragged nets flapped in the wind. Crabbing pots and the like were stacked higgledy-piggledy in careless disarray. Here and there a thin wisp of smoke emanated from a hovel and was instantly snatched by the breeze.

Up ahead, the figure he had been tracking suddenly darted in amongst the crude dwellings. Sheridan halted. It would be foolhardy to follow them into this warren. Sheridan should turn back. He had surely been mistaken. A rumble of thunder growled in the distance. He would soon be drenched to the bone if he did not find shelter himself. Dead men did not rise from the grave, travel fifty miles, and take a stroll along the promenade amongst the pleasure-seekers of Brighton.

Sheridan had merely set out for a short amble in the late afternoon sun to take stock before the revels of the evening ahead. He knew that he should be considering what stratagem to employ next with Mr Nathaniel Parker Forth. He had not quite taken the measure of the man and he felt unsettled by him. But the more he tried to focus on his mission for the prince, the more his thoughts flew to Marceline.

That moment when she had held the Duc d'Orléans within her aim — had Sheridan imagined the murderous glint in her eye? No. He had seen it. He had felt every nerve in his body shudder and thrill to her dangerous power. For all her grace and beauty, here was a nature that was wild and untamed. She was daring, and not only in her costume and style. Marceline LeClaire readily flouted conventions. She symbolised the new enlightened image of womanhood which the Revolution in France had embraced. The baroness enthralled him. He wanted to clasp her in his arms. To possess her. And yet it was her very wildness which aroused him and fired his blood. He did not want to subdue or conquer her. What he wanted, he realised, was for Marceline to choose him.

His thoughts had been thus engaged when from the corner of his eye he had observed the Chevalier de Saint-Gelais further along the promenade. The young French nobleman also seemed to be on a solitary perambulation. Should he catch him up and engage with him? Pass flattering comment on his heroic faith in Marceline's aim with bow and arrow? The image of that extraordinary moment assailed him again. What a William Tell act that should be on the stage. Top Billing. Monsieur Dubois would be put quite in the shade.

As Sheridan dithered over whether or not to approach Saint-Gelais, another man, in rough attire, fell into step with the young chevalier. A hawker, he supposed. He had noticed how the small fishing town had begun to change. When he had first ventured down to Brighthelmstone, it had been centred on an industry of fishing, the agricultural land being so poor in the area. There was no natural harbour, fishing boats were left on the beach, exposed to the elements, and the shoreline could be lashed by fierce winds. On a number of occasions, the town had been near destroyed by violent storms. Now, with the increase of visitors in the summer months in search of the medicinal benefits of sea bathing and other entertainments, the locals had embraced other opportunities. The beach was interspersed with bathing huts on wheels which could be trundled into the sea. The town could become fairly overrun with sellers of gimcracks and ribbons as well as cockles and winkles. Performers too, balladeers and jugglers. The hawker must have something of interest to sell. Saint-Gelais, although he feigned to ignore the fellow, did not shoo him away.

As Sheridan drew nearer, the pair ahead slowed their pace. He was close enough that a word or two drifted to him between the sharp cries of the seagulls circling above the beach.

'…act soon … no knowing when…'

Some sales patter. But for what? Sheridan could not help his natural curiosity and edged closer still.

'…and Monsieur Danton…'

Sheridan shook his head. Had he heard aright? Had this fellow really spoken the name of the French revolutionary? Surely not. He had misheard. A gull shrieked overhead and swooped down on the waste from a stall selling dressed crabs.

Ahead, the chevalier suddenly halted, nodded curtly, then turned and strode away from the beachfront. The young hawker paused a moment, shot one backward glance towards the retreating figure of the Frenchman, then pulled his cap lower over his brow and continued his path.

Sheridan froze with shock.

A ghost. Had he just seen a ghost? It had been a mere glimpse and it was many months since Sheridan had last seen Jack Champion, but sure as day this was the fellow or his double. He observed the back of the fast-moving figure up ahead. Tendrils of dark curls escaped the flattened cap.

'Try our fresh crab, sir? Only caught this morning.' A gnarled hand waved the produce before him.

Sheridan shook his head and increased his pace. Jack Champion? The same that was interred in a Huguenot cemetery, whose funeral he had paid for. He needed to know. He needed to be certain. If this fellow really were Jack then … then what? Nothing made sense. He tried to make order of the jumble of his thoughts. The body which had been found in the cellars of Old Dame Drury. Two possibilities had presented:

Gaspard Bernon or Jack Champion. Both had disappeared. But the Huguenot Cross had been identified by Champion's sister. How could it not be the remains of Jack Champion that they had discovered? But if this young fellow now striding away towards the coastal path was the same man — then what did that mean?

And what did it signify that he had appeared to be in conversation with the chevalier? A discussion that mentioned Monsieur Danton. If this rough fellow was Handsome Jack, then was the dead Harlequin Gaspard Bernon after all? Sheridan hastened his step in pursuit as the gamut of questions tumbled through his head.

Then the squall rose, and now the man disappeared between the ramshackle abodes of this fishing community. Sheridan might lose him in a moment if he did not act. At least, if nothing else, he might find a Christian soul who would give him shelter from the driving rain. A sheet of lightning flashed across the glowering sky. He ran towards a gap between the hovels and in the narrow passage his eyes flitted from side to side in search of the man with the dark curls.

A figure loomed up at his side, arm raised. Sheridan felt the weight of the blow at the back of his head and then all went dark.

CHAPTER FIFTEEN

Sheridan blinked. His head throbbed. He closed his eyes and moaned.

'Sheridan. Sherry. Are you all right?' Someone was shaking him gently.

He moaned again. 'Devil take it.'

There was a sigh. 'You'll live, I think, old fellow.'

With an effort Sheridan opened his eyes again. As they adjusted to the gloom, a face appeared above. Sir Roderick Howgill peered down at him with a frown of concern.

'Howgill?'

'Yes. Let's sit you up.'

He was lying on a crude mattress stuffed with straw. As his senses returned, he could smell the dank stench of the place and the reek of a fish oil lamp. Howgill eased him up into a sitting position. His clothes were sodden and he shivered.

'You were fairly drenched in that earlier downpour, Sheridan. What the deuce possessed you to wander this far?'

Sheridan began to take in his surroundings. They were inside an upturned hog boat. The furniture, what there was of it, was mean and shabby. Howgill gestured towards a young man who was sitting at a small table, his weather-beaten features picked out by the glow of the lamp.

'This good man, Gabriel, spied your attacker as he returned to his home and at his cry the rogue fled. You were carried within.'

Sheridan nodded, though the effort hurt his head anew. 'My heartfelt gratitude to you, sir.'

A bunch of rags stirred beside the crude central hearth from which smoke drifted up towards the blackened underside of the hog boat and a makeshift smoke-hole. An old woman leaned over and stirred the simmering pot which dangled over the meagre fire.

'Mrs Gimmell here recognised you as one of the Prince of Wales' regular guests. Apparently, Mrs Gimmell is a fortune-teller with a stall on the promenade. She sent her grandson up to the Pavilion for help. I happened to be passing and when I heard that you had been injured, I felt it only right to offer my assistance.'

'Decent of you, Howgill.'

'Seems you may have wandered too far abroad, Sherry. It is not all pleasure in Brighton, you know; there are villains aplenty, and it seems you have been waylaid by a vicious footpad.'

'Footpad...' Sheridan felt for his waistcoat pocket and pulled out his pocket watch. 'Then he is not a very clever cove. I do not think I was struck by a footpad, Howgill.' He touched the back of his head tenderly with his other hand. 'I very much believe a dead man is responsible.'

Sir Roderick looked puzzled. 'A dead man? A ghost, do you mean? Banquo, heh?'

'I do not think ghosts cosh you over the head. That blow felt not in the least supernatural. No, I talk of a dead man who is not dead after all.'

'Are you sure your mind has not been noodled by the blow, Sherry?' Howgill asked.

Sheridan was not of a mind for flippancy. 'I could not be certain, so I followed him. I did not see his features for long, and yet I know it was the fellow.'

'Damn it, then he is a dangerous fellow.'

'It would seem so.'

'And yet you gave chase?'

Sheridan nodded and winced.

'Damnably brave or damnably stupid, Sherry. Both, I would say. He should have done you some wrong, I suppose, that you would pursue him in amongst these hovels?'

'An actor of my company, Jack Champion.'

Sir Roderick shrugged. 'I might know him by his role.'

'Harlequin. A very tricky fellow.'

'Harlequin?' Howgill's eyes narrowed. 'I heard there was a spy in your company who was a Harlequin, a Frenchman.'

Sheridan shot a look of surprise at Howgill.

The younger looked embarrassed. 'Some time ago, I overheard my relative Dundas speak of it to Mr Pitt. I own I was intrigued and tarried a little longer than was polite.'

'What else did you hear?'

'I really shouldn't say; I have been indiscreet already.'

'If there is an agent amongst my company, I should know, Howgill.'

Sir Roderick hesitated and then nodded in concurrence. 'Dundas did mention a name, but it was not...'

'Jack Champion.'

'No. It was...' Sir Roderick strained to remember. 'Bernard ... perhaps?'

'Bernon?'

Howgill clapped his hands. 'That would be the fellow.'

'Spying for whom?'

'The émigrés. Marquis de Penaud-Mortain: bit of a firebrand, lucky to get out of France alive after the Day of Daggers — that botched plan to rescue King Louis. The marquis is pressing on all sides for England to go to war with France, restore the *ancien régime*.'

'Why would they need a spy at Drury Lane?'

Howgill shrugged. 'You theatre people, you are known for a hotbed of radicals — damned if you aren't one yourself, Sherry!'

'Bernon has disappeared.'

'You don't say?'

'It was thought he was escaping from some dangerous creditors.' Sheridan heaved a sigh. 'Now I fear another more perilous fate may have befallen him.'

'I do enjoy a mystery, Sherry.'

'Well, if this fellow I have seen today *is* Jack Champion, then he has proven himself a very devilish trickster and quite possibly a murderous one.'

'Dangerous times, Sherry. I should keep clear from all skulduggery if I were you, or it may be more than a knock on the head you receive. Do you feel able to walk? The carriage is but a little way along the path.'

'I think so.' Sheridan edged himself up from the rough cot as Howgill placed a hand under his elbow in support.

Sheridan nodded towards the wiry young man at the table and then to Mrs Gimmell. 'I must express to you again my deepest gratitude and if you will allow, I shall send some small token of appreciation for your help and hospitality.'

'Think nothing of it, sir,' Gabriel Gimmell said with a shrug.

The old woman beckoned. 'I sense you are troubled, sir. If you will give me your hand, I can tell your fortune.'

Sheridan stretched out his arm. 'Pray, tell me only what is good.'

Mrs Gimmell reached out and clutched his hand in hers, raising her face up to Sheridan as she did so. Her sharp eyes seemed to pierce his. She pressed and felt around his palm.

After some moments, she spoke.

'Joy and sorrow walk hand in hand, sir. Life and death. One follows the other as night does the day. There will be death and there will be a child.'

For a moment Sheridan felt unsettled but then rejoindered blithely, 'Joy and sorrow, that is true for all of us, is it not, my good woman? Is there not something more particular?'

Mrs Gimmell screwed up her features. 'Beware! The devil has a handsome face and demons speak with silver tongues. You have a kind nature, sir, and must have a care, for you are also a very great fool.'

Mrs Gimmell released his hand and turned back to tend her pot.

Sir Roderick laughed. 'She holds a mirror, does she not, Sheridan? I think I shall refrain from seeking any pronouncement from Mrs Gimmell for fear of hearing truth unvarnished.'

'Very wise, Howgill.'

'Come, Sheridan, we must get you back to the Marine Pavilion and into a hot bath and dry clothes before you catch your death.'

His death, he mused. He might very well have caught his death at the hands of his attacker if young Gimmell had not heard his cry.

Sheridan was forced to excuse himself from the dinner table and take to his bed with a compress and a bottle of brandy. Major Hanger arrived at his bedside soon after to convey the general solicitude.

'Of course, His Royal Highness is peeved that you do not attend. He fears the evening shall be frightfully dull without you. I can't think why.' The equerry perched on the edge of the bed and sniffed at the rose in his buttonhole. 'And that young

French baroness, her astonishing prowess with a bow and arrow is on everyone's lips — rather sorry to have missed that show, but there were compensations.'

'What about Madame LeClaire?'

'The lady expressed herself most particularly disappointed that she should not enjoy your company this evening. It seems the baroness had set her heart upon sitting next to you at dinner, had requested it, my dear fellow.' Hanger gave a sly wink. 'Apparently she's a great admirer of your scribblings — Lady Teazle, Lydia Languish and all that.'

Sheridan was encouraged by Marceline's regret at his absence and experienced a flutter of anticipation. The baroness sought him out. She wished to be in his company. Perhaps a little delay might work in his favour; he might feign indifference — not too much, of course — and tease her out into declarations of feeling.

'Mrs Fitzherbert was most distressed to hear of your injured state. That you had been waylaid by some villain. As are we all, my dear fellow. Though it has been cause for jest in some quarters. What the devil were you doing in that squalid place?'

'It was foolish of me — I am told I am a very great fool by a Mrs Gimmell.'

'That lady knows you well, then.'

Major Hanger rose to take his leave.

'Hanger...'

There was another besides Marceline whom Sheridan had lost the opportunity to cultivate that evening, but it occurred to him that the equerry might be a source of useful information. 'What can you tell me of Mr Parker Forth?'

'Nathaniel Parker Forth?'

'Yes, the agent to the Duc d'Orléans.'

'Well, let me see. An Irishman, though born in this country. Sometime wine merchant but largely he is a broker. And he has played many other parts too. You may know that he was the king's special envoy to Paris during our late troubles with the American rebels. An irregular position.'

Sheridan's eyes narrowed. 'He does not sound like a king's man.'

'Perhaps not, but he has proved very useful, I gather. Parker Forth has a veritable spider's web of connections amongst men of very different rank. And he gathers all sorts of private information...' Hanger smiled urbanely. 'I daresay Mr Parker Forth may have intimated that he had influence.'

So, Sheridan thought, Nathaniel Parker Forth was no stranger to suggestions of *influence*, a polite euphemism for blackmail.

'I heard a rumour that some while ago he brokered bonds on behalf of the royal brothers.'

Sheridan's ears pricked; how much did Hanger know of that dangerous business?

'Matters went awry, apparently, and Parker Forth tidied up the business. The royal brothers are indebted to Mr Parker Forth and I believe he has been promised a future reward.'

Sheridan had to admire Hanger's talent for gathering up snippets of gossip. He wondered how far these rumours had spread. Not to the ears of the king. Not yet. Sheridan waited.

'In consequence, I rather fancy that Parker Forth considers himself to be a very great friend of the Prince of Wales.' The equerry looked askance. 'He seems to have one foot here, having recently taken up a residence in Chelsea, but the other foot is firmly in France. But his time for sitting on the fence may be drawing to an end. It may seem to him that the duc's political fortunes are in the ascendant, and Orléans is without question a very wealthy individual.'

Whereas the Prince of Wales may as well be a pauper, given the amount of his debts and the king's rude health. He is as far away as he ever was from sitting on the throne, Sheridan concluded privately.

'You are remarkably well informed, Major.'

'I keep my ear to the ground. As must we all in these disturbing times.' Hanger regarded Sheridan shrewdly. 'You consider that Mr Parker Forth may present some difficulty for His Royal Highness?'

'The Prince of Wales surrounds himself with difficulties.'

'And good Sheridan shall act as a moat?'

Sheridan groaned as he felt a spasm of pain at the back of his head and pressed the compress to the swelling bump.

Hanger bowed. 'So, I am to tell His Royal Highness and all who enquire that you are laid low, but that this is a mere excuse for playing chicken-hazard and muggins with the maidservant. They shall be deeply envious.'

As Hanger retreated, Sheridan threw a pillow after him. He then lay back on the remaining pillow and thought over the equerry's information and the crowded events of the day.

CHAPTER SIXTEEN

By the time Sheridan had returned home to Isleworth he was in a raging fever. He had coughed and spluttered throughout the entire journey. Having blasted his nose into four handkerchiefs until they were miserable sodden rags, he requested that John, his coachman, stop in Croydon at a parade of shops to purchase another half dozen. How was it possible for one nose to produce such a deluge? Not only that, but his head felt like an overstuffed cushion. He was only thankful that the blow to his head which he had received on the previous day had broken neither his skull nor skin but only caused a bruising lump, which was painful enough.

Mrs Tucker had stayed awake in anticipation of his return. She tutted and shook her head in disapproval when he confessed to having been drenched in a thunderstorm. Suitably chastened, John helped him into his bed and Mrs Tucker arrived with tonics and a poultice and orders that on no account was he to rise the next morning. He had not the strength to argue that there was business to be attended to and a prince to mollify, but nodded imperceptibly and allowed his eyelids to droop.

It was approaching midday when a late breakfast of coddled egg on a bowl of porridge oats and millet was brought up — Mrs Tucker's habitual recipe for all invalids. And knowing Sheridan's sweet tooth, she had also dribbled a little honey over the gruel. Tom arrived in Mrs Tucker's wake and flopped onto the bed.

'Well, Pa, I had as well live in a hospital! That is you and mother both taken to your beds.'

'Your mother is unwell?' Sheridan asked with sudden panic as he stirred the egg into the porridge mixture.

'She has not been seen for days and will not let me near her — and you are ordered to keep your distance too, with your dastardly fever. But you know I am made of sterner stuff than either of you!'

For all Tom's bluff, Sheridan knew this not to be the case. He had often worried that Tom had inherited the tubercular tendency of the Linley family.

'Nevertheless, do not come too close, Tom,' Sheridan ordered, fighting the urge to sneeze.

A handkerchief appeared in his hand just in the nick of time. He sneezed explosively.

Tom grinned.

'Thank you, my dear boy. I am sorry you are disappointed with your poor parents, and I had promised to take you to the spectacular at Astley's, had I not?'

'I have made my own arrangements, Pa. I shall go with the Cannings,' Tom responded blithely. 'I know you are never to be relied upon. Now, I must away; I go swimming this afternoon with Freddie.'

Sheridan looked up with quick alarm. 'Do you think that wise, Tom? These summer chills!' He sneezed again as if to underline the point.

Tom laughed. 'Pa, you may not wrap me up in cotton wool! And I have promised Mrs Tucker faithfully that I shall take an umbrella with me wherever I go — though what good that contraption shall do me when I am quite soaked through in the river, I do not know!'

Tom bounced off the bed and headed to the door. At the threshold he turned and looked severely at Sheridan. 'And Pa, you are to stay abed and rest — the world shall turn very well without you!'

The boy was gone before Sheridan could reply. He muttered to himself nevertheless. 'My dear Tom, I fear the world is very much tilted from its axis already.'

Sheridan was confined to his bedchamber for two whole days. Neighbours called to enquire and all were sent away by Mrs Tucker as she held the household in a strict quarantine. Tom had been invited to stay with good Mrs Canning in Wanstead and Sheridan was thankful. The boy would enjoy the company of that lively family. On the third day, Sheridan was beginning to feel restless. He dressed and took himself to the library, where he could not sit still but paced about the room.

The enforced imprisonment of the invalid, whilst irksome, had allowed Sheridan plenty of time to think. He kept returning to the moment when he had been struck down outside Mrs Gimmell's hovel. The figure had loomed up beside him in ambush. As the blow had come, an object had flashed in the man's other hand. A blade, Sheridan now felt certain. The fellow had meant to knock him senseless and then finish him off. That was not the action of an ordinary footpad but of an assassin. Jack Champion. The actor must have sensed that he was being followed, then realised that it was his former employer in pursuit and feared to be recognised. The intent of the attack had been murder, plain and simple.

The remains in the cellar must be the unfortunate Gaspard Bernon. Bernon the French spy. There was only the puzzle of the Huguenot Cross. Why would Gaspard be wearing such a cross if he too was not a part of the Huguenot Brotherhood? And if he was a member of the Brotherhood, then why should he be killed by a fellow member? Sheridan shook his head in frustration. Bernon was employed by the counter-revolutionaries, but Margaret Bedwell had remarked that he considered himself a clever fellow. Perhaps he had infiltrated the Brotherhood and had then been unmasked and dispatched by Champion. Yes, that might make sense.

Or Sheridan may have the whole matter upside down. Perhaps Bernon had been double-dealing all along — he could have deceived the Marquis de Penaud-Mortain on behalf of the Huguenot Brotherhood, spread false information to the marquis and even gained access to counter-revolutionary plans. A very clever Harlequin. Too clever for his own good — and so he had been murdered by an assassin from the émigré faction when he was found out. In which case Jack Champion may have fled into hiding a month later, in fear of his own life.

Sheridan sighed. Then there was the Chevalier de Saint-Gelais. Where did he fit into the puzzle? Did the encounter on the beach suggest some connection between the Brotherhood and De Saint-Gelais? Was the chevalier the end of the chain, or was he a mere conduit? To whom?

Sheridan felt immediately that he knew the answer. The Duc d'Orléans. That might be the connection. The Brotherhood were acting in support of the Revolution. The duc had used the Palais Royale and his huge network of influence to place himself close to the heartbeat of all the political developments in Paris since the Storming of the Bastille a couple of years previously. If he favoured secret societies like the Freemasons, then why not also embrace the Huguenot Brotherhood? It should be at a discreet distance, of course. And Sheridan should not be surprised to learn that the duc funded the group — perhaps through the agency of the enigmatic Nathaniel Parker Forth.

The ruffian on the promenade had mentioned Monsieur Danton. Sheridan had not misheard. What might that mean? He strained to remember what else he had overheard. Something about needing to *act soon*. If only he could be entirely certain that it was Handsome Jack that he had seen on Brighton beach. All was supposition. More proofs were needed. He determined to write to Constable Nicholls. That young officer of the law had already shown himself eager in the matter.

On his return from Brighton, there had been a report waiting for him. The Runner had requested a watch might be kept on Henry Champion. Manpower was stretched, but Sir Sampson had agreed; the Home Department now took an active interest in this secret society. Nicholls had been tasked with gathering information from within the Huguenot community. As yet he had been unsuccessful, which led him to the conjecture that the group was likely to be small and tight-knit, jealously guarding its secrecy. Not unlike the Freemasons, Sheridan had mused. Nicholls would keep Sheridan updated if there were further developments.

Well, perhaps there was another way to crack a nut. Sheridan wondered if the actor's lover, Mrs Jeffreys, was privy to his activities. She had attended the funeral, but her tears might have been a sham. The arrival of Captain Jeffreys had drawn attention to her presence. Someone had let slip to the captain that his wife attended her lover's funeral. Had that been deliberate? Another stratagem to convince all that Champion was dead? Did Mrs Jeffreys in fact know that Champion was still very much alive? Did she assist to hide him?

Sheridan decided to write to Nicholls, suggesting that he might try speaking first with Mrs Jeffreys' maid. The young woman had clearly been an accessory to her mistress' relations with Champion. If the servant could be teased into talking about that relationship, then they might learn more than by going directly to the horse's mouth. Servants saw and heard to a greater extent than their masters ever knew.

Sheridan rubbed his eyes. He wished his head did not feel quite so sluggish. He felt weary and could not winkle out the nature or purpose of the intrigue. All his senses told him that peril lay ahead, but in which direction and for whom he could not tell.

CHAPTER SEVENTEEN

Sheridan was sitting with a bowl of chicken broth, another of Mrs Tucker's favourite recipes for the indisposed, when a visitor was announced.

His manservant, Michael, grinned. 'Mrs Tucker has told the gentleman that you may receive no visitors, sir. But Mr Fox will not have it and insists that he will not be budged. That should indeed be some task, sir.'

It would, for Charles James Fox was of a considerable weight and girth. Sheridan clapped his hands, delighted by his party leader's intransigence.

'Please show Mr Fox to the library. And Michael, bring up my best claret.'

After they had exchanged polite enquiries about Mrs Sheridan's health and the well-being of the *de facto* Whig leader's paramour, Mrs Armistead, the two parliamentary colleagues quickly settled themselves by the window. Outside the sky was grey and it threatened to rain again. Sheridan and Fox took comfort in the rather fine claret which Sheridan kept for special occasions.

Fox drummed his fingers on the arm of the chair. 'I have received an intriguing snippet, Dick. It appears that Mr Christie has a most interesting houseguest.'

'Monsieur Danton,' Sheridan croaked as he blew his nose loudly. 'Excuse me.'

'You have also heard this news?'

'I have met him, Charlie.'

'Is that so?'

'And he would very much like to meet you.'

'Ah.' The Whig leader's eyes gleamed for a moment.

'However, he appreciates that a meeting should be discreet.'

'That is wise — we would not want there to be any suggestion of plotting with the French Jacobins.' Fox shook his head sadly. 'Our dear Burke has thrown the apple of discord amongst us with his *Reflections on the Revolution in France*. I fear our party increasingly divides and we shall be the few, Dick.'

'Miss Wollstonecraft rebutted very well, I thought, and —' Sheridan blew his nose again — 'Tom Paine's tract gains favour, I believe.'

Fox waved a hand in dismissal. 'They do not speak to the common man, to John Bull. Whatever else he is, John Bull is a patriot and the ordinary man in the street shall never lose his loathing of a Frenchman. The Revolution in France daily scuppers our chances of reform here. And you and I are painted as friends to the Jacobins. Who knows what Mr Pitt's dogs might sniff out, and the government would be only too eager to have us arraigned for treasonable activity. Now that Mr Pitt has placed his dear old Dundas in the Home Department, we may expect his agents shall be poking their snouts into every nook and cranny of our business.'

'That I do not doubt.'

'I trust that you have a care, Dick. I know you to be sometimes impetuous.'

'You see what has happened in Birmingham? Shall the legitimate voice for reform be silenced by such villains, worked up by the agent provocateurs of the government? We cannot allow ourselves to be muzzled, Charlie.' Sheridan sat back. 'But I do understand that we must choose our words with care.'

'Some of our friends do not tread so warily.' Fox eyed Sheridan. 'My cousin Fitzgerald, for instance. I know the love you bear him and he is a fine young man, whose heart is true, but his enthusiasm for events in France may light the torch for rebellion in Ireland. Be careful that you are not scorched by such a flame.'

Sheridan flushed. How could his future not be entwined with Edward Fitzgerald now that his wife was to bear the young lord's child?

'We speak of Monsieur Danton...' Sheridan leant forward. 'He asks that I might assist to bring about a conference.'

'Does he? And what is your plan?'

'That you do not meet in some dark room sequestered at the back of a tavern off the Strand but in the most public of arenas, the Pleasure Gardens at Vauxhall.'

Fox laughed. 'Capital.'

'You might perhaps collide as the fireworks commence.'

'And what is your impression of Monsieur Danton?'

'He keeps a pistol in his pocket, which I rather fear is loaded, and he pointed it my way. What can I say? He grabs one's attention. I can see why the mobs in Paris are so in thrall to him.'

'What does he do here?'

Sheridan hesitated. Should he share some of his recent speculation?

'For all that Monsieur Danton reminds one of a bull, not unlike the one which may have disfigured him in childhood, and should not be let loose in a china shop, he is nevertheless of a dainty mind and keeps his cards very close to his chest.'

Fox chuckled. 'Dick, I shall now have to suffer an image of a bull playing cribbage while surrounded by crockery. Come, you must have some notions. Was he behind the business in the Champ de Mars?'

'I suspect that he may have played a part in stirring up the feeling against Louis. Which then drove those poor people to protest and demand the king's removal, only for them to be mown down by Lafayette's troops. But Danton himself keeps a safe distance, and whether or not he truly wishes to advance, the republican cause is another matter altogether.'

'The National Assembly in Paris is busy drawing up their constitution — you think Danton might favour a constitutional monarchy if there was someone other than Louis XVI on the throne of France?'

'This I will hazard — that the Duc d'Orléans imagines that Danton might be persuaded of that option.'

'Why?'

'He is a Freemason.'

Fox laughed again.

'I do not jest. These secret societies, they wield tremendous power behind the scenes.' Sheridan hesitated. Should he also speak to Fox about the Huguenot Brotherhood? Too soon, he thought. He had no clear idea yet of their agenda.

'Monsieur Danton seeks our friendship, but how may we be useful to him? We are further than ever from government.'

'He should imagine we have influence with the Prince of Wales.'

Fox steepled his hands together. 'Would he not be wiser to court Mr Pitt?'

Sheridan paused. Real and practical support for a constitutional monarchy in France with acceptance of a leading role for Monsieur Danton would best come from Mr Pitt's government. The prime minister had thus far avoided being drawn into open hostilities against the revolutionaries and expressed the view that France should be considered *neither heaven nor hell but as a country in a state of some chaos which should be left to her own devices.* Pitt did not wish to join the clamour for war from countries like Austria. But there would come a point, Sheridan felt sure, when everyone must make a choice. Neither Mr Pitt nor Monsieur Danton could hedge their bets forever. Could Pitt afford to allow the French revolutionaries to be left to their *own devices* entirely?

'There is nothing to say Monsieur Danton does not parlay with Mr Pitt, through an intermediary.'

Fox nodded. 'That would be a reasonable conjecture.'

Sheridan had a sudden thought. 'And that is the whole purpose of his visit. We are a mere sideshow.'

'Perhaps ... unless he sees that the wind blows towards a republic in France, and then our friendship may be of some worth after all.'

Sheridan buried his nose in his handkerchief again and blew. When should this damnable fever be finished with him?

'I begin to see schemes everywhere, Charlie. How should a man know who to trust?'

'He should not, by Jupiter!'

After Fox had departed, Sheridan remained in his library and reflected on how few men he could, with sincerity, trust. There were those within his own party since the Regency Crisis who he knew did not trust him; they had painted him as a schemer and tried to turn Charles James Fox against him. He sighed. Truth be told, he *was* prone to scheming. But always for a good cause, he reassured himself, for the sake of reform and a society which recognised merit as well as privilege.

He finished off the second bottle of claret and felt that he must lie down awhile. On his way to his bedchamber, Sheridan rapped lightly on the door to Eliza's apartment, so as not to disturb her should she be asleep. A permission to enter came from within. He did so and closed the door gently behind him.

Eliza half rose to greet him from a chair by the small fire which had been lit in the room, but he gestured for her to be seated again.

'I shan't come any closer, my dear; this is a thoroughly nasty fever. Thankfully, I may be over the worst of it. I am concerned for you, however, Eliza.'

Seeing his wife only served to increase that concern. Eliza seemed thinner than ever and looked weak. She shook her head slightly at his solicitude.

'In your present delicate condition…'

'Poor little mite… It might be better if…' Eliza closed her eyes and bowed her head.

Sheridan felt a stab of pain in his heart. His eyes pricked to think of those earlier unborn children and the boy who had died at birth. How they had both grieved. Eliza should not lose this child as well.

'No. All will be well.'

Eliza looked up, catching the feeling in his voice. 'How shall that be?'

'You will take copious amounts of Mrs Tucker's chicken broth, which perhaps she may vary with a white soup — and I, well, I would recommend a tot or two of warmed brandy and honey in the evening.'

'It shall be done, Dick.' Eliza laughed softly and smiled at him in a way which she had not done for some time.

He bowed his satisfaction and quit the room. But he was not satisfied. He felt nothing but a growing concern that he might lose his wife for ever.

CHAPTER EIGHTEEN

A full moon was rising in the clear August night sky, casting a silver shimmer on the surface of the Thames. The wherry which carried Sheridan and Fox across to the south side of the great river rocked as the waterman bent his oars to the task. As they approached Vauxhall Stairs and joined the queue of similar small ferries jostling to discharge their fares, Sheridan fancied he saw the lights of the Pleasure Gardens already twinkling ahead of them.

He was still chesty, but it felt good to be out on such a fine, warm evening and to be once again abroad about the great metropolis, a party to its thrum and heartbeat. He felt those stirrings of anticipation and excitement in his breast which always accompanied a visit to Vauxhall. The season was drawing to a close, and before the end of the month the Gardens would be quite shut up. In consequence, there should be a good showing of the *bon ton* that evening, at least those who were not otherwise engaged in taking the waters in Bath or indulging in country pursuits on their estates. Chief among them should be the Prince of Wales, who had invited Fox and Sheridan to join him in his box for supper.

They entered at the gates fronting the River Thames to join the milling crowds who had paid their shilling and were gathering in their thousands. Here, the very highest of the land might rub shoulders with tradesmen and their wives and even find working men who had saved a week's wages for the occasion and wore their best. Fox and Sheridan were recognised at once, their features long familiar from the hundreds of prints and cartoons by the likes of Rowlandson and Gillray. A murmur of that recognition rippled through the throng. Some tipped their hats or made a short bow. For all Mr Pitt's iron grip on government, he would never have the common touch or popularity of Charles Fox.

As the hour was already approaching nine o'clock, they proceeded swiftly along the walkway of the Grove towards their engagement. Sheridan caught sight of the massive figure of Monsieur Danton in the crowd up ahead. He nodded to himself, pleased to see that the Frenchman had arrived. Everything should fall into place for the planned rendezvous later in the evening. Danton reached down and in the next moment was lifting a child up onto his great shoulders. The boy looked exultant as he was thus enabled to see above the heads of the swarming masses. Sheridan paused a moment, open-mouthed, and almost tripped over himself as the flow of the crowd pushed from behind. Little Billy Legge!

What on earth was that scamp doing at Vauxhall and with Monsieur Danton? It was then that he noticed Timothy in animated conversation with Mr Christie. Well, young Timothy should be quite beside himself to be in company with the revolutionary Frenchman. Sheridan only prayed that the enthusiasm of the young lawyer could be sufficiently contained to keep him discreet about the encounter between Charles James Fox and the Jacobin. Timothy had not been informed of the ruse and would be an innocent to the scheme, unless Monsieur Danton had broken that confidence. It was a complication Sheridan could well do without.

'Mister!' Billy's keen eyes had spotted Sheridan. His high, excitable voice reached over the noise and babble of the surrounding pleasure-seekers. 'Hey, Mister Sheridan!' The boy waved at him enthusiastically.

Sheridan gave a rapid half-wave in return and scurried forward to catch up with Charlie Fox.

His Royal Highness' party had commandeered a section of the fifty or so supper boxes, each compartment accommodating between eight and ten guests, from which they could enjoy the foremost view of the orchestra building. The raised octagonal bandstand housed the musicians above the spectators and allowed for the concert to be appreciated on all sides of the Grove. They were presently playing a piece composed by Thomas Arne, which drifted over to Sheridan as he settled himself into the one remaining seat at the table, having paid his respects to Prince George. Beside him Lady Lade fanned herself and complained of the heat of the day that was still present.

Across the table Sheridan was greeted by Lord Derby. He had a fondness for the diminutive earl, a man of sound principles. Derby was in company with the comedy actress, Miss Eliza Farren, chaperoned as usual by her mother, the silent presence at the far end of the table.

Liveried waiters were already arriving with the usual fare of wafer-thin slices of ham, salads and cheese custards, which would be followed by tarts and assorted puddings. A mere picnic to the Prince of Wales. But who should have a care when the champagne was so plentiful?

The Muse of Comedy leant over towards Sheridan. 'I am pleased to see you, Mr Sheridan. I had read in *The Gazetteer* that you and your dear wife had caught a chill and that Isleworth is quite overtaken with fevers this summer. I do hope that Mrs Sheridan recovers?'

Sheridan smiled to make light of any concern. 'We are hale and hearty, Miss Farren. Our good Mrs Tucker saw to it that we were fed plenty of chicken broth, which we can all recommend as a restorative.'

'I am gladdened. And our company is to play at the King's Theatre next season, I believe?'

Sheridan could scarcely refrain from grunting. 'Though I may be beggared in the process. But our audience expects, and until the new Theatre Royal shall be completed, we must make do.' It still rankled with him that he had been forced to agree to the onerous terms for the residency. His company of actors should know they may not command any rise in their salaries, however popular they might consider themselves, and that included Miss Farren.

Attention was drawn by the Master of Ceremonies to the appearance of Miss Anna Maria Leary, or as she was affectionately known, the Siren of Vauxhall, sporting the headdress of three ostrich feathers for which she was celebrated. The orchestra launched into the most popular song of the day, 'The Lass of Richmond Hill'. Then the milling crowds ceased their perambulation and moved as one closer to the stage, enraptured by the lyrics and that clear, natural voice which held so much emotion.

'On Richmond Hill there lives a lass,
More bright than May-day morn…'

The lyrics had been written by a fellow Dubliner, Leonard MacNally. Their paths had crossed over the years. Whilst Sheridan had abandoned the study of law in his youth, MacNally had persisted and forged a career as a barrister. Sheridan had made his success in the theatre, whilst MacNally had merely dabbled in the writing of comic operas and satirical plays — including *The Apotheosis of Punch*, dedicated to

Sheridan, which he had taken to be a somewhat back-handed compliment. It amused Sheridan that MacNally's authorship of 'The Lass of Richmond Hill' should be so disputed and the piece often ascribed to the Prince of Wales, who in declining to make comment enjoyed the accolade and on this occasion deigned to join in with the refrain.

> '...*Whose charms all other maids' surpass,*
> *A rose without a thorn.*'

A rose without a thorn. As the concert continued Sheridan found his thoughts drifting to another rose, of the French variety: Marceline. He had read that the Duc d'Orléans intended his daughter, Mademoiselle Adelaide, to remain in England with her governess, and rather hoped that the duc and his entourage would likewise tarry awhile, or at the least be frequent visitors. He must see the baroness again. His blood stirred to recall her declarations of high regard. How had she expressed her admiration? Ah yes, she held herself *the premiere fanatic*!

He was brought back to the present by the blowing of a whistle. Prince George clapped his hands in anticipation. Night was falling rapidly. This was the signal for the lamplighters to scurry to their allotted stations around the Grove. At a second whistle the cottonwool fuses were lit, guiding the flames swiftly from one oil lamp to another. To a rousing accompaniment from the orchestra a thousand or more glass lamps, hung amongst the trees, were lit in an instant. The effect was truly spectacular. The myriad magical illuminations elicited gasps of surprise and wonder all around, in particular from those who had never witnessed the display before.

The prince's party continued with their buffet, the liveried waiters hurrying back and forth serving the various supper boxes. One, he could have sworn, was Jack Champion! Sheridan shook his head; it had been but a fleeting impression. Perhaps he now imagined that he saw that trickster everywhere after the encounter in Brighton. There was a restless impatience among the Prince of Wales' guests to join the promenade. They were to view the new Gothic Temple which had been unveiled only the previous day. At last Mr Tyers, one of the owners of the Gardens, arrived to escort His Royal Highness with much obsequious attention. Their path was eased, and the gawping masses kept at bay, by the lines of officers of the Vauxhall Gardens police — a private force of whom Mr Tyers was inordinately proud.

The prince did, however, manage an aside to Sheridan en route. 'How do you progress with that other business, Sherry?'

'By elimination, Your Royal Highness.'

'And how long should that take?'

'If the fellow would show his hand —'

'But he does not! Devil take him!'

'No, sir.' He really must put his mind to this business for the prince and quit his hopeless deliberations over dead Harlequins.

Prince George was beginning to look thunderous and Sheridan was relieved when Derby joined them. The diminutive earl was in jolly humour and began to turn the mood of the prince with his enquires about the horses which the prince intended to run at Brighton. The two men were soon happily discussing form and jockeys and the challenges which the course might present.

The new temple had been decorated with coloured lamps in a perpetual motion, designed by Martinelli and already attracting the appellation 'The Moving Temple'. The prince expressed himself delighted. His humour further improved when the party encountered the Duc d'Orléans with his entourage. They too had come to admire the new temple.

Sheridan found Sir Roderick Howgill at his side. 'You are quite recovered, Mr Sheridan?'

'A mere sniffle or two — thank you for your kind enquiry, sir.'

'I was referring to that other injury you received in Brighton. Your brain has not been addled, I trust?'

'On the contrary, I believe it has been whetted.'

'Then you will excuse me if I step away from so sharp a blade.' Howgill chuckled.

'Monsieur Sheridan, how wonderful to find you here in these enchanted gardens. My pleasure is complete!'

Marceline glided towards him. Strikingly elegant, she wore a soft turban over her short curls, complemented by a tasselled Indian silk shawl draped casually about her shoulders over a loose, flowing dress. He could see other young women casting sly, appreciative glances, whilst their chaperones or mothers looked grim with disapproval. One would never fail to notice Marceline LeClaire, her fashion being so daring and modern.

'*Enchanté*, madame.' Sheridan bowed low and groaned inwardly with frustration. The appointed time for the rendezvous with Danton approached. It now loomed as an irksome distraction from this opportunity to further his acquaintance with the delectable baroness.

'Sherrie, or I may call you Dick?' She laid a hand on his arm and hurried on without waiting for a reply, her enthusiasm brimming over. 'We want only for the fairies, Titania and Oberon, to make of this magical evening a midsummer night's dream!'

'I see the Fairy Queen before me even now, my dear Marceline, and we are all under your spell.'

She laughed gaily and gestured towards the Chevalier de Saint-Gelais, who approached. 'And here is my most mischievous Puck!'

'I shall need to have a care then that he does not turn me into an ass.'

'Does not Titania fall in love with an ass?' Marceline reminded him coyly.

'That is mere foolery. It is Oberon she loves in truth.'

'Ah yes, Oberon… Who should be my Oberon?' Marceline looked Sheridan directly in the eye.

He wanted to clasp her then and declare that he should be her Fairy Lord and make away with her to gambol and frolic in the dark woods close by.

'*Cher* Baronne, is the temple not indeed a moving spectacle?' The chevalier nodded curtly to Sheridan and offered his arm to Marceline. 'Come, His Serene Highness wishes to introduce you to a dear friend, Monsieur Fox.'

Marceline inclined her head to Sheridan. 'You attend the dance, sir?'

Sheridan smiled in reply.

'You will mark my dance card; it is a royal command, Mr Sheridan, from your Fairy Queen. Now, I must thither to meet your clever Monsieur Reynard!'

Sheridan could see at once that the meeting of the wily and amorous Fox with this glorious Titania would not be hurried. He prayed that Monsieur Danton was a patient man and would pardon their delay.

In the meantime, he felt a pressing need to relieve himself. He had drunk rather too much of the champagne. He took the opportunity to slip into the nearby woodland. A sly cove sidled up to him almost immediately, a Hector, plying for trade.

'I've a proper bevy of beauties, sir, to suit all tastes. Young or buxom? Fair or dark? What say you?'

Sheridan shook his head.

'Only ten pennies, sir.'

Sheridan continued into the woods.

'Nine, since you're a gent.'

'Cannot a man take a quiet piss?'

The pimp grunted and slid away in search of other customers.

Once the myriad lamps were lit and the respectable families of the middling sort had drifted away from the Gardens, the fall of night ushered in other pleasures. The walkways and darkening woods rapidly became a haunt for the Vauxhall demirep and practised ladies of the night. Men prowled in search of their favours, and in their wake came pickpockets and other villains. A man must keep a watchful eye, despite the Gardens boasting their own police force.

As Sheridan sighed his relief into the undergrowth, he cast his eyes warily about. A man's voice drifted over to him. One that sounded familiar. He strained for a view through the trees and glimpsed a distinctive figure caught briefly in the outer glow of a hanging lamp. Sir Roderick Howgill. Sheridan smirked. Was the young dandy cavorting with a doxy? Sir Roderick spoke in urgent whispered tones. Then Sheridan heard a male grunt in response. No strumpet.

Sheridan raised an eyebrow. Somehow the notion that the elegant fop's sexual preferences were inclined towards other men did not entirely surprise him. It would be a piece of information useful to know, although he could not immediately imagine how he might use such a titbit of scandal.

Another thought flashed into his mind. Were Howgill's attentions towards Marceline all a game? A masque to deflect from his true tastes? Such a scenario suited Sheridan very well; there were rivals enough for the baroness' favour.

He was about to turn away and regain the party at the Gothic Temple when the other man's heavily accented voice caught his attention. That voice too seemed familiar, although he could not make out more than a few words. Keeping himself out of sight, Sheridan edged closer on tiptoes. Sir Roderick was conversing with none other than Monsieur Danton!

The two men were now speaking *sotto voce* in French, but Sheridan was certain that he heard Howgill giving the Jacobin an assurance: 'You may depend on it that Mr Pitt shall express his gratitude in a fulsome manner…'

Sheridan frowned with confusion. Was this an overture from the Prime Minister to Monsieur Danton? And was Sir Roderick in the role of Pitt's intermediary in the business? He had speculated on such a possibility but had not considered it in all seriousness. But if Danton schemed with Mr Pitt, what then did he want from Charles James Fox?

CHAPTER NINETEEN

'By Jupiter, Sherry!' Fox exclaimed as they hurried along the Grand Walk towards the Fountain of Neptune. 'But that lady is Helen of Troy incarnate!'

Sheridan sighed. 'A face that should launch a thousand ships.'

'Do you know anything of the husband?'

Sheridan shook his head as he tried to hurry their pace. 'The Baron LeClaire is notable only for his absence.'

'I daresay the duc has already staked his claim on her.'

'If the Comtesse de Buffon will allow — I would not be so certain.'

'That young chevalier shoots daggers at any man who will come near her; he is worse than any duenna. Still, I do believe the lady smiled on me.'

'You have always had a way with the ladies, Charlie.'

Fox grinned with satisfaction.

They arrived at their destination through a final triumphal arch at the end of the Grand Walk. Sheridan reduced their pace to a saunter and they both proceeded with nonchalance towards the fountain as though they merely strolled companionably.

Moments later, they were hailed by Timothy Legge.

'Mr Sheridan!' The young lawyer darted over to them, weaving through the courting couples. 'And Mr Fox.' Timothy flushed with delight as he bowed to the Whig leader. 'This is a most unexpected pleasure. Such a fine evening for a stroll in the Pleasure Gardens.'

'Charles, allow me to introduce Mr Timothy Legge, a young man of my constituency who will no doubt one day make his mark in the law.'

'Pleased to make your acquaintance, sir.'

'See, I told yer Mister Sheridan was 'ere.' Billy sniffed to underline his assertion.

'And who may this young fellow be?' Fox asked.

'This is Billy, sir — my ward.'

Sheridan raised an amused eyebrow. So, Billy was to be Timothy's ward now, was he?

'And shall you be a lawyer also, Billy?' asked Fox.

'Nah, mister, it's the dragoons for me!' Billy's eyes lit up at the prospect.

'A fighting fellow, are we?' Fox made playful sparring motions with his fists.

Billy frowned and then struck out at the portly figure in front of him, landing a punch in that capacious belly.

'Oof!' Fox staggered back. 'By Jupiter, you'll make a fearsome foe!'

'He has been nursed at the bosom of one Battling Poll, a pugilist of the fairer sex,' Sheridan explained. 'I should have a care he does not hit below the belt, Charles.'

Sheridan grinned as Timothy tried to admonish Billy and elicit an apology from the boy.

Thomas Christie ambled over. 'Good eve, Mr Sheridan.' He kept his voice low and drew Sheridan to one side. 'My regrets, but we appear to have lost our houseguest. One moment he was behind us, and the next he is quite gone.'

'Losing oneself is a frequent hazard of Vauxhall; one might even say it is one of the Pleasures of the Gardens.'

He had said nothing to Fox as yet, but Sheridan suspected that Monsieur Danton's intended rendezvous that evening had not been with Charles at all. The Frenchman had instead used the occasion of this visit to Vauxhall to connive with a representative of the government — for that was the part he must consider Sir Roderick had been chosen to play. He was reminded that Howgill had a family connection to Henry Dundas.

'I thought I caught sight of Monsieur Danton earlier, near the Moving Temple,' Sheridan continued conversationally.

'Ah yes … the new spectacle! Moths gathering about a flame. And it was not just the flicker of the lamps that were the attraction — we heard tell the Prince of Wales was about to arrive. I suggested that we should move on to avoid the crush — and to hasten to our *rendezvous*.' Dr Christie touched his nose confidentially and nodded towards Timothy. 'Young Mr Legge knows nothing of this scheme, I assure you. Our meeting is quite *accidental*, though all in vain at the moment.'

'You have made the acquaintance of Mr Legge, I see, without the necessity of any introduction on my part.'

Dr Christie smiled broadly. 'A most zealous and promising young man! He has submitted an article for the *Analytical Review* on the recent disturbances in Birmingham, and I must say that I am greatly impressed — as is Monsieur Danton. He is quite taken with Mr Legge — and the boy, Billy. I believe our mutual friend misses his own little son —' Dr Christie raised an eyebrow — 'though I doubt his boy to be such a scamp as Billy. Timothy kindly offered to show my guests around the city and they have been often abroad. I am grateful for this service, as the calls on my time have been most pressing.'

'An eventful summer.'

Dr Christie nodded over to an elderly gentleman standing by the fountain. 'You must allow me to introduce you to

Monsieur Recordain. You did not meet Danton's stepfather when you called on us some fortnight since.'

'Sadly no. Monsieur Recordain was busy chasing the spinning jennies — has he succeeded in catching one yet?'

'*Pardon*! *Pardon, mes amis*!'

Monsieur Danton lumbered towards the group with his arms spread open in an act of contrition.

'Such crowds to see the prince! Then we are separated, alas! Turn right, Danton — turn left...' Danton shrugged his great shoulders. 'I am a clumsy fellow. *Pardon, pardon...*'

'Oh, I imagined monsieur to have met an acquaintance.' Sheridan's eyes narrowed as he searched the Frenchman's face for any sign of falsehood. 'I am sure you have made many acquaintances on this trip, and being too polite, Monsieur Danton, you could not tear yourself away.'

'Monsieur Fox, if I am not mistaken!' Danton turned to Sheridan's companion and beamed widely.

Fox laughed and bowed towards the imposing Frenchman, whose size quite outmatched his own. 'Monsieur Danton, a pleasure, and there is no need for apology. Sherry, here, describes perfectly his own disorder. He is notoriously tardy and it is a truth that he is often delayed by virtue of having more acquaintances than any other man in London.'

'Why, Sheridan should be late for his own funeral!' Christie quipped.

They decided to stroll along the quieter path that ran parallel to the Grand Walk. There were fewer lamps lit along this path, but the moon was now high in the clear night sky. Dr Christie led the way in company with Monsieur Recordain, pointing out the occasional piece of statuary or decorative ruin situated in the woods. All was a marvel to the merchant from the small provincial town of Arcis. Fox and Danton sauntered side by side and spoke occasionally in a low, conversational tone. Sheridan followed in their wake and strained to catch snatches of their exchange, but this proved impossible, not least because Timothy was full of animated chatter.

Timothy's eyes gleamed as he talked of the excursions he had taken with the famous Jacobin — in particular their attendance at a lecture given by John Thelwall, at which Monsieur Danton had voiced his pleasure at finding the radical voice expressed with such fervour.

'I assured Monsieur Danton that there are many here in England who will speak up for the Revolution, despite Mr Burke's *Reflections* and despite the fact that the king and his government seem determined to silence us.'

'Do you not wonder that Monsieur Danton has not remained in Paris?'

Timothy shook his head vehemently. 'His life was threatened! He has many enemies. The Revolution cannot afford to lose such a great leader at this juncture, Mr Sheridan. There is every fear of regression! That General Lafayette should have been party to the massacre of all those poor people at Champ de Mars, who only wished to make a petition! There are those in the National Assembly who would limit the achievement with force and repression. Who stifle rational debate, sir. It is Danton, when he returns to Paris, who shall light the way to a new and brighter future.'

Timothy was clearly in the grip of a feverish devotion to the French revolutionary. Sheridan's own views on Monsieur Danton, on the other hand, were now sinking into a quagmire of mistrust.

Billy had been following behind, dragging a spindly stick along the path. He beat his stick against the ground and grumbled, 'When's the fireworks, Mr Legge?'

'Soon, Billy, soon.'

'How soon?' The boy whacked the stick on the ground and it snapped.

Timothy shook his head with annoyance and turned back again to Sheridan to resume his conversation. 'It is a pity that parliament is in recess for the summer; Monsieur Danton regrets that he has not the opportunity to view our House of Commons and to listen to the debates…'

'But when?' Billy interrupted, running ahead and waving his broken stick in the air. 'Will mi'ssur know? He'll know when we see the fireworks!'

Billy scampered towards the hulking figure of Monsieur Danton. 'Mi'ssur, mi'ssur!' he called.

Timothy heaved a great sigh of exasperation and sprinted off in pursuit of his young ward to cut short the boy's advance on the leading political figures of the day.

All at once an explosive shot sounded at close quarters. It took a moment for Sheridan to realise that this was no firework. He watched with rising horror as Timothy crumpled to the ground behind Monsieur Danton. The startled Frenchman span about with a look of astonishment to see Timothy collapsing at his feet. Fox let out a loud groan of horror and dismay.

In an instant Dr Christie rushed back to the party and crouched by the young man's side.

Sheridan looked about wildly. 'Did anyone see the villain?'

Danton had drawn his pistol from his pocket and was likewise wheeling about. '*Merde*!' He slapped his head.

Two men ran towards them.

'You are attacked?'

'Did you see the fellow — which way he went?'

They shook their heads and spoke one on top of the other.

'In the trees —'

'Too dark and he too far away, sir!'

'He did not pass us —'

'— the villain has run through the woods back towards the Grove.'

'And will lose himself in the crowds,' Sheridan growled.

'What may we do?'

'A hackney — we must get our friend to a hospital, as soon as possible.'

The younger of the two men nodded in sharp agreement. 'We are close to the stable gates — there will be cabs on Kennington Lane.'

Both men sprinted away in the direction from which they had come.

Christie had lifted Timothy's tailcoat to examine the wound. The bullet had entered on the left side of his back and blood seeped from the injury. Christie hastily divested himself of his cravat and stuffed it up against the wound to stem the flow of blood.

'Your neckerchiefs, gentlemen! Tie them to make a dressing. I must bind the wound as tight as I can!'

Fox was about to untie his own cravat when Sheridan seized him by the arm, dragged him aside and whispered urgently, 'You must not be here, Charlie — you may be recognised.'

Fox hesitated. 'Mr Legge, he shall —?'

Sheridan nodded vehemently. 'He is a strong young man. I shall see he has all care, Charlie. There is nothing you can do — go. Now!' With insistence Sheridan pushed Fox and was glad to see him turn and walk reluctantly from the scene.

Sheridan had expressed an optimism he did not in truth feel. Timothy Legge must not die. He could not bear to lose him. And yet that terror seemed all but certain.

His heart pounding, Sheridan turned to console his young friend and give what aid he could when he noticed that Billy was staring into the trees.

'Billy, what did you see?'

Billy blinked. 'I saw the devil.'

Sheridan placed a hand on the boy's shoulder. 'This is the devil's work and no mistake.'

'He had a mask.'

'A mask? You mean a scarf? About his face?'

Billy shook his head, his brow creased in memory. 'Same as what that other devil wore in the cellar. Only this was a man — I saw that when he took it off and ran.'

'A handsome man?'

Billy shrugged. 'I suppose.'

At that moment a member of the Vauxhall police arrived breathless on the scene.

'I am told there is a murder, sir!'

'That may be the sorry outcome, officer,' Sheridan responded, keeping his voice low so Timothy should not overhear. 'But for now, our friend hangs on to life and if we may get him to the hospital —'

The police officer nodded. 'I passed the fellows on their way to fetch a cab; they should not be long.'

Christie looked up from his patient and spoke to the officer directly. 'Can you dispatch a fast rider to St Thomas to enquire for the surgeon Mr Cline? If he be not there, the rider must in all haste to Mr Cline's residence in St Mary Axe and plead for his attendance. He is to tell the surgeon it is Dr Christie who asks.'

'Yes, sir.' The Vauxhall policeman shouted over to a fellow officer who had hurried in his wake and relayed the urgency of the message.

'Henry Cline is the best fellow for this operation, a most excellent surgeon — if anyone can help Mr Legge, it is he.'

With Danton's assistance, Christie continued to secure the makeshift bandages around Timothy's torso. The young man let out a low moan.

Sheridan wrung his hands. Timothy lived still. That was something. He prayed that he would hold on until they should get him to the surgeon's table.

The Vauxhall officer addressed him. 'Can you say what happened, sir?'

'A shot was fired and has struck Mr Legge in the back.'

'Did you see the fellow?'

Sheridan shook his head. 'The devil lurked in the trees. This boy has said he wore a mask.'

'And he was dressed in uniform,' Billy piped up.

'A soldier?'

'Nah, like them coves what carries the plates about.'

Sheridan's eyes narrowed. 'A waiter's livery, I think he means. How many of those fellows should there be at Vauxhall?'

The officer blew out his cheeks. 'A great number and mostly employed in a casual way. I am sorry, sir, but I doubt we can find the rogue. This seems like a deliberate assassination — who might have cause?'

'None that would wish to kill poor Timothy.'

They transferred Timothy as gently as possible into the waiting hackney. Dr Christie was to accompany Sheridan and the injured young man to St Thomas's whilst his French guests proposed to bring Billy back to Soho for the night to await news.

Sheridan felt every jolt of the journey as the cab made its way from the Pleasure Gardens to St Thomas's Hospital. He cradled his friend's head in his lap and stroked his unruly auburn hair back from his brow. All colour seemed to have drained from Timothy's features and his lips were a worrying shade of blue. Christie maintained an additional pressure on the wound, sharing a look of concern with Sheridan. Much blood had been lost already. Timothy's moans subsided and he appeared to be slipping into unconsciousness.

Christie squeezed his shoulder. 'Mr Legge, you must remain awake. You must stay with us!'

Sheridan closed his eyes and thought of all that he should give if Timothy Legge would only live.

CHAPTER TWENTY

Sheridan sat alone on a bench in the dismal corridor. Dr Christie had rushed away with one of the medical assistants and a night nurse to oversee Timothy's care until the surgeon should arrive. There was nothing more that Sheridan could do but wait. The events of the night did not seem quite real but cloaked in nightmare, the dark, whispering woods hiding their conspiracies and masked assassins. He began to try to make sense of all that had happened.

Monsieur Danton. He had been the target of the assassin's bullet. He had been at the heart of all the plots and scheming of the night. The furtive meeting with Howgill, the 'chance' encounter with Mr Fox and who knew what other arrangement? Someone of the Duc d'Orléans camp, perhaps? Sheridan should not be surprised. Who had known that Danton would be at the Pleasure Gardens? Sir Roderick, clearly; and that might imply the foreknowledge of persons at the Home Department if Howgill acted for Dundas and the government. Fox may have inadvertently let slip something of the planned rendezvous — Dr Christie likewise. And then who should want Danton dead? There was a stumbling block indeed. Sheridan sighed. Half the world, in all likelihood, should want to see the fiery Jacobin dispatched.

Two thoughts nagged at Sheridan. First, the overheard report to the Chevalier de Saint-Gelais on the promenade at Brighton. That the man was Jack Champion, he was convinced. And certain also that the slippery Harlequin had mentioned Danton by name. There had been something about *our cause* and the need to *act soon*. It would suggest that the Huguenot

Brotherhood and the chevalier were in cahoots. Did this implicate the Duc d'Orléans as a puppet master? Or did De Saint-Gelais' loyalties lie elsewhere? If the Huguenot Brotherhood wanted Monsieur Danton dead, what might be their reason?

The Brotherhood supported the Revolution. Would they not welcome a republic? Then why should they want to kill so influential a leader as Danton — a man who teetered on the edge of espousing republicanism? Unless ... either the Brotherhood believed Danton to be a traitor, or Orléans had convinced the Brotherhood that he was the man to succeed to the throne and restore their property and fortunes and that Danton would offer no such guarantee. If the liveried waiter with the devilish mask was Sheridan's erstwhile Harlequin, he was a tricky and murderous character indeed.

Sheridan held his head in his hands. A great weariness overtook him. What did any of this matter beside the life of Timothy Legge? A trusting, kind and honest young man who cared for the well-being of others before himself. A porter passed along the corridor at that moment, carrying sheets and bedding. Sheridan accosted the fellow to ask that ink and paper be brought to him. He must write a note at once to Josiah Legge in Stafford and have the missive dispatched on the earliest mail coach. Josiah should receive it on the morrow, and Sheridan hazarded he would then arrive in London by the following evening. He fervently hoped that he would not then have to tell good Mr Legge that his youngest boy was dead.

As if in answer to his prayer, Henry Cline swung through the door at the far end of the corridor and strode swiftly towards the surgeon's ward.

Sheridan rose to greet him. 'Mr Cline — I thank God you are here, sir!'

'Mr Sheridan.' The surgeon grasped both of Sheridan's hands in his. 'Timothy Legge is a very decent young fellow. We shall do all in our power to save him, be assured.'

A nurse, having heard the approaching footsteps, opened the door and the surgeon swept on through.

Sheridan dozed fitfully, finding little comfort on the hard bench. He was roused in the early hours by someone taking a seat next to him. When he blinked open his eyes, it was to see the solid form of Constable Nicholls at his side.

'Nicholls…'

'Sir. Is there any word of Mr Legge?'

Sheridan shook his head. 'Not yet. What hour is it?'

'It approaches three o'clock.'

'We shall know soon enough if he shall live or die.'

Nicholls nodded. 'I came straight when I heard Mr Legge's name spoken at Bow Street and that there had been a murder attempt. I confess to being surprised that anyone should want to hurt that young man.'

'And so should I be, Nicholls, were Timothy the intended target.'

Nicholls stared at Sheridan. 'If there was someone of note in your party, they must pay heed to their safety. This assassin is still at large.'

Sheridan hesitated. Could he trust this Runner's discretion? He had agreed with Dr Christie that every attempt should be made to keep Monsieur Danton's name from appearing in the Grub Street press. The Runners were notorious for their questionable relations with the criminal fraternity and were known to accept bribes. This may be choice information. Was Nicholls a man to be trusted?

Sheridan chewed his lip and then resolved to confide at least one suspicion. 'The assassin is Jack Champion, I believe.'

Nicholls looked up sharply. 'You have seen him again?'

Sheridan sighed. 'No. And neither can I swear that it was he who dealt me the blow in Brighton. And yet, I feel in my very bones that his ghost walks among us.'

'We may know, soon enough.'

Sheridan sat up straight. 'How so?'

'I have arrested Henry Champion this very evening. That is why I have been abroad so late. He stays tonight in the cells at Bow Street.'

'On what charge?'

Nicholls smiled wryly. 'Conspiracy to riot. You may know that some years back there were troubles among the silk weavers of Spitalfields?'

'Ah yes, you spoke of that upheaval.'

'Discontent is brewing among the weavers; that they may riot again is not implausible, for times are hard. It is as good a charge as any on which to hold Henry Champion. I have been keeping a watchful eye and an ear to the ground with the aid of my informants. This evening Henry was followed to a tavern near Petticoat Lane and from there a number of men proceeded to the back room of a lodging house. With the local parish watchmen, I forced an entry and found a stash of knives and an old musket. We were near overpowered as the men tried to break out, but we succeeded in capturing Henry and the man whose room it was, Phillip Millais. I have found a Huguenot Cross about Henry's neck, one with a phial attached.'

'The Brotherhood.'

Nicholls nodded. 'Henry refuses to speak. Millais proclaims his innocence. I shall allow them to enjoy our accommodation overnight. Tomorrow, once they have been before the magistrate, they will be transferred to Newgate. But I will interview them again before dawn.'

Sheridan's jaw stiffened. 'He must speak to you! Once at Newgate it will be agents of the government who will press for information, which I — we — shall not be privy to.'

Nicholls nodded in agreement.

'I should very much like to be with you, Nicholls. I believe Henry can tell us that his brother is alive. I suspect he knows where Jack hides and what his purpose may be. I should know the reason Timothy lies even now on the surgeon's table. And may not survive,' he added, forlorn.

'It is irregular, sir.'

'Then what must I say to Timothy's dear father? That it is all a mistake? His son died because he stood in front of the bullet intended for another man?' Sheridan looked squarely at the Bow Street Runner. 'Constable Nicholls, I believe you to be a man of integrity. A man who desires to see justice done. Please, help me in this matter.'

There was silence and then Nicholls turned his dark eyes on Sheridan. 'Then first you must place your full trust in me, sir.'

Sheridan sighed and nodded slowly. 'The bullet was intended for Monsieur Georges Danton.'

Nicholls' eyes widened. 'The Jacobin? What does he in London?'

Sheridan glanced around to ensure they were alone. 'He meets secretly with rather a lot of interesting people, and he schemes, Nicholls.'

Sheridan sat back in the cab which was heading for Bow Street. He felt some relief that he was doing something. Mr Cline had emerged with Christie at his side. It was fortunate, they both declared, that Timothy Legge was a fit and strong young man. He had lost a lot of blood from the wound. It had been necessary to search deep for the bullet, a great difficulty whilst avoiding a too great enlargement of the wound.

Cline looked to his friend. 'It was invaluable to have the assistance of Dr Christie; he had already done much to staunch the wound, else young Timothy should have bled to death before you got here, Mr Sheridan. A great pity Thomas has given up the practice of medicine.'

'I have not Mr Cline's refinement. There is no man who knows more about anatomy. I wondered at his skill when he was at last able to extract the ball with the locked forceps. But...' Christie shook his head sadly.

'But?' Sheridan looked anxiously between the two medical men.

Cline spoke. 'It is hoped there shall be no infection; that is all too often the real cause of death with such injuries. The bullet's force and passage takes shreds of garment and the like into the body. I have done what I can, and I hope that has reduced that likelihood.' Mr Cline straightened. 'However, there is another matter of grave concern should Mr Legge survive.'

Sheridan found that he could scarcely breathe. 'Which is?'

'Given the entry point, it is not unusual in injuries of this kind for the very force of a bullet to cause fractures in the bones of the spinal column. We must be prepared that Mr Legge may not regain the use of his lower limbs.'

Sheridan put his hand to his mouth in shock.

'He must rest and he must be kept very still,' Cline continued. 'He has been given a tincture of opium which will check the pain, and that prescription will continue for some time. We must hope that he mends. The rest is up to fate.'

Constable Nicholls led Sheridan down into the underground regions of the Public Office at Bow Street. A dank and acrid smell rose to greet them. Sheridan imagined the dark, moist earth pressing in through the brick and coupling with the stench of unwashed bodies and their effluences. And more — the bitter scent of fear. How many desperate souls had known that these stinking cells were but the first stage on a journey that might take them to the fatal tree? There to hang by the neck and dance for the delight of the crowds who found their entertainment in such macabre sights. That, or a leaky barque which would transport them to the new penal colony on the other side of the world, another death sentence in all but name. Sheridan shuddered.

They had decided to speak first with Phillip Millais.

He was a small man of middle age with a bald head framed by a thin line of lank grey hair. Millais squinted and blinked as the lantern light held up to the bars in the door caught his eyes and dispelled the darkness of his corner. He sat up on a rough bench.

'Phillip Millais?'

'What do you want with me, sirs?'

'A word. Stay back.'

'I have done nothing to warrant this arrest. And yet I am placed in here with this —'

Millais looked with dread across the cell to the mean-looking ragged man who crouched opposite him, the rogue's sinister shadow cast behind by the thin, flickering light which came through the bars.

Nicholls sneered. 'Nothing to warrant arrest? Is it nothing to gather with six men and to conspire destruction?'

Nicholls nodded to the gaoler, who proceeded to unlock the door. He scowled at the wretch in the other corner. 'You can stay put an' all, Ben Grudge.'

The door was swung open and Nicholls stood on the threshold, a short truncheon grasped in one hand. He placed the lantern on a hook. Sheridan was at his side and kept one anxious eye upon the snaggle-toothed Ben Grudge, who grunted in the corner.

Nicholls glared at Millais. 'Is it nothing to store weapons for that purpose — and a musket amongst them? We shall see what the magistrate, Sir Sampson Wright, shall say on that.'

Millais flinched. 'The musket belonged to my brother, sir. He fought in the American War. Lost an arm and lame in one leg. And what reward did he have, but destitution? Never recovered proper. My wife and I cared for him 'til he passed away, but she took a fever and died not long after. That musket —' Millais rose with urgency.

'Sit down, sir!' Nicholls roared.

Millais promptly obeyed. 'You may ask any of my neighbours if the musket did not belong to Robert Millais. It was kept more in memory than for any other use — it has not been fired in four years or more.'

'And the knives?'

'I keep a grinder, sir. If you had looked more closely, you would have found it under cover in the yard. My wife's father left it to me. It was his trade — knife grinder. I sharpen knives and such for neighbours, a way to make a little extra.'

'We must take the word of your neighbours on all your business, it seems,' Sheridan put in.

Ben Grudge was now preoccupied with picking the lice from his hair and then devouring the creatures. Sheridan felt emboldened.

'What other business explains so many gathered in your lodging? Do you perhaps run an illicit taphouse? Ah no, pardon, you are a law-abiding man! It was the grand opening of a gentleman's outfitters that Constable Nicholls interrupted?'

Millais looked distraught. 'It is the weavers, sir — they come to me to speak for all.'

'How so? Speak for them?' Sheridan asked.

'I am a weaver myself but employed as a supervisor at the factory of Mr Logier, on the new machinery. Mr Logier still buys from the journeymen but it is all piecemeal, and he has cruelly dropped the price he will pay till it almost makes beggars of the cottage weavers. They ask me to plead for them only to be paid what is right and fair.'

'Or they shall riot? And burn down his factory?' Nicholls slapped his short truncheon into his palm.

Phillip Millais quailed at this accusation. 'No. No, I know nothing of rioting, I swear!' Millais turned to the kinder face presented by Sheridan. 'I swear this, sir.'

'These gentlemen would jump out of your window without good cause? And raise a hand against the Watchmen as they made escape?'

Millais wrung his hands in distress. 'In that they were foolish, I do concede, Constable. They are rough fellows, some, and may have a natural fear of the Watch — but they are by and large as law-abiding a group of men as any, sir.'

'And what of the Brotherhood?'

Millais looked confused. 'Brotherhood?'

'You are a Huguenot, Mr Millais, and do not know the Brotherhood?' Sheridan asked with feigned amazement.

Millais shook his head. 'I know not of what you speak.'

'Only think, sir,' Sheridan continued. 'If you can tell us something of the Brotherhood, then you may find a different outcome today. Altogether different.'

Millais bit his lip, his shoulders heaving as he sobbed. 'How can I tell of something I do not know?' He wiped his nose on his sleeve. He looked hurriedly at Nicholls. 'If you can tell me what I should say…?'

Nicholls shook his head. 'Come, Mr Sheridan, we waste our time.'

'That is a pity.'

Millais lunged forward and swiftly found Nicholls' truncheon prodded forcefully into his chest.

'Only tell me, Constable, and I shall say it!' the weaver pleaded with desperation as he fell back onto the bench.

Sheridan sighed with exasperation as the door was slammed on the prisoner. 'I am half-inclined to believe the poor man.'

'You are too trusting, Mr Sheridan. He may not know the Brotherhood, but Mr Millais plays a dangerous game, acting as a broker between the weavers and the masters. He expects some reimbursement for his efforts from both sides of this dispute, to forestall the need of a more direct threat. I would hazard the charge of "conspiracy to riot" is not far off the mark.'

'Still, these masters with their greed are in great part to blame, Constable. I have some sympathy with these journeymen, indeed, no little sympathy.'

'I shall have to have a care or you shall soften my heart, Mr Sheridan. First, I allow that rascally sneak-thief Billy to avoid arrest, and now you would press me to release Phillip Millais.'

Sheridan regarded Nicholls with expectation.

Nicholls heaved a sigh. 'All right, sir, I shall have Mr Millais discharged with a warning — a dire warning — to have a greater care with whom he consorts.'

Sheridan allowed himself the merest twitch of a smile.

CHAPTER TWENTY-ONE

As Sheridan and Nicholls stood in the dank corridor, they could hear a commotion coming from above. Voices were raised and ribald insults coloured the air. A drunken woman, her hair and clothing in disarray, was manhandled down the stairs.

'Get a move on, Bella!'

'Lemme go, yer rotten traps! 'E's the one what stole from me!'

'Stole what, Bella? You ain't got nothin'!' the bull-necked constable snorted.

'Me livelihood — whad'yer fink? Fink he can take my snatch and not pay!'

'Might not have thought he got his money's worth.'

'Never 'ad any complaints from your lot, yer gorbellied, dog-hearted jolthead!'

Nicholls raised an eye as his fellow Runner pushed Bella towards the cells.

'Had it comin', that stingy bung hole!'

'We'll see what Sir Sampson 'as to say, shall we, Bella?'

Nicholls turned to Sheridan. 'Sir, I suggest we might seek some refreshment before we interview Henry Champion. It has been a long night.'

Sheridan nodded. 'Yes, Constable, I think I am in need of some revival.'

'If you will excuse me, I shall be a moment and shall find you at the entrance.'

Sheridan nodded and ascended the stairs. As he came into the lobby of the Bow Street Office, the first sliver of a dawn light edged through the open doorway. Two figures entered with anxious hesitation. He recognised the couple at once.

'Mr Forster, Mrs Forster.'

'Sir!' Louise Forster rushed towards him. 'Is it true? Henry has been arrested and brought here?'

Simon Forster moved beside his wife and bowed deeply. 'Good morrow, Mr Sheridan.' He took his wife's arm. 'Louise, I am sure Mr Sheridan knows nothing of Henry. How should he? He must be here on business of his own. I trust all is well, sir?' The weaver looked at Sheridan with polite concern.

Sheridan paused. 'All is not well, Mr Forster, I am sorry to say. A young friend that is dear to me was attacked last night and is gravely injured.'

'I am distressed to hear that, sir. You have the villain detained?' Forster gestured towards the innards of the building.

'No. But an accomplice to the assassin, I believe, is in custody.'

'That is some good news, sir.'

'I do not think your wife will agree, Mr Forster.'

Louise started in alarm. 'Henry? You do not mean Henry?'

At that moment Constable Nicholls appeared with Phillip Millais following close on his heels.

'You will take heed of what I have said, Mr Millais, will you not?'

Millais nodded energetically. 'That I will, Constable. I do not wish my actions to be misunderstood again! I thank you, sir, most humbly.'

'Good day then.'

'Mr Millais?'

Millais turned to catch sight of Simon Forster at the entrance.

'You are released, sir?'

'And Henry?' Louise darted forward. 'Henry was with you, was he not?' She looked from Millais to Constable Nicholls. 'Is he also to be released?'

Nicholls looked impassive. 'Henry Champion is detained.'

Simon looked narrowly at Millais. 'Do you say something against Henry, Mr Millais?'

Phillip Millais had a sudden look of alarm. 'I have said nothing against Henry Champion. You will not say I am an informant, Mr Forster — I am none such.' He shuffled nervously. 'I have only told the truth to Constable Nicholls about the reason for my conversation with Henry and his fellows — it was they that came to my lodgings and asked for my help to speak to Mr Logier.'

Simon continued to look doubtful.

Nicholls interposed. 'I bid you good day, Millais — or have you taken a liking to our accommodation?'

Millais needed no further prompt and nodding his farewells, hurried to the exit.

Louise placed herself in front of the Runner. 'Constable Nicholls, what do you say Henry has done?'

At that moment two officers, one with cutlass drawn, pushed a corpulent man through the entrance. The man was in a fit of temper and loud with it. The officer with the cutlass yanked the prisoner forward.

Sheridan leant over to Nicholls. 'Is there a room where we might speak with Mrs Forster? I have a notion she may be able to persuade her brother to co-operate with your investigation.'

Nicholls nodded slowly. He addressed the couple before him. 'You wish to help your brother? Let us speak somewhere —' he gestured about — 'less public.'

Nicholls nodded to the clerk and led Sheridan and the Forsters into the rear of the building. They arrived at the private chamber of the magistrate behind the courtroom.

'Sir Sampson shall not be in session until mid-morn.'

Sheridan perched against the desk.

Louise had taken time to compose herself. She looked now at Nicholls. 'Constable, we would know what the charge is against my brother?'

Nicholls regarded Mrs Forster not without some sympathy. 'Your brother Henry is something of a hothead, is he not?'

Louise did not reply. Her husband took her hand and looked anxiously at the constable.

'He is young, sir.'

'And handy with his fists. As one of the watchmen will testify by virtue of the bloodied nose and black eye he has received.'

Louise took a breath. 'I have heard account that the Runners broke in on what was no more than a —' she searched for the right words — 'a social gathering. In the confusion, Henry may have thought himself under attack by villains and sought to defend himself. I am sure he intended no harm to an officer of the law. The magistrate must see this. Henry is a good, honest working man. We shall speak for his character. Others will speak for his character.'

Nicholls removed the Huguenot Cross from his pocket and held it out for inspection. 'And this? I found it about Henry's neck. It is one worn by initiates of a secret organisation, as you know.'

Simon paled. 'The Huguenot Brotherhood. Henry has become a member?'

Louise rose and pointed to the cross lying in Nicholls' palm. 'No! No, sirs, you have it all mistook! This is the cross that belonged to Jack! Look, here — see where the link has been mended to re-attach the phial.'

Nicholls frowned as he discerned the truth of Louise Forster's observation.

She continued with heated animation. 'After Mr Sheridan returned the cross to me, I had it repaired and gave it as a memento to Henry. I wanted him to know that Jack had not abandoned our faith, or our community, but had latterly sought to further their cause.'

'You encouraged Henry to join the Brotherhood?'

'No. No.' Louise shook her head vehemently.

'How should you know?'

'It was a memento only. What time has Henry for politics? He wants only to support my mother and my poor witless father who rely on him entirely.'

'That may be. But he refuses to speak, thus far. Why is that?'

'He is afraid,' Louise retorted, her voice rising in distress.

Nicholls held up the Huguenot Cross. 'Government officials will wish to speak with him. If Henry is deemed a troublemaker, then the least he can expect is to be sent to Botany Bay.'

'How shall my parents and sisters survive without him?' Louise wailed.

Mrs Forster's fraught question hung in the air.

'There is one way... He has not been brought before the magistrate as yet.' Nicholls eyed Mrs Forster shrewdly. 'But time is running very short.'

'What do you mean, sir?' Simon interposed.

'Someone else might divulge the information which will be wanted. The Home Department might never know that Henry was apprehended in any connection to the Brotherhood.'

There was a moment's silence as this proposition was digested by the Forsters. Time for Sheridan to admire the way in which the young Bow Street officer had steered the interview to an interesting juncture. Nicholls suspected that the Forsters knew more of the activities of the Brotherhood than they claimed. By suggesting that they divulge what they knew, he held up the tantalising prospect that they might yet save Henry Champion from falling into government hands. He waited with bated breath for the response.

Simon rose to stand beside his wife. 'How may we help Henry? You want us to give you information we do not have. We know nothing, Constable. How could we? I am not a part of this Huguenot Brotherhood — it was I who alerted you to their existence.'

Louise glanced at her husband in surprise.

The weaver continued. 'But I know Henry, and I believe him to be innocent of any involvement in their activities. He thinks only of how we might make an honest living at our trade. Yes, he is sometimes hasty. We are so often at the mercy of the silk merchants, men like Mr Logier. Henry will not stand idly by as they exploit and abuse the weaver at his loom. He will protest. But that is all.'

Nicholls shook his head. 'If there is nothing you can tell me, I must show Sir Sampson this cross and tell him what it signifies. That is my duty.'

Louise wrung her hands in despair. The conversation, it seemed, was at an end.

Sheridan stepped forward. 'Mrs Forster, do you love your brother?'

'Of course I do — most assuredly!'

'Both of your brothers?'

Louise's brow creased.

'In protecting one, you may condemn the other…'

Simon looked bewildered. 'But Jack is dead. There is no other brother now.'

'Madame?' Sheridan urged gently. 'Shall Henry be transported on the next Fleet, never to be seen again by those that love him? Or shall he rather face a fine and —'

Nicholls quickly calculated. 'A month in prison, perhaps? For his good character. His assault on my poor watchman — that cannot go entirely unpunished.'

Louise put a trembling hand to her brow. 'What must I do?'

'Only tell the truth, my dear,' Sheridan urged.

She began to sob.

'What is this? What do you ask of my wife?' Simon placed an arm about Louise.

'You must save Henry, Mrs Forster. Jack is still alive, is he not?' Sheridan prompted.

Hesitantly, Louise nodded.

Simon frowned. 'Louise? Do you say it is not Jack that we buried? That you know him to be still living?'

Louise turned to Constable Nicholls. 'Henry knows nothing, I swear to you. He does not know that Jack lives. Henry has always been angry with Jack for leaving the family these ten years.'

'Go on.'

'When Jack returned to us, like my mother, Henry refused to recognise him and would accept nothing from him. He was furious when he heard of the gift that Jack had made to us.' She glanced quickly at her husband. 'Henry went to have it out with Jack and to insist that he keep away.'

'When was this?' Sheridan asked.

'The night that Captain Jeffreys confronted Jack and near enough killed him. Henry said he took pity on his brother then and helped Jack back to his lodgings. He urged him to leave the city for good and make a new life elsewhere, to leave us all in peace. That is the last Henry saw of him. Then you came to us, Constable, to speak of murder. When Henry learned that our brother had been killed, he was convinced that Captain Jeffreys had returned, with renewed fury, and done away with Jack.'

'But you knew, Mrs Forster, the day that we first spoke with you, that it was not your brother's remains that had been found in the Drury Lane cellars — is that not the case?'

Louise put a hand to her mouth and again nodded.

Sheridan regarded her. 'Jack did quit his lodgings, and he went into hiding. It fit his purpose; he had a new master. But he continued to meet with you in secret, did he not?'

'Can this be true, Louise?' her husband asked plaintively, his hand slipping from her shoulder.

'He begged me, Simon. He said there were larger dangers which I could not be privy to, but that a time would come when all would be well.'

Simon shook his head. 'And you believed him?'

Sheridan interjected. 'When we discovered the remains in my theatre cellars, of a man I now believe to be Gaspard Bernon, it must have been distressing for you, Mrs Forster — that body in the Harlequin costume. You knew it was not your brother, but you feared something worse.'

Louise paled and looked as though she might faint. Nicholls rushed over with a straight back chair for her to sit on.

Sheridan knew he must continue. 'It was when we produced the Huguenot Cross — then your shock was very real, my dear. Was it then that you suspected it was Jack who had killed the man?'

'In defence, he said,' Louise whispered.

'In defence? Yet he planted the cross deliberately to deceive. Jack must have known that the corpse would be found during the demolition of the building. It suited his plans very well to be considered dead and for you and your husband to confirm that this cross was his.'

'The devil — he has used you! Used us!' Simon spluttered.

Sheridan studied Louise. 'That was quite a performance that you gave. Jack would have been pleased to see his sister shared the same inclination for the stage. Perhaps then he also laughed up his sleeve as he attended his own funeral. I begin to believe your father did catch a sight of him that day, but who would listen to the poor man?'

'Where is Jack, Mrs Forster? I cannot delay if I am to help Henry,' Nicholls urged.

Louise shook her head. Sheridan could see the conflict racing across her features. She must choose. She must betray one brother for another.

'Louise,' her husband urged, 'you must do what is right.'

She took a deep breath. 'He has a room in an attic, Wilkes Yard. Please —' she looked pleadingly at Constable Nicholls — 'do not tell Jack it was I who told you.'

Nicholls nodded curtly.

Sheridan bowed. 'Thank you, Mrs Forster. It is a good and brave choice that you have made.'

CHAPTER TWENTY-TWO

Constable Nicholls had not been pleased when Sheridan had insisted on joining the Bow Street Runner and his assistants on the mission to Spitalfields.

'This is a dangerous man that we deal with, Mr Sheridan. One who may be in company with other desperate coves.'

'I shall take my chances, Nicholls, if I can finally look Jack Champion in the eye and see justice done. He has murdered one of my company, Gaspard Bernon, leaving another bereft and with a fatherless child. And this villain may yet be responsible for another death — I will not bear it if Mr Legge...' Sheridan swallowed hard. He had kept those feelings at bay since leaving the hospital earlier that morning.

Nicholls had muttered but pressed a short sword into Sheridan's hand. 'Take this then. I hope you shall not need it.'

'So do I — it is many years now since my lessons at Signor Angelo's School of Arms.' Sheridan raised an eyebrow as he felt the weight of the weapon in his hand. 'And in neither of the duels that I fought did I acquit myself with any great skill.'

The remnants of the night were giving way to dawn, the city streets now stirring to life. Lamplights were snuffed out. A night-soil man, attired in filthy rags, trundled his load wearily towards the cesspit, from which it would be sold on as fertilizer. The last of the night's streetwalkers, fuddled by gin, wove their way to whatever bed of their own might await them.

In their stead, carts trundled up through the main thoroughfares towards the old market at Spitalfields, laden with produce from the nearby countryside to feed the burgeoning suburbs outside the crumbling city walls. A farmer and his boy led two squealing pigs towards their slaughter at the Shambles. Live fowl flapped within the confines of their cages and lent their voices to the dawn chorus. Yawning shop assistants and apprentices set about opening their master's businesses. Sombre-looking clerks quickened their step, only stopping to purchase muffins or hot gingerbread from the street sellers along the way. Sheridan was reminded that there had been no time to halt for the promised refreshment and his flask, he realised, was sadly empty.

As they neared Hawksmoor's Christ Church, Nicholls stopped the Bow Street wagon. They were met by two of the parish watchmen and Nicholls set about deploying one of these men and his fellow Runner at the narrow entrances to Wilkes Yard. He and the other man of the parish, one Samuel Dibdin, then drew close to the door of the house tucked into the Yard. The four-storey tenement was steeped in darkness and no lights could be seen in any of the windows, those that were not broken and patched with board or canvas. Sheridan suspected that even when the sun was at its height, little light would penetrate the ground level to dispel the gloom and odours of mouldering decay.

Sheridan narrowly avoided the contents of a piss pot emptied from a window above as he hurried to follow Nicholls. The area they were entering was a warren of houses whose occupants lived one on top of the other — the weavers and their families catching what light they could to work their looms in the attics above. The inhabitants were stirring. An old man appeared on the threshold and spat out into the yard. He looked with a cutty eye at the armed men who approached and then whistled high and sharp before taking out a clay pipe and preparing a plug.

'Stand aside, sir, if you would,' Nicholls addressed the man.

The old man leant against the doorpost. 'Who is it you'd speak with?'

'That is not your affair, sir.'

'Only I may save you a climb of them rotting stairs if the cove is not within.'

The old man chewed on the end of the unlit pipe and regarded Constable Nicholls from under thick brows.

Nicholls smiled without humour. 'We'll take our chances. If you will let us pass.'

The old man flicked his brows. 'Now, if it is Davy you want, he is gone to his sister up Shoreditch.'

'I will not ask again, sir.' Nicholls advanced until he was abreast of the old man.

The man shrugged and moved aside. 'As you please. I do not stop you, sir.'

As they passed into the house and launched up the narrow staircase, they heard the old man chuckle behind them. A door opened above. A woman peered out and then at the sight of the constable and his cutlass slammed it shut again. A barefoot boy hurtled down the stairs and eyed them warily as he made to squeeze his way past. Dibdin snatched him by the shoulder.

'How many?'

The boy shook his head but looked frightened.

Dibdin grunted and shoved the boy down the rickety stairs.

Sheridan could feel his heart quicken as they reached the final set of stairs that led up into the garret. He was struggling to catch his breath and could feel the rasp of his throat from his recent illness.

Nicholls pounded on the only door. 'Open up! It is the officers of the magistrates!'

Sounds came from within but none advanced to the door.

Nicholls nodded to Dibdin and together they heaved their shoulders to the door. On the third attempt it gave way with a great splintering of wood from the rotting frame. The force of their effort carried both men into the room under the pitch of the roof. Dibdin was met at once with a savage blow to the head, which sent him reeling and unconscious to the floor.

Nicholls regained his footing and whirled about with his cutlass. The brawny assailant jumped back, but not before he had been slashed in the side by the blade. Another man then set about Nicholls with a cutlass in hand. There was the sound of metal clashing as the constable swiftly parried.

Sheridan stood on the threshold, his gaze fixed on the man at the open dormer window. Jack Champion. Their eyes locked. Sheridan saw surprised recognition flit across the features of his former actor, and then Handsome Jack raised his pistol and fired.

Later, Sheridan would swear that he actually saw the bullet pass within a hair's breadth of his nose as he threw himself sideways, the blast ringing in his ears. He yelled from fear as much as fury and hurled himself into the attic room with his short sword raised.

The other man, grasping at his injured side, had backed towards the window, blocking Sheridan's way with a thick staff, which he waved from side to side.

'Run for it, Jack! Make away!'

Jack, needing no further urging, was already clambering through the opening onto the roof.

Sheridan lunged forward with his short sword, but the thickset man in front of him was a seasoned fighter and avoided the thrust whilst dealing Sheridan a clout across his knuckles. Sudden pain seared up through Sheridan's arm and he staggered back. He would need a more cautious approach.

From the corner of his eye, Sheridan could see that Nicholls was engaged in a deadly battle with his adversary in the cramped space, the pair crashing and grunting together as they clashed weapons and knocked over the furniture. A trickle of blood ran down Nicholls' cheek. The constable prepared himself for another onslaught as the man let out a cry and sliced at him again. Sheridan prayed that Nicholls was a better swordsman than he himself was.

Adding to the clamour, booted steps could be heard thundering up the stairs from three floors below. Then shouts arose in the yard as the other Runner saw Jack Champion making his escape over the rooftops.

Sheridan eyed the man in front of him. 'Throw down your weapon! It is all up for you!'

The lumbering brute sneered and lashed out with the heavy staff, forcing Sheridan to jump back. The weapon was raised again and this time Sheridan dodged to the side as it swept down. Then there was a sharp yelp, and Sheridan snatched a glance to see that Nicholls had skewered his opponent. It was a fatal strike, and the man dropped his cutlass as he began to crumple forward onto Nicholls' blade. The constable hastily withdrew it and sidestepped, allowing the man to slump to the floor.

Seeing his comrade thus felled, Sheridan's attacker hesitated and then lurched backward. He felt for the windowsill at his rear and hoisted himself through the frame, hurling the thick staff towards Sheridan and catching his cheek with a sharp, searing pain. The big man swung himself out onto the pitch of the roof. But being neither as light nor as agile as his predecessor, he scrambled to steady himself on the incline, which was slick with morning dew. Moments later, a desperate cry signalled that he had lost his balance.

Sheridan rushed to the open window in time to see the shocked expression on the man's face as he clutched desperately at the rotten wooden guttering. It would not hold his weight. Sheridan closed his eyes when the man fell, but could not block out his fearful cry nor the deadly thump as his body hit the ground below.

The watchman arrived in the doorway and, struggling for breath, called out to Nicholls. 'Sir, we heard a shot fired!' He then saw his fellow patrolman splayed on the floor and with a strangled cry dropped to his knees beside him. 'Samuel! Is it Samuel that is struck?'

Nicholls did not reply. He was staring between the body of his assailant and the bloodied cutlass in his own hand. 'I never killed a man before now.'

Sheridan cast his own weapon aside and moved towards the young constable, placing a hand on his shoulder.

A low moan came from Dibdin, followed by an oath.

His friend sobbed a laugh. 'He has a thick skull, Samuel Dibdin, the very devil he has!'

Nicholls had pulled himself together and rushed out to see whether or not Jack Champion had made good his escape. By the time he returned to the attic room, that search had been abandoned as a lost cause.

'Blast the villain!' Nicholls cursed.

His fellow Runner had been tasked with enquiring of the tenants living around the yard what they knew of the men holed up in this garret. And if any could identify the thickset man now lying dead in the cobbled yard below.

Sheridan had not been idle. He had set about searching Champion's sanctum to see what he might find. Stepping gingerly around the lifeless body in its pool of oozing blood, he had started from the further end of the garret. There had been the liveried waiter's costume, worn the night previous, discarded on the bed together with the Harlequin mask. An open trunk had held other costumes and wigs that might help Jack blend into any number of differing environments. And yes, here was the misshapen hat which the villain had sported all those days past in Brighton, evidencing a man who relished disguise.

By the upturned table were writing materials and papers which had become scattered on the floor in the affray. Sheridan picked up a scrawled note written in French and unfinished. He translated as best he could.

My dearest Sister

I have failed, but shall see all righted when I join you in B and our Sister.

Louise Forster. What more did she know? She was steeped in her actor brother's activities to a greater degree than even he had suspected. Perhaps it was not young Henry Champion who was in imminent danger of transportation to the new prison colony but his older sister.

On a cabinet near the bed, Sheridan found gazettes — one from Brighton, he noted — and newspapers open on the society pages that spoke of the comings and goings of members of the Royal Family, the *bon ton* and other notables, himself included. And beneath the gazettes was an advertisement for the Vauxhall Pleasure Gardens, which heralded the opening of the new temple. How easy it was to track the movements of society's celebrities.

Stuffed at the back of a drawer he found a purse. Here was not pennies and farthings but coinage that was no mean sum.

Someone was funding Jack Champion in generous amounts. The Brotherhood was more than a gathering of poor weavers and apprentices. There was someone of note behind the formation of this secret society. Someone who directed their activities. What was it that these Huguenots wanted alongside a guarantee of religious freedom? A return to wealth and power. Rudderless, ambitious men, like Jack Champion, had been lured into the group with the promise of both. And something else, it occurred to Sheridan. Revenge for the dragonnades, revenge for the massacres, revenge for the persecution, revenge for the ancient theft of land and property.

From beneath the purse Sheridan retrieved a cache of letters and was still puzzling over their contents when Nicholls returned.

'Anything of interest, sir?'

'My Harlequin has been busy, it seems —' he indicated the contents of the trunk — 'and moved amongst us at will.'

Sheridan held out a bundle of papers to the constable. Nicholls took them and as he perused the contents, his brows creased in consternation. 'It is gibberish.'

Sheridan nodded. 'The letters are in code. Something of a fashion, I gather, within secret societies.'

'They must go to the Home Department; they may have a chance to decipher them.'

'It is out of our hands…'

Nicholls then looked up expectantly at Sheridan and offered him two sheets from the pile. 'Two heads may be better than one. If you discover the code, it can be passed on.'

Sheridan took the proffered pages. 'I shall attempt it, and if I can make neither head nor tail, so be it.'

Nicholls regarded the dead man on the floor. 'If only we had one of these villains alive, they should be made to talk.'

'You must speak again to Mrs Forster.' Sheridan held out the half-written note.

Nicholls' features set hard. 'We shall have him, Mr Sheridan. I promise you, we shall have him!'

From without they heard a peel of bells, coming from Christ Church. The sun was rising above the rooftops. It was to be another fine summer's day, and Sheridan was reminded that it was a Sunday, a day of rest — and how he longed for that.

CHAPTER TWENTY-THREE

It was Thomas Christie himself who ushered Sheridan into the house in Soho.

'My dear Sheridan, come in, come in! You are exhausted, my poor fellow!'

Sheridan knew that he looked more than simply exhausted. His hair was dishevelled, his clothing stained and scuffed, his cheek grazed raw and his right hand bruised and swollen at the knuckles — he looked like nothing so much as a drunken libertine who had come off the worse in a tavern brawl. Dr Christie made a fuss of Sheridan's battered hand and insisted he would put a salve and dressing on his wounds, leading him immediately to the kitchen.

'What news do you bring from Bow Street?'

Sheridan sighed wearily. 'I know who he is, the assassin. But the villain has escaped us for now. And Timothy?'

Christie inclined his head sadly. 'We must wait. He sleeps — let his sleep be long and deep. I would give hope, but you should know his recovery is by no means certain.'

'This is a bad business.' Sheridan winced as the stinging salve was applied.

'The bullet was not intended for Mr Legge.' Christie's response was more statement than conjecture.

'No, it was meant for Monsieur Danton. Your guest was shaken, but perhaps not so surprised as we have been. Does he say anything?'

Christie shook his head. 'But you may ask him yourself. He is busy entertaining young Billy.'

'Billy, yes, Billy. That is another reason why I call.'

'You are here to take the boy into your care? That is most kind of you, sir.'

'It is what Timothy would want, I know.'

'I myself would offer, but —'

Sheridan shook his head. 'You have guests enough, Christie.'

As they returned to the front vestibule, they could hear shouts and laughter coming from within the front parlour.

Christie smiled. 'Monsieur Danton went to the nick-nackatory last week and purchased a board for playing Fox and Geese to set about teaching Billy — but the boy appears to need no lessons in cunning!'

They entered and received scarcely an acknowledgement as the game was reaching its tense climax. Danton was in the part of the fox and Billy had command of the geese. Sheridan observed that the Frenchman made moves not obviously to facilitate Billy's triumph but which nevertheless had that desired effect.

Billy whooped with triumphant glee as his piece cornered the hunted fox in an arm of the cross-shaped lattice board. 'That's got yer, Mister Fox! Yer done for now!'

Danton threw his hands up in the air and exclaimed in grand oratorial style, 'Ah, *sacré bleu*! Reynard has been ambushed — by the silly goose!'

Christie patted Billy on the head. 'Well done, Billy, you have shown Monsieur Danton what we British are made of. Now, Mrs Scrope has made a treacle tart for you. They are her speciality.'

The boy's eyes lit up at the prospect.

'You are excused and may go to the kitchen without delay. Mr Sheridan shall be ready to take you with him after he has likewise received refreshment.'

Billy needed no further prompt and made swift his exit. Christie smiled. 'The way to that boy's heart, I should think. And you, sirs, a glass of claret?'

'That would be very welcome, Christie.'

'Excuse me then — I have a special bottle,' Christie said as he left.

Danton rose from the card table and stretched his limbs.

'Monsieur Sheridan, you surprise me. I did not take you for a man of action.' Danton nodded towards the bandaged hand.

Sheridan shook his head. 'I fear Sir Sampson Wright will not be recruiting me to his Bow Street Runners any time soon! Though, come to think of it, should the building of the new theatre bankrupt me, then it may present as a career alternative to the debtors' prison.'

Danton chuckled. 'We are all bankrupt, monsieur. We merely pray that our creditors do not speak to each other.'

'Do you have a theory yet, Monsieur Danton? About who tried to shoot you last night? Not a creditor, I think,' Sheridan added with a smile.

'One of our noble émigrés. *Le case-cou* Le Marquis de Penaud-Mortain, I imagine.'

'Monsieur, do you know of a society called the Huguenot Brotherhood?'

Sheridan was sure that he caught a twitch at Danton's left eye.

'Huguenots?' Danton shook his head. 'They are now free from persecution in France. I do not doubt there are societies of friendship, a *brotherhood* that may have formed. Why do you ask?'

'This society is a secret one. Similar to the Freemasons and the Illuminati.'

Danton shrugged. 'I may have heard something. Paris has been awash with societies and clubs since our Revolution.'

'I can well believe that, monsieur. This Brotherhood, however, may have some deadly purpose — since it was one of their members that tried to assassinate you.'

Danton's eyes flickered with interest. 'One of their members? You are certain of this?'

'Jack Champion, formerly employed in the role of Harlequin at Drury Lane, I am sorry to say. From a family of Huguenot weavers. I wondered if you might know why you are their target?'

Danton barked a laugh. 'As I have told you before, Monsieur Sheridan, there are many who may have a price on my head.' He patted his pocket, which held the pistol.

'But the Huguenots? That does seem odd to me.'

Again, the large shrug of the shoulders. 'I do not know what I may have done to displease them so much that they want to execute me.'

Sheridan nodded thoughtfully. 'In these tumultuous times, it may not always be clear who may be on which side. Indeed, there may be any number of "sides" — a veritable hexagon.'

Danton grinned. 'I think in that you are correct.'

'Which side are you on, Monsieur Danton?'

Danton broke into loud guffaws. When he had caught his breath, he spluttered an answer. 'My own, Monsieur Sheridan, my own.'

Sheridan had toyed with the notion of taking Billy down to the villa at Isleworth, for the country air would do him good, but he decided the journey would be too far that day. He needed to sleep, urgently. As he prodded Billy towards the hackney, he directed the driver to the house in Grosvenor Street. The ruddy-faced man looked down with a squint.

'Right you are, sir — reckon we know where that is.' He gave the reins a slight tug and addressed his horse. 'Don't we, Billy-Boy?'

Billy stopped for a moment, as though stunned.

'What is it, Billy?'

Billy turned back to look at Dr Christie's door. 'Can I not stay here with mi'ssur?'

Sheridan put a hand on his shoulder. 'No, Billy. You must come with me. I shall take good care of you, do not fret. And then tomorrow, God willing, we shall visit Mr Legge.'

'Does yer 'ave a pistol? Mi'ssur 'as a pistol.'

'Somewhere; it is not something I carry about with me, Billy. They are a dangerous weapon — as you have unfortunately witnessed.' He nudged the boy around. 'Now come, let's make haste. I am very much in need of my bed.'

By the time they had arrived at the house, Sheridan had begun to nod off and needed to be shaken awake by the boy.

'Need a hand up them steps, sir?' The driver dismounted.

'Nah, we're all right,' Billy cut in. 'Ain't yer, Mister Sheridan? I can help.'

Sheridan shook the sleep from his head and stepped from the cab. 'Thank you for the offer, Driver. I can manage with my boy.'

'Good lad you got there, sir. Knows his place.'

Sheridan pressed a coin into the man's hand. 'Yes, he has surprised me.'

Sheridan gave a long sigh of relief as he slipped between his bedsheets. His manservant pulled across the thick curtains and the light of day was extinguished at last.

'Thank you, Michael. That will be all.'

Sleep arrived almost at once, but it was uneasy with half-dreams and recurring images. Foremost, the lithe young man standing at the window, his eyes glittering dark pools that seemed to mock him. And then the man wore a mask and his eyes were hollow beneath the cockaded hat, and he moved closer to Sheridan in his diamond-patterned jerkin. He waved a slapstick, but then the stick was a pistol. Sheridan wanted to swipe the man away, but he was frozen to his place and the figure loomed over him, and below the nose of the mask was a gaping mouth stripped clean of flesh.

He woke, sweating, and tossed the bedding aside. He sensed a presence lurking in the shadows.

'Who's there?' he said aloud, his eyes raking the darkness.

A whispered response came. ''S'only me... I was scared...'

'Nothing to be scared about, Billy... Go back to sleep...'

And then he gave in to the tugging tendrils of sleep pulling him back into the dreamscape.

Michael yanked the curtains aside and the morning sun pierced the gloom. Sheridan blinked at the rude awakening and covered his eyes.

'Did I call you?'

'No, sir.'

'Then why the devil do you wake me?'

'It could not wait any longer, sir. We've been robbed in the night.'

'Robbed?' Sheridan hoisted himself up against the pillows.

'I sent to Bow Street, sir. There is a Runner below who awaits you.'

'Robbed?' Sheridan repeated. 'How is that possible? Are we not securely locked up at night?'

'The thief has come from within.'

Sheridan frowned in disbelief. 'You cannot mean —'

'No, sir. None of your loyal servants.'

'Then who?' Sheridan groaned as realisation dawned. He heaved himself out of the bed and pulled on the brocaded banyan which Michael held out for him together with the loose turban. He felt the rough stubble at his chin and the sting at his cheek. His toilette should have to be delayed.

Constable Nicholls was waiting in the parlour.

'This is a pretty pass, is it not, Nicholls?'

'Yes, sir. Very unfortunate.'

'I had begun to imagine that I was wrong and that Billy might be changed from a sneakthief after all. I take no pleasure in having been proved right in my first estimations of the boy.'

The constable nodded. 'Mr Legge shall be most disappointed.'

'Yes, poor Timothy… I don't know how I shall inform him of this. But that may be left for now; Mr Legge needs no further upset.'

'Do you have a list of what has been taken, sir?'

'I shall ask my manservant to compile the full directory. There are items of some value, I believe.' Sheridan shook his head, aggrieved. 'The boy took his opportunity all right. He waited 'til he had our trust and might snatch items of real worth.'

Nicholls nodded. 'We may still be able to find some of your property, Mr Sheridan. There is a man I know that sometimes handles stolen goods. He is useful to us as an informant. He may get word of this haul.'

'I daresay Billy has now returned to Battling Poll.'

'Well, he was nurtured in the bosom of that wicked family, sir. He will no doubt re-join his blackguard brothers and grow in villainy until he will most likely dangle at the end of a rope.'

'I'd almost allowed myself to grow fond of the little chit.'

They were silent for a moment.

'On other business, sir, we have identified those men in Wilkes Yard.'

'Well done, Constable.'

'The man who fell from the roof was one Giles Rivers, a local of Spitalfields. Had worked as a drayman until he argued with the brewer. Known as a brawler and was said to have fallen into bad company. The other villain was a Frenchman. The neighbours didn't seem to know much about him.'

Sheridan shrugged. 'It suggests there is some link back to France.'

'Louise Forster, however, did know his name — Leonard. He came from the region of Guienne, apparently, somewhere near the port of Bordeaux. That was once an area where there were many Protestants.'

'And the note left for her by her brother?'

'She swears blind it cannot have been meant for her. She does not know what it means and besides which, she herself has not been taught to read.'

'Her husband can read. What have you done with them?'

'Nothing for now. But they will be watched.'

'And Henry?'

'In Newgate. With a fine of ten shillings and a month in prison for his drunken assault on the parish watchman.'

'While their brother Jack still haunts our streets.'

'I fear so.'

Sheridan rubbed his brow.

'Mr Sheridan, you have done all that you can. His description has been posted. I believe Champion shall be found,' the constable reassured.

'Before he kills again, or after?'

Nicholls did not respond.

Sheridan's eyes narrowed with a sudden remembrance. 'Mrs Jeffreys — were you not going to make some enquiry in that quarter?'

Nicholls flushed. 'Yes, sir.'

Sheridan raised an eyebrow. 'And?'

'Well…' The young constable shifted uncomfortably.

Sheridan regarded him with a mischievous smile. 'You have used your charm to gain some titbit, I can tell.'

Nicholls nodded. 'I made the excuse of examining the security of the house, warning of a spate of burglaries in the neighbourhood — which is partly true, sir.'

'Naturally, you were not intending to deceive.'

'The lady's maid, Emma —'

'A young woman not immune to your attentions?' Sheridan said with a smirk.

'I did learn something of interest.'

'Yes?'

'Captain Jeffreys' commission in the Life Guards was paid for by his wife. It was the marriage portion, in a manner of speaking.'

'Ah, and how did the lady come by her fortune?'

'The Duc d'Orléans.'

Sheridan spluttered a laugh of incredulity and then, correcting his reaction, he nodded sagely. 'Margaret Bedwell did hint that Mrs Jeffreys had a past.'

'As Sophia Goodwin, sir. She often frequented your theatre, and that is where she made Orléans' acquaintance some five years gone. Unlike many of her kind, she used the proceeds of that liaison to turn respectable. Jeffreys was a trooper in the Grenadiers and she gave him that opportunity in the Life Guards. Emma was delighted with the change in her own prospects, the chance to become a proper lady's maid. It seems her mistress had not expected Jeffreys to turn into a jealous husband, but Mrs Jeffreys is a very attractive woman, so it is understandable. Only she had always loved another.'

'Handsome Jack.'

'Precisely, sir.'

'Hmm. I do not know where this fits. But something tells me it is not insignificant. Thank you, Nicholls. I hope the task was not too onerous?'

'Ours is a rum profession. I'll bid you good day then, Mr Sheridan.'

After Nicholls had been shown out, Sheridan's manservant returned to the parlour.

'We draw up the inventory, sir, of what has been taken, but we must add your pocket watch to the list. It was in your waistcoat yesterday when you returned — but it is gone now.'

'The little rogue! He was rummaging in my room even whilst I slept!'

Michael nodded. 'That would be the conclusion, sir.'

The watch had been a gift from Eliza. Sheridan beat his fist against his palm before remembering that it was still painfully bruised.

'Devil take it!'

CHAPTER TWENTY-FOUR

Despite being still out of season, it was a surprisingly lively evening at Brooks's Club. Sheridan enjoyed a hearty meal of beef and dumplings washed down with a good bottle of claret. He felt in the mood to be inebriated and ordered a bottle of port, for he had spent the afternoon at his desk attempting to decipher the letters he'd found in the garret. In less than an hour, he had been at his wits' end and after two hours he felt he might indeed be consigned to Bedlam. Nicholls was right. He had done all that he could do. He must try to forget the whole dreadful business of dead Harlequins and would-be assassins. Never mind thieving rascals. Only the thought of Timothy Legge's potential demise nagged at him and drew him with increased alacrity to the succour which the port of Douro obliged him with.

He sought forgetting, but the events at Vauxhall Gardens were not to be forgotten. He had scarce downed his second glass when Charles James Fox appeared in front of him and made solicitous enquires after the young lawyer.

'Henry Cline is a damn fine surgeon — damnably fine,' Sheridan slurred. 'Mr Legge shall come through, no doubt — no doubt.'

'I sincerely hope so, Dick.' The politician tapped his cane on the floor and lowered his voice. 'After all, that bullet was not intended for him.'

'No, egad! It was not. It did not have his name on it, Charlie.' Sheridan stabbed at the occasional table with his finger. 'No, no, no.'

'Mr Tyers has been most aggrieved to hear that such a dangerous highwayman was lurking in his Gardens. He intends to increase his police force.'

'That is what they are saying, is it?'

'What else? A robbery gone wrong. Pistol misfired. Unfortunate consequence. Villain escaped. That is the general consensus.'

'It is as well. Our French friend should not welcome the attention.'

'Let us pray there will be no further attempts on his life. We do not need such a crisis here in England. Paris may have been long prone to volatility, but London is not immune to disturbance either. The Prime Minister is beginning to consider that we have too many émigrés here, and at this juncture I feel inclined to agree.'

'We cannot become a fortress, Charlie. Men, like ideas, should move freely.'

Fox nodded and changed the subject. 'Do you join us at cards?'

Sheridan could tell that Fox was itching to be at the gaming tables; it was his weakness. 'Later, perhaps — you go on, Charlie.'

He was not to be left alone for long. Major Hanger arrived by his side, waving his own bottle of port.

'Mind if I join you, Sheridan?'

"S'a free country. Sit down, Hanger.'

'Free, by God, it is — down with tyranny, I say!' Hanger slumped into a chair.

'You sided with the Bostonians then, did you?' Sheridan chuckled over his own poor jibe.

'I think all of us — by the end of that misbegotten war — had some sympathy with our deputed enemy; in their situation, I should probably have had a tea party myself.'

Sheridan straightened his features. 'Major, you served, you did your duty in the Americas — if somewhat recklessly, I gather. But yes, *down with tyranny* — wherever it may reside!'

'To freedom!' The major topped up their glasses.

'Hanger, you're a military man… Did you ever need to use coded messages?'

'All the time, always been a part of warfare, sir.' Hanger sat back, dribbling a little port in the process. 'A means to send messages behind enemy lines.'

'There are many different forms, I imagine?'

Hanger nodded. 'From the fairly simple to the near impossible to decipher if you do not hold the key.'

Sheridan withdrew from his pocket the sheet of paper found in the attic room at Wilkes Yard and held it out. 'What d'you make of this?'

Major Hanger looked at the jumble of letters. 'Well, it is letters rather than marks…' He sucked at his teeth. 'So, it is not a pigpen…'

'Pigpen?'

'A kind of grid where you group symbols.' Hanger took a draught of his fortified wine. 'Did you come across any books lying about where these pages were found, by any chance?'

'Books?'

'A bible? Treatise…?'

Sheridan tried to cast his mind back to his search of the garret. 'Gazettes, newspapers — any number of such literature. But a book, I do not recall.' He scratched his head. 'Also, the code may be in French.'

Hanger groaned.

'It is impossible then? Well, so be it.' Sheridan sighed in resignation.

Hanger shook his head. 'Can you leave it with me a day or two, Sheridan? I may try some basic combinations. I have always rather enjoyed a puzzle.'

'Thank you, Major. You're a good fellow… Now, I think I must find my carriage. I never have slept comfortably in these chairs.'

'Sheridan … forgot to say, His Royal Highness expects —'

'I know what the prince expects!' Sheridan snapped.

'Charades. Expects you for charades, Wednesday. Did you think I was talking about something else?'

Sheridan sighed as he heaved himself up from the chair. 'Apologies, Hanger, I was unpardonably rude. A lot on my mind…'

Sheridan was waiting in the vestibule for his carriage when Nathaniel Parker Forth entered the club, on his own.

'Good evening, Mr Sheridan.' The agent bowed politely.

'Not sure about that, Mr Parker Forth.' Sheridan swayed. 'Whether it's a good evening.'

'I am sorry to hear that, sir. Have you lost at the tables?'

Sheridan shook his head. 'Not my vice. The duc not with you?'

Parker Forth smiled in a conspiratorial fashion. 'His Serene Highness is otherwise engaged.'

'And what engages you, Parker Forth? Another round of chicanery?'

Nathaniel Parker Forth bristled. 'Sir, you are quite right to go home; it is evident that you have drunk an unseemly amount.'

'I've kept good company then, sir. I bid you good night.'

Sheridan lurched and felt a sudden rise of nausea. He swallowed hard to hold it down, but before he could request a receptacle or issue any warning, the contents of his stomach had disgorged onto the tiled floor.

Parker Forth regarded the splatter on his elegant shoes with distaste and moved swiftly away, presumably in order to have them cleaned forthwith.

'Apologies,' Sheridan called after him. 'The dumplings, avoid the dumplings.'

The porter nodded in recognition as Sheridan made his way to the recovery ward of St Thomas's Hospital the following morning. His head throbbed pitilessly. His stomach growled a reprimand. He had baulked at consuming anything more than a hunk of toasted bread for breakfast. He also was in need of the so-called 'recovery' ward, he mused. The matron greeted him at the threshold.

'Good morning, sir. You have come to visit Mr Legge?'

'If that is permitted, my good woman?'

'You may not see him for long. Mr Legge is awake, but he tires quickly. There have been visitors enough this morning.'

'I shall not overstay my welcome, Mrs —?'

'Merriweather, sir.'

'Mrs Merriweather, I must commend you on the diligence with which you conduct your office, and you have my complete assurance.'

For a fleeting moment the woman brightened at the compliment but then fell back to a critical regard. 'You look rather pale, if you don't mind me saying so, sir. You are not ailing yourself, I trust? We cannot have any fevers brought into the hospital.'

'Nothing of that nature, Matron — something I ate last night … merely.'

She looked askance, judging what that might imply, but stepped aside to allow him to enter.

'Oh, and you will find his father with him, sir.'

Sheridan nodded. It was as he had anticipated. He could see his good-hearted constituent across the room, sitting by the cot, his large paw resting on top of the limp hand of his son.

'Josiah ... Mr Legge.' Sheridan bowed a greeting.

The older man rose awkwardly from the cricket stool, his joints stiff, and bowed in turn. 'Mr Sheridan. I am right glad ter see tha.' He spoke in the strong accent of his native Staffordshire.

Josiah spread his arms and Sheridan allowed himself to be drawn into a bear-like embrace. Tears glistened in the old man's eyes when he stepped back. He nodded, unable for a moment to express himself in words.

'This is a most dreadful business, Mr Legge. I am heartbroken.'

Josiah continued to nod and then clutched Sheridan's hands in his own. 'I am only pleased that tha were with him, Mr Sheridan, and did everything that could be done.'

'Thank you, sir, but it is Dr Christie who is our hero.'

'Aye, I had the honour of meeting with that gentleman this morning, just after I arrived. There were another with him that were most solicitous, though to look at the man you would think him a devilish brute. A Frenchman, would you credit? I don't think I had ever met with a Frenchman afore. Everyone has been most kind.'

'Timothy is very highly regarded, Mr Legge, and has many well-wishers.' Sheridan bent down towards the young man. 'How do you fare today, Timothy?' Sheridan asked softly.

Timothy's unruly auburn locks framed a brilliant smile. 'Today? Yes, a lovely day. My dear father has come to see me... Do you meet him, Mr Sheridan?'

'Yes, Timothy, your father is right here beside you.'

'And shan't leave tha side until thee are well again, my boy,' Josiah Legge exclaimed with feeling.

That should be a long time yet, Sheridan deduced. Young Mr Legge had clearly been given a great quantity of laudanum to relieve the pain he should otherwise experience.

'And Billy? Shall I see Billy? Do let it be soon.'

'All in good time, Timothy. You must mend.' How should he tell him that Billy was gone, along with a very fine pocket watch, a brooch that belonged to Eliza and various items of silverware?

'He takes his cod liver oil? Christie says that cod liver oil is good for Billy's constitution. He is so very small...' Timothy's eyelids began to flutter as he drifted back into his laudanum haze.

Sheridan patted the young lawyer's hand and stood up straight again.

'Yer look after this boy, Billy, I believe, Mr Sheridan? That is very generous of thee. It will do Timothy good to see the little fella, for he is ever so fond, but you are right to wait awhile — a small boy can be a spirited creature, and Timothy needs rest for now.' Mr Legge shook his head sadly. 'A pleasant evening stroll in the Pleasure Gardens — tha could not imagine such an outcome. Do they catch this murderous footpad yet?'

'No, sir, but I have faith in the Bow Street Public Office,' said Sheridan. 'Mr Legge, do you have a place to stay? If not—'

'That is very thoughtful, Mr Sheridan, but I have sent my luggage ahead for a room at Nerot's Hotel. It is closer than Timothy's lodgings. More convenient.'

Sheridan nodded. 'Very good — I have stayed at Nerot's often myself; you will be made comfortable. I shall return soon, then.'

Sheridan walked from St Thomas's with a heavy heart. He encountered the surgeon, Mr Cline, on his way out and asked for the medical man's view.

'I am more hopeful today that Mr Legge shall survive. But the feeling in his lower limbs has not returned as yet.'

Sheridan strode across the bridge at Westminster, enjoying the breeze off the river and feeling the need to stretch his own limbs. He imagined the horror of not being able to do so. Mr Cline's words reverberated. To lose the ability to walk. To be confined forever to a bath chair. Always to be dependent on others, on servants. That would be a crushing blow. Sheridan himself was not yet forty and knew that he could not countenance the prospect in like circumstances.

And at some point, he should have to deal another blow to the young idealist. He must tell Timothy that his protégé, little Billy Legge, had proved beyond redemption and was a blackguard youth after all. Perhaps if these terrible events had not occurred and Timothy had continued to keep a close watch on the boy — who knew? He might have saved Billy from that birthright. Sheridan doubted it. Nevertheless, he felt the weight of his responsibility; he had had charge of the boy when the thefts had occurred, and he was the man who must soon puncture Timothy's faith in the essential goodness of all mankind.

These thoughts assailed Sheridan as he stepped up to his front door. A voice hailed him from across the street.

'Monsieur Sheridan!' Danton marched across the thoroughfare, holding up a hand to the approaching traffic.

'Monsieur Sheridan, I hoped to find you at home. We must speak.'

There was a fire in the Frenchman's eyes. Sheridan wondered what should have caused such animation.

'Why yes, Monsieur Danton — I am at your service.'

The door was opened and Sheridan gestured for Danton to enter.

Danton did not wait until they were seated in the reception room. 'We have received word that Billy is gone! The kitchen maid is sent round with a treacle tart, for the boy likes them so well, and she is informed that Billy is absconded and he is a thief! Is this true?'

'Please, Monsieur Danton, do be seated. A glass of claret?'

'Is this true?' Danton demanded.

Sheridan nodded to his manservant and the man went to fetch a bottle.

'Sadly, it is true, Monsieur Danton. Some valuable items were taken during the very first night of his stay. The boy even had the audacity to enter my bedchamber whilst I slept in order to filch a rather fine pocket watch given to me by my wife.'

Danton shook his great bull's head. 'I will not believe it!'

'The facts are incontrovertible, my dear Danton. We must remember that the child was brought up and nurtured in a den of thieves. It is, unfortunately, not so very hard to believe at all.'

Danton paced about the room. '*Non. Non. Non.* I am a lawyer, Monsieur Sheridan. I know the criminal mind very well. This boy, he wants to be a child, not a villain. He wants to please, and of course that can be manipulated by wicked people, but he craves affection, not reward. He would not do this bad thing unless he must.'

'Must?'

'This is not Billy's doing. He is afraid, monsieur. He is very much afraid. He told me, when we made the tours of the city. He said they will "nab" him, they will beat him — they will *kill* him. So, I showed him my pistol and I said, *Billy, when you are with Danton, no one will take you!*'

'There is no evidence that the boy was taken or forced in any way.'

Danton glared at Sheridan. 'Something has happened!'

'Nothing happened. We left Soho and came immediately here. We saw no one.'

'No one?'

For a moment Sheridan felt that if he were to be in the dock and that if Monsieur Danton were the prosecuting barrister, he should feel very much intimidated.

'No one that I can recall.'

'Then recall.'

Sheridan shifted nervously. What on earth possessed Monsieur Danton that he should make such a fuss? But he did not wish to make an enemy of the Jacobin; that would not be a comfortable position to be in at all. He strained to think back to that afternoon two days previous.

'Well … only the jarvey, the driver of the hackney. He was very praising of Billy, said what a good boy he was, a boy who knew his place. Funnily enough, his horse was called Billy-Boy.'

'*Sacré bleu*! It is this man! He is telling the boy they come for him, and Billy must know his place! He is saying to Billy, his place is with that monstrous dam!' Danton gestured extravagantly with his hands, just as he might in a courtroom with twelve good men assembled before him. 'So, of course the boy must save himself. He takes what he can — because that is what these villains will expect! He knows that otherwise it will go very hard for him. These people, they are extremely wicked! He is in the gravest danger, Monsieur Sheridan!'

Sheridan stared at him. 'What can be done?'

'We go to your police — we get him back.'

Sheridan snorted. 'Constable Nicholls tells me that even the Runners dare not enter parts of St Giles and have no proofs to arrest Battling Poll. She is a clever dam, it would seem, and keeps her own hands clean, running a laundry or some such enterprise, I believe.'

'Then it is we who must do it.'

'*We* must do it?'

'It is our duty, Monsieur Sheridan.'

'My dear Danton, forgive me, but I fear this is a lost cause.'

'I shall say when the cause is lost,' Danton declared fiercely.

Sheridan quaked. Billy had clearly touched some nerve with the Frenchman. Sheridan was reminded that for all his conniving, Danton was also a man of action, and here was a cause, of no great consequence perhaps, but one which he felt he could command.

Sheridan raised his hands in a placatory gesture. 'Of course, if I can assist you, monsieur, in any small —'

'Three days — and you should bring a man with you, a strong man.'

It was an order. Sheridan gulped and was rather relieved when Michael arrived with the claret.

CHAPTER TWENTY-FIVE

That evening at Carlton House the Duc d'Orléans was not of the party but Marceline arrived in due course, escorted to the entertainment by the Chevalier de Saint-Gelais and Sir Roderick. Her entrance caused Sheridan's heart to skip a beat. And he was left quite without any breath at all when, after the customary niceties with the Prince of Wales, he saw that she hurried in his direction. Until, that is, he realised that it was not with a smile that she greeted him but a face of thunder.

Marceline rapped him on the chest with her fan and her brow creased furiously. 'Monsieur Sherrie! You are the most terrible man! And cruel! To break a woman's heart — pah! It means nothing to you!'

She rapped his chest again forcefully and pierced him with glowering violet eyes.

He struggled for a moment to identify the shortfall in his conduct. And then it came to him. Of course, four nights previous he had promised to dance with her in the ballroom at Vauxhall Gardens.

'My apologies, Baronne! My most heartfelt and sincerest apologies. Forgive me! I beg you to take pity — although I am entirely worthless. It is unpardonable that I did not send word to plead your patience and explain that I was called away by events quite beyond my control.'

'I see only that I am of no importance to you whatsoever, monsieur.' Marceline pouted becomingly.

'I should have written to you the following day to excuse my lapse in manners and must blame all such negligence on the most extenuating of circumstances.'

'Which are?' she demanded with a piqued expression.

Sheridan sighed. 'It is a very sad tale. A young friend of mine was shot at Vauxhall. Even now he clings uncertainly to life.'

'That is most tragic.' Marceline pondered a moment. 'A duel?'

'No, not a duel, Marceline, an accident of fate at the hands of a villain.'

'How very dramatic! I do hope the young gentleman shall make a full recovery.' She paused. 'You are forgiven, Sherrie, but must make penance nevertheless.' Marceline bestowed a mischievous smile on him.

'I shall endeavour to make amends.'

Prince George clapped his hands. The party were to be corralled into groups for the playing of charades. Howgill immediately appeared at Marceline's side and proffered his arm. She leaned towards him with a flirtatious smile and accepted.

'Sherry!' the prince called over gaily. 'You are with me.'

His Royal Highness opened the entertainment with a simple pleasantry.

'My First I hope you are;
my Second I see you are;
and my Whole I know you are.'

The prince spread his arms wide to all assembled. The gathering responded in merry chorus:

'Well come, sir!'

Lady Lade nudged Sheridan and asked, 'Tell me, my dear Sherry, are you yet "well come" with our young ingenue?' She nodded imperceptibly towards Madame LeClaire in the opposing group.

'I appear to be in the doghouse, Lady Lade.'

'We are all agreed that is where you belong.' Lady Lade's eyes twinkled with the urge to tittle-tattle. 'But you are not the only one who has failed to gain entry. It seems the lady will flirt and tease but cannot be mounted with any great ease.'

'Laetitia, I would you could, for the honour of all Lades, save your appalling rhymes for our little charades.'

Lady Lade laughed uproariously.

Sir Roderick presented the next riddle.

'My First is company;
my Second shuns company;
my Third collects company;
and my whole amuses company.'

Prince George clicked his fingers. 'Oh, I know this one! I'm sure I do! Sherry, Sherry, you certainly must.'

Sheridan turned to the prince and prompted, 'If the first is company, then it should be as writ, *co.*'

'Egad, I think you are right.'

Lady Lade snorted. 'And who should shun company but a *nun?*'

'Which could never be said of you, my dear,' her husband smirked.

'I should think the third might be a military allusion, sir, and in which case might refer to —' Major Hanger sniffed at the rose in his lapel and then declared — 'a *drum.*'

'And then the whole should be —' the prince waved his hands with exuberant excitement. 'Ah yes!' He pointed triumphantly across the salon to Sir Roderick. 'A co-nun-drum, sir!'

Howgill bowed in acknowledgement.

A *conundrum* Sir Roderick most definitely was, Sheridan mused as he himself stepped forward.

He kept it short and to his mind very sweet.

'My First is a substance that's light,
My Second makes many things tight,
My Whole is the key to delight!'

It was Nathaniel Parker Forth who wheedled out the answer.

'A corkscrew, Mr Sheridan. I should imagine you are rarely without this device.'

'I am rightly skewered, good sir!' Sheridan conceded, rather generously, he thought.

The entertainment continued with much hilarity as the riddles became increasingly risqué. After which the assembly repaired either to the card tables or to some comfortable nook.

'What the deuce are you up to, Sheridan?'

Startled, Sheridan turned to find the equerry at his shoulder with a rather smug look on his face.

'Major?'

'You are all very cloak and dagger. I never thought to ask at Brooks' how you came by those ciphers. Clearly you are embroiled in a deal of espionage.' Hanger's eyes narrowed. 'First, in Brighton, all that business of *perfidy and treachery* and True Sons of Albion — and don't deny you didn't squib that ridiculous note — and now this! Coded messages from some Frenchman, by the looks of it.'

'Frenchman?'

'And should I be concerned who you work for?'

'You need not be concerned, Major.'

Hanger looked quizzical. 'I never took you for a friend of Mr Pitt.'

'Indeed, I am not.'

'So —?' Hanger's look continued to pose the question.

Sheridan shook his head in frustration. 'I do not work for anyone.'

'Do you want the translation or not?'

'You've cracked it then?' Sheridan's eyes brightened.

Hanger took the piece of paper from his pocket and unfolded it. 'It makes very entertaining reading; you can be assured of that.'

Sheridan reached out to take the page from Hanger, but the equerry immediately held it tantalisingly out of his reach.

'I need to know what I involve myself in, Sheridan. You do have some reputation as a schemer, you know.'

Sheridan looked affronted. 'I am besmirched, Hanger. You must know that. My friendship with His Royal Highness has caused jealousy in some quarters. There is no passion so strongly rooted in the human heart as envy. I am more schemed against than scheming, I can assure you.'

Hanger continued to wave the sheet of paper out of reach. 'Nevertheless...'

Sheridan admitted defeat and through gritted teeth indicated for Hanger to follow him, for he had noticed that Sir Roderick eyed them both with interest, though he pretended to listen to Lady Lade. 'Come away then, Major — the walls have ears.'

They slipped through the servants' door into the back corridors.

The Major grinned. 'So what is this all about?'

Sheridan kept his voice close to a whisper. 'Murder.'

Hanger raised an eyebrow. 'How very dramatic.'

Sheridan continued hurriedly. 'A month ago, the remains of a performer were found in the cellars at Drury Lane. It has transpired that the fellow was acting as a spy. For the émigré cause, a Marquis de Penaud-Mortain, we believe. The killer was a fellow performer. We believe the victim may have discovered this man's secret and that was why he was murdered.'

'The secret being —?'

Sheridan hesitated. 'The killer, Jack Champion, is a member of a dangerous and subversive organisation.'

Hanger looked expectant.

Sheridan responded reluctantly. 'The Huguenot Brotherhood.'

'Never heard of them.'

'Nor will you.' Having said so much already, Sheridan decided to continue. 'Not only has this fellow murdered my poor Harlequin, but he has also attacked me and then attempted the assassination of a notable figure. Which attempt sadly resulted in a near fatal injury to a very dear friend of mine. That is my interest, and I merely assist an officer at Bow Street in this matter. Confidentially,' he added, to underline the need for discretion.

'Monsieur Danton?'

Sheridan looked alarmed.

'The notable figure,' Hanger asserted.

'How the devil do you know that?'

The equerry waved the sheet of paper. He grinned and then passed it over to Sheridan with a flourish. '*Voila*!'

Sheridan grabbed the sheet with alacrity. Between the lines of the original, Hanger had pencilled in the interpretation.

'I think I have surpassed myself, Sheridan. It was no easy matter, I'll have you know. But I had the bit between my teeth, as they say, and I was curious.'

Sheridan scanned through, muttering the lines beneath his breath.

The Bros. salute you. How very clever and devious you are! To have disguised the remains of that worthless mercenary as yourself. Did you enjoy your funeral? I have heard that Mrs J. attended and wept most profusely. She has been useful in more ways than one, the silly goose!

Mons. Danton's unexpected arrival is of the greatest interest. Follow him closely. Find what you can of who he meets with. I fear he may prove a traitor.

Renard

Sheridan nodded vigorously throughout. The letter confirmed much of what he and Nicholls already knew. The Harlequin in the cellar was indeed that poor fool, Gaspard Bernon, and Jack Champion had left the Huguenot Cross around his neck deliberately to mislead any that might find the body. Indeed, it seemed Champion very much hoped the body would be discovered when the theatre was demolished.

Champion had then orchestrated his own disappearance. He had provoked Captain Jeffreys deliberately, although he had probably not anticipated such an immediate and violent response. Mrs Jeffreys he had used in other ways too. It must be her connection to the Duc d'Orléans, Sheridan hazarded. And then there was the final part of the note, which suspected that Danton was a traitor.

Danton had been followed, his various meetings and dealings had been noted, and the Brotherhood had then clearly decided that the French Jacobin needed to be eliminated.

But a traitor to what? To whom?

Did Danton have an existing pact with the Brotherhood which he had broken in some way? Or was it simply that they did not trust his intentions or his commitment to the Revolution? More than that, Sheridan speculated. They had expected a shared commitment to end the monarchy and establish a republic in France. Even as the National Assembly in Paris were spending the summer preparing to enshrine a constitutional monarchy, the Brotherhood were plotting with those who would do away with the monarchy altogether. They suspected Danton supported Orléans' bid for the throne and presented a threat, a very real threat to republican ambitions. Danton was a fiery orator and held great sway with the Paris mobs. Sheridan knew his force at first hand. Wasn't he even now being dragooned by Monsieur Danton into some misbegotten mission to 'rescue' that thieving scamp Billy Legge?

Sheridan was pleased to have got to the bottom of the whole business. This was their plan, then. To bring the French Bourbon dynasty to an end and to do all in their power to bring about a republic. The Brotherhood were fanatics. And men like Jack Champion who had been recruited into their number were prepared to do anything to further that cause. Including murder.

'Thank you, Hanger.' Sheridan squeezed the major's shoulder. 'You have been of great service to your country.'

'So, what do you intend to do now?'

What did he intend to do? There was nothing left that he himself could do. His only course of action was to take the information to the magistrate. The letter was proof, if further evidence were needed, that Jack Champion had murdered Gaspard Bernon. Champion would be hunted down. Sir Sampson would pass the decryption to the Home Department. If they had not already decoded the other letters, then they could now do so. Pitt's agents might even be able to identify the members of the Brotherhood and thwart their plans in England. For once, he very much hoped that Mr Pitt would succeed.

CHAPTER TWENTY-SIX

'Perhaps there is somewhere that we could converse, *mon* Sherrie. Somewhere that is, how shall we say, beyond prying eyes.' Marceline whispered close. Sheridan felt her soft breath tickle his ear.

She could intend only one thing, surely. She was a married woman, by no means virginal, although everything about her had a most charming lack of artifice and a simplicity suggestive of purity. Nonetheless, she was a woman of flesh and blood. There was enough of that on display to fire the ardour of any man, and the lady was fully aware of the effect.

The baroness spread out her fan with a flourish. Sheridan used the concealment to lean in and whisper in his turn. Eagerly he hastened to give her the directions to the bedchamber which the prince had designated for his use at Carlton House.

Marceline immediately snapped her fan shut and walked swiftly away from him towards Mrs Armistead and engaged the actress with a beaming smile. Was that assent, or had he just insulted her? Really, she was the most tantalising of women.

How long should he wait? Well, there was no time for hesitation now. He ordered champagne to be sent to his room. As an aside he complained of a little indisposition to one or two people. If Marceline did not arrive, so be it; he would know that he had misjudged her. Sheridan was about to slip away when he was apprehended.

'Do you get anywhere, Sherry?'

He turned to find himself facing His Royal Highness.

'Well, sir?' The prince regarded him with thin lips.

Sheridan found himself lost for a reply. Was Prince George referring to his seduction of Madame LeClaire? Or the other matter?

'You have been tardy, I fear. I do not enjoy suspense, don't you know.'

The anonymous letter. Sheridan felt a momentary relief that he was not to be called out as a rival for Marceline's affections. And then he pinked. For he had been tardy, it was true.

'I work on the matter, sir.'

'Then work a little harder, if you will!'

'One thing occurs…' He lowered his voice. 'The bonds, which you and your royal brother burnt, are you quite sure they were all genuine? No forgeries amongst them?'

The prince blinked. 'How should I recall? York and I were in something of a flap that night, egad.'

Sheridan nodded. 'Understandably, sir.'

'You think there may be one extant?' The prince was aghast.

'The letter suggests the writer is informed.'

His Royal Highness gulped. 'What the devil does he want?'

Sheridan took a breath before ploughing on. 'Sir, I suggest that you limit your dealings with His Serene Highness, as a precaution.'

The prince looked affronted. 'Orléans is my friend.'

Sheridan wavered. How should he remind the Prince of Wales that friends could not always be trusted? He stood firm.

'Very well. But you must not disappoint me in this matter, Sheridan.'

The prince waved across to Sir John Lade and Sheridan knew himself dismissed. He stood for a moment in contemplation; his eyes followed the heir to the throne as he crossed the salon. Sheridan had let the business of the anonymous letter slip from his mind; affairs of murder had rather stolen his attention from his promise to His Royal Highness. He must make amends. There, hovering at the prince's shoulder, was Nathaniel Parker Forth drawn like a bee to the pollen, or a fly to — well, yes, the stinking dunghill of His Royal Highness' debts. Parker Forth seemed to be everywhere and ubiquitous in everyone's business; he must keep a closer eye on him. But not tonight. That affair could safely wait until the morrow. Sheridan allowed himself a sly smile; tonight, a more urgent affair needed consummation.

It being summer, there was no fire in the grate to lend an appealing warm glow to the bedchamber. Sheridan drew the heavy damask curtains on the starry night sky and set about lighting candles and positioning them so as to create a pleasing chiaroscuro. The room must not be so dark as to appear sinister, but not too well lit as to curtail seduction. He stood back to admire the results. Long years of theatrical production had honed his skills in the construction of atmosphere. He loosened his necktie. His heart was racing in anticipation. Would she come? Pray let her come. His mind was given all to lust.

A light rap at the door answered that prayer.

Sheridan flew across the room and then composed himself. He should not appear unseemly in his eagerness, but neither should he keep the lady waiting conspicuously at his door. He grasped the knob and opened it smoothly.

A footman bowed and presented a tray laden with champagne and glasses.

Sheridan forced a smile. 'Thank you, Simpson.' He opened the door wider and pointed to an occasional table. 'That table over there will do.'

'Can I be of any other service, sir?'

'No, that will be all, Simpson.'

Was the young man smirking as he left the room?

With a sigh, Sheridan went over to the bed and idly smoothed down the cover. He was sorely tempted to open the champagne immediately.

A lighter rap then came. But he had scarcely turned to the sound when Marceline flew into the bedchamber with a titter of delight. She raced across the Persian rug, flung her arms about his neck and kissed him full on the lips.

This was beyond anything which Sheridan could have scripted. He had imagined such a scene when his senses were aroused but had not thought it plausible. Not at the very first stage of seduction. As he had been busy placing the candles about the chamber, he had taken the time to revise and rehearse various sweet nothings and flatterings which had garnered pleasing results in the past. But here was Marceline already in his arms, and all call for polite preamble seemed unnecessary. She really was the most thrilling young woman. He clasped her about the waist and was about to throw her onto the bed and get to the lovemaking straight away when Marceline pulled away from him with a laugh.

She wagged a finger and tutted. 'I see that you are as impatient as I am, my darling Sherrie, but is it not most gloriously delicious to wait?' She clapped her hands. 'And you have champagne!'

Such a tease, he thought with a shake of the head as he crossed the room to close the door which she had left ajar in her haste. He slipped the lock. But she was right; the pleasure was doubled by anticipation, for had she not already acknowledged her conquest? Let him savour that certainty.

Sheridan strode over to the small table and uncorked the champagne.

'I raise a toast to beauty, celestial and fair —'

Marceline clinked his glass. 'And I to genius never dimmed, though on another stage that light must shine!'

They drank and filled the glasses again. Marceline moved about, admiring the paintings on the wall, part of the Prince of Wales' celebrated collection. Sheridan's eyes followed her greedily.

'But, Sherrie, tell me you will write again. The world longs for another great play.' She pouted. 'I long for it. One that you will dedicate to me, perhaps?' she added with a twinkle.

He bowed. 'You cannot doubt that dedication, my dear Marceline. If I should be moved to pen another offering for the stage, it shall be all your inspiration.'

'I should very much like to be your muse.'

Marceline had placed herself with an unerring intuition at that spot in the room where the candlelight most exquisitely enhanced her countenance.

Sheridan stood entranced. In that moment Marceline appeared to him a Greek statue brought alive. Aphrodite. Diana. Galatea flashed into his mind. She was perfection. On the stage at Drury Lane, she would be a sensation.

With an elegant gesture Marceline undid a clip at her shoulder and her dress slithered to the floor, leaving her in a thin, gossamer sliver of undergarment, which concealed very little. Sheridan's heart thudded. She really was the most ravishing creature he had ever laid eyes upon.

'I have dreamt of this moment, Sherrie,' she crooned. 'I envisage myself as Lydia and you are my Jack Absolute!'

Sheridan shrugged off his tailcoat and could have wished it were not quite so fashionably tight-fitted. He then fumbled for the buttons of his waistcoat. Marceline's eyes held his as she glided towards him across the Persian rug. He was frantically divesting himself of the brocaded garment when she reached out and, with elegant gestures, slipped the waistcoat from his shoulders. She laid it reverently over the back of a chair. Next, she loosened his cravat, a smile twitching at the corner of her lips. Sheridan allowed his fancy full rein. He was a Turkish sultan and she was his odalisque, a perfect vision of beauty from the hareem. It was one of his most frequently recurring inventions, one that he had played out with any number of the Covent Garden roses. But it was a long time since Sheridan had felt so utterly aroused.

Marceline stood back from him and struck a charming theatrical pose, raising a hand to her brow.

'*I ne'er could any lustre see*
in eyes that would not look on me.'

She was quoting his own lines to him! And Sheridan could not pretend to be anything other than flattered. How he wished that he had not consumed quite so much claret earlier.

'*I ne'er saw nectar on a lip*
but where my own did hope to sip.'

She began to advance towards him and pressed herself up to his heaving chest.

'Marceline...' he gasped.

With that, she pushed him forcefully back onto the bed.

Sheridan groaned. With a light tinkle of laughter, Marceline climbed on top of him and yanked his shirt loose. She ran her hands underneath the fabric, kneading at his chest. Panting, he gripped her shoulders and swung her round onto the bed, then reached for the buttons of his breeches. He could contain himself no longer. He must have her.

'*Assez!*' a voice hissed. Then louder and more insistent. '*Assez!*'

Startled, Sheridan looked up to find a small, thin figure standing in shadow at the end of the bed. In the flickering candlelit chamber, Sheridan made out the chiselled features of the Chevalier de Saint-Gelais.

Where on earth had he come from? How long had he been there?

The chevalier tapped the floor with his elegant cane, twisted the silver top and with a flourish withdrew a long, thin rapier. The dangerous tip arced with a flash of menace.

For a delirious moment Sheridan was reminded of Tom's playful notion of a blade-tipped umbrella.

'*Violeur!*'

Sheridan shook his head vehemently. '*Non, non*, monsieur!'

He found the point of the rapier whipping around to hover a mere fraction from his open throat.

Sheridan raised his hands and then shuffled himself awkwardly back up onto his haunches. The rapier followed his movements, dangerously close to pricking his skin.

'Chevalier, this is most uncalled for, I assure you.'

The chevalier continued to regard him with steely eyes. The young French noble flicked the rapier to indicate that Sheridan should remove himself entirely from the bed. Clumsily he obeyed, his hands spread in a placatory gesture.

'Please, monsieur, you misunderstand.'

The chevalier rounded the bed and delicately pressed the tip of the rapier into Sheridan's chest. To his horror, a small bead of blood stained his shirt. He gasped and took a step back. My

God! Did the young lunatic mean to run him through? Sheridan felt a shiver of fear course through his body.

'You may name your weapon, Monsieur Sheridan,' the chevalier intoned slowly and deliberately.

Sheridan looked desperately towards Marceline. She was rolling about upon the bed. In a paroxysm of shame? No, devil take it — she was laughing! Her hand was balled tight to her mouth to suppress the sound. 'Madame? Marceline?' he cried.

'Your weapon, monsieur?' the chevalier spat.

Marceline sat up and stifled her mirth. 'Oh, Pierre — Pierre, desist at once! Do you not see how you terrorise our dear Monsieur Sheridan?'

Marceline slid off the bed and sauntered across the chamber. Placing her hand over that of the chevalier, she pressed down and forced the tip of the rapier to the floor, allowing her to slip into the space between the two men.

'You are very naughty, Pierre.' Marceline mocked rebuke with a wagging finger. Then she turned to Sheridan with a bright smile. 'You must forgive my cousin, Sherrie. The chevalier has so long desired to fight a duel that he looks for any meagre excuse. He pretends to be jealous of my honour. Do you not, Pierre?' Marceline flicked her head back towards De Saint-Gelais.

The chevalier grunted and looked peevishly sour.

Marceline laughed and reached back; she stroked the young man's face tenderly. 'Oh, *mon petite frère*. In truth, Pierre detests my husband.' The baroness turned her winsome smile again to Sheridan. 'As do I.'

'Madame, it is one of the hazards of marriage.' Sheridan attempted a light tone but found that he was still quaking.

'You must put your silly toy away, Pierre. You make Mr Sheridan nervous, though I don't know why.' She placed a finger on Sheridan's chest and gently circled the bloody stain. 'Since he is quite notorious for his duels.'

'Oh, I wouldn't say that,' Sheridan said modestly — besides which, the chevalier had yet to withdraw.

De Saint-Gelais continued to shoot daggers at him. This was no game. For all that Marceline attempted to make a comedy of the encounter, Sheridan had no doubt whatsoever that the chevalier was a very dangerous young man and he should never like to be left alone with him.

'Would you really fight for my honour, Sherrie?' Marceline's face was alive with mischief.

'I would … I would be most honoured…' Sheridan stammered.

'Of course. You are heroic.' She smiled at her cousin. 'And you also, *mon frère*. Now, all this talk of honour and duels, it is so boring.' Marceline sighed with exasperation. 'I am perfectly capable of looking after myself, Pierre, as you know very well. Enough, now go!'

The chevalier pursed his lips then obediently went to retrieve his cane and re-sheathed the rapier with a dramatic flourish. He marched to the doorway, hovered at the threshold, raised his chin and glowered at Sheridan with menace. 'Monsieur, do not give me cause to challenge you again, if you value your life.' With a sharp bow the young nobleman departed.

'What a pity,' Marceline said with a sigh. 'My dear cousin — he is of a very jealous temperament. I fear he has quite spoilt our fun.' She gazed with a deep yearning into Sheridan's eyes until he felt his heart catch again.

'Marceline…' He made a move towards her.

With an artless gesture she slipped out of reach and stepped into her chemise to be dressed again in moments. She ran her hands through her short-cropped curls. '*Et voila!*'

His spirits plummeted. 'Another time, perhaps?'

Marceline smiled sweetly. '*Au revoir, mon* Sherrie.'

In a whirl of flowing gown, she was gone before Sheridan had found the wit to respond. The door slammed shut.

Sheridan reached for the bottle of champagne, raised it to his lips, and glugged down the remainder of the contents.

CHAPTER TWENTY-SEVEN

A sliver of light stole around the edge of the curtains. Sheridan rubbed the sleep from his eyes. He turned and sighed. He felt the hunger of a lovesick fool. To have been so close, on this very bed... Surely that could not be the end of the affair? For all his threats the chevalier was a mere braggadocio, wasn't he? And Marceline? Marceline was a woman, Sheridan realised, who would have whatever she desired. She would ensure that there would be other opportunities to satisfy their mutual lust. Sheridan allowed himself to savour the taste of a conquest which was merely suffering a delay in its consummation. But he must not lie abed for too long. There were matters to which he must attend. He should go immediately to Bow Street.

Simpson arrived with hot water and assisted him with his toilette and dress. The manservant had collected the waistcoat and other items of clothing from the previous evening, including the shirt with the pinprick hole and the bloody circle.

'Ah yes, bit of a scratch... Can it be mended?'

As only a servant could, Simpson raised a discreet eyebrow. 'As you wish, sir.'

'The waistcoat —'

Simpson handed over the brocaded garment and Sheridan searched the pockets. The encoded letter. Where had he put it?

'Simpson, do you have a note there? In the tailcoat?'

The manservant turned out the various pockets and shook his head.

In the tumbling of the night the folded piece of paper must have dislodged. Sheridan knelt to check under the bed. Nothing but a pair of old slippers.

'You have lost something, sir? Dropped it in the corridor, perhaps? Shall I make enquiry?'

Sheridan frowned and shook his head. It could not be. The letter had been snug. And then it came to him. The Chevalier de Saint-Gelais. The chevalier had witnessed the encounter with Major Hanger. Hanger waving the letter out of reach, for all the world to see. The hurried tête-à-tête with Hanger behind the servants' door. De Saint-Gelais had deduced that the note was one retrieved from the garret in Spitalfields. Because … because the chevalier knew Jack Champion. They had rendezvoused in Brighton. More, it must be that De Saint-Gelais was also a member of the Huguenot Brotherhood. The chevalier suspected that the note had been deciphered, but he needed to be sure. So, he had entered Sheridan's bedchamber to retrieve it. That had been his purpose all along.

Whatever plans had been spelt out in those messages might all be abandoned or altered as a consequence. Whatever opportunity there had been to ensnare the Brotherhood was now lost. Sheridan felt himself deflate. Nevertheless, he must hasten to Bow Street and seek out a meeting with Sir Sampson Wright. He could at least share the system to decode the messages and summarise the contents of the letter he had read the night before, for that had confirmed, beyond all doubt, that Jack Champion had indeed murdered Gaspard Bernon.

'This note, sir?' Simpson stood in the doorway and held up a sheet of paper.

Sheridan snatched at it. The coded message. 'Where was it, Simpson?'

'Under the door, sir.'

'Right, right…' He had dropped it after all. He blew out his cheeks; he really must rein in his imagination. He was beginning to see subterfuge at every corner.

On his way to the magistrates' court, Sheridan stopped briefly at Grosvenor Street to pick up the second, shorter note. Then as the carriage rattled through Covent Garden, he applied Hanger's decryption. The messages were in English, that much was a relief, Sheridan's French being so inadequate. Three letters of the alphabet forward and then the words backward. Simple enough when you knew the key.

LW WVXP HE HQRG QL E.
GUDQHU

He raced through the alphabet, jotted down the corresponding letters and transcribed in reverse.

It must be done in B
Renard

What must be done? A meeting? An assassination? And where was B? A place, Sheridan supposed. But that could be a house or a part of London or somewhere else entirely. And Renard? The name itself was an obvious alias. The French word for *fox*. But this was not any old fox. This was surely the wily character known from medieval tales. Hero or villain? Renard could be either, depending on the story or one's point of view. This was the man behind the Huguenot Brotherhood, and he was just such a slippery character.

Sheridan's thoughts flew back to the chevalier. Could the leader be De Saint-Gelais himself? There could be no doubt of the man's physical bravery. Sheridan recalled the moment the young noble had placed the apple on his head and faced Marceline's arrow with complete confidence. But *Renard* was not known for bravery so much as guile, and how much of that did the young man possess?

Thoughts of Monsieur Fox inevitably brought Sheridan's own parliamentary leader to mind. Beyond a hurried enquiry as to whether there was any further news of young Timothy Legge, there had been no opportunity to have a quiet word with Charles at the soiree. Fox had avoided Sheridan's company. He had shared nothing of his conversation with Danton. Though the evening had been interrupted somewhat dramatically, Fox and Danton had nevertheless conversed for a good twenty minutes or more. They must surely have gone beyond pleasantries. Sheridan felt a little aggrieved that Charles had not drawn him into his confidence.

The carriage drew to a halt outside the Bow Street Magistrates' Court. A sudden torrential downpour caught Sheridan unprepared and he could have wished for the umbrella that Mrs Tucker advised should always be carried in readiness for just such a deluge. Most people were scurrying for shelter, whilst the remainder seemed willing to accept that they must be drenched quite through. Sheridan made a dash for the entrance, his light summer shoes splashing through the fast-forming puddles.

It was astounding how a distance of a mere twelve feet in such rain could leave a man feeling like a bedraggled mongrel. Standing in the lobby, Sheridan attempted to restore his dignity as best he could. He approached the desk and asked the clerk if he might have an audience with Sir Sampson Wright.

'The magistrate is in session at present, sir.'

Sheridan thought for a moment and then responded. 'I shall wait. Can you send a note that Mr Sheridan wishes to speak on a matter of some importance? Meanwhile, I shall observe the proceedings.'

Sheridan passed through to the back of the court and edged in amongst the spectators. A young girl stood in the dock, perhaps fifteen or sixteen. She was small, dressed in plain but clean attire, and fair and pleasant enough in appearance, save for a bruise forming on her right cheek. She was pleading against a shopkeeper who had charged her with lifting half a dozen linen handkerchiefs. A crime for which she was likely to be transported if found guilty.

'T'weren't me, honest, sir!'

'But you were found with the handkerchiefs in your possession, were you not?'

'Yes, sir, but —'

Sir Sampson looked about the court. 'Where is the constable that apprehended the girl?'

Constable Nicholls stepped forward. 'Constable Nicholls, Your Honour.'

'Ah, Nicholls, you're a sound fellow. Give me an account, if you will.'

Nicholls placed himself in front of the magistrate. 'I was patrolling in the area and was alerted to a hue and cry for a thief. I arrived at Maiden Lane to see a young man, the shop assistant, grab hold of this young woman —' he nodded across to the girl in the dock — 'Dorcas Roberts, as I later discovered. There was a bit of a tussle. The lad was perhaps a little overzealous on his master's behalf.'

'What do you mean, precisely?'

'That he struck the young lady a heavy blow. I hastened to intervene. The accusation of theft was made, and I requested Miss Roberts to turn out her pockets. The young lady obliged and almost immediately produced the said handkerchiefs.'

'I see. So, she was caught red-handed?'

'So it appeared, sir, though she protested her innocence.'

'Go on, Constable.'

'I brought her to the shop and the handkerchiefs were identified as belonging to the shopkeeper, Mr Wattling. He insisted on an immediate arrest and so Miss Roberts is here before you, sir.'

Sir Sampson turned to Dorcas. 'And yet you claim to be innocent, Miss Roberts?'

The girl nodded. 'There was another customer in the shop at the same time as myself, sir. Then there was a cry of theft and she pushed by me, sir. And that is when she placed the handkerchiefs on my person and hurried herself away. When the assistant ran out from the shop, he headed towards me in a fury. I was frightened, sir, that is why I made to escape — and I knew how it should look.'

Sheridan found himself quite moved by the girl's tale. He imagined the horror. To be accused of a crime of which one was innocent but with so much evidence stacked against one must be a very nightmare.

Sir Sampson turned to the shopkeeper. 'Mr Wattling, come forward, sir.'

Mr Wattling, a very dapper little man, stepped out.

'Is it true there was another lady in your shop?'

'Yes, sir, but she was of a very well dressed, respectable type.'

'Do you imply that Miss Roberts is not respectable?'

Mr Wattling smiled nervously in response.

'Is there any that can speak to the character of this girl, Dorcas Roberts?' Sir Sampson asked.

A man pushed in from the entrance to the courtroom, a little out of breath.

'Yes, sir, if you please. I have just heard my niece has been taken and I have come to Bow Street with all haste.'

'You are?'

The man bowed and removed his tricorn hat. 'Ezekiel Brough, Your Honour. Dorcas, here, is my niece. Me and the wife took her in when she was orphaned. She is honest and hardworking. A seamstress — that is why she looks in the shops, sir. She may not afford the wares, but she can see what is the latest style and stitch.'

Sir Sampson nodded thoughtfully and then addressed the courtroom. 'I am minded that Mr Wattling's handkerchiefs have been retrieved; therefore, he suffers no loss of property. It is my judgement, since the actual act of theft itself was not witnessed, that Dorcas Roberts be deemed to have given a true account. The case is dismissed and you are free to go, Miss Roberts.'

The girl's face lit up. 'Why, thank you, Your Honour, thank you!'

Sheridan felt a well of gladness at the outcome.

Mr Wattling shook his head with displeasure.

Sir Sampson turned to the shopkeeper. 'Mr Wattling I fine three shillings in the matter of the assault by his assistant on the young lady's person. Said amount to be rendered to Miss Roberts in compensation.'

Sir Sampson Wright rose and exited the courtroom, leaving a general hubbub in his wake.

Sheridan grinned. The law was not always an ass, he thought.

Dorcas ran to her uncle with an expression of relief. They turned to depart and Sheridan caught sight of Ezekiel Brough's face for the first time. To his astonishment, he recognised the man as the jarvey who had delivered Billy and himself to Grosvenor Street. The man clasped the girl by the wrist and pushed his way out of the crowded court.

Sheridan frowned. This was the man whom Monsieur Danton had been convinced was the villain behind Billy's sudden departure. His whole theory of Billy's innocence rested on that argument. Sheridan should have to inform Danton that he was mistaken. Mr Brough was a respectable driver who had kindly taken in an orphaned niece; he was not some criminal overlord.

With this thought circulating through his mind, Sheridan went in search of Sir Sampson. As he crossed the lobby, he found himself passing close behind Ezekiel Brough and overheard his vicious snarl as the jarvey yanked the girl close. 'Don't you get nabbed like that again, yer poxy baggage, or yer will be out on the streets! Wait'll Poll hears 'bout it!'

Sheridan's mouth dropped open. Poll — the man could only mean Battling Poll! The girl was no honest seamstress at all but one of Poll's legion of snafflers. And the jarvey — why, the jarvey was a loathsome rogue. And Monsieur Danton may be correct after all.

It was in this state of stupefaction that Constable Nicholls found him.

'Mr Sheridan, sir? Is there something ill?'

'There is something very ill, Nicholls.'

Sheridan proceeded to relate to the Runner what he had overheard. 'That girl is no innocent; it is all a sham.'

Nicholls nodded. 'A common trick, sir. Two of the villains will enter a shop separately. One distracts the shopkeeper and assistant whilst the other pilfers. They will leave one after the other and turn in different directions. If the one with the stolen property is caught, they will play all innocent and blame the other customer. Just as you have witnessed.'

'But if you know this, then…?' Sheridan looked confused.

'We do, sir, but in this instance the property is returned and the poor girl is likely to be but a pawn — and then Sir

Sampson cannot abide that a young woman be struck in so violent a manner. Hence his judgement.'

Sheridan nodded slowly. 'There is sense in it. No one would wish to see the poor girl transported to Botany Bay.'

Nicholls was at that moment nudged off balance in the crowded lobby.

'Oh, I do beg pardon, Officer.'

The constable steadied himself and they turned to find a broad-shouldered man of similar height presenting an apologetic face.

'Mr Drewe,' Nicholls almost spat through thin lips.

The man smiled, but this pleasantry did not reach his eyes as he extended a finger and delicately flicked imaginary dust from the constable's jacket. 'You always was a very smart fellow, Mr Nicholls — neat and tidy, is that not right? And are you clever too?' Mr Drewe nodded and then pouted. 'Clever enough to keep out of my way? We wouldn't want any accidents, would we?'

Nicholls remained tight-lipped.

Drewe patted Nicholls' chest. 'Good day to you, gentlemen.'

When he was gone, Sheridan exhaled. 'Who was that deuced impertinent rogue?'

'Zachary Drewe, the very devil, sir, spawned in St Giles.'

'I wonder that so many of these fellows walk abroad.'

'We do what we can, sir. The law is oftentimes a blunt instrument.'

'Sadly so. And that brings me to the matter of Billy. That shop thief Dorcas' uncle — which I doubt he is — Ezekiel Brough, may be the man that caused Billy to steal from my household,' Sheridan confided.

Nicholls inclined his head with interest. 'That might be no surprise, sir. And on that matter, I do have some good news to convey.'

'Billy is found?' Sheridan's eyes lit up.

'No, not that, sir. But we have this morning retrieved some of your stolen property. Your pocket watch and, from your description, the brooch that belongs to Mrs Sheridan. My informant, who sometimes comes by goods of questionable origin, has been very useful, and it seems more than likely that these items passed through the hands of Battling Poll.'

Sheridan hesitated over whether or not to confide in the constable something of Monsieur Danton's intended mission to rescue Billy Legge from the wicked dam. Not least to confide his own nervous misgivings about the whole enterprise.

'We owe you a debt of gratitude, Mr Sheridan. You have been of great service.' Sir Sampson nodded as he read the notes which Sheridan had handed over, together with the key to decryption.

'It was Major Hanger, in truth, who cracked the business,' Sheridan admitted modestly.

'This information shall be passed on to Henry Dundas and Mr Pitt at once. A description of this Jack Champion will be posted. The reward you offer may tempt some barker to betray the man.'

'I sincerely hope so.'

'Nicholls mentioned your concerns regarding the Chevalier de Saint-Gelais. I have made enquiry. There does not appear to be any Huguenot ancestry.'

'I see. Well, he may have no direct involvement with this group. I should be glad to be mistaken.'

Sheridan shook his head. He had done all that he could in the matter. There was only one sad duty remaining to him. He must call on Margaret Bedwell and her fatherless babe to tell her that it was Gaspard Bernon who was the dead Harlequin after all. He very much hoped that little Antoine would continue to thrive, and he would do his utmost to see to it.

CHAPTER TWENTY-EIGHT

A piece of loose daub skimmed off Sheridan's battered old tricorn and skittered to the ground. He looked up at the rooftops of the decaying tenements in time to see a young boy rein in his neck and disappear from view. The streets and houses were still shrouded in gloom, the sun not yet risen. A waning moon lent an eerie half-light as it peered through the scattering clouds.

'That'll be a lookout,' Jedidiah grunted. 'They jump about them rooftops like little goats. Only it's no play.'

There were no streetlamps in this part of the city. St Giles was a dark world within itself, removed from all vestiges of true civilisation and rarely entered by outsiders unless they had pressing business. A man should need a guide through the maze of narrow alleys and passageways that had originally given access to the stables and courtyards of the old medieval dwellings. Those buildings which had been thrown up since the Great Fire had been swiftly packed to the gunnels by unscrupulous landlords answering the demands of a rising population. All was crumbling squalor. A hundred tenants or more might be dependent on a shared standing pipe or pump at a well, sharing likewise one or two sheds that housed the 'necessary accommodations' which drained into an open sewer. Men pissed in the street and none collected the waste that mounded into dunghills. The street-borne filth oozed and dripped through the grates of those unfortunates who lived, and died, in cellar dwellings. These streets were a wilderness where the most savage beasts of all were hunger and disease.

London was ripe with a rich variety of smells, but the worst parts of St Giles smelt like death, to Sheridan's mind. He imagined an open graveyard, putrid with the stench of decay and the reek of noxious gases. Yet daily it seemed the numbers swelled as the city took in the desperate and the destitute from all parts — many of his fellow Irish countrymen amongst them. They might be poor but honest on arrival, but that would not long survive the ravages of want, nor the temptation to forget all woes in a jug of cheap gin. This was a place where no one asked questions so long as the rent might be paid, and none would judge. It was a safe harbour for thieves and villains of every kind and those most unfortunate of women who had no way to survive but by selling their own bodies.

Sheridan would not choose to enter this dismal place. Neither would he choose to think on it, except fleetingly, for what could be done? In truth he viewed the rookeries as a problem too overwhelming to countenance. If a man were to allow himself to think on the misery for too long, he should sink into a pit of despair. Sheridan steeled himself and wondered for the umpteenth time why he had been cajoled into this venture. But such was Monsieur Danton's persuasive power.

'We must keep a cutty-eye from here on in, sirs,' said Jedidiah. 'Our presence is probably already noted.'

Although Sheridan had dressed in the plainest fashion with borrowed clothes, he felt the party stood out immediately by virtue of being well scrubbed. He was glad to have the burly labourer by his side. Jedidiah had grown up near to these streets and was familiar with many of the routes through the warren of St Giles. The man had been offered a handsome bonus to accompany them. Releasing Jedidiah from his other duties, good Mr Knatchbull had shaken his head in astonishment at their objective.

'You risk a den of thieves and villains for the sake of that little chit?'

Sheridan nodded. 'I have come round to the view that the boy may be turned away from the life of crime that would await him otherwise. But in truth, Mr Knatchbull, it is not for his sake; in larger part it is for my young friend, Mr Legge, who is entirely certain that Billy can be saved.'

'Ah yes, sir, I was sorry to hear about that misadventure. There's some desperate rogues roaming the city.'

Sheridan risked a glance to either side of the narrow street. A barefoot man was slumped against a wall and might be thought dead but for the dribble from his mouth and the snore which followed. A thin waif with thick, matted hair slunk along the side of the decrepit buildings, clutching a bag to her. She pressed herself into invisibility. Two well-built young men emerged from an alley with brisk purpose. Their impenetrable dialect marked them out as recent arrivals from Ireland. Labourers off to work, Sheridan supposed. Less reassuring was the sly-looking cove on the corner, sucking on a clay pipe and peering at them from beneath hooded eyelids. At his side a scrawny dog bridled, snarling and baring his teeth.

Sheridan had spent some of the previous day in Soho with Monsieur Danton. The Frenchman had not been idle. Sheridan had to admit that he was impressed by the range and scope of Danton's network of information, given that this was London and not Paris. The general opinion had been that Mistress Polly Dearlove was nigh on untouchable. She was the 'mother' of a veritable army of villains, many of whom had been educated in her nursery. Monsieur Danton, however, was blithely convinced that he could persuade her to give up Billy

Legge. He assured Sheridan that he had secured an informant who would lead them to the very lair in which the dam might be found.

'*Bonjour*, gentlemen.'

A tall man stepped out of a narrow passage under the sign of a pawnbroker. He was darkly handsome, with a rakish tilt to his hat.

Danton bestowed a beaming smile in return. 'Monsieur Sylvain!' He clasped the broad-shouldered man in an affectionate embrace, kissing both his cheeks.

'Come, my friends!' the man said with a heavy French accent.

Sylvain set off at a brisk pace. As they followed, Danton spoke in an aside to Sheridan to explain that Sylvain was himself a former pugilist and would act as interpreter should Danton's vocabulary fall short of what he desired to communicate. Sylvain, it appeared, had Poll Dearlove's ear — and more besides, Danton intimated with a saucy wink.

The group followed in Sylvain's quick footsteps as he led them back down the dark passageway and then through a maze of narrow streets. Sheridan's heart raced, fearful that at any moment they might be ambushed and attacked. They traversed a moonlit yard where a drunken couple were swearing and shouting at each other. In the far corner a hog was penned, grunting and snuffling through the filth. A young lad was perched on the rickety gate, no doubt set to guard over this most prized possession. He cast a wary eye at their approach. Sylvain made a feint towards him and laughed as the boy lost his balance and tipped to the mucky ground.

Then they were diving into an opening, along a corridor and out into a smaller courtyard, on to which no windows gazed, for all were boarded up. Sylvain approached a door and rapped loudly. After some moments a hatch was raised and suspicious eyes peered out.

'Wha's yer business?' an old man croaked.

'I come to speak with Madame Dearlove,' Monsieur Danton intoned deeply and with a purpose that would not be denied.

'Who wants to see 'er?'

'If you will please tell your mistress it is I, the Frenchman.'

The doorkeeper muttered, 'Wait 'ere.' Then snapped the hatch shut.

Wait they did. Ten long minutes passed and the door remained shut. Sheridan twitched his head about nervously at the slightest sound. The four high brick walls of the courtyard loomed darkly above and seemed to press in on them. There were eyes upon them, watching their every movement from spyholes, he felt sure. Jedidiah shuffled beside him and drew out a pipe, which he readied. How could the man remain so calm? They were caged. There would be no easy escape from this place. It was little wonder, he thought, that the Runners would not venture so deep into the rookery.

Another five minutes. What the devil was going on? Sheridan cursed Billy Legge under his breath. He cursed Monsieur Danton, who was laughing and conversing in French with Sylvain. From what he could follow, Sheridan deduced that Sylvain had been a former client in Paris and considered himself still indebted to the lawyer. The man was a rogue. That was certain. Nonetheless, Danton appeared to place his trust in him. That must be some reassurance, Sheridan supposed.

Then all too quickly the door was flung open and a gap-toothed young thug grinned at them, his hands on his hips. Two others behind him looked stony-faced.

'Mistress Poll sends her apologies for keeping you waiting, gentlemen.' His grin widened. 'Now, if you will kindly divest yourselves of any, how shall we say, weaponry? Not in ladies' company, you understand.'

Danton nodded slowly and withdrew the pistol from his pocket.

'A fine piece, sir.'

'I am become very attached.'

'Not to worry, sir, you'll have it back when you leave.'

Sylvain surrendered a knife and Jedidiah likewise, if more reluctantly. The young thug looked then to Sheridan, who shook his head hurriedly.

'The sharpest thing I have about me is my wits, and I fear they are sorely blunted today.'

'This way then, gentlemen.'

With the two lackeys bringing up the rear, they were led up through the old tenement and then to Sheridan's surprise conducted through a mean dwelling, where in the gloom he could just make out a ragged woman sitting by a man on a pallet. The unfortunate soul's hacking cough suggested he was long past the point of recovery. At last they came out onto a narrow wooden bridge that linked into yet another building. Sheridan looked down three storeys into a fetid alley.

As they began to descend the stairs, Sheridan glanced through a half-open door. It was a dormitory of some kind, a long row of cots packed close. The young girls within were stirring and at the end of the nearest bed Sheridan caught sight of Dorcas Roberts dressing a child of some four or five years. The little one was tearful and sniffling as Dorcas tried to comfort her with soothing words.

So here it was. The school for pickpockets and who knew what other villainy. Sheridan halted, transfixed, but was soon shoved along from behind.

'Move along there, gents.'

By further circuitous routes the party eventually arrived at a solid double door. The young thug gave a jaunty rap and grinned at his charges.

Sheridan heard a key in the lock and the door was then opened with a dramatic flourish by two boys done up in red livery, as though they were regular young flunkeys. The group entered a dim, candle-lit vestibule. This was no pokey little hole but looked to be decorated in high fashion. A rather fine bust stood on a pedestal to his left, and he noticed then its equal on the opposite side. The door to the reception room stood open and, on the threshold, there stood an older man in a powdered wig and the same red livery, but more ornately trimmed as might befit a butler.

'How do, James?' The thug saluted. 'Gentlemen here to see Mistress Poll, if you please.'

The older man bowed neatly and addressed himself to Danton. 'Monsieur Danton, if you will come this way.' He swept a hand behind to indicate that they should enter.

As Sheridan passed, the butler regarded him with his one eye, the other hidden behind a black patch, an old wound no doubt, as indicated by the livid scar which ran down one side of his face. 'And Mr Sheridan, I believe.'

Sheridan nodded curtly. If the experience thus far had been calculated to disconcert him, then on entering the salon, he felt that effect had been arrived at beyond all expectation. They had been catapulted from the meanest poverty of St Giles to a room which might fittingly grace a palace. The reception room was an Aladdin's cave, all aglitter. The mirrors alone might rival the fabled Versailles. As he took in the artless jumble of *objet d'art* and fine paintings, he fancied that he recognised one or two. This was, he realised, Battling Poll's treasure trove of stolen goods all on display, here in the heart of the rookeries.

Whilst those beyond her doors lived in stench and starvation, within was beauty, of a sort.

By the nonchalance of his demeanour, Sylvain had clearly gained entrance to this inner sanctum on previous occasions, but Danton and Jedidiah seemed as stupefied as Sheridan himself by this display of opulence and wealth. First came wonder and second a fierce stab of indignation. Only moments before, they had passed through streets of filth and degradation. They had intruded on a man dying in gloom and despair, glimpsed a crowded and fetid dormitory of wretched waifs. What a monstrous dam was this who could revel in such riches and ignore the misery on her very doorstep! Foster it, even, for her own wicked ends!

Jedidiah grunted, as if in unspoken agreement.

'Gentlemen.'

They turned as one to see Mistress Poll Dearlove standing on the threshold behind them. She was a large-boned but surprisingly handsome woman of fifty years or thereabouts. Her nose must have been broken in some past conflict then reset to give an almost Roman profile. Sheridan didn't know what he had been expecting, but certainly not a statuesque and haughty dam decked out in lavender silk.

A bejewelled hand lay on the shoulder of young Billy Legge, who was clutched at her side.

Sheridan caught the expression of surprise and sudden hope which the sight of Danton aroused in Billy's urchin features. *Mi'ssur*, he mouthed.

'It seems you are become an item of value, my lad.' Poll chucked the boy under his chin. She looked then from Monsieur Danton to Sheridan. 'Tell me, what is he worth, gentlemen?'

CHAPTER TWENTY-NINE

It was on that morning that Sheridan learnt Monsieur Danton would be perfectly prepared to do a deal with the devil, if it so suited him.

Danton rubbed his hands and beamed at Mistress Poll. 'A woman of business, Madame — I am in admiration.' He looked about the palatial room with an appreciative eye. 'Such splendour, such a display of wonders as I have never seen, and in France, as you know, we have an eye for beauty. Truly it is magnificent!'

He swung about the salon, his huge bear-like presence somehow dominating the room as he swooped to admire an object here, a vase there, a painting by Reynolds. Sheridan was reminded of the proverbial bull in a china shop and wondered what Poll's reaction would be should anything be broken. He need not have worried. Danton was surprisingly dainty for so large a man. But what on earth was he up to? Did he think he might persuade Battling Poll to hand Billy over simply by flattering her good taste? Which, as far as Sheridan could see, had no particular rhyme or reason. There was no schematic design to the interior; it was simply a jumble of wares. Ill-gotten ones at that; Sheridan was sure he had seen the Reynolds before, hanging on the wall of some earl or other — Lord Derby, perhaps.

He stole a glance in Poll's direction. She was eyeing the Frenchman with something like indulgence. Could he actually have charmed her with his ridiculous effusions?

Then her features hardened again.

'The boy, monsieur. I believe you wish to discuss terms.'

The young thug hovered behind his mistress and began to play at cleaning his fingernails with his clasp knife.

'If you are agreeable, madame.' Danton bowed and smiled broadly.

'What do you intend to offer?'

'Ah, Madame Dearlove, it is not what we may offer...' Danton made one of his large gallic gestures. 'It is what you may want — and not yet know it!'

Poll sighed. She signed towards her one-eyed factotum. 'James, bring us the punch, will yer? Looks like we've got a haggler here.' And then she surveyed the party. 'Gentlemen, you may take your ease.'

The lady herself settled onto a commodious chaise longue and smoothed out her silk dress. 'Mr Sheridan, we are not acquainted, but I have enjoyed the hospitality of your "house", you might say, and been right royally entertained. Mrs Jordan is a particular favourite —' Poll chuckled — 'though I should have had thought to take a different husband!'

The young thug sniggered at this witticism from his mistress. Sheridan was sure that Dora Jordan must be heartily sick of being reminded that a *Mrs Jordan* was a common name for a chamber pot.

'And that young Grimaldi — he's a one! Such larks!'

'He is indeed, ma'am.'

'I hear as you're looking for investors for the new place?'

'We sell debentures, ma'am, yes.' Sheridan felt his stomach lurch. Did the villainess mean to buy into the Theatre Royal, Drury Lane?

'Only I hear your creditors have the devil of a time.'

Sheridan shifted awkwardly. Was this extraordinary woman making play with him?

'Funny, innit, the way the rich can rob a man blind with some fancy scheme or bankrupt an honest tradesman 'cause they never pays their debts, and yet the likes of my Dorcas or young Billy here might get sent to Botany Bay for lifting an 'ankerchief? Rum I calls it.'

Sheridan squirmed in his seat and was rather relieved when the punch arrived. They were each presented with a glass.

Danton raised his tumbler with a show of bonhomie. '*Santé*.'

'Y're health,' Poll responded. 'Now, what is it you think I want, monsieur, and yet am ignorant of it?'

'To be esteemed, madame — to be recognised for your talents and industry.'

'I'm recognised well enough in this neighbourhood, sir.'

'Ah, but who here really appreciates your achievements, or comprehends all of this?' Danton cast his eyes about the salon.

'And what do you suggest then, that I hold a soiree?'

'Paris.'

Sheridan sat up with a start. What the deuce was Danton proposing?

Poll looked flummoxed. 'What? Paris? Do you mean in France, sir?'

Danton nodded enthusiastically. '*Mais oui*! In Paris we are creating a new world, madame. A future where merit and intelligence may be valued irrespective of birth. You could retire from your current enterprises, let us say, and establish yourself in a fine house in — in my arrondissement. As an honorary citizen of our great city your natural gifts would be desirable; there should be innumerable opportunities worthy of your business acumen. Madame Dearlove, you should have a place of honour and standing in Paris,' Danton finished with a flourish of the hand.

Poll's brow furrowed as she listened closely to Danton's proposition. After a pause, she threw back her head and laughed uproariously, slapping her thigh. When she had regained her composure, she shook her head. 'You are quite the comic, sir!' She looked towards a man who had now entered the room. 'D'you hear this, Ezekiel? The monsieur invites us to live in Paree!'

The man joined her in amusement at the joke. It was the jarvey.

'My brother, gentlemen, Mr Brough. Honest as they come. Runs a company of hackney cabs — there shall be one at your disposal when you depart. Paree!' She shook her head again and snorted.

'I make no jest, madame. It is, how you might say, like for like.' Monsieur Danton heaved his great shoulders and extended his arms as though it were obvious. 'Monsieur Legge offers young Billy the opportunity of a respectable future as his ward. In exchange, I offer to you the same chance to make a new life, Madame Dearlove. And, just as the young lawyer offers his guardianship, I offer my protection in Paris.'

Poll leant forward. 'You have a silver tongue, monsieur, I'll give you that. I hear you are a great speaker and a leading man in your country, such as might very well make large promises. But I am also informed that fortune's tide is not currently in your favour and that there is a price on your head. Someone has tried to take a pot shot at you already.'

'Tha's right, Poll,' Mr Brough concurred with his sister. 'Down Vauxhall way.'

Danton shrugged. 'Pah, that is nothing — as you would say, a storm in a teacup.'

Sheridan bridled; it was no small matter to Timothy Legge.

Danton continued. 'And the tide it is changing, madame, as tides are wont. You can be assured that my word shall be made good.'

'Now, for the sake of amusement, how should this miracle be brought about? I am to simply up sticks? And a magic carpet shall fly me to Paris?' Her arm swept about the room with proud ownership. 'You see my collection is no mean thing?'

'It would be improved in Paris, madame,' Danton offered nonchalantly. 'There is, how shall we say, a very fluid market at this present time. So many of our noble houses have reason to sell at a very reasonable price, perhaps before those possessions might be — confiscated.'

'In which you might have a pecuniary interest, monsieur?'

Danton shrugged.

'And how am I to know that you do not set a trap and would sell me out to the magistrates?'

'As to the first: the entry papers to France may be arranged without delay. A ship will stand by to transport you and —' he nodded towards Ezekiel Brough — 'your family and any possessions you might reasonably carry. Contrary to expectation, there is much traffic across the Channel. In Paris, you need have no concern. No one shall query your origins, madame. As to the second, why, Mr Sheridan shall stand as guarantor to our agreement, and he is by all accounts a gentleman who does not break his word in such matters. In any case, I should not imagine he would want to risk the vengeance that would be wreaked on his person were you to be betrayed, Madame Dearlove. Is that not so, my friend?'

Sheridan found himself looking into Danton's smiling face with an astonishment which rendered him speechless. Now he was being called upon to aid and abet the flight from justice of a known felon.

'Furthermore,' Danton continued before Sheridan could contradict him, 'Billy shall be handed over only when you are safely on board the ship, which will be bound for Calais.' Danton winked at Billy and displayed his huge paws. 'Into these very hands, *mon garçon*.'

Billy allowed himself a tentative smile in response.

'It's a lot for me to give up all this on a Frenchman's fancy.' Poll tapped impatiently on the arm of the chaise longue. 'Can we not simply agree a figure for the lad?'

'It is more to gain, I assure you, madame,' Danton insisted with great force.

They were blindfolded and jolted along some circuitous routes before one of Brough's fellow jarveys deposited Danton, Sheridan and Jedidiah at Charing Cross. Sylvain had remained behind in company with his mistress.

Once out of earshot of the leering driver, Sheridan rounded on Monsieur Danton. 'God's blood! What do you mean by all of this tomfoolery?'

Danton patted his stomach. 'You will join me for lunch, my dear Sherrie, my good honest Jedidiah. I have found there is a very passable steak house not far from here and I am ravenous.'

With that, he placed a hand on the shoulders of both men and steered them in that direction.

Jedidiah was soon rewarded for his part in the morning's exertions with a plate piled high with beefsteak and all washed down with a jug of porter. Sheridan was not so easily recompensed for the ordeal to which he had been subjected in St Giles.

'Monsieur, you heard that villainess — could we not simply have haggled a figure for Billy?'

'*Non, non, non*. Sherrie, my friend.' Danton shook his enormous bull's head. 'The elastic, it is too tight. You have seen this for yourself. She has only to snap the finger and the boy bounces back into her clutches. The link, it must be severed, completely.'

Really, Monsieur Danton was the most impossible man with whom to do business. And yet, he was right, damn him; Sheridan acknowledged his perspicacity. Truth be told, Sheridan was beginning to realise that the Frenchman was exceptional. He did not wonder that he held such sway with the people of Paris. Were Sheridan to abide in that city, he too might succumb to the force of the man's personality. He felt that he beheld a man worthy to be a leader, a giant amongst men, however trying and exasperating he proved to be.

'Battling Poll will never rise to this. It is too great a risk, and I cannot clearly see the advantage to her.'

'Oh, she will agree to this plan. Trust me, Sherrie. There is a greater risk for Madame Dearlove if she stays put,' Danton declared triumphantly.

'How so?'

Danton grinned like nothing so much as a serpent that had swallowed a man whole. 'Because, my dear Sherrie, her days in the ring they are numbered, and being the experienced fighter that she is, she understands this very well.'

'What do you mean?'

Danton tapped the table with the end of his knife. 'There is always the next villain ready to throw in his hat. One who is more vicious. One who is hungrier. One who might destroy her. His name, it is Zachary Drewe.'

'Zachery Drewe — the devil. You knew this?'

'Sylvain has always been a rogue, but a reliable informant. He misses Paris — who can blame him? Behind this madame's skirts, it may now be possible for him to return. He tells me that in this past month alone, two of Poll's lieutenants have been skewered by Monsieur Drewe, pickled and delivered in a barrel. The choice is war, which will not be pretty and of uncertain outcome, or...' Danton drove his fork into a piece of bloody steak.

'Exile,' Sheridan completed for him. 'And —' he must be diplomatic, he supposed — 'Mistress Dearlove might be useful to you in Paris.'

Danton beamed. 'The steak, it is good, yes? Just as I like it, very rare — I have to demand this of the cook or I am presented with the piece of charcoal which you English prefer.' He pointed with distaste at the blackened slab of meat on Sheridan's platter.

Sheridan grimaced and pointed with equal distaste at the bloody mess of Danton's meal. 'And that to my mind is pure savagery, sir. You may as well consume the meat raw for all the cooking it has had.'

CHAPTER THIRTY

Two days later it appeared that Danton's conjectures had been correct. Battling Poll was agreeable to considering a permanent change of location. Sheridan felt able to return to Timothy's bedside with a lighter heart. Billy should be brought back, Sheridan would hand him over to Mr Legge, and he would have discharged his duty of care. Timothy himself was not yet quite beyond the danger of infection. But despite these continued anxieties and concerns as to his future mobility, Josiah reassured Sheridan. With his usual robust optimism, he declared that rest and three wholesome meals a day would soon have his son restored to full health.

Timothy had naturally enquired after Billy. 'You have him in Isleworth, I should think, Mr Sheridan; the country air will be most efficacious for Billy after so many years of London fug.'

'It is very pleasant in Isleworth,' Sheridan asserted with conviction.

'How I long to see the boy again. I had not thought to become so attached. You know we had started on his letters; he has a quick and lively mind. It is most encouraging. And Monsieur Danton remarked to me only yesterday that Billy had thrashed him most soundly at Fox and Geese.' Timothy glowed quite as much as any proud parent might.

A general contagion of buoyancy prevailed and Danton called to inform Sheridan that dates had been mooted with Mistress Poll and plans were now set in motion. Sheridan also found himself in motion as his carriage rattled along the well-worn roads south through Sussex. The Prince of Wales had taken himself down to Brighton for the races in the second half of the month, and Sheridan was expected to be of the party.

Prior to departure, he had sought out Constable Nicholls at Bow Street.

'Ah, Mr Sheridan, I am sorry to say I have nothing further for you at this juncture.'

'I have something for you, however, Constable.'

'Sir?'

'Zachary Drewe.'

Nicholls blew out his cheeks. 'Now, there's a nasty cove and no mistake!'

'An opportunity is about to come his way which I am determined he shall not have.'

'Then how might I be of assistance?' Nicholls offered with enthusiasm.

'In a week, a man shall come to you; you will know him.'

Nicholls looked suspicious. 'Am I not to have his name beforehand?'

'I pray you trust me in this matter. There is much at stake, Louis-Pierre.' Sheridan used the presumption of familiarity to press his suit.

Nicholls nodded a cautious acceptance. 'Go on, sir.'

'He will guide a party of your men — let them be in numbers and well-armed — to a school. One that is for snafflers and pickpockets. The children there are in need of your protection. They will be frightened. There is a young woman, Dorcas — you will remember her recent visit to the magistrate — she may help to calm them. The prize for the kindness that may then be bestowed on these unfortunate wretches shall be found close by. A treasure trove of ill-gotten property. The larger pieces, anyway. Which, with any luck, may be returned to the rightful owners for a sizeable reward. You will also have the satisfaction of knowing that you have thwarted the immediate ambitions of Mr Zachary Drewe.'

Nicholls' eyes narrowed. 'Ambitions to take the place of Battling Poll? And what of her?'

'Constable, I have come to hold you in the highest regard. Without impertinence, I hope, I consider you a friend, as you must consider me.'

For an anxious moment, Sheridan wondered if he had miscalculated.

The young man shook his head with exasperation. 'It seems I am called upon to trust your judgement, Mr Sheridan. Let me not be in error.'

Mistress Poll Dearlove. It troubled Sheridan greatly that he was a party to engineering her escape from justice. The woman was a cunning battler and no mistake. It must have been something to see her engaged in fisticuffs. Most female pugilists spent themselves in the sport, fighting on for longer than their broken bodies could sustain. Then they turned to gin in order to dull the constant pain. Not Poll. She had abandoned her wastrel husband and assiduously saved the purses which she won. Poll might then have pursued a life of modest respectability, but no, she had returned to the rookeries whence she had sprung, to those very ginnels and dens where she had earned her keep as a thief, and proceeded to make a greater fortune by teaching that trade to another generation.

Sheridan's carriage drew up outside the Star and Garter, a favourite watering hole on this route. The horses were to be changed, and he should have enough time to partake of some refreshment. It had been hot and humid in the carriage, and he welcomed the dark coolness of the old tavern's nooks and crannies. Sheridan breathed in the smells of ale, sawdust and old candlewax mixing with the aroma of meat juices wafting from the kitchen beyond.

From her position at the counter, the barmaid greeted him familiarly.

'A small beer and a dish of whatever repast assaults my nostrils, if you would be so kind, Mary.'

He was heading towards a quiet corner when a voice arrested him.

'Mr Sheridan.'

Sheridan turned to find himself facing the Duc d'Orléans' agent, Nathaniel Parker Forth.

'Would you care to join me, sir?'

Another time Sheridan might have attempted some whimsical excuse, but nothing came to mind other than that he really should become better acquainted with Parker Forth — if for no other reason than to further his task on behalf of the prince.

'I should be delighted, Mr Parker Forth.' He took the seat opposite.

'You are en route to Brighton, Sheridan?'

'It is my good fortune and pleasure to attend His Royal Highness.'

'Mine also — not to stay at the Pavilion, but to be invited to Brighton.'

'His Serene Highness —?'

Parker Forth nodded. 'The duc shall presently attend the races.'

'Naturally, the races, a great interest that both men share. I cannot say I have ever felt a passion for horseflesh — except in a pot perhaps, with onions and carrots.'

At which moment Mary approached and laid out a steaming bowl, tankard and jug.

'Ah, Mary! What have we here?'

''Tis only my mother's beef stew, sir, and suet dumplings.'

'Only? Why, there is no "only" about it, but the finest fare to be had in all the land!' Sheridan beamed at the young barmaid, who rolled her eyes and retreated to her counter to serve the local custom.

Sheridan tucked in to the simple dish and smacked his lips in satisfaction.

'You are about the duc's business, I daresay, Mr Parker Forth?'

'Amongst other matters.'

'I believe the duc's daughter, Mademoiselle Adele, is now installed in Bury St Edmunds with her governess?'

Parker Forth nodded. 'Madame de Genlis.'

'I shall look forward to renewing that acquaintance — Madame de Genlis is an authoress of formidable achievement.'

'His Serene Highness re-joins our party in Brighton, before we return to Paris.'

'Paris! I hope to visit Paris myself — such stimulating times.'

Parker Forth grunted. 'At present it would seem that Paris has come to these shores.'

'We have our share of émigrés, to be sure.'

'I was alluding in particular to Monsieur Danton. You have met him, no doubt?' Parker Forth probed.

Sheridan speared a dumpling. 'At one of Mr Johnson's dinners. It amused him to tell me that there is a price on his head and to show me the pistol he keeps in his pocket as a consequence. Such a considerable personality, almost as large as his person. Does he meet with His Serene Highness?'

A wary look flitted across Parker Forth's features. 'Danton commands notice, that is for certain.'

'So many stars that rise and fall in the glittering firmament of Paris. The duc shall be foremost in the ascendant — he has always favoured a constitutional monarchy and must be delighted that the National Assembly is engaged in drawing up that constitution as we speak. Pleasing for you, Mr Parker Forth, to have so illustrious a master.'

Parker Forth raised an eyebrow. 'I am the duc's agent and advisor, not his servant, sir.'

'Pardon, that was not my implication.' Sheridan continued his advantage. 'Let us hope that the calls for England to take up arms against the revolutionaries go unheeded. You should be in a delicate situation then, Mr Parker Forth? Were we to be at war.'

Parker Forth stiffened imperceptibly.

'My first loyalty has always been to His Majesty, King George. It may not be widely known, but in the past I have acted as His Majesty's special envoy.'

Sheridan noted the gleam of pride in Parker Forth's disclosure. 'You are too modest, sir. I also believe that the Prince of Wales owes you a debt of gratitude and more, perhaps?'

Parker Forth flushed. 'His Royal Highness has spoken of me?'

'In the most glowing terms. The prince assures me that you are the soul of discretion.'

'I do believe I have given many proofs.'

'Then I am reassured.' Sheridan thumped the table. 'I shall give no credence whatsoever to the fellow who claims that you have been involved in dubious financial transactions and furthermore, sir, that you have cast aspersions on the patriotism of His Royal Highness.'

Parker Forth's eyes started wide. 'Who would dare to voice such an outrage?'

'Quite. Only a low sort of fellow who fancied he might take advantage of your disgrace in order to curry his own favour.'

'I would have his name!'

'So would I sir, so would I!' Sheridan declared with fury and thumped the table again.

Nathaniel Parker Forth looked momentarily bewildered.

A footman arrived at the table and nodded to Parker Forth.

'Ah, it seems we are ready to depart.' Parker Forth rose with a look of anxiety. 'You must forgive my haste, Sheridan. It has been most — most —'

'Refreshing and enjoyable! Let us agree to be great friends.'

'Of course. Honoured.' Parker Forth bowed. 'Good day to you, sir.'

Sheridan smiled and waved the duc's agent on his way. He suspected that Parker Forth was no more than a sycophant, a man whose greatest pleasure was to be in proximity to wealth and prestige, preferably royal. He sighed. He seemed further than ever from knowing who the anonymous letter-writer might be.

Sheridan was thrilled beyond measure to find that Marceline was already installed in Brighton and that she welcomed his own arrival with effusive enthusiasm. The baroness was in the throes of organising a theatrical entertainment for Prince George, and Sheridan's genius should be indispensable to her.

'A harlequinade, my dearest Sherrie. And you shall assist me, won't you?' Her eyes gleamed.

'Harlequinade?' Sheridan could not disguise his lack of fervour. He felt that he had had rather enough of Harlequins of late. 'Why not consider something a little…?'

She pouted becomingly. 'You don't like my idea?'

'Oh, it is a fine idea — I just wondered, Marceline, perhaps whether something more original…'

'*Exactement!* That is my notion — you shall help me to create a new version!' She leant in close to his ear. 'Something surprising!'

Marceline's scheme was for them to adapt the scenario of *The Two Harlequins*, a lesser-known piece of the repertoire. Traditionally set in Paris, it was Marceline's suggestion that they relocate the scene to Brighton and make playful reference to topics of current interest and titillation.

'Our own *School for Scandal, mon* Sherrie!'

Her coup, as she enthused to Sheridan, was to have persuaded Orléans into the part of Gerontes, whenever he should join them. Sheridan would naturally play the part of Harlequin with Marceline as Columbine. Sir Roderick had eagerly accepted the role of Harlequin's double — referred to as Harlequin Junior in the *dramatis personae*. The chevalier was cast as the Commissary, an officer of the law. Lady Lade, who had a pleasing voice, should play the songstress Marinetta. They planned to rewrite her part as an orange-seller, in a nod to Nell Gwyn, and in order to allow Lady Lade a line in bawdy asides. Various others of the party had been cajoled into the roles of Pierrot, little Piquelard and the two young lovers. The Marine Pavilion fairly buzzed with the excitement of imminent theatricals and the Prince of Wales had to be teased and shooed away from learning too much of their production.

Marceline approached the project with her customary gusto. Sheridan soon found himself happily ensconced in a secluded corner of the gardens with the object of his affections. Together they perused the hackneyed storyline, in which the older Gerontes desires the hand of the beautiful Isabella, seeking to woo her with a gift of precious jewels, and enlists his servant, Harlequin, to assist. Confusion and mayhem arising when Harlequin's twin brother unexpectedly arrives in town.

They knuckled down to give the script a thorough tweak, added current jokes and witticisms and laughed infectiously at each other's sallies. *The Two Harlequins* held plenteous opportunity for the comedy of mistaken identity resulting in the furious tiffs between Harlequin and Columbine which should be a dramatic highlight.

Sheridan felt thoroughly revived after what, he realised, had been a fraught and trying summer. How utterly agreeable it was to flirt and snatch furtive kisses in the fragrant shade of the arbour with the promise of further intimacies. As much as he expressed his ardour and pressed for the consummation of his desires, Marceline took equal pleasure in keeping herself tantalisingly just beyond reach.

'I fear that you trifle with me, *mon* Sherrie. I am of no consequence, of course, to a great man such as yourself, but I would not be a mere plaything,' she chided.

It was all delicious play. Not even the cold stares of the chevalier, as he eyed them from behind the rose bushes, could entirely dampen Sheridan's spirits. The chevalier. Sheridan wondered fleetingly whether the extent of his earlier suspicions were warranted. He had leapt to assumptions with the disappearance of the coded letter, only to find that he had dropped it after all. The young man was scarcely more than a boy; if he had liaised briefly with Jack Champion on the beach, it was surely as a messenger for Orléans — the duc perhaps sought to use the Huguenots in some way but, Sheridan felt sure, would not condone assassinations.

The Duc d'Orléans arrived and Brighton became an exhausting carousel of pleasures. Dining, recitals, promenades, the Assembly Rooms, and above all the excitement occasioned by visits to the racecourse up on Whitehawk Down — a frenzy of gambling which saw the prince lose more wagers than he won.

Sheridan could not suppress a smile to see Mr Parker Forth so anxious to ingratiate himself with His Royal Highness at every opportunity. More seriously he suspected that, although Parker Forth may not be the True Friend of Albion, he nevertheless continued to play a devious role. From the intent expression on the face of the Prince of Wales whenever he came upon him ensconced with Parker Forth, Sheridan deduced that negotiations had not been abandoned, despite the warnings and threats posed by the anonymous letters. Perhaps His Royal Highness imagined his position as heir to the throne was unassailable. Sheridan felt the prickle of anxiety. Others must note that the prince continued thick with Parker Forth. Would there be a final warning from Anon? So many eyes were watching His Royal Highness, and one amongst them might not be a friend at all.

CHAPTER THIRTY-ONE

Sheridan stifled a yawn. He had decided to keep a watch but had almost called it a night, when the man appeared. He pressed himself into the shadows and kept an eye on the figure descending the staircase. All those rich sauces had given Howgill dyspepsia again, he supposed. Then Sir Roderick drew out a sealed note from the pocket of his robe and placed it swiftly on the salver in the vestibule before retreating silently back up the stair. Well, this was something of interest.

When the young baronet was out of sight, Sheridan tiptoed over to the dish. He picked up the missive and held it aloft to the sliver of moonlight which came in through the windows. It was addressed to His Royal Highness and there was something quite familiar about the plain block letters.

'Can I be of assistance?'

Sheridan dropped the missive with sudden fright. He swirled about. The voice seemed to have come out of the darkness itself.

'Apologies, Sherry, did I startle you?'

'Hanger.'

Major Hanger stepped out from the servant's doorway into the foyer, taking a bite from a biscuit as he did so. 'Found myself a tad peckish on the way back from a jolly old romp with Sukie — you remember Sukie?' He leered and outlined the comely barmaid's hips.

Sheridan recovered his composure. 'Quite. Sukie. Yes … indigestion. Walking about has relieved the symptoms, thank you.' He backed away towards the stairs with an exaggerated yawn.

The equerry approached and stooped to pick up the note. 'You dropped this, I believe.' Hanger held it out towards him.

Sheridan hesitated; Hanger would surely notice to whom it was addressed. Yet he desperately wanted to know the contents. He was on the prince's business, after all.

'Thank you, Major.'

Sheridan was about to take the note when Hanger snatched it back.

'Ah, I see it is for the attention of His Royal Highness...' The equerry regarded the note with pursed lips. 'Do I recognise the hand — or something like it?'

Then, with a look of realisation, Hanger waved the note and observed Sheridan with a wry smile. 'A True Friend of Albion, perhaps?'

'I believe so,' Sheridan admitted reluctantly.

'You are charged with this matter, are you not?'

'I have the confidence of the prince.'

'Then let us brook no delay in his service.'

Hanger broke the seal and held the contents of the letter up to the sliver of moonlight.

'Major!' Sheridan looked stern.

Hanger squinted. 'Damn, I can hardly see a blasted thing in this light. I've a decent brandy in my room. Follow me.'

Devil take the impudent fellow. Sheridan found himself scurrying in the equerry's wake.

Hanger had not lied. It *was* a decent brandy. Sheridan took a pleasing sip as he scanned the contents of the letter.

Sir,

The races are begun, but be warned, the Finishing Line approaches.

Have a care which horse you back! Or you may find one that is put out to pasture. Nay — and gelded furthermore!

A TRUE FRIEND of Albion

'I see our friend's wit has not improved.'

'You got a glimpse of the fellow, I think?' Hanger probed.

Sheridan paused and considered. He may as well have an ally. 'Howgill.'

'Ah, yes, Sir Roderick. He is his cousin's eyes and ears.'

'Then Dundas at the Home Department is behind this?'

'Mr Pitt, I shouldn't wonder.'

'You consider Pitt?'

Hanger shrugged. 'Our Prime Minister is such a sneaking fellow and weaves a perfect web; he likes to be in the know. Howgill is a charming young fop who has cosied himself into many a different corner.'

'But what do they intend with these threats?' Sheridan slapped the note.

'Well, let me see... What might we suppose?'

Sheridan's eyes narrowed with inspiration. 'Pitt thinks that by cutting off all other sources of finance, the prince may be —'

Hanger nodded in amused anticipation.

'— persuaded into marriage,' Sheridan concluded.

'Bingo.' Hanger raised his brandy glass. 'Like his brother York, whose considerable debts you note are only partly solved by this recourse.'

Sheridan grimaced in understanding. 'All the royal brothers' debts will be paid off by King George and his government, if only the heir to the throne himself will marry a German princess!'

'In a nutshell. I believe it is not simply a matter of money; the government views such royal marriages as a cornerstone of diplomatic relations with the German states. The only fly in the ointment is these financial dealings with Parker Forth and the Duc d'Orléans.'

'And this nonsense —' Sheridan flapped the letter — 'is to frighten the prince out of his negotiations with Orléans.'

'So it would seem.'

Sheridan sank back in his chair. 'Do they really threaten a scandal if he does not heed the warning?'

'Sadly, I don't doubt that possibility. York will marry the Princess Frederica in a matter of months, and, in all likelihood, he will produce a kindergarten with the Prussian mare. When there is a veritable stable of little princelings — what need then of our dear prince? There is no love lost between His Majesty and his firstborn, as we all know. A dirty, treasonous scandal — that should be an excellent way for His Majesty to be rid of him, exiled to Ireland or Scotland, poor devil.'

Sheridan blew out his cheeks. What were they to do? No — what was *he* to do?

The costumes and accessories for the *commedia* had been delivered from London and the various players were extracting their rigs and props.

Sir Roderick Howgill twirled the black harlequin mask between his fingers. 'To mask or not to mask? That is the question. Marceline seems determined that we wear these disguises throughout and only reveal ourselves when we take the final bow. What's your opinion, Sheridan?'

'I should have imagined that wearing a mask would be your natural bent, Howgill.'

Sir Roderick smirked. 'Certainly, I am fond of disguise. That I will not deny.'

'You might do very well at Drury Lane; Joseph Surface is a role that might suit you — being all Surface.'

'Who should know who is true? Or what a man's real worth might be, in truth?'

Sheridan nodded and responded *sotto voce*, 'How many, for instance, may lay claim to being a True Friend of Albion?'

'I should hope that we are all True Friends of Albion,' Howgill responded blithely.

'These are turbulent times, Howgill. Traitors move amongst us and like moths to a flame gather around the light of power. His Royal Highness must have a care of treachery.'

'None more so.'

'We are agreed.'

Sheridan picked up the slapstick which was lying next to the cockaded hat. He flexed the instrument and then whacked it against the table to produce the distinctive sound of the slap.

'An anonymous letter might do the trick as a reminder — is that not so, Howgill?'

'If it serves to forestall — what is the term you theatricals use? A pratfall.'

'Pratfall, heh?' Sheridan took Howgill by the arm and yanked him away from potential eavesdroppers. 'Was it your idea? Shall I inform the prince and allow him into the joke? He should find the prank very amusing.'

Sir Roderick smiled benevolently. 'There are those whose only wish is to save the Prince of Wales from his own poor judgement — and from causing His Majesty the King further apoplexy by bringing the Royal Family into any more disrepute than Wales already does.'

'It does not solve the problem of his debts.'

'Then His Royal Highness must spend less.'

Sheridan raised a cynical eyebrow in response.

'He must refrain from redecorating his house every month. Forgo the gaming tables and the monies squandered at the racetracks.'

'You think to frighten the prince away from his dealings with the Duc d'Orléans? But what are his alternatives, pray?'

'Why, to marry.' A slow smile crept across Howgill's features. The two men regarded each other.

'He will not be persuaded. You must know that. Mrs Fitzherbert…' Sheridan trailed off.

'That liaison can never be legitimate.'

'He sees no great necessity now that his brother York marries the Princess Frederica — is that not enough? Can't the king be satisfied and encouraged to be more generous?'

It was Howgill's turn to raise an eyebrow.

'Does Mr Pitt seriously mean to threaten scandal?' Sheridan asked in disbelief.

'Relations between England and France stand at a precarious juncture. This mischief with a foreign prince is not in the national interest, Mr Sheridan.' Howgill looked suddenly very serious. 'Were His Majesty King George to know of the negotiations or their full extent, it should have dire consequences.'

Sheridan paused in deliberation. He must acknowledge the full gravity of the situation. He owned that he had been idle in the matter; his princely friend might truly be under the most serious threat. There was a ruthless streak in young Mr Pitt. He paled to think of it. Howgill was right, damn him. The prince must be saved from his own poor judgement.

'You have succeeded in alarming the prince. That is no bad thing, Howgill.' He bit at his fist. 'Perhaps a further, more tangible, scare might underpin that alarm and discourage attempts to curry rescue from foreign quarters.'

'You have something in mind, Sheridan?' Howgill's eyes gleamed.

'Your masters must assure me that if we succeed, then the Prince of Wales is safe. Do you understand me, Howgill? This matter shall never see the light of day.'

Sir Roderick nodded curtly.

Sheridan took a deep breath. He was almost too nervous to put into words the plan that was already forming in his mind.

'*Mes chers*!' Marceline slipped in between the two men, kissing both lightly on the cheek. 'Is it not splendid?' She stepped back and twirled about to display her Columbine costume, a colourful patched dress cut daringly low at her bosom and short at the ankles, the better to display her steps in the dance sequence. A pretty little apron to denote her servant status and a jaunty feathered hat set at an angle completed the outfit.

'Enchanting as always, my dear Marceline.'

The baroness snatched up the cockaded hat and placed it onto Howgill's head. She stood back to admire him.

'Now you begin to look the part, Roddy!'

'These masks, Baronne, must we?'

'It is *commedia*. Sherrie can explain — when you wear the mask, it hides the expression on your face, and so you must of necessity use the movement of your body to make that expression. *N'est-ce pa?*'

With that, Marceline picked up a colourful parasol and twirled it about as she struck a series of flamboyant and exaggerated poses. She laughed gaily as her two would-be suitors competed to guess which attitude she represented.

CHAPTER THIRTY-TWO

Sam Chifney shifted his weight in the saddle and eased his horse, Escape, forward from his position at the back of the field. The reins were unusually slack in his hand. He seldom used the whip other than to tip the flank; instead, by tightening his grip at the knee, he urged the horse past the flagging steeds on either side and on to that final effort — a finishing style which had been dubbed 'The Chifney Rush'.

The Prince of Wales fairly leapt from the ground as his distinctive colours, the crimson waistcoat, purple sleeves and black cap, could be seen to overtake three other horses in the race and then Escape surged up the field to sit behind the leader. A fifty-guinea sweepstake and His Royal Highness had enjoined Sir John Lade to wager a further hundred guineas on the outcome for him.

'Do you see, Sherry? Now you shall wish that you had placed your coin on Escape rather than Lord Grosvenor's tired mount!'

Only two days previous Escape had been the favourite but had only managed to come third. Today his odds were much reduced against many of the same field over a greater distance. Sir John Lade had muttered to the prince that Escape must be out of form, but Chifney had assured His Royal Highness that the horse had 'cleared his pipes' in the earlier race and would be a better ride for it. If Chifney were to ride Escape to victory today, that should be a very profitable win. The prince would recoup all losses and add a satisfying profit to the whole enterprise.

The gap narrowed. Escape was gaining on the leader.

The prince cheered and waved his hat as though to speed him on.

Neck and neck the finish line approached. Grosvenor's horse, Skyscraper, strained to stay in front, but Chifney had momentum now and Escape struck out a further head to secure a decisive victory.

Lord Grosvenor and his party groaned, the owner casting narrow, suspicious looks at the jubilant prince.

'Well done, Georgy, your fortunes have quite revived today!' It was the Duc d'Orléans who clapped his friend on the back.

Sheridan wondered fleetingly if there was something underhand going on. The delight of the prince at the success of his favourite horse seemed innocent enough, but might his recent losses have tempted a deceit? He questioned if Chifney could be entirely trusted. Had the jockey pulled the horse in the earlier race and then placed his own discreet wager with the change of odds? Well, Sheridan knew little to nothing about horses or their form, and his losses that day reminded him that he should keep from betting on them.

The afternoon was balmy with a light breeze off the sea, which subdued any unpleasant heat up on Whitehawk Down. The added attractions of a fair had brought throngs of locals to the event. Race enthusiasts and tourists mingled with excitable townsfolk. The stewards attempted to keep order as the crowds pushed and jostled for their viewpoints during each race and then dispersed in crushing masses to beer tents, sideshows and pie-sellers.

Sheridan emerged from the jakes and made his way back up through the grandstand. His eye caught Sir Roderick Howgill, who gave an imperceptible acknowledgement in return. Plans had been put in place. There should be two more races, after which Sheridan was to keep close to His Royal Highness as they made their way from the course. He felt a queasy flutter of anxiety. There was still time for him to call off the whole ludicrous business. He had surely suffered a fit of insanity to suggest the scheme in the first place. As his mind tussled with this burning quandary, his wandering gaze alighted on a familiar figure amongst the crowds teeming below. He caught his breath. Monsieur Danton.

The Frenchman was parading arm in arm with Battling Poll. The brazen dam was decked out in all her finery. And there was Sylvain at her other side, equally sartor and swinging a silver-topped cane with practised insouciance as he conversed with Danton's stepfather. But what did Mistress Dearlove do in Brighton? Should she not even now be en route to Dover and the promised passage to France? What on earth was Danton up to?

And then he could see very well what Danton's game might be. For there was Orléans in company with the chevalier and a handful of courtiers. A brief exchange saw Danton peel away from Poll to draw alongside Orléans. Danton moved momentarily from view, but His Serene Highness was all courtesy and smiles from what little Sheridan could observe. Well, this was an interesting development — particularly at this time. The National Constituent Assembly in France was due to dissolve once they had finished devising the new constitution. A self-denying ordinance barred them from sitting in the proposed successor, the Legislative Assembly. Both Orléans and Danton would have ambitions to take leading roles in that new body. If they were to forge an alliance behind the scenes, then who knew what the outcome might be? The burgeoning calls for a French Republic might yet be silenced, and Orléans offered to the people as their constitutional monarch.

'You are surveying the field, *mon* Sherrie?'

'Marceline! I did not think you had an interest in the track?'

Marceline sighed. 'In truth, it bores me.'

'I confess to a similar disinterest.'

'But do not tell the duc,' she laughed gaily. 'It is his only topic at the moment, and I must pretend to hang upon his every word.'

Her eye was caught then by his figure in the crowds milling below the grandstand. 'Speak of the devil — isn't that your expression?' Marceline pointed. 'Do you see? His Serene Highness strolls amongst the hoi polloi.'

Sheridan affected to follow the direction of her finger. 'Ah, yes. The duc is in the thick of it.'

'He so enjoys to mix with the common people.'

'Why do you think that is?'

'Oh, he believes that they love him.' Marceline strained over the rail to inspect more closely the man sauntering at the duc's side. 'And can that truly be that brute, Monsieur Danton, with whom he converses? Here, in England — in Brighton?' Marceline turned with a look of astonishment to Sheridan.

Sheridan laughed. 'He assists his stepfather in the purchase of a spinning jenny.'

'How exquisitely ridiculous.'

'I have suggested he might also consider the spinning mule.'

'Then he has already taken your advice. Do we not see him consorting with the duc?' Marceline eyed Sheridan with a wicked grin. 'But their meeting it is intriguing, *n'est pas*?'

'It should raise an eyebrow, I imagine.'

She indicated the horses beyond, gathering on the field for the next race. 'And who should be the front runner? Do you have a favourite?'

'After my earlier loss, I am sorely tempted to hedge my bets.'

'Oh, but where is the thrill in that, *mon* Sherrie? In Paris we have all learned to live dangerously; it is so exhilarating. One must make a choice. Which horse shall I back, win or lose?'

'In Paris, you stand to lose more than mere coin.'

Marceline's hand fluttered to her neck and a shiver coursed through Sheridan as he contemplated her elegant fragility. The thought that she might suffer harm appalled him. He very much hoped that she chose well. The mob in Paris had shown how easily it might be stirred to anger and violence. He sought to reassure himself; surely Marceline was safe within the orbit of Orléans? The new constitution would settle the political ferment in France. The Revolution had succeeded; it had overturned the tyranny of Absolutism. There was no further need for bloodshed and cataclysm to bring about change. The events at the Champ de Mars were unfortunate but should only serve to focus the minds of sensible men; men like Orléans and Danton, who must pave the way to further gradual reforms and a greater democracy.

'We live to the full whilst we have the chance!' She leant in closer. 'Speaking of which ... you know where I stay, *mon* Sherrie, and that door should not be locked tonight.' She held out her hand for him to kiss.

Sheridan felt a surge of panic as he pressed his lips to her proffered fingers. How could he explain that tonight, of all nights, he would not be free? He found himself struggling for words.

Marceline squeezed his hand and smiled coyly. '*À bientôt.*'

'I beg you will not take it ill —' he began, but she had already turned and was moving swiftly towards the Comtesse de Buffon.

'Damn and blast,' Sheridan muttered to himself, as a roar from the crowd signalled the start of the next race.

The party made its way from the grandstand and headed towards the waiting carriages. The Prince of Wales was in ebullient mood at his success.

'I consider Mr Chifney a very sound investment, Howgill. There were those who derided the notion of keeping a retained jockey, egad!'

Sir Roderick nodded in fawning agreement. 'I wonder you do not have a stable of the fellows, sir.'

'If all might be winners —'

Their pleasant conversation was drowned by sudden shouts and cries from a surge amongst the crowd. Sheridan could see that a disorderly group of rough-looking coves were breaking through.

'There he is!' one shouted above the others. 'The insolent pup!'

'Yer blubby lummocks!' another yelled.

It was clear that these insults were directed towards the heir to the throne. Mr Townsend, His Royal Highness' bodyguard for the occasion, read the situation at once and called his men about, rapidly ordering a ring of defence.

'Long live the king!' came the cry.

'Away with Georgie Porgie!'

This crew, for they were hardly yet a mob, had been worked to a frenzy of feeling for the king by some practised provocateur, Sheridan deduced.

'Ingrate!'

'*Georgie Porgie, pumpkin pie!*
Kissed the girls and made them cry.'

A loud refrain was taken up to raucous cheers, and others seemed to be drawn into the demonstration.

'*When the boys come out to play,*
Georgie Porgie runs away.'

A bottle hurtled through the air and narrowly missed Major Hanger. Another object followed immediately and caught the side of the prince's coat. A lump of horse dung — a readily available missile, for another soon followed.

Mr Townsend and his men swore vivid oaths at the blaggards. They pushed back at the heaving, drunken protestors, threatening with short swords. Heavy truncheons smashed into the skulls of any who pressed forward. Calls rang out for the militia. In the mayhem which ensued Major Hanger, with the aid of Sir Roderick, forged a path in retreat and Sheridan took the opportunity to place himself beside the royal heir.

'Sir, sir — come, you must away! My carriage stands very close. You would draw less attention if you were to ride in that vehicle, sir. We must get far from here at once!'

Before the prince had time to respond, Sheridan was guiding him towards his vehicle. A footman jumped to open the door and lower the step.

Once they were both inside, Sheridan leaned out of the carriage window and urged his driver to make haste from Whitehawk Down. The coachman flourished his whip with a crack above the heads of the two horses, exhorting them forward. With a volley of florid curses, he yelled at all before them to give way as he forged a path between the milling crowd and other vehicles. Sheridan fell back within and drew the curtains tight.

'I do not think we have been seen by these ruffians, Your Royal Highness, but you must keep hidden within until we are safely away from the track.'

The prince gulped. 'Sherry, I do believe they meant me harm!'

The carriage lurched and swayed as the coachman drove them at all possible speed across the sward and onto the thoroughfare. The shouts and clamours of the racetrack fell away.

'We are safe for now, I'll hazard. To be certain, I could instruct my man to take a back route? In case this disturbance may have spread into the town.'

The order given, Sheridan sank back and forced a smile.

'Well, that was more sport than we bargained for, sir!'

A blood-red sky streaked over the Sussex Downs as the carriage lurched along rural byways on its circuitous journey back towards the Marine Pavilion. Sheridan peered from behind the drape, trying to gauge their whereabouts, tense with anticipation. At any moment the hasty design which had been formulated with Sir Roderick would be put into action.

As the vehicle swayed around another bend in the road, His Royal Highness groaned. 'Surely we are safe to return now, Sherry. I do think you have overreacted. Those fellows were a bunch of drunken ne'er-do-wells; they cannot have meant any serious harm. Order your man back to the town.'

'As you wish, sir.'

Sheridan rapped on the roof to draw the attention of his coachman. He felt a sudden relief that the plan might have to be abandoned.

At that moment they were assailed by the sounds of thundering approach, loud shouts and the blast of pistol fire.

'What the devil?'

The carriage rocked to a sudden halt as the horses were reined in, neighing and stamping their hooves in alarm.

Sheridan risked a peek through the gap in the curtain. He swallowed and turned with wide eyes to the prince. 'I do believe we are stopped by highwaymen, Your Royal Highness.'

'Highwaymen? Do they dare to waylay the Prince of Wales?'

Sheridan held up his hand in a sudden panic and hissed, 'Sir, I would urge you, do not reveal your identity. We must offer a purse and pray that they will let us go!'

Prince George looked flustered. 'But I have no purse about my person.'

Sheridan sighed. A prince should not carry a purse; it might spoil the line of his costume, for one thing. 'They shall have mine.' He fumbled in his pockets and brought out his coin.

At that moment, the door of the carriage was flung open.

'Step outside!' a man on horseback roared. A black tricorn sat low over his brow and a black neckerchief was pulled up to cover his features so that only his dark eyes were visible; with a black cloak swirled about, he looked every inch the highwayman of legend. In his gloved hand he held a pistol which pointed directly at the Prince of Wales.

The prince clutched at Sheridan's arm. 'Offer him the coin, there's a good fellow!'

Sheridan held up the small leather purse and reached out towards the masked man.

It was waved away with disdain by the highwayman, who all the while kept his weapon fixed on the heir to the throne. 'I will not ask twice!'

Sheridan nodded quickly and stumbled from the vehicle. He was at once grabbed and his arms pinioned behind his back by another of the gang. As he cast his eyes about, he could see that three other masked rogues made up the numbers. His driver and footman had already been bound and gagged and were lying in the ditch.

'I demand to know what you want with us, sir!'

Sheridan turned back to see that the Prince of Wales had paled appreciably, his lips trembling as he struggled to assert some authority.

The dark eyes of the masked man narrowed. 'Do you not hear me? Have I not made myself sufficient clear? Be you dead or alive, I care not, sir.' The last was said with a coarse, sneering emphasis.

'Sir, you must climb down,' Sheridan implored.

'This is most irregular!' the prince whined as he edged cautiously out of the carriage. He was yanked to the ground by a stocky fellow, and at once a blindfold was wrapped about his eyes.

'Unhand me, damn you!' the prince wailed. 'I am — I am —'

The highwayman scoffed. 'You are what?'

'A gentleman,' the prince responded. 'A *gentleman*,' he repeated with greater force.

'No, yer snivelling dog!' The masked man leaned down from his mount and prodded the chest of His Royal Highness with his musket. 'You are no gentleman but a blubbery gollumpus!'

Sheridan gulped with a sudden dread. This felt all too real. Was it possible that they had actually been ambushed by real villains?

'I give you fair warning, you rogue, release me at once or you shall pay most dearly.' His Royal Highness straightened and attempted a dignified stance. 'It is the Prince of Wales that you address!'

This declaration was met with a rumble of laughter which built to a roisterous crescendo. When at last the man had spent his mirth, he nodded slowly. 'Then we have hit the mark, my lads. We have hit the mark.'

CHAPTER THIRTY-THREE

An owl hooted somewhere close outside. The moon waxed nearly full and a sliver of light stole through the slits in the thick walls of the keep. His Royal Highness shivered; the old stone walls to which they had been shackled were cold but thankfully dry. Sheridan was relieved that they had at least been taken to an upper room of the Tower rather than, God forbid, down into the dank and unwholesome dungeons. There was little else of comfort to be had. A rough straw mattress had been laid out on the flagstones. One flickering lantern lit by an evil-smelling tallow candle showed that within reach they might share a chamber pot for the necessary and a beaker of water, but there was nothing to eat.

Sheridan supposed that a certain member of parliament must be thanked for providing the night's accommodation, but at this precise moment his thoughts were consumed with how best he might exact a dire vengeance against the Independent member for Lewes for his contribution to the charade.

The charade. It did not feel such at the moment. And yet it had been Sheridan's suggestion to have the prince arrested and imprisoned in the Tower. Sir Roderick had leapt at the notion and assured him that all might be arranged. With remarkable alacrity, Sheridan mused wryly. During the disturbance at the track, Sheridan simply had to guide the prince into his own carriage and suggest a back route to avoid the crowds teeming from the races.

If His Royal Highness should ever discover the part played by Sheridan, he doubted that any forgiveness would be forthcoming. And to think that he had sacrificed an invitation to frolic with Marceline LeClaire. He sighed. Instead, here he was, shackled by the wrist and stewing in this abysmal condition for some three or four hours. Meanwhile, the Prince of Wales was becoming increasingly petulant and morose.

'What the deuce is happening here, Sherry? Do they mean to ransom me? Why have we not yet been found?' he wailed. 'Surely my absence has long been noted and there must be a hue and cry throughout the county? The dragoons must be called out from their barracks. And where is that man Townsend? I shall want to know the reason for the delay. These rogues that have subjected me to this unpardonable treatment shall hang, every last one!'

'Perhaps it is some prank, sir,' Sheridan offered lightly.

'Prank? You call this usage a prank, Sherry?'

'I only consider that if this were some act of tomfoolery on the part of say, your brother York, or ... or ... that jackanapes Hanger, then we might all be laughing into our cups at any moment, sir.'

'You are trying to cheer my spirits, are you not? That is kind of you, I am sure. You never do take any matter seriously — it is your nature, Sherry. It is the sort of prank you might devise, only more cruel, I think, than you are capable. And of course you are here also, incarcerated in this —' the prince pulled a grimace of disgust — 'cesspit. If this is some piece of foolery, Sherry, I feel it strains all capacity for hilarity.'

Sheridan's ears pricked. He was certain that he heard footsteps on the stair. He held up his hand.

'Do you hear, sir? Someone comes. We should pretend to be the most merry of fellows, and then might we not have the last laugh?'

'And how should I laugh, tell me that?' the prince grunted.

Sheridan took a breath and gathered his wits. With a dramatic flourish of the hand, which jangled his shackles, he launched into verse.

'You must know of that pisspot called Sherry
Fond of grape, brandy, malt and hop-berry...'

He paused momentarily for further inspiration.

'He consumed by the gallon
From boudoir to salon
And was caught all at once Necessary.'

The corner of the prince's mouth twitched and he let slip a reluctant chuckle. Sheridan took the cue to continue; perhaps something a little more ribald would tickle His Royal Highness.

'You have heard of a scoundrel named Sherry
Who was known to be damnably merry
He once took a fancy
To a maid name of Nancy
Now her cheeks flame as bright as a berry!'

The prince smirked. 'Cheeks — damn you; we should all know what you might mean!'

There was a sound at the door. Sheridan hastened into another rhyme in the same vein.

'A well-endowed devil named Sherry
Was known to be quite mercenary
He found at her ease
A young girl he would please
And left with the gift of her cherry.'

'Devil take you, Sherry!' The prince guffawed loudly and slapped his thigh.

A key rattled in the lock. After some moments, the heavy oak door began to creak open. A huge, broad-beamed man filled the doorway, his face shrouded by an executioner's hood. A flaming torch was placed in a sconce. Three shadowy figures entered and the door clanged shut behind them. Each was robed in a floor-length scarlet gown, faced with grey taffeta and girdled by a black cincture. On their heads each wore a full bottom wig, but their identities were obscured by masks which covered eyes and nose.

The prince continued to snort into his sleeve and the sight of the masked judges only increased his mirth.

'Damn you, York — is this your notion?' he spluttered.

'Something amuses you, sir?' The man at the centre addressed himself solemnly to the Prince of Wales.

Not recognising this voice, His Royal Highness peered at the robed men on either side. 'Game's up, brother. I know your foolery. Show yourself.'

No response came.

The prince's laughter became uneasy and subsided into a heavy silence which fell upon the room.

The judge to the left spoke in the sonorous tones of an older man. 'We are convened in the arraignment of George Augustus Frederick, Prince of Wales on the charge that he did commit an act of treason.'

The judge on the right continued. 'And did treasonably consort with divers parties against the person of His Majesty the King and this great nation.'

'How do you plead?'

The prince scanned the men before him. 'Not York then, eh?' He clapped his hands and wagged a finger. 'Unless he has put you up to this performance? What? He has his ear to the door?'

'Again, must we ask: how do you plead, sir?'

The prince held up his shackles with irritation. 'Enough. The jest is all sour. I command that you unchain me at once.'

'I would second that, sirs, damnably uncomfortable,' Sheridan interposed, pulling a piece of straw from his hair and twirling it between his fingers.

'Sir, you have heard the charge. It is treason. That can never be a matter for mirth.'

'These masks —' His Royal Highness waved a hand in their direction. 'If you act with authority, then why should you hide yourselves? Tell me that!' Pleased with the sagacity of this point, the Prince of Wales' eyes gleamed brightly. 'This is all some ridiculous charade, and when I discover who has devised it —'

The robed figures remained stock-still.

The prince presented an attitude of exaggerated disbelief. 'As if the Prince of Wales should be arrested and — and —'

'Brought to the Tower, sir,' the chief amongst the judges completed with a thin smile.

'Quite.' He harrumphed, glancing about the bare stone walls with distaste.

'We are instructed to acquaint His Royal Highness with the charges against him.'

'By whom?'

'The True Friends of Albion.'

The Prince of Wales flinched.

Sheridan leapt to his feet and surged forward, as far as his shackles would allow. 'Are we not True Friends of Albion, sir? I should like to see the man who suggests otherwise!'

'You are an Irishman, are you not, Mr Sheridan?' the judge countered with a sneer.

Sheridan did not like the tone of the fellow's voice; there was a cutting edge to it. 'And proudly so, as are many of my fellows who serve His Majesty and the nation at Westminster.'

The judge allowed himself a slight smirk and then turned once more to the prince.

'Should His Royal Highness acknowledge his error, demonstrate his remorse and contrition —'

'Contrition! Egad. Do you hear this, Sherry?'

'— then His Majesty the King might be spared learning of the full extent of his heir's transgression. The scandal and humiliation of a public trial might be avoided.'

The prince snorted. 'Trial? The devil. What are the grounds?'

The older judge produced a rolled-up paper from his pocket and waved it above his head. 'Do you deny, sir, that you have put your name to this bond? A document which speaks of the death of the king, your father, His Majesty King George the Third?'

The prince paled. 'That is a forgery, a damnable forgery,' he exclaimed, but the spirit was gone from his protest, for he knew, forgery or not, that such a bond had indeed existed.

'Do you deny having signed such a document?' the judge pressed. 'Or that Your Royal Highness continues to connive with a foreign prince to mortgage the Crown Lands of this Great Nation?' The bond was unfurled.

'As a consequence of dissolute and debauched pursuits,' the man on the right contributed with disdain.

'This is an outrage!' the Prince of Wales floundered.

The chief judge drew himself up. 'We are minded that you have been led astray, Your Royal Highness, by those you would keep company with.' The judge inclined his head towards Sheridan.

Sheridan blinked. All eyes were now trained on him.

'Perverse and devious radicals at home and abroad who have supported rebellion and revolution first in the Americas and now in France and may yet be plotting insurrection nearer to hand, in Ireland and closer yet — within the borders of England.'

Sheridan stiffened with sudden dread; the spotlight of this inquisition had all too rapidly and unexpectedly turned. Was this part of the ruse? Had Howgill seized an opportunity to trap Sheridan himself? Had he been proffered a traitor's kiss?

'You know the punishment for treason, Mr Sheridan?'

He knew it all too well. Every man did. It was to be hung, drawn and quartered. And the last man to suffer such a fate — for correspondence with the French — had been but nine years previous. The execution site was along the coast at Southsea. It was reported that after the unfortunate Tyrie had been interred, a mob of sailors, not content with the normal quartering, had dug him up and sliced him into a thousand pieces for their grisly amusement and as souvenir.

'I am no traitor.'

'You have spoken loudly in support of revolution, Mr Sheridan —'

'Against tyranny, sir. I have spoken out against tyranny.'

'And the Irish Volunteers?'

Sheridan was momentarily left speechless as their eyes locked. He should imprint those insolent and calculating orbs in the recesses of his memory, and should this actor ever come looking for an opportunity at Drury Lane, then he would take great pleasure in giving the audacious fellow short shrift — but only after he had made him audition as Caliban and crawl about the floor.

The chief judge turned once more to the Prince of Wales in a conciliatory manner. 'It is our humble opinion, sir, that you are in need of wiser counsel.'

The prince bristled. 'You do not imagine, sir, that I pay any heed to Sherry, here?' He shuffled uncomfortably before he continued blithely, 'A mere player's son?'

The slight cut Sheridan to the quick.

'The True Friends of Albion only offer advice, sir,' the judge pronounced pointedly. 'Our sole purpose here tonight is to avert catastrophe. To forestall the charge of treason which might be occasioned by these ill-advised financial dealings with foreigners.'

Again, the bond was waved ominously in the air.

'In these dangerous times, His Royal Highness might judiciously reaffirm that he is first and foremost a patriot.'

At this point the second judge presented the tome which he clasped in front of him. It was a King James bible.

'You would not baulk, sir, at taking an oath of allegiance to His Majesty King George?'

Sheridan could see that the prince did indeed baulk even as his hand reached out towards the proffered bible.

CHAPTER THIRTY-FOUR

The following afternoon, Sheridan emerged from a troubled sleep and went at once in search of Howgill. He found him rehearsing the musicians who had arrived to accompany the harlequinade.

'Ah, Mr Sheridan, you are abroad at last.' The young fop bowed with a welcoming smile.

'Damn and blast you, Howgill. A word, if you please.'

Sir Roderick excused himself to the musicians. 'If you will pardon me, gentlemen, our esteemed producer —'

Sheridan grabbed Howgill's coat sleeve and dragged him out of earshot.

'Producer? And in whose production did I perform last night, pray?'

Howgill examined his nails, which were perfectly manicured. 'You will agree, I feel sure, Mr Sheridan, that our event needed to convince a certain party of the right course of action. I don't doubt that your contribution was a most natural performance. I merely wished to guarantee that you would play your part with the utmost conviction —'

'Conviction? I damn near was convicted.'

'— and prove persuasive.'

'I was accused of treachery.'

Howgill raised an eyebrow. 'But did we not succeed in our objective?'

'The means do not always justify the ends, sir.'

Howgill inclined his head in apology. 'I pray you will pardon me, Sheridan. If it is any comfort, personally, I have no doubts as to your loyalty to the Crown.'

Sheridan glared at Sir Roderick. 'I do not need your judgement or recommendation, Howgill.'

'Don't suppose you do.'

Sheridan was about to turn away when a question occurred to him which he hoped Howgill might answer, being on the back foot.

'One puzzlement I have, which I wish you would answer.'

'Ask your question and if it is politick, I shall.'

'At Vauxhall Gardens, you met with Monsieur Danton in the woods — I cannot but imagine the rendezvous was pre-arranged.'

'Ah, you observed our little tête-à-tête? I had thought to be more discreet.' Howgill smiled wryly. 'Sherry, I do believe you might have the makings of a spy.' Then he added with pointed amusement, 'Would you consider it?'

'I have had quite enough of deceit lately, thank you.'

'Well, let me see … you may keep a secret, I think? I am sure I can rely on you. For one, you would not wish the prince to hear any insinuation as to your involvement in last night's caper. He would not "see the joke", I imagine.'

'I can be trusted.'

Then, for a passing moment, Sheridan caught sight of the gravitas which lurked beneath Sir Roderick's foppish veneer.

'I have been charged to open negotiations with Monsieur Danton.'

'For Pitt?'

'We shall meet again tomorrow morning — a chance encounter as we both admire the display of fish in the market near the Old Ship Inn; I hear that Monsieur Danton is rather partial to a species of shark that is to be found in our waters.'

'I rather suspect that it is Monsieur Danton himself who is the shark to be found in our waters.'

So, the government was reaching out to the foremost Jacobin — a communication which Mr Pitt should certainly not want broadcast.

'To what end?'

'To save the life of Louis.'

Sheridan started with surprise. He had expected Pitt might try to tempt Georges Danton into the role of informer with attractive promises of remuneration, but this signalled dealings of another order entirely.

'And his family, of course,' Howgill went on. 'Austria would insist on the inclusion of their sister, Marie Antoinette.'

'You think the jeopardy is real? What of the constitution which the Assembly in Paris draws up even as we speak?'

'Exactly. It is a piece of paper. Who really believes that the people of France want Louis as their king? Constitutional or otherwise. Their tolerance has been stretched to breaking point by his attempted escape in June. Our Majesty King George fears for his royal brother's safety. If the French make one change, why not another?'

'The Duc d'Orléans?' Sheridan posited as nonchalantly as he could.

'The very thought of that libertine scoundrel on the throne of France appals His Majesty, as you would no doubt surmise, but the king is advised that it is a case of better the devil you know than the one you do not. The notion that royal heads could roll, that is the concern which keeps His Majesty awake at night. He recalls all too well the fate of Charles I in the last century.'

'And so, Pitt hints that he supports an abdication in favour of the duc? And you keep a close eye on the Orléans camp... Meanwhile, His Majesty's government would barter with the Jacobin devil?'

Howgill nodded curtly.

'Where would poor Louis go?'

'The Americas.'

That rather took Sheridan aback as well, but he could then immediately see the sense of it: it was somewhere far enough away that the abdicated king should not pose any threat as a rallying point for the counter-revolution. And it was a country which still held Louis in esteem for the support the French monarch had provided for their own revolution.

'You have been busy, Howgill.'

Sir Roderick's eyes glittered darkly. 'There, you have hit the mark!'

Sheridan blinked. He almost had to look twice, but yes, there he was — that devilish highwayman. What a performance — he must give Howgill credit for that.

Sir Roderick turned from Sheridan and bowed extravagantly low towards Marceline, who had appeared at the threshold of the salon.

'Ah Baronne… *If I could write the beauty of your eyes*
And in fresh numbers number all your graces
The age to come would say —'

Marceline strode across the room and poked Howgill with her parasol. '*This poet lies*! And I will brook no contradiction; enough of your Shakespeare, Sir Roderick. You know I will not be flattered. And certainly not by dissembling poets,' she added with vehemence.

Sheridan pinked; the barb could only be meant for him. Marceline had very deliberately avoided looking toward him as she crossed the salon and now pointedly showed him the elegant curve of her back as she took Howgill's arm and steered him towards the quintet, who were playing snatches of the composition which had been chosen for the harlequinade.

'How are my musicians?'

Marceline pressed herself close to Howgill's side. Sheridan felt a sharp stab of envy. Their heads came together in a whispered intimacy and the peals of laughter which ensued reached Sheridan as an assault. What was he to do to make amends? Or was all lost? Well, there was little he could do at this present juncture to rescue his cause. He was dismissed. He turned on his heel and walked rapidly to the door.

So preoccupied was Sheridan with the sorry state of his *affairs amour* that he stepped straight into the path of Nathaniel Parker Forth, almost knocking that gentleman off his feet, for he too was proceeding down the corridor with some alacrity.

Sheridan reached out clumsily to the staggering agent. 'Mr Parker Forth —'

Parker Forth steadied himself and scowled at Sheridan.

'My most heartfelt apologies, sir. You see before you a blundering buffoon. I should look where I go.'

'So you should, Sheridan.'

'You are in haste; let me not detain you.'

Parker Forth heaved a sigh and looked abject. 'In truth, I am not rushing toward, sir, but rather I am hurrying away, and you must pardon my ill humour.'

'Ah, something has distressed you? I am sorry to hear it.'

'I had a most pressing meeting arranged with His Royal Highness and now I am informed that he is abed and indisposed — for which, of course, he naturally has my solicitude,' Parker Forth hastened to add. He then continued with a sigh which signalled his incomprehension. 'But the prince conveys that he shall not be disposed to meet with me at any time in the foreseeable.'

Sheridan regarded the aggrieved man sympathetically. So, the scare had worked. The Prince of Wales was minded to abandon his negotiations for financial assistance from the Duc d'Orléans. He felt a wave of relief.

'Most aggravating. You have undoubtedly been supremely industrious on His Royal Highness' behalf and now find your business thwarted.'

Parker Forth frowned at Sheridan's apparent acuity.

Sheridan lowered his voice. 'I have often found His Royal Highness to be contrary. Apt to change his mind,' he offered confidentially. 'Other than that, the prince is the most genial companion.'

'The foremost gentleman of the land,' Parker Forth concurred, but still with some trace of annoyance.

Sheridan patted Parker Forth on the back. 'Will you join me in a stroll, my dear sir? The sea air might revive our spirits, for I confess that mine have also been dealt a severe blow. And if chance favours us, I may introduce you to a Mrs Gimmell and she will tell you your future. She is remarkably adept.'

'Thank you, Sheridan, you are most sympathetic; another time, perhaps, and I don't think my future bears contemplation at the moment.'

Sheridan watched as the agent scurried away — he felt sure that Parker Forth would not be out of the Prince of Wales' favour for long. His Royal Highness would always have a use for such a man.

Prince George did not emerge to join the party that evening and a subdued atmosphere prevailed amongst the guests assembled in the salon. Sheridan found the conversation lacklustre and banal. He felt reluctant to entertain the gathering with forced bonhomie, nor could he summon the energy to join the tables of whist. Marceline, when she arrived escorted by Sir Roderick and the chevalier, brought a refreshing burst of gaiety and laughter into the room, but she studiously avoided Sheridan despite the soulful looks which he cast in her direction.

He was all at once overcome by a general ennui. The adventures of the previous night had taken their toll and cost him dearly in the affections of the baroness. He felt inclined to proffer excuses to the company and retire early. This thought was scarcely formulated but Sheridan acted upon it. As he passed from the assembly, he ordered a bottle of brandy to be sent to his bedchamber. He might uncharacteristically enjoy his own company and recover some of his equilibrium.

Sheridan rummaged amongst his luggage and dug out the well-thumbed copy of Dryden's poetry with which he proposed to indulge his occasional taste for melancholy. Lingering a moment by the open window, he looked out on a canopy of stars in the warm night sky. The myriad twinkling lights in the heavens contributed to his wistful humour. How vast was God's creation and, he considered, how small his own place within the scheme of history? Should he leave a mark at all? Such thoughts, one upon another, led him to a tally of those who might sincerely miss him should he exist no more. It was a pitifully short list if he were candid. Of course, his notoriety should earn some passing acknowledgement and regard, but in truth a man died alone. And he might only feel less alone by virtue of the love he inspired. Love bestowed by friends and family. Sister, son, wife...

Eliza. Dear, sweet Eliza. Sheridan swallowed hard at the lump in his throat. How he had wronged her. Over and over. That she was now lost to him could be the fault of no one but himself. His shameful neglect. All his promises to her broken. The judges were right: he was a traitor — a traitor to the sacred vows of his marriage.

Sheridan felt a sudden stab of jealousy. Other men desired Eliza. Numerous men had laid siege to her heart. That great booby, the Duke of Clarence, for one. No matter for surprise. The years had not tarnished her beauty. Only now, after so many years of enduring his own philandering, she had succumbed. She had lain in the arms of another man. Edward Fitzgerald. A young man of soldierly bearing with large, soulful eyes framed by dark lashes — lashes which might be coveted by any courtesan. But Fitzgerald was no idle fop or preening macaroni; rather, he was a man of vigour and intelligence, in the fullness of his prime. He was the son of the Duke of Leinster. The young lord had declared his ardent love for Eliza, and she had given herself to him. The image assaulted Sheridan's senses. His wife in intimate communion with another man. The thought cut through to his heart. She must now love Fitzgerald as she had once loved him.

He suddenly had to sit down. His feelings were at war within — painfully so. Eliza knew the extent to which she risked her delicate health by the physical act and yet the young Irish lord had unleashed a passion which set aside all caution. For Fitzgerald she had not only risked her frail constitution but cast aside the vows and protection of marriage. The fruit of that communion would soon be all too evident. How easily might

Sheridan fling her off and no word of censure would he receive.

He would not, could not, do that. Fresh resolve took hold of him. Should Eliza survive the birth, as he prayed most fervently that she would, and the child live also, then he would behave not only as a father, but he might be a true husband again. This coming infant allowed him a chance to make all well in his marriage. He resolved that he should win Eliza's heart once more. She would know his devotion.

CHAPTER THIRTY-FIVE

Sheridan was half-dozing in the chair by the window, the Dryden anthology open on his lap, when a skittering of small stones against the windowpane startled him from his reverie. Had he imagined the sound? A bird on the window ledge? The hour must be late — the candle had burnt down almost to the wick. He stretched his stiffened limbs. He must put himself to bed. And then again, there was a dash of pebbles at the window. Someone wanted his attention.

Perplexed, he rose and leant out the window, but could discern nothing on the path or the lawn. Sheridan frowned. He had heard something; of that he was certain. Was this some schoolboy prank? Hanger or Howgill? They had seen the curtains still undrawn, the candlelight flickering at the window.

'Go to bed,' he mumbled to no one in particular. 'I have had enough of japes lately.'

Sheridan took a deep breath of the fragrant summer night and was about to retreat into his chamber when a figure emerged from the bushes below his window and stepped into the moonlight.

'Sherry,' a light voice whispered.

It was a boy in breeches and jerkin, a soft felt cap pulled over his brow. Sheridan strained to make out his features. What the devil did he want? Was he some messenger from Howgill? And be damned with the familiarity. Then the lad began to shin up the drainpipe which ran alongside Sheridan's room and, looking upward, the impertinent youth grinned puckishly.

No boy!

It was Marceline whose short black curls Sheridan now discerned beneath the cap. Her beauty was not entirely disguised by the smudge on her nose or the easy swagger of her climb. Sheridan had scarcely digested this astonishing turn of events when a man hurtled from the shadows and jumping upward, made a grab at Marceline's ankle in an attempt to yank her back down to the ground. Startled, she kicked out and yelped with dismay, clinging with desperation to the drainpipe and then pulling herself further out of reach.

'Get down here, yer poxy thief!'

John Townsend, who had a care for the security of the prince, had woken to his duty. Most assiduously, so it would appear. Clearly, he had felt humiliated by his own shortcomings during the disturbance at the racetrack and now sought to redeem himself in the opinion of the heir to the throne by catching a burglar single-handed.

With alarm, Sheridan saw Townsend grab at the drainpipe with the intention of pursuing the intruder.

'Get down here or I'll break both yer legs for yer impudence!'

The Bow Street officer was surprisingly agile and in his next attempt succeeded in grasping a shoe. Marceline shook her foot with fierce determination and kicked free of her footwear. But it could not be long before Townsend would pull her to the ground and the force of the fall might cause serious injury. Townsend threw the shoe behind and managed to grab hold of Marceline's thrashing foot.

Sheridan had to act to avert disaster.

'Mr Townsend!' Sheridan called down with as much merriment in his voice as he could muster. 'I would you might have a care of my son's limbs!'

'Your son, sir?' Townsend called up with a puzzled frown.

'Do you not recognise my boy? It is Tom, Mr Townsend. He is ever full of mischief and see here — he thinks to surprise me with his entrance! But —' Sheridan wagged his finger at 'the youth' clutching the drainpipe — 'I am happily forewarned and have been lying in wait to box my son's ear!'

Townsend hesitated, then shook his head in chagrin and let go of the slender ankle. 'I should box it sound, Mr Sheridan, if I were you. The boy needs a good lesson — for if I had had my cutlass in hand, he might have lost the ear entire!'

'My midnight visitor shall be well taken care of, I can assure you, Mr Townsend. Tom bids you goodnight and apologies for disturbing the peace of this house, do you not, my boy?'

Marceline gruffed her voice and made murmurings of apology.

Sheridan bit his lip to suppress the grin which threatened to break across the serious composure of his features.

Townsend grunted and turned away into the dark shadows of the night to continue his patrol.

Marceline hurriedly clambered up the remaining distance to be unceremoniously tugged into the bedchamber by Sheridan. Collapsing onto the floor, the baroness allowed herself to explode in a fit of giggles.

Sheridan put a finger to his lips, urging her to be quiet. But, after her narrow escape, the lady now seemed altogether unconcerned that she should be discovered.

'Marceline, what the devil do you do here? And in this disguise?'

'I have decided to forgive you, *mon* Sherrie.'

'That is very gracious, but —'

'Roddy has taken your part and informs me that your absence last night must all be laid at the door of His Royal Highness.'

'And did he tell you the reason?'

'No, but I am sure it is an entertaining story. I am, how do you say, *all ears*!' She flicked her ears for emphasis.

'I am not at liberty — indeed, I have almost lost my liberty in truth.'

'Affairs of state?' Her eyes brightened with interest.

'In a manner.'

'How very intriguing. Paris is full of intrigue; there are spies simply everywhere. Under every table, hanging from the rafters, swinging from the chandeliers, dropping from the eaves.'

'I think you may find that we have our fair share of eavesdropping and espionage on this side of the Channel also, my dear Marceline.'

'Do you consider, perhaps, I may be a spy?' Marceline asked coyly.

'Are you, Baronne?'

Marceline laughed and then adopted a serious expression. 'I think I should be a very good spy, Sherrie. Every bit as good as your Mrs Elliott.'

Sheridan shook his head and smiled wryly; the Scottish courtesan who resided in Paris as a mistress of the Duc d'Orléans was often rumoured to act as a government agent for Mr Pitt.

'Are you jealous, Marceline? I rather suspect Grace Elliott started those rumours herself, for effect. One moment, please —'

Sheridan stooped to look under the bed and then began to search behind the drapes and the larger pieces of furniture.

'No sign of the chevalier as yet — that is one blessing.' He ventured finally to the door of the chamber and flung it open swiftly, as though to catch an eye or an ear bent at the keyhole.

He turned back to Marceline and whispered, 'It seems that I am not under surveillance.' He closed the door gently. 'I am almost offended.'

'*Incroyable*, monsieur!' Marceline concurred. 'I always believed you to be at the heart of your nation's intrigues. I have been told that you are a paramount schemer, *mon* Sherrie.'

'Who tells you that?'

Marceline shrugged elegantly. 'You are a friend of the prince, and he is always scheming. I have seen the duc's agent, Monsieur '*Back and Forth*' — *alors*, he is most certainly a spy, *mon ami*.'

Sheridan wondered momentarily if the baroness knew about the financial negotiations and the treasonous bonds — the matter could be common knowledge amongst the duc's inner circle. They might laugh into their sleeves at the pickle His Royal Highness found himself in. The prince did very well to be out of the whole business.

'And am I to expect another challenge from your cousin, the chevalier?'

Marceline placed her hands on Sheridan's shoulders. 'We are quite alone, I can assure you. My cousin has his own rendezvous tonight.'

'He confides everything to you, does he?'

'We have no secrets.'

'Secrets … ah yes, I am heartily sick of secrets myself.'

'You may be honest with me, Sherrie,' Marceline suggested tenderly as she stroked his cheek.

Sheridan looked at the young woman in front of him. Perhaps it was the boyish disguise which made him hesitate to clasp her in his arms. Her short curls, her smudged nose and cheeks — all of this accentuated her youth. What was she? A married woman of twenty? Twenty-one? And yet she seemed at this moment like a child playing a game. She liked to take risks, was thrilled by danger. He had a flash of that moment when Marceline had directed her arrow at Orléans.

He took a handkerchief from his pocket, tipped his tongue to it, and wiped the dirt from her nose and cheeks.

'For a moment, you had me fooled by your breeches disguise, Marceline.'

Marceline grinned triumphantly. 'No one notices a boy — I have often wandered the streets of Paris quite freely and unrecognised.'

'You will return there shortly?'

'Yes, very soon.' Her violet eyes blazed.

He nodded, sadly.

'But let us not think of tomorrow — or the future,' she insisted.

Sheridan took her hands in his and sighed. 'Oh, Marceline…'

She gazed at him with concern. 'Something troubles you, *mon Sherrie?*'

Sheridan shook his head, not in denial, but in an attempt to shake off the melancholy which still lurked beneath the surface of his mind.

'Come,' she said kindly, 'let us sit.'

Marceline led him over to the bed and they sat, side by side. It was she who this time took his hand in hers.

'I am so afraid…' He spoke so quietly that Marceline leaned closer to hear him. He squeezed her hand. Why had he voiced his inner dread? What had prompted him to divulge so much? Here was one of the most beautiful women of the age, who had come to his chamber in search of romance — what sort of bloody fool was he?

'Speak with me, *mon cher*. I will listen…'

He hesitated a moment and then with some perverse fit determined to be honest. 'You are everything any man could desire, Marceline... I am greatly honoured by your favour, truly, but...'

'But?' she prompted gently.

'My wife...'

Marceline's eyes widened. 'Your wife?'

The sight of Eliza as he had last beheld her, fragile and pale, had haunted him all through the evening and that image now assailed him with even greater force.

'I fear that I may lose her...'

Marceline frowned, perplexed by this declaration.

'...and the child she bears.'

There. He had spoken his anxiety aloud. He had given voice to a truth. In doing so, he knew that he had scuppered all possibility of a tryst with this dazzling creature sitting so close beside him in the privacy of his own chamber. And yet he felt glad.

'Your wife is with child? Oh, *mon cher*...' Marceline crooned.

His feeling welled up within him and Sheridan shook with the silent sobs of a grief that seemed inevitable. If he were to lose Eliza, then the man he knew he once was, that better part of himself, might too be lost irretrievably, leaving only a vacuous shell.

It seemed an age before Sheridan found that he lay on his bed, with Marceline at his side, stroking his head. Her soothing words gave way to a lullaby sung in French, and then at some point he slipped into sleep.

CHAPTER THIRTY-SIX

When Sheridan was ushered into the Prince of Wales' bedchamber the following morning, the younger man was still lying in bed, picking at a plate of pastries in a desultory fashion. The two men eyed each other for a moment with some uncertainty.

Sheridan gave a cursory bow. 'I bid you good morning, Your Royal Highness. I trust you make a fulsome recovery.'

'Sherry…' The prince affected bonhomie and nodded to his valet to vacate the bedchamber.

'You wished to see me, sir? Can I be of service?' Sheridan regarded his feet and continued under his breath, but loud enough to be heard, 'Being "a mere player's son", perhaps I might perform a jig?'

'Sherry…' the prince whined in a pleading voice.

'Or sing a ditty? "The Lass of Richmond Hill", which you are reputed to have composed, should be a favourite I'd hazard,' Sheridan offered with a touch of sarcasm whilst avoiding the searching eye of the prince.

'Sherry, my dear friend…'

'Friend, sir?'

'None dearer to me.' The prince patted the coverlet to indicate that Sheridan might sit on the bed beside him.

Sheridan pretended not to have noticed the invitation.

'We have both been sorely abused, Sherry,' the prince insisted. 'Any offence was wholly unintended. A ploy, you understood. Thought those beastly devils were going to string you up there and then if they imagined you my chief advisor.'

'So, I am reduced to the role of a court jester.'

'Damn it, Sherry — you know your worth to me.'

Sheridan blinked back the sudden tears which pricked at his eyes.

'I rely on you, Sherry.' The prince put his plate aside and regarded Sheridan with a rare sincerity. 'No man knows my heart as you do.'

'I have only sought to serve you and our great country.'

'I know, I know … though I will own there is no finer wit in the land,' the prince flattered in an attempt to lighten the too sombre mood.

'Some men may appear the statesman but are fools, whilst I may act the clown but am —'

'The very epitome of sagacity!' the prince concluded, and patted the coverlet again.

This time, Sheridan found himself succumbing to the invitation.

'Damnable business, Sherry. Believe me, if ever I should discover who these men are that have the impudence to call themselves True Friends of Albion, I shall not be held responsible for the consequences.'

From beneath his pillow the prince drew out a sheet of paper in an all too familiar hand.

Sheridan frowned. 'They have sent another?'

'Hark at this!' The prince proceeded to read aloud:

'*Sir,*
The True Friends of Albion congratulate His Royal Highness on his splendid
   show of patriotism!

The prince slapped the paper. 'Pah! As if that should ever be in question.' He read on:

'We trust that the prince has been reminded where his DUTY lies. A prince must be wary of the many snakes which lurk in the grass…'

Was that a poke at him, Sheridan wondered, as well as at Orléans?

'I should say it is these so-called Friends that have behaved as snakes in the grass. And so on and so on in the same tedious vein.' The prince refolded the missive. 'We shall say no more on the matter, Sherry. Our incarceration shall be entirely forgotten.'

'Quite right, sir. I am only too eager to erase the whole night from my memory as a bad dream.'

'Here, take this damnable doggerel and burn it to a crisp.'

'It shall be dust.' Sheridan stuffed the letter into his pocket.

'Bad dream, eh? I find the best cure for a nightmare to be a bottle of champagne — what do you say, Sherry? Shall I send out for one at once?'

'One, sir?'

The prince laughed. 'Did I say one? Quite right, Sherry; it shall be two — or three?' He slapped his great thigh.

'As you wish, sir. Let us raise the flag before breakfast.'

That morning Sheridan also received a letter, one which gladdened his heart. Josiah Legge had written to reiterate his heartfelt thanks for everything which Sheridan had done for his son. Timothy was now past the danger of infection and was able to sit up. He had been taken out into the gardens of the hospital in a bath chair for a brief perambulation. He was a strong youth and the surgeon, Mr Cline, whilst urging a restraint of hope, was ever more cheerful about his progress.

Sheridan responded with his own effusive optimism, his head still a little light and frothy from the champagne breakfast. He was reminded of that other business which was afoot, the matter of that young scallywag, Billy. It should be a great relief for Sheridan to return him into Timothy's care. All being well, Billy might soon be released from Battling Poll's clutches.

The remainder of the day was taken up with the preparations for the performance of *The Two Harlequins*, scheduled as the main event of the evening's entertainment. As the company gathered, all was frantic industry. The stage was being set by a team of carpenters. The painted backdrops were secured: scenes of a sun-drenched Brighton town. Stagehands scurried about with swathes of drapery and green branches to decorate arbours and entrance arches.

The Duc d'Orléans arrived late as usual with the Comtesse de Buffon on his arm and his entourage in train. Marceline bounded over to draw His Serene Highness away from his comely mistress and to take command of his rehearsal, for he had made little effort to learn any of his lines thus far.

'That precocious minx quite has Orléans wrapped about her little finger,' Lady Lade opined in Sheridan's ear. 'How the devil did she persuade him into the part of an old man?'

'Or to perform at all. Being stiff as a poker, it is not his natural bent,' Sheridan sneered. He had wondered at Marceline's determination to secure the duc for their theatricals, the French royal's talent for the stage being so questionable. But he supposed it must be considered as something of a coup for the young baroness, a flagrant demonstration of her influence. De Buffon should need to have a care that she was not soon usurped in Orléans' affections. Sheridan felt a stab of jealousy. Did Marceline really mean to ensnare the duc? Had he always been nothing more than a dalliance? An additional feather in her cap?

'I suppose the role of Gerontes is not the usual cuckolded buffoon,' Lady Lade mused. 'The character does acquit himself with dignity and with some honour at the finale.'

'I daresay the Duc d'Orléans would welcome being considered a Man of Honour.'

'The reality should remain to be seen. I've always considered the duc a blaggard and have told him to his face.'

Sheridan grinned. 'As only you could have the gall to do so, Laetitia. No man is safe from the lashing of your tongue!'

'You do well to remember that yourself, Sherry.' Lady Lade poked him with her elbow before setting off to welcome the comtesse.

Sheridan found Sir Roderick at his side.

'She is really quite a marvel, don't you think?'

'Who? Laetitia?'

'Lady Lade? Of course, always splendidly colourful, but I refer to another.' Howgill sighed somewhat longingly.

'The baroness?'

He nodded. 'You have bested me, Sheridan. I bow from the field.' Howgill lowered his voice. 'I saw the lady leave your room this morning, before the house was awake.'

'You spy on me, Howgill?' Sheridan turned sharply to the government man.

'Not at all, my dear fellow — simply an observation in passing as I dashed to my rendezvous at the fish market. And don't worry, madame did not see me — not that any fear of tittle-tattle would temper the lady's actions, she is so devil-may-care.'

Sheridan sighed in turn. 'I would not be so hasty in your retreat from the field, Howgill.'

Sir Roderick eyed Sheridan with curiosity.

'I find I may still be in love with my wife.'

Howgill smiled and patted his shoulder. 'Now there's a thing! I always knew you to be a man of feeling, Sheridan, be it ever so fleeting.'

'How was the shark?'

'Slippery creature. You are just thinking that you may have hooked the rogue and then the line goes slack.'

'It is those teeth which I find so damnably alarming.'

'But my expedition was not altogether fruitless, Sheridan,' Howgill concluded enigmatically.

Prince George was returned to his usual high spirits, Sheridan was pleased to observe. The terrors and anxieties of the preceding days were all cast to one side. The Prince of Wales wanted only entertainment and play at the Marine Pavilion and all were determined to provide it.

Nathaniel Parker Forth was notable by his absence from the luncheon table. Sheridan sat next to the Comtesse de Buffon and learned from her that the agent had been called away to business elsewhere. That should be his excuse, Sheridan mused, although he did not doubt that Parker Forth had his fingers in a great many pies.

'He is a man of trade, of course.' The comtesse dismissed the agent with hauteur. She suddenly regarded Sheridan. 'I have always considered the arts and the theatre a higher calling, though I daresay it is a commerce too.'

'We make shift, madame,' Sheridan responded with a small smile, despairing that he should always be reminded of his dependence on business.

'My cousin considers you the most perfect gentleman, monsieur. She told me as much this morning.'

The remark brought a genuine smile to Sheridan's face.

'Marceline, poor girl, married off to a decrepit when she was barely sixteen. No other option — her family's fortunes have been in decline since they were exiled from Versailles. Thankfully, her husband already has an heir, so at least the poor girl has been spared that obligation. I took pity, monsieur — her talents were quite wasted in the provinces. I do so admire Marceline's spirit; she is a creature of passion, rather like myself.'

Sheridan concurred politely. He eyed Marceline across the luncheon table. She did indeed look full of a *joie de vivre*. The baroness was describing an encounter with a fortune teller on the beachfront. The prince laughed with delight at her vivid storytelling.

'An absolute crone!' Marceline screwed up her face. 'I fancied I was in *Macbeth*, sire. *Double, double, toil and trouble!*'

'And did the old witch say you should be a queen?'

'She did, in fact, say that I should be foremost amongst my brethren, a leader of men.'

'Egad!'

'I should say the lady leads men by the nose,' Mrs Fitzherbert interjected from her seat at the prince's right side.

'The hag gave me a warning, Your Royal Highness, as all good soothsayers should — I must *beware the hog*.'

'And who should that be?' the prince tittered. 'There are any number of boars in our party, and not just of the swinish variety; bores — d'you get me?'

'Most droll, sire.'

The violet of the young Frenchwoman's eyes flashed as she caught Sheridan's stare. He felt a moment of deep regret. How had he been such a fool as to decline her favours? Yet, it appeared she thought the better of him for it. What a quandary.

The Two Harlequins got off to a resounding start. Within minutes the assembled audience were in paroxysms of laughter. By the end of Act II Sheridan sensed that a triumph was imminent. During rehearsals he had appreciated that Marceline possessed a natural talent for the stage, but in front of an audience she was a true revelation. He had to be on his toes to match her for liveliness and sense of comic timing in every scene they played together. He reflected, with satisfaction, that they had managed to turn a hackneyed old pantomime into a fashionable satire. Sheridan even began to toy with the possibility of rehashing a version for the Drury Lane Theatre Company when they should take up residence at the King's Theatre in the autumn.

He sensed something else, too: a looseness gurgling through his entrails. He should not have eaten so much of the salmagundi for lunch, a favourite dish, and there had perhaps been a raw prawn somewhere in the mix. He should need the jakes at once. He had time. Lady Lade was about to enter for her solo scene as Marinetta. She was a rousing songstress, and she would no doubt embellish the ribald asides he had scripted in her inimitable fashion. She would fondle her oranges and the audience should take great delight in her teasing of Nell Gwyn's descendent, the bashful young Earl Burford. Laetitia would milk the audience for all it was worth and Sheridan would not be in the least surprised if she elicited an encore.

Then there should be all the comedy of the mistaken identity scene between Gerontes and Harlequin Junior before Sheridan's next entrance. He felt the urgent pressure of his bowels. Yes, he had time to reach the privy if he made a run for it, before the 'runs' should scupper him.

CHAPTER THIRTY-SEVEN

Returning from the jakes, Sheridan realised that he had left his slapstick beside the privy seat. There was not sufficient time to fetch it and be certain he would be on cue for his entrance. Damn and blast! Then a thought came to him as he passed the door of the small chamber which had been commandeered for costumes and props. He might find something there; a short riding whip would do. He hastened to the entrance and flung it open. Dresses and sundry outfits were either hung along a rail or flung over chairs. On a small table he could see a basket and a flagon, a large knapsack and a clump of artificial greenery. Perhaps there might be something amongst the pile he might use for comic effect.

Pulling his mask down about his neck to better see, Sheridan rummaged through the flotsam of items shipwrecked on the table. Nothing struck him as plausible. A pile of clothing was heaped in the corner of the room; perhaps there might be something underneath. As he threw the first dresses from the mound, Sheridan was startled to find Harlequin slumped underneath. Sir Roderick? Sheridan hurriedly swept the rest of the costumes aside. A fringe of powdered hair fell over the face of the masked man. A thin gush of blood appeared at the edge of his mouth and ran down his chin to drip onto the diamond-patterned costume.

With a surge of apprehension, Sheridan grasped the Harlequin's shoulder and his head lolled back to expose a thin, livid line about his neck. With mounting horror, he raised the disguise. His worst fears were realised. The young baronet had been strangled, garrotted. Sheridan was overcome with confusion. Was not Harlequin Junior even now on stage for the confrontation scene with old Gerontes? Along the corridor he could hear the play in progress. The Duc d'Orléans was loud in the role of the old man.

Sir Roderick's eyelids suddenly shot open. Startled, Sheridan leapt back. Howgill still lived. He must call for assistance at once, but before he could do so the young man's lips moved, struggling to make a sound.

Removing his hat, Sheridan squatted forward in an attempt to catch whatever it was that Howgill was trying to say — the name of his assailant?

'Who has done this, Howgill?'

Sir Roderick shook his head imperceptibly. 'Sss—ave,' escaped with a choked, sibilant sound.

'Or… Or…'

'Orléans?' Sheridan hazarded with equal urgency. 'Save Orléans?'

Howgill blinked slowly in acknowledgement. There was a soft, strangulated rattle and then the life slipped from his eyes forever.

For a moment Sheridan was frozen with disbelief. Howgill had been murdered. Orléans must be saved? There had been the utmost urgency in Howgill's message. He must save Orléans. But Orléans was at this moment performing on stage in front of a sizeable audience. From what or whom should Sheridan save him?

Harlequin!

If Howgill was not in Act III Scene Three, then who was? At the sound of a soft footfall, he turned to find Marceline standing in the doorway. She entered swiftly and silently, closing the door behind her.

Did she anticipate a snatched embrace, Sheridan wondered fleetingly?

'Marceline…' He stumbled to his feet, divesting himself of the theatrical mask entirely. 'It's Howgill — he's been murdered. I must get to the duc!'

'This is unfortunate,' Marceline whispered lightly. 'So unfortunate.'

'A little more than unfortunate! Come, we must —'

Marceline shook her head. 'No, *mon* Sherrie. You do not understand.' She regarded him with sorrowful eyes. 'How unfortunate this is for me.'

Did she not understand what he had just said? Sheridan moved to the edge of the table but was halted in his tracks. Seizing the handle of her colourful parasol, Marceline drew out a sharp, thin blade.

Sheridan's first thought was that here was Tom's very suggestion for an umbrella that should double as a weapon, save that in this instance it was a parasol. He should remember to tell Tom to include that addition in his patent.

The razor-sharp dagger flashed in his direction and Sheridan was brought back to the moment.

'Marceline?'

The baroness sighed softly. 'Such a pity, I wrote the scenario myself. Gerontes mistakes Harlequin Junior for the real Harlequin; they argue and come to blows. Gerontes collapses to the stage. The audience think it all part of the action.' Her eyes glittered. 'That is my conceit. Then, the chevalier, in the role of the Commissary, discovers the truth and cries foul murder on the Duc d'Orléans! He gives chase to the assassin who has fled from the stage.'

Sheridan paled as he began to understand the chicanery of the plot. 'Jack Champion is playing Harlequin…' he mouthed under his breath.

'The chevalier pursues the monster into this room, but he is cornered by the villain. The life of my heroic young cousin is in imminent danger. I chance on the scene.' Marceline struck a pose of horror. 'And, without any thought for my own safety, I grab the chain from my throat —' she fingered the chain around her delicate neck — 'and fling myself at the rogue's back.' She nodded towards the slumped figure in the corner of the room. 'You see the consequence. Sir Roderick, treacherous assassin of His Serene Highness, lies dead. A tragedy.'

'You have murdered Howgill.'

'Sir Roderick was a government agent. He knew that he played with fire.'

'Marceline, this madness must stop — let me get to the duc.'

She stamped her foot angrily. 'And now, you foolish, foolish man —' there was a catch in her voice, as though she might suddenly burst into tears — 'you force me to rewrite my play.' Marceline held up the blade with its fearsome point. 'But you shall be a hero, I promise, *my* hero. It will be that you also tried to stop Sir Roderick, and fought with the utmost courage.'

'Only to be fatally stabbed. Is that how you would write my end, Marceline?'

'As I have said, it is most unfortunate. But we must all make sacrifices for our greater cause.' She withdrew the pendant nestled in her bosom. As she clutched at the Huguenot Cross, her features set with determined resolve. She raised the dagger and took aim.

With deft anticipation which amazed even himself, Sheridan sidestepped and in the same movement snatched up the heavy knapsack from the table and swung it around towards

Marceline's head with all the force that he could muster. Even as he did so, the blade whistled past, missing him by the merest fraction, to thwang violently into the frame of a rather fine portrait by Van Dyke.

At the force of the blow from the knapsack, Marceline dropped to the floor with a gasp of surprise. Sheridan pushed past her and flung the door open wide. At the end of the hallway, coming from within the salon, he could hear the performance still in progress.

Sheridan hurled himself along the length of the corridor. There was still time, he prayed, to put an end to this murderous pantomime.

Up ahead, Orléans was declaiming as Gerontes. 'Hold, sirrah! You shall not … not…'

'Escape with my jewels,' the prompter urged.

'Escape with my jewels, *mon dieu*!'

And the response came: 'Let me go, you old rogue!'

Sheridan had a moment to admit that Champion mimicked Sir Roderick's foppish tones to perfection even as he realised how dangerously close the two characters were to the end of the scene.

'I'll pluck your beard to the last hair,' the false Harlequin continued.

'Thief! Villain!' Gerontes cried out. 'Help! Help!'

'You court your own misfortune,' Harlequin declared ominously.

Sheridan grasped the door handle and threw himself across the threshold into the screened area at the side of the stage. Red-faced and wheezing, he stumbled straight into the arms of the Chevalier de Saint-Gelais.

'Sheridan!' the chevalier hissed as he steadied the playwright. 'Are you drunk?'

On stage, Gerontes raised his fists against Harlequin Junior in the comic stance of a pugilist. 'Rogue! Hand over my jewels!'

'My cue, I think,' Sheridan spluttered.

'Here, you shall take payment!' Harlequin Junior approached the belligerent old man with menace.

Sheridan thrust the startled chevalier aside and catapulted across the stage, diving for the legs of the would-be assassin. The pair crashed loudly to the boards.

A startled audience whooped and cried out in amazement at this sudden dramatic turn of events. Those who knew the traditional harlequinade were taken aback and delighted by this unusual twist in the plot. But none were more surprised than His Serene Highness, the Duc d' Orléans.

'*Sacré bleu!*' the duc gulped as he staggered backwards, only to catch a heel on the hem of his outer robes and trip up onto his posterior.

Harlequin Junior twisted about to see who had brought him down. Sheridan caught the furious glare in the eyes behind the mask. Those same eyes had pierced him with their murderous intent in the Spitalfields attic. Handsome Jack. The man who had shot young Timothy Legge. An instant later, both men glanced towards the flashing blade which had skittered upstage. Champion kicked out viciously, catching Sheridan just above the groin. Steeling himself against the spasms of pain, Sheridan clutched desperately at the killer's torso and heaved his greater weight onto him in an effort to keep Jack from reaching the dagger. Blows rained down on Sheridan's head as Champion strained to retrieve his weapon.

'Devil take it!' Major Hanger cried out. 'What a show!'

Sheridan and Harlequin Junior rolled upstage as they tussled to gain the upper hand. Harlequin's cockaded hat was knocked from his head. Sheridan's outfit ripped at the shoulder as he pulled away and landed on top of the knife. He could feel the contours of the handle pressing into his back through the thin costume. Hands flailing, Sheridan grabbed at the killer's curls only to find a powdered wig, which came away to reveal the short, dark hair beneath. The audience must now realise that this was not Sir Roderick Howgill in the part of Harlequin Junior but some devilish imposter. Someone would surely come to his aid. But not a bit of it.

'Have at it, Sherry!' the prince encouraged.

'Tally-ho!' Sir John Lade concurred.

To his dismay, Sheridan saw that it was His Serene Highness who had staggered to his feet. Clearly sensing that something was very much awry, he was fast approaching the contest.

'Orléans!' he managed to cry out before Champion clasped his throat and began to throttle him. Frantically, Sheridan waved his free hand to shoo the French royal away. In doing so, he lost his grip on the would-be assassin and Jack found just enough leverage to reach beneath for the knife.

Sheridan closed his eyes. Was this to be his end?

An object whacked into the side of Jack's head, ricocheted and bounced onto the floorboards. Sheridan squinted an eye open in time to see another orange reaching its target. Jack Champion fell away, but in a moment, he had leapt to his feet, dagger in hand. Yet more oranges rained in his direction. Realisation flashed across Champion's furious features: it was all up for him; his cover was broken. He looked about for the one object of his mission. But the Duc d'Orléans had finally understood the danger and at that murderous glance he leapt from the stage into the lap of the Prince of Wales.

With a bellow of anguished frustration, the false Harlequin took exit stage right, waving the blade before him against any who might try to impede his escape.

Members of the audience were at last on their feet, crying out for the chase.

Sheridan sat up, groaning at the twinges of pain in his groin. Lady Lade stood over him with her basket, throwing and catching her one remaining orange.

'Good shot, Laetitia,' Sheridan managed to compliment, his throat hoarse from near strangulation.

'All those childhood years shying at the Aunt Sallies,' Lady Lade smirked. 'Who was that? It was not Howgill.'

'No. Poor Howgill is done for.'

Townsend had rushed to the scene backstage and, from the corner of his eye, Sheridan spotted the officer hastening out of the servant's door. He had been misdirected by the Chevalier de Saint-Gelais.

'The chevalier — he must not escape!' Sheridan squawked to a bemused Lady Lade.

He lurched awkwardly to his feet as Lady Lade hurled her last piece of fruit into the wings. The chevalier staggered a moment and clutched his head. He shot a glance at the stage. Lady Lade answered with a blasé shrug.

'Stop him!' Sheridan shouted.

The chevalier turned and fled into the hallway.

'Stop him!' Sheridan cried again as he threw himself into pursuit. Still shouting, he dashed through the door in time to see that De Saint-Gelais' retreat was blocked by members of the audience. Pushing to their head were the Prince of Wales and the Duc d'Orléans.

'I say, what the deuce is occurring, Chevalier?' His Royal Highness asked.

The chevalier drew forth his Commissary sabre and wheeled around and about.

Sheridan could read the confusion which flashed across his face. Should the young man persist with the plot to assassinate His Serene Highness — an undoubtedly suicidal act? Or should he turn about and take a chance of escape, with Sheridan as the only obstacle?

Sheridan paled as he realised that he himself had no weapon to hand. But to turn his coat tails in front of such an audience... He felt his own indecision reflected in the chevalier's desperate gaze.

'Saint-Gelais?' Orléans wailed with a plaintive comprehension at this betrayal of friendship.

With nonchalant bravado, Major Hanger stepped forward to place himself in front of the duc and addressed the young nobleman. 'Come, sir, you must drop your weapon. The play-acting is done now.' He sniffed at the rose in his buttonhole.

The chevalier turned frantically back towards Sheridan and made a step in that direction.

'The curtain falls, Chevalier.' Sheridan urged reason.

The chevalier took another three strides towards him, his face alive with fury. He flashed his sabre mere feet away, urging retreat.

Sheridan flinched. This was madness; he must run for cover at once.

Lady Lade appeared at his shoulder. 'No oranges left, I'm afraid, Sherry — but damned if I can't throw a low blow.' She clenched her fist in readiness.

Sheridan grinned. 'That should be enough to floor any man, Laetitia. By Jupiter, if I can't manage half your pluck!'

The Frenchman hesitated. Then he raised his weapon and drew a deep breath. Letting out a great roar, he made a half turn and hurled himself through one of the large windows which lined the hallway, glass shattering in his wake.

Sheridan rushed to the jagged hole in time to see De Saint-Gelais rolling and tumbling over the lawn some fifteen feet below. Winded, and clearly in pain, the young man staggered to his feet, clutching at his side. The last rays of sunlight sliced through the darkening trees and caught the withering look which he cast up to Sheridan. His face was streaked with blood, lending him a ghoulish aspect. The chevalier bowed and turned to head into the gloom and the cover which the narrow streets of Brighton might afford.

A figure rode out of the darkness towards him from that direction and brought the Frenchman up short. Sheridan could not contain a smile of relief as he recognised Constable Nicholls.

CHAPTER THIRTY-EIGHT

Mr Townsend had taken charge of the investigation. The hue and cry for Jack Champion was to be spread about the town and further afield into Sussex. All the parish constables and watchmen were alerted that there was a savage assassin attired in a diamond-patterned costume on the loose. Mr Townsend fumed. One of his own men had been stabbed as Champion had made good his escape from the grounds. It was only fortunate that the wound was superficial.

The news that Madame LeClaire was also a part of the devilish plot caused consternation amongst the guests at the Pavilion. The Duc d'Orléans regarded Sheridan with incensed amazement. 'That I have taken such a viper to my bosom! Who does she act for? That is what I wish to know.'

Despite the furore surrounding her disappearance, it was not considered seemly to put out a description of the baroness to the general public. She would be hunted down by other means.

The chevalier, however, had surrendered or rather collapsed into the custody of Constable Nicholls. A shard of glass had pierced the young man's side and the tip had wedged within. His Serene Highness would no doubt have liked to string De Saint-Gelais up without delay, but the doctor hastily called to attend Townsend's man was diverted to him on arrival. The chevalier was carried into a room off the kitchens and laid on a table for the medical man's inspection.

Constable Nicholls turned to Sheridan with a short bow. 'Sir, it seems I arrived too late to prevent the attack. I was sent post-haste by Sir Sampson.'

'You had information?'

Nicholls nodded. 'Mrs Forster has at last come to fully realise that her loyalty to her brother Jack was misplaced. She admitted that he used her to act as go-between with certain members of the Brotherhood, and she gave up a name. This Mr Courteney has been persuaded to cooperate with our enquiries. It was he who divulged that Champion was to make an attempt on the Duc d'Orléans here in Brighton.'

'That assassination has thankfully been averted.'

'Courteney also revealed that they received instruction from a French aristocrat matching the description of the chevalier.'

'So, it was all the chevalier's doing. I suppose that should have been clear enough to me from the day I observed the assignation on the beach. Without their leader, the Brotherhood is surely broken.' Sheridan sighed. 'I could but wish that De Saint-Gelais had not lured his cousin into his scheming.'

'The baroness?'

Sheridan nodded sadly. 'A passionate creature, whose head might all too easily be turned by the chevalier's notions of heroics.'

'I hear she might have killed you, sir. I should not be so understanding in your place.'

You were not a little in love with her, Constable, Sheridan might have retorted, but he kept the thought unspoken.

Nicholls frowned. 'And yet one thing still puzzles me, Mr Sheridan; we found no Huguenot ancestry in the chevalier's history.'

Sheridan cast about for an explanation. 'Perhaps he merely took advantage of their cause for his own ends. We shall hopefully get to the bottom of the matter now we have him.'

At that moment the doctor emerged from his examination to convey the sad news that he could not hope to stem the internal bleeding. He had treated the other injuries as best he could. The Frenchman's end might be slow but it was inevitable. There was little to be done but to keep the patient comfortable.

'Comfort be damned!' the prince exclaimed. 'That devil was all set to murder us.'

Townsend was ordered to interrogate De Saint-Gelais forthwith.

Sheridan asked that he might be present and received a curt rebuffal. 'This is no business for a playwright, Mr Sheridan.'

Nursing his disappointment, Sheridan retreated to his chamber to divest himself of his tattered costume. He must let the officers of the law do their work and trust that Jack Champion would be apprehended soon. His actions had undoubtedly saved the Duc d'Orléans from assassination, though none had thought to commend him for his bravery. They were all still astonished by the events of the evening, he supposed, and for the moment all attention was focused on the chevalier.

Sheridan suddenly found that he was shivering. The shock of his close call with death not once, not twice, but three times in quick succession had all at once caught up. With a shaking hand he poured a bumper of brandy, pulled a blanket around him and slumped onto his bed. For all that he relished drama — more than most, he could safely claim — this evening had seen an excess of thrills. His heart fluttered in his breast. He took a deep breath and downed his drink in one.

Images of Marceline assailed him. He felt an acute sense of bewilderment and betrayal which led to no other conclusion but that she had fully intended to dispatch him. But there had been a moment, he felt sure, when he had sensed a genuine regret before her attempt on his life. Was that merely a wishful fancy? He had wanted to believe that he was her hero, that she had admired him above other men, that her avowed devotion was sincere. It had been, surely? There had been no subterfuge. What end would it have served? Her mission had clearly been to keep Orléans close and to lay the way for his assassination. Sheridan was of no real consequence, a mere bystander to their machinations. No. Her feelings for him had been true, he assured himself. It was only that her passion was eclipsed by a greater desire. Revenge.

Sheridan paused.

Marceline was a Huguenot. She had seemed like a woman possessed, in the grip of a fury when she had clasped the sign of her religion, the Huguenot Cross. It was her ancestors, not her cousin's, who had been cruelly persecuted by a tyrant. It was she who had nurtured a thirst for revenge in her bosom from childhood. She who had been coerced to marry an aged baron at scarcely sixteen. The Revolution of 1789 had merely unleashed the forces which might bring such vengeance about. She had been no innocent dupe at all. There had always been something inherently wild about Marceline — hadn't that been a part of the attraction from the first? Part of his nature could even find sympathy with the motives which propelled her — the Irish self, he supposed, which had always been dangerously drawn to the outcast and the rebel. Sheridan heaved a sigh. He rather hoped that she had made good her escape.

As he was refilling his glass, there came a soft rap at the door.

'Enter,' he called.

A servant appeared.

'What is it, Jenkins?'

'I am sorry to disturb you, sir, but you were a friend to Sir Roderick…'

'In a manner … I daresay.'

'Only, he is going to be laid out in the cellars before removal to his family. He is still in costume, and I am sent to fetch his suit.' The servant indicated the clothing he held in his arms.

'And?'

'And there is a note stuffed in the waistcoat. I did not know who to give it to, sir.'

'Is it not addressed?'

Jenkins shook his head. 'I don't rightly know, sir. It is in French. I thought you might…?'

'Of course, let me take a look.' Sheridan waved the manservant over.

Jenkins held a scrap of paper in his hand, which Sheridan took and unfolded. Scrawled in Howgill's hand in French was a date, the morrow — no, it was gone midnight, it should be that very day, and one word: *L'Amphitrite*. Sheridan strained to sieve through his French vocabulary, but it was decidedly blank on the meaning of *L'Amphitrite*. And then in a flash it came to him: it was all Greek! Not a French name, but a Greek goddess, the wife of Poseidon. But where did that get him? He was none the wiser.

But there was one man who might know the meaning — the chevalier.

Sheridan leapt from the bed. 'Thank you, Jenkins! Can you help me dress? Quick as we can — this is most urgent!'

Sheridan knocked peremptorily on the door of the poultry room. After some moments the door was opened a little by one of Townsend's men, a local watchman.

'I must speak at once with the chevalier,' Sheridan commanded as he pushed through the entrance.

A strong whiff of game came from the brace of pheasants and other birds hanging on hooks around the chill room and assailed Sheridan's nostrils as he entered.

Townsend glowered at the interruption. 'Mr Sheridan, your reasons for intruding on my investigation had better be substantial or there shall be consequences, by Jupiter!'

'And do you get anywhere, Mr Townsend?'

The officer's lips set in a tight, thin line.

From the table where the chevalier was laid out came a strangled laugh and an accompanying groan.

'You do not, I hazard.'

Constable Nicholls ventured, 'The chevalier refuses to talk, sir. If Mr Townsend will allow, perhaps you might be able to persuade him otherwise.'

Townsend cast a sharp eye at Nicholls to silence him.

Nicholls kept the eye of the Principal Officer. 'Mr Sheridan has shown an aptitude for interrogation, sir.'

Townsend grunted and stood aside. 'The stage is all yours, Mr Sheridan.'

Sheridan took a deep breath and approached the young French nobleman, the pallor of his face in stark contrast with his luscious dark locks.

'You are made as comfortable as possible I hope, Chevalier?' Sheridan swallowed hard. 'The pain must be unconscionable.'

A glimmer of a sarcastic smile crept across the chevalier's face as he turned to confront Sheridan. 'You would make it worse, is that your method, Sherrie?'

'No, of course not. And no one could ever doubt your bravery, Chevalier. I would alleviate your suffering. You may ease yourself into sleep; there is laudanum to hand, if you will only tell us where we might find Jack Champion.'

The chevalier's smile broadened and then fell into a grimace of pain. 'I will not.'

'I know you to be a man of honour, sir. But in recruiting adventurers like Jack Champion, you do not serve a worthy cause. Champion is not a man of honour. Give him up, I beg you.'

'You know nothing, Monsieur Sheridan.'

'The Brotherhood is finished.'

The chevalier closed his eyes and shook his head. 'It is just begun. It is not I who lead the cause.'

'Then who?' Townsend cut in, charging towards the wounded man and striking his baton against the edge of the table.

The chevalier's smirk twisted into a mask of agony.

Townsend turned to Sheridan. 'You waste our time, I fear, Mr Sheridan.'

Sheridan hung his head. Townsend was right; he was getting nowhere. How should he get any information from the chevalier that made sense, never mind wrest the meaning of *L'Amphitrite*? And then he was struck, as though by epiphany. He stared at the chevalier. Could it be that he already knew the answer? 'Your leader ... Orléans...'

Townsend snorted. 'The Duke of Orléans plans his own assassination?'

'No, interesting notion though that may be...'

'Then what nonsense is this?'

'Perhaps the Maid of Orléans...'

Nicholls started. 'Jeanne d'Arc?'

Sheridan nodded slowly. A young girl in armour, her hair shorn to a mannish crop. A maid who was a leader of men, courageous and without fear. Marceline LeClaire.

The chevalier's eyes flickered. 'Not quite the fool —' his breath slowed and rattled — 'I took you for.' The chevalier's eyes rolled and he passed into unconsciousness.

There was a moment of silence punctuated only by the strangled breath of the young man, and then Townsend, casting a look of fury, moved to lay his hands on the chevalier to force him back to consciousness.

Sheridan stretched out to stop him. 'Leave him, Townsend. Damn it all, leave him. De Saint-Gelais will never betray his cousin's safety.'

Townsend frowned. 'You are saying it is the baroness that is at the head of this Brotherhood? We must find her at once!'

Sheridan nodded. He pulled Howgill's note from his pocket. 'Sir Roderick left this. A codename, perhaps … and something that may happen today.'

Townsend snatched the note and scanned the contents. 'The Amphitrighty?'

'Amfeetrighty?' the local watchman exclaimed.

All heads snapped in his direction.

The local man shifted awkwardly at the sudden attention. 'It is a ship, sir. French. One that frequently makes passage to and from Brighthelmstone across the Channel.

Sheridan's eyes glittered. 'Townsend, send one of your men to find out when this ship might next be anchored here. I'll warrant it will be today.'

The local man stepped forward. 'Oh no, sir, it arrived yesterday, and will leave with cargo and passengers on the high tide.'

'What time should that be?'

'Why, it should be at any moment, sir.'

'Devil take it!'

CHAPTER THIRTY-NINE

The lanterns of *L'Amphitrite* twinkled in the distance where the brig sat at anchor. It was a clear, starry night, dark under a moon that had scarcely begun to wax. On the far horizon, a sharp eye might just make out a bank of clouds, roiling up and rolling in with a gathering speed. The calm stillness of the waters was giving way to a gradual rise in the waves that dropped upon the shingle.

They had hurtled down the Steyne with all haste, lanterns swinging, and had been forced to veer around a cart which blocked their way. Then they had lurched across the pebbled foreshore with renewed urgency. Casting about in the gloom, one of Townsend's men sprinted ahead to find there was a rowing boat at the water's edge which was making ready to ferry across to the French merchant ship. This lay some distance away, there being no harbour or jetty at Brighton.

A grizzled sailor and his young helper grumbled and swore as they stowed and secured the last of the luggage and cargo that needed to be transported. They nodded out to sea to indicate the boat which ferried passengers. It had only just set off and could be seen cresting over the incoming waves.

'And Champion is on board, I'll be bound!' Townsend thumped his fist into his palm.

The sailor continued to mutter his gripes that the lady had caused no end of lag and fuss in the transfer of goods from her cart. *L'Amphitrite*'s captain would be in a filthy temper at these delays, the man snorted, and he should not be at all surprised if the captain were to set sail with neither of these last passengers nor their baggage if they did not hurry.

The sailor jerked his head towards the horizon. 'The tide is already on the turn. Captain Lefebvre, he won't like to tarry long, and the weather is also for changing! She's a sprightly rig and he'll want to outrun any storm that might be brewing.'

'You must take us with you!' Townsend commanded.

''T'ain't possible, sir. We're loaded to the gunnels.'

'We are officers of the law, my man — there is a villain that would flee on that ship and his escape shall be prevented!'

'We'll like as drown.' The sailor dug his heels in.

Townsend looked at his men in a fury. 'Here, throw this cargo overboard.' Townsend confronted the old salt before he could object. 'You shall make room for us or know the consequences. The magistrates will answer for my actions.'

'All of you?' the sailor wailed as he watched his carefully stowed crates and packages hurled from within the vessel onto the beach.

Townsend spun around to Constable Nicholls. 'Nicholls, you are to stay here on duty and await our return.'

'And I, Townsend?' Sheridan stepped forward impetuously.

Townsend grunted in response. 'I thank you, sir, for the part which you have played, but we have no further need of your service.' He turned back towards the sailor. 'Damn it, that should be enough. Come, we must not risk that the ship ups anchor.'

As the craft was hauled into the surf, Townsend jumped aboard before his feet should get too wet.

'Damn and blast!' Sheridan slapped his thigh in frustration.

Nicholls shrugged and backed away from a surge of seawater. 'Townsend is right. They are already laden. All that we can do, sir, is wait.'

Sheridan wheeled around and groaned. 'Whoever said that patience is a virtue never wanted for anything.'

The lid of one of the crates had broken open. The edge of a rug was discernible and the Runner picked out a silver candlestick. 'Someone is moving their home, by the looks of it.' He shook his head in bemusement. 'That is contrary to the usual flow of refugees, if they settle in France.'

'They have good reason, I believe,' Sheridan said with a snort. He glanced about at the cargo strewn on the tideline. 'I should take stock of these goods, Constable — you may find that all are ill-gotten.'

'What do you know of this, Mr Sheridan?' The Bow Street Runner's eyes narrowed with suspicion.

Before Sheridan might feel obliged to respond, Nicholls was hailed by a parish watchman rushing towards him from the town.

Sheridan's own attention was distracted by the arrival of a fishing boat along the beach, one of the distinctive hoggies of the local fishermen. The rig of square sails was being furled and the hog boat rode in on the waves to crunch up onto the shingle. Sheridan recognised the man working on deck, his features snatched by the swaying lantern. It was young Mr Gimmell. The other fisherman leapt out of the vessel and rushed up the beach, carrying a coil of rope to loop around the capstan which would winch the flat-bottomed boat up above the tideline. A sudden thought assailed Sheridan.

'Mr Gimmell!' Sheridan ran towards the hog boat, splashing through the surf. 'A word, if you please! Mr Gimmell!'

Sheridan gulped deep breaths of salty air as he clung to the mast. The red sails of the hog boat's spritsail rigging unfolded, and with her bluff bows the craft was able to rise up over the incoming waves and spring forward. *The Dotty* sped along before the wind that was picking up, despite her heavy cargo of men and fish.

Sheridan had pleaded with young Gimmell to turn his craft around and make after the boats which were being rowed out to the ship at anchor.

Gimmell shook his head. 'Mr Sheridan, we have made a large catch this night which must be unloaded for the market.'

'I can pay you, sir.'

'We are first of the night's fishing and I can sell the lot. There is cod and —'

'Mr Gimmell, I shall purchase it all.'

At that moment Nicholls hurried to their side with the watchman hot on his heels and gasping for breath.

'Gabriel Gimmell. Stop! You must turn about to sea!' The parish officer waved his arms wildly. 'I've found the ferrymen Jemmy and Amos trussed up; Jemmy is near done for by the villains.'

Young Gimmell's eyes opened wide in shock. 'My cousin Jemmy?'

The watchman nodded, struggling to speak. 'Ambushed, robbed of their clothes and their boat taken.'

Nicholls grasped hold of Sheridan. 'Jack Champion — he is not a passenger but is disguised as the ferryman. If he reaches L'Amphitrite, the rogue shall slip aboard and it will be the devil to find him before this captain sails.'

Gabriel Gimmell shouted to his crewman and then all sprang into action.

Sheridan and Nicholls secured their place on board. The parish watchman, a cordwainer by trade more often to be found at his lapstone, had experienced enough shocks for one night and volunteered to stay on land to guard the luggage.

Now here they were tacking away from the shore as the sea began to swell around them. The hold was crammed and overflowing with the creatures of the deep. Sheridan was disconcerted to see that some still retained a vestige of life and one large fish flapped onto the deck before fixing him with its eye. The crewman busily moved back and forth from bow to stern. Gimmell shouted out his instruction as he tried to catch every shift in the wind that was rising to make headway in pursuit of the rowing boats. Nicholls squeezed up beside Sheridan, who was perched on a mound of netting, some smaller fish still caught in the gillnets. The officer gulped and put his hand to his mouth. Sheridan fancied he saw a greenish tinge to the young constable's face.

'You are not a sailor then, Nicholls?'

Nicholls shook his head. 'I have had no occasion to be at sea before, sir.'

'We are in good hands, I think, with young Mr Gimmell. These boats have a remarkably broad beam, I am told, which makes them very steady in a rough sea.'

'Steady?' Nicholls groaned.

They could hear the timbers creaking and the sails straining overhead.

'He pushes her, but she will not capsize.'

'I am glad to hear it, for I cannot swim.'

Across the churning waves they heard a voice shouting up ahead. It was Townsend.

Sheridan jerked himself up onto his feet, clutching the mast, his court shoes unsteady on the slick decking. He peered into the pitch. A swinging lantern identified Townsend's craft; it must be gaining on the other rowboat, with the passengers bound for *L'Amphitrite*. Sheridan felt certain he knew who those passengers might be. Mistress Dearlove, her brother Ezekiel Brough and Sylvain, together with Monsieur Danton and the boy, Billy.

He could hear now that Townsend was issuing threats and warnings as he called for the ferryboat to pull in its oars.

No response could be discerned. The ferrymen continued their progress to the French vessel.

Townsend shouted again, with more insistence.

This time there came a reply. The crack of gunshot fractured the air.

CHAPTER FORTY

Another shot followed almost immediately from a second musket. *The Dotty* was sailing close enough that Sheridan could hear the curses of the old salt. A hole had been blown through the bow of the boat. The vessel being as laden as it was, the breach was dangerously on the waterline. The sailor yelled at Townsend's men to throw another crate overboard to lighten their load and swore that he and his fellow would row no further in pursuit of such murderous coves.

Townsend swore bloodier oaths in turn. Sheridan saw the flash from his Brown Bess as the officer aimed towards the boat that was pulling ahead in the darkness. Within seconds he had reloaded the musket and fired again. A faint cry in the distance suggested that Townsend had hit his mark.

Glimmers of the new day had appeared to the east as a tumult of thoughts hurtled through Sheridan's mind. Who had fired the shots? Not Champion, if he and his comrade continued to row throughout the altercation.

Nicholls scrambled awkwardly to his feet beside him.

'It is Battling Poll!' Sheridan said aloud. 'She recognises Townsend and believes that she has been betrayed to the Runners.'

Nicholls scowled, 'I wondered what part you had played in her flight, sir. Jedidiah came to me the day before my journey here; I had an inkling then.'

'The children are safe? And Dorcas?' Sheridan asked anxiously.

'Yes, the children are cared for.' Anger flashed in the constable's eyes. 'We shall speak on this matter later, Mr

Sheridan. For now, we have more pressing business, and I have no firearm, only my cutlass.'

They were sailing up behind Townsend, and in the light afforded by their lantern Sheridan could see that the patrolmen were desperately ditching the last of Poll's cargo. Townsend himself had taken off his jacket in an attempt to plug the breach in the bow. All the while he berated the two sailors to put their backs into the oars or they should find themselves before the magistrates. The men rowed but their efforts seemed to produce little in the way of forward movement.

'Do you need assistance, Townsend?' Nicholls called over as the hog boat drew in behind them.

'Nicholls, you must cut them off!' Townsend cried as he waved the sailing vessel on. In the gloom it was difficult to make out his features, but Sheridan imagined them to be enraged.

'Mr Gimmell,' Sheridan called back over his shoulder, 'we must try to warn the *L'Amphitrite.*'

Gabriel grimaced. 'I doubt we could keep out of the range of their firearms, sir, to get by them.' He nodded towards the rosy tips of dawn edging over the horizon.

Sheridan clutched at his hair in frustration. He could not ask the fishermen to risk their lives. It seemed that Battling Poll would prove an unwitting guardian to Jack Champion.

'I have but one course, Mr Sheridan. You do best to keep your head down, and the constable.'

Gabriel Gimmell shifted the tiller until *The Dotty* was making directly for the faint outline of the ferryboat ahead. With the wind whipping into the sails, she fairly leapt forward.

Sheridan stared in horror at the young fisherman. 'You mean to ram her?'

Gimmell nodded. 'Jemmy is my cousin, sir. If he is done for by these villains, they will not escape me — and their muskets shall be of little use in seawater.'

Sheridan gulped. 'I have reason to believe that there is a child on board, Mr Gimmell, whose life is of great value to me.'

Gabriel's face fell as he digested this information and his grip on the tiller loosened. 'Then all is in vain.'

Sheridan's mind raced. He was certain that Mistress Dearlove and her brother Ezekiel had fired the shots at Townsend. Champion in his disguise as the ferryman would act as though he and his fellow were petrified to find themselves rowing a brace of villains out to *L'Amphitrite* and make show of rowing all the faster. But, if Champion believed that the pursuit by the Runners was to apprehend Poll Dearlove and nothing at all to do with his own escape, then his guard might be down. How could this be turned to advantage?

A thought came to Sheridan. *The Dotty* was a local fishing boat; if he and Nicholls lay on the deck and remained out of sight, the hog boat could approach as though merely going about its usual business of fishing. It could get near enough that Gimmell might hail them in some way that would alert Monsieur Danton to the danger on board. Champion would likely be keen to complete that assassination, having failed in his attempt on Orléans. If only Sheridan could somehow apprise Danton of the situation.

He turned to Gabriel Gimmell. 'Perhaps all is not quite lost...'

He quickly communicated as much of a plan as he could muster to Gimmell. The young fisherman nodded agreement at once. He would tack out and then sail across in front of the ferry and pretend to be dropping nets; when in range, Gabriel should call over to his *cousin* as Sheridan instructed.

The waves heaved beneath them as *The Dotty* mustered all speed. Sheridan and Nicholls splayed on the deck of the hog boat, a rough cloth laid over them for added concealment. The smell of salt and fish was strong in Sheridan's nostrils and he tried not to think of the blood and guts which mixed with the sea spray sluicing up and down the boards and ruining a very decent frockcoat. Constable Nicholls had a hand across his mouth, muffling the low moans of increasing nausea.

It was fear that Sheridan gulped down. Young Billy Legge was still in the hands of one wicked villain whilst another, a murderous fanatic, was dangerously unpredictable.

The Dotty came around and the crewman began to reef the sails. Gimmell waved an arm in greeting towards the ferry. 'Ahoy! Jemmy!'

There was no response, only the sound of the oars dipping steadily into the brine.

From his prone position on the deck, Sheridan signalled to Gimmell to repeat the salutation.

'Ahoy, Jemmy — a message from our grand dam.'

There was a pause and then a grunted greeting came across the water in reply. Champion would try to bluff this encounter.

'Most upset she be.' Gimmell laughed as directed.

His crewman made a show of readying the nets.

Gabriel persisted. 'I am to tell you a fox is amongst the geese. And this fox is a villain if ever there was one.'

Sheridan prayed that Danton's ears were pricked now. He nodded encouragement up to Gimmell.

The fisherman shouted across the water. 'Her favourite is lamed by this devil.'

Another grunt came in reply.

'We're to lend a hand, Jemmy — she fears for the young.' Gimmell laughed again.

A guttural laugh came in response.

Gabriel gave a final wave and turned away to join his fellow on the other side of the hog boat.

Sheridan held his breath. He could hear the oars dipping in and out of the waters. The ferryboat was about to pass them on its route towards *L'Amphitrite*. Then a familiar stentorian voice spoke in French.

'Sylvain, you must persuade madame. Sadly, her brother does not survive his gunshot wound. It is time to bid *adieu*. Mr Brough must be slipped beneath the waves. If not, Captain Lefebvre will want to know why one of his passengers is a corpse.'

Sylvain's plea was cut short by Poll. 'I know what the monsieur says.' There came a moaning wail from her, then a moment of silence, followed by a barked order. 'You men, still the oars. Let us be done with my poor brother Ezekiel.'

The oarsmen obeyed.

'Sylvain can assist you,' Danton suggested. 'Send the boy up to me, madame. He has had fright enough.'

'These men at oars can... And I am minded...'

Sheridan pushed the canvas covering aside with frustration and strained his head as far as he dared to catch the drift of Poll's words.

'...Billy as surety.'

The sounds of movement on the boat came, and then there were grunts of exertion. Sheridan assumed the boatmen were lifting Ezekiel's body, which they must have weighted.

'Farwell, my brother,' Poll intoned solemnly. 'Forgive this end. God give you peace.'

These last rites were followed by the splash of the body as Ezekiel Brough was delivered into the waves. Up ahead, a ship's bell began to clang the three bells of the Morning Watch, as though to add finality to the occasion.

The ferrymen resumed their positions and took up the oars.

'Monsieur Danton,' Poll addressed herself again to the Jacobin, 'some conk 'as squealed, else why are we being pursued by Mr Townsend? Are you one that deals treachery? Am I to be handed into chains on board the ship?'

Danton heaved a great sigh of exasperation. 'Madame Dearlove, please consider if you will. If they wait with chains on *L'Amphitrite*, then why does the Runner try to stop this boat? Would the officer shoot when there is a child with us? It is because Mr Townsend does not know there is a boy. He does not know that you are on this boat. He seeks another villain.'

'What other villain, pray tell? Unless it is yourself you speak of.'

'The one who sits in front of you, madame. The man at whose back I have aimed my pistol, and who will please raise his arms very slowly above his head.'

Bravo! Sheridan felt a surge of relief. Perhaps now should be the time for he and Nicholls to show themselves? Cautiously, Sheridan pulled himself up so that he could peer over the side of the hoggie. The rowing boat was drifting just ahead of them. In the faint glow of early dawn, he could make out Danton sitting in the prow wedged up against the samson post, his pistol aimed at the back of the taller oarsman. Poll also held a flintlock, but hers was pressed to Billy's chest.

'This sailor?' Poll snorted, waving her firearm towards the ferryman. 'What game is this you play, monsieur?'

'Why, Fox and Geese. And it appears the silly gooses have caught Renard.'

The man who was pretending to be the ferryman had ceased rowing and raised his arms above his head as ordered. He stood, looked between Mistress Dearlove and Danton, then shrugged as though to signal his innocent, befuddled incomprehension to both parties. A knitted cap was drawn low over his brow, but he could not disguise a shifty quickness in his eyes. Sheridan recognised Jack Champion at once.

Battling Poll frowned, unsure who she might trust, and looked across to Sylvain seated beside Danton for some further prompt.

Champion's movements as he stood in the centre of the craft had started a gentle rocking of the boat. He now lurched heavily from side to side, crouching low, increasing that momentum rapidly as he made a grab for the pistol in Poll's hand.

All was sudden confusion. Sylvain instinctively sprang forward, calling out a warning to Poll. His action only added to the sway of the boat; he lost his footing on the bench, was pushed by the second oarsman, and slipped overboard with a despairing cry.

Sheridan could see that Danton tried to brace himself against the tilting motion of the boat, but all was movement and he cursed loudly as he grappled to keep his pistol trained on Champion. Jack wrestled for the firearm held in Poll's grasp, all the while turning her about so that she shielded him from Danton's aim.

'Mistress Dearlove,' Champion shouted into her ear, 'we mean you no harm. It is the traitor Danton who must die. Then we can all make good our escape. Please, I beg you, surrender your pistol!'

Billy had broken free of Poll's grasp in the melee and was scrambling up the boat, his eyes fastened on Danton. The other ferryman, a slight fellow, snatched Billy around the waist, yanking him to the middle of the rocking boat. Sheridan paled as he caught the glint of a knife.

'Monsieur Danton, drop your weapon or it is the boy who will die!'

Sheridan's heart plummeted. His worst fear was realised. There was no attempt at disguise in Marceline's voice as she uttered her threat, and he knew she was very capable of carrying it out.

'Mr Gimmell — now!' Sheridan hissed.

Already primed, Gabriel and his crewman leapt to place *The Dotty*'s oars in the tholes. Sheridan nudged the waiting Nicholls. The constable half crawled, keeping low, as he moved up to the prow, cutlass in hand, his eye searching out Champion. Sheridan hurriedly divested himself of the ruined frockcoat. He clutched at the side of the hog boat and waited for impact, his gaze fixed on the wide-eyed boy and the knife at his throat.

The Dotty surged forward and within half a dozen powerful strokes rammed into the side of the ferry. With a splintering of timber, the loose oar was smashed and the boat knocked sideways.

At the moment of impact, a number of events happened all at once. Billy and his captor were hurled together into the sea. Poll and Jack catapulted forward into the belly of the boat, with the flintlock at last secured by Champion, whilst Danton's great bulk slumped backward into the prow. Nicholls leapt onto the swaying craft, cutlass in hand, and Sheridan dived into the dipping waves.

When Sheridan resurfaced, gasping from the shocking chill of the sea, he looked about frantically. Treading water, he tried to raise his view above the waves. Yes, there they both were!

Thrashing and flailing in the open water. Billy's spluttered cries of panic rent the air. Marceline struggled to keep a grip on the squirming boy as his head dipped below the surface.

Sheridan struck out in their direction, his heart pounding as he swam. He could hear shouts and commotion coming from the ferryboat and then the deafening blast of gunfire. All he could do was offer up a quick prayer for the safety of Constable Nicholls. He had one sole purpose. Another stroke and then he was within easy reach. Billy, his mouth spilling seawater, was desperately gasping for air. The knife was clutched tight in Marceline's hand as she tried to keep them both from slipping under the rolling waves.

'Marceline!'

'*Mon* Sherrie!' Marceline managed a sharp laugh of surprise as she recognised the man bobbing before her in the sea. 'You have a talent for unexpected entrances.'

'You must give yourself up. The child — let me have him.'

The knife flashed as the baroness considered Sheridan with her arresting violet eyes.

'Marceline,' Sheridan spluttered. 'The boy is a rascal and has been a sore obligation to me — but there is one who loves him very much.'

Sheridan could see that *The Dotty* had swung about and was approaching cautiously.

'It is all up for the Brotherhood — let me plead your case; it was the chevalier who forced you to these actions,' he promised in desperation.

'*Petite* Pierre…' She shook her head sadly but dismissively. '*Non*, Sherrie, it is the cause for which I have always lived.'

'Marceline!' Sheridan cried out again in anguish.

'The boy — take the boy.' The baroness managed a smile. 'I always knew you for a hero, *mon* Sherrie.'

Marceline thrust Billy towards him and then she disappeared beneath the waves.

The boy thrashed wildly as he too slipped below the surface. Sheridan kicked down. Through the murky gloom his eyes desperately sought out the small, sinking figure. He stretched out to grab Billy's writhing frame. Clasping him tight, he pushed them both back up to the surface. He heaved in great lungfuls of air. The boy felt limp in his arms. Treading water, Sheridan shook him and as best he could in the choppy seas, pounded at his back. After a few heart-stopping moments, a spume of seawater and a strangled cough brought a return of hope.

'I have you now, Billy. You are safe.'

A silver-gold ray of light splintered the eastern horizon. The sea sparkled. Mr Gimmell was close at hand, throwing a rope towards them, then pulling them in and reaching down for the boy. Sheridan clambered back on board to the welcome safety of the little hoggie. As he righted himself on deck, was he deceived or did he catch sight of a figure swimming towards the shore? Marceline, could it be? Forlorn, he stood and yearned that even now it might be so.

The hog boat sailed in close to *L'Amphitrite*. Men were clambering through the rigging as the mainsail unfurled.

'Ahoy!' Gimmell shouted.

A sailor hollered back. '*Ficher le camp!*'

Gimmell shook his head and cried out for a ladder. They could all hear the sound of the windlass as the anchor was being raised.

A large, bearded man looked over the rail and regarded the small sailing craft below. He reiterated the injunction to be gone.

The bulky figure of Danton rose up from the prow of the small fishing boat. 'Citizen Lefebvre!' he roared. '*Vive La France! Vive La Revolution!*'

The man suddenly bellowed in amazement. 'Citizen Danton! Citizen Danton *é arrivé!*'

He turned away and shouted orders. A rope ladder was flung over the side, Gimmell quick to seize it.

The young fisherman signalled to Battling Poll. 'Mistress, quick, you must make haste.'

Poll clutched a bag to her side and lurched towards the ladder.

Nicholls stretched out a hand. 'Here, allow me, Mistress Dearlove…' He nodded to the bag. 'I think you will do better without this encumbrance.'

Poll glowered as she reluctantly handed over the small valise.

Nicholls felt its surprising weight and heard with satisfaction the jangle of coin and other riches within.

He nodded curtly to the treasure still worn on her fingers. 'You have a chance to do good, madame. Take it. I do not want to regret this decision.'

Sylvain grinned, wringing the last of the seawater from his jacket between his powerful fists. 'A school for pugilists — that shall be our plan, eh, *chérie?*' He tugged the garment back on before following his mistress up the ladder.

'Thank you, Constable Nicholls.' Sheridan slapped the Bow Street Runner on the shoulder.

Nicholls grunted. 'I daresay Battling Poll has saved my life.'

'I should like to have seen her in action.'

'It was a sight, Mr Sheridan. Champion scarce knew what hit him. She dealt a fearsome uppercut and no mistake. Caught him squarely on the jaw. His head shot back — reeling, he was, with such a stunned expression as to be almost comical. And then he collapsed onto the monsieur, causing the pistol to discharge into his back, straight through his heart, I should say. Most unfortunate…' Nicholls trailed off and shook his head in disappointment. 'I would have liked to see that blaggard hang.'

'Better he should be forgotten, Louis-Pierre. There are those who might make a martyr of him, as though he acted from conviction, when in truth he was a self-serving wretch.'

Sheridan regarded Monsieur Danton as he spoke. He had not yet determined whether the Frenchman might also fit this description. But in one true sense Georges Danton differed from the villainous Harlequin. The Jacobin had a heart, a very large heart, which at that moment he was using to comfort the frightened, shivering child gathered to his breast beneath his capacious coat.

CHAPTER FORTY-ONE

The funeral of Sir Roderick Howgill was a private affair held at the small chapel on the grounds of the family estate of Bedfont. His mother, Alice, Lady Howgill held her two younger sons close on either side and contained her grief with admirable fortitude.

As the congregation moved sedately towards the interment in the ancestral crypt, Sheridan found himself joined in step by Henry Dundas.

'I hear you were with young Howgill at the end, Sheridan,' the Home Secretary intoned with the soft burr of his native Edinburgh.

Sheridan nodded.

Dundas heaved a sigh. 'Sir Roderick was a brave young man; he died in the service of his country.'

'A pity none should know it.'

'Howgill would have understood. As you must understand too, Mr Sheridan. These are troubling times and sparks may yet fly from the bonfires that have been lit across the Channel.'

'So, you would stamp out the radical voice, Dundas, and all reasonable calls for reform with it?'

'We take precautions.' Dundas pursed his lips. 'And you must agree that this affair of the Huguenot Brotherhood should not be broadcast.'

Sheridan had indeed arrived at that same conclusion, if perhaps for different reasons. 'The Huguenots are a settled and peaceable community and certainly should not be viewed as scapegoats for your King and Church mobs — who seem to need little encouragement to be stirred to riot and violence.'

Dundas raised an eyebrow at the barb. 'Thankfully this Brotherhood is a limited affair, a society of fanatics, their tempers fired up by the Revolution. They seized upon the chance for acts of revenge against the monarchy of France and were willing to resort to mayhem and assassination.'

'I still do not understand why they sought to put Sir Roderick in the frame for the assassination?'

'A clever ploy, Mr Sheridan. Not only would they be rid of the Duc d' Orléans, but they also hoped to undermine and damage any chance of rapprochement between the new French Legislature and the British Government. Orléans would be hailed as a martyred hero of the French Revolution assassinated by an agent of the British Government, implying that Mr Pitt is really in cahoots with the émigrés who threaten war and counter-revolution. Without Orléans as an alternative to that unfortunate Louis, France will be edged closer to declaring a republic.'

'Is the threat over?'

Dundas nodded uncertainly. 'We must remain vigilant, but I believe so. We have rounded up the remaining members in London. They were largely known thugs, such as that man Rivers who fell from the roof in Spitalfields, or young adventurers, like your Mr Champion. Fair game to promises of standing and property in the new world of a French republic.'

'He always fancied himself in a gentleman's outfit, from what I gather.'

Dundas sneered. 'We are told Champion fell for the charms of the baroness and she encouraged his slavish attachment. Perhaps he saw some opportunity with her.'

'Handsome Jack…'

'The baroness was a fanatic, Sheridan. It appears that one of her ancestors on the maternal side was a Vicomte de Castras, a

Protestant noble, who lost land in the purges and was forced to convert to Catholicism by Louis XIV; however, the family continued secretly in their Protestant faith. The baroness nurtured many grievances against the Bourbon dynasty; in the Revolution she saw opportunities for restitution and revenge. She used the devotion of her cousin, De Saint-Gelais, towards that end.' Dundas snorted. 'She was not a woman afraid to use her charms, from what I have heard.'

Sheridan blanched and swiftly changed the subject. 'You have been cultivating Monsieur Danton, have you not? That was another part of young Howgill's efforts.'

'Danton may be a republican sympathiser, but he is also a man who enjoys the finer things in life and he has expensive tastes. He is a pragmatist. It is no secret that he is corruptible.'

'Immensely charming. I should always prefer a corrupt charmer to a puritan.' Sheridan looked at Dundas. 'Do you really think he might save Louis?'

Dundas looked askance. 'There is always that possibility, provided that the French king will abdicate.'

'And if not?'

'I very much fear that we shall be dragged into a war, Sheridan. Which, I can assure you, Mr Pitt desires no more than you do.'

The day was fine and warm in Isleworth. It was decided to take a picnic down to the riverside, and Eliza had insisted that she was well enough to join the party. Mrs Tucker huffed and shook her head but set about organising rugs and parasols, cushions and shawls. All that might be necessary for Mrs Sheridan's comfort was then transported across the lawns to the riverbank.

Sheridan took his wife's arm and begged her to lean upon him.

'Dick, you are as much a fusspot as Mrs Tucker. I shan't break, you know.'

Up ahead they could see that Tom was already in the river, teaching young Billy to swim. Billy had been uncertain at first, given his recent experience of deep waters, but Tom had teased him in. Now, the rookery rascal seemed keen to demonstrate his newly acquired prowess as he splashed about like a veritable water rat. Sheridan was pleased to note that the boy had begun to plump up with Mrs Tucker's insistence that he be fed on puddings of every kind.

'It seems that this child desires to live.'

Sheridan knew at once that it was not to Billy that his wife referred.

'I am glad of it.' Sheridan patted her arm, although he wasn't at all sure that this should be cause for celebration; he feared for the toll that a continued pregnancy would take on his wife's delicate constitution.

'I have informed Fitzgerald.'

'I see.'

'He insists that he will recognise the child.' Eliza shook her head in exasperation. 'He is most excitable at times, as all Irishmen are, it seems, and I believe he has even written to inform his mother.'

Sheridan felt his stomach lurch. 'Is that what you would wish, my dear? Surely Lord Edward must realise that if he persists, then —'

'— then I shall be considered a social pariah and the infant a bastard, albeit with a duke for a grandfather. Mrs Canning has already discerned the truth of my condition and will not suffer me.'

Eliza did not shy from bald reality, Sheridan had to admit.

'Fitzgerald will provide. He is a man of honour.'

'Perhaps my child does not need a man of honour, but a father.'

Sheridan brought them to a halt and shuffled awkwardly. 'Then ... let it be so.'

Eliza sighed, but he observed that she suppressed a smile. 'Oh, Dick, how can that be? You know yourself to be amongst the most unreliable of men.'

'This is a promise I will keep.' He took his wife's hand. 'Give me this one chance, Eliza, to redeem myself.'

Eliza hesitated.

'It is the only possible course,' Sheridan urged.

She squeezed his hand and nodded slowly.

Sheridan brightened. 'I shall persuade Fitzgerald. And I shall write to Mrs Canning; she shall not be allowed to cut you.'

'You would change the world, wouldn't you, Dick, with a wave of your wand.'

He gave a short chuckle. 'More a slapstick, I fear. But nothing shall hurt you, Eliza, that I vow.'

Billy shouted across to them from the river. 'Did you see, Mr Sheridan? Did you see? I was swimmin'!'

'I saw, Billy. You made a good splash of it.'

The following day Sheridan took Billy to St Thomas's Hospital. Word had been sent ahead and Timothy Legge was dressed and sitting in his bath chair in readiness to greet his ward. Sheridan was pleased to note that the young man had recovered some of his former rude health.

Josiah Legge stepped forward at their approach.

'So this is the boy, is it?' Josiah clapped his hands and beamed widely as he leaned down towards Billy. 'Tow rate, Billy? And shalt tha' com wom wi' us?'

Billy screwed up his face in confusion.

'Mr Legge wishes to know if you are all right, Billy?' Sheridan translated.

'Aye.' Josiah nodded eagerly. 'Well, I must go make arrangements, Mr Sheridan. We may leave at th' end o' week.'

Timothy watched his father depart and then turned shyly to his visitors. 'Billy looks very well, Mr Sheridan. You have taken good care of him, I see. I am most heartily grateful to you.'

'We have Mrs Tucker's pigeon pies and apple puddings to thank for filling him out.'

'And he has been much out of doors, I think.'

'Ah, for that you must thank my son Tom. It is he who has put the colour into Billy's cheeks with their games of cricket and croquet, and he has taught him to swim — Billy is quite the little salamander.'

'Should you like to take a turn in the garden, Billy?'

Billy shrugged. 'If yer like.' He had been eyeing both Timothy and the bath chair with some uncertainty.

Sheridan offered to push the chair and dismissed the porter. They set off along the gravel path, Timothy steering the three-wheeled contraption. Billy lagged behind, kicking at the dirt.

'Constable Nicholls visited. I have heard that my attacker has met his end, and is the same rogue that murdered the poor Harlequin we found in your cellars.'

'The very same. Billy was right — it was the devil that he saw, or rather the devil's work.'

Timothy shook his head. 'He has experienced many horrors for one so young. But I understand from Mr Nicholls that he need have no more fear of Battling Poll?'

Sheridan nodded and grinned. 'That dame has slung her hook.'

Timothy lowered his voice. 'Mr Sheridan, I beg you to give me honest advice. I only want what may be best for Billy. Mr Cline has been admirably blunt; I may not regain full use of my legs, and if I do walk again, it will most certainly be with a crutch. I shall not be much use at cricket or for kicking a ball about. What might such a poor fellow offer? Would Billy do better, do you think, to be amongst other boys at Coram's? And I should then gladly pay for an apprenticeship when he is of age.'

'You have an abundance of affection, my dear Timothy; that is more than enough for any boy you might think to call a son.'

Timothy looked yet to be convinced.

'Let us ask, shall we?' Sheridan called back over his shoulder. 'Billy, what say you? Would you return to your playmates at Coram's? Or should you like to take a ride with Mr Legge in his contraption?'

Sheridan turned the bath chair about to confront the boy.

Billy looked puzzled for a moment.

'I think I can muster a good speed,' Sheridan tempted.

Timothy tentatively opened his arms. Billy grinned and ran to jump onto the frame of the vehicle. Sheridan took a deep breath, dug in his heels and pushed with all his might. Timothy let out a series of whoops as the momentum picked up and he grappled with the steering rod to keep them straight. Billy clutched around Timothy's neck and let out his own loud hoots. A startled nurse jumped from their path as Billy laughed with glee. Sheridan would have joined in with the laughter if he had had any puff left with which to do so.

The balmy days of summer were fast receding. The end of September ushered in a week of grey skies and perpetual rain.

The marriage contract between the Duke of York and the Prussian Princess Frederica had finally been settled, and the marriage took place on the 29th of September in Berlin. It was to be followed by an English ceremony at Buckingham House in November — much to the expressed joy of the king's household, relieved no doubt that at least one of His Majesty's sons had done the right thing. Eyes now turned towards the Prince of Wales; would he follow suit? The issue of his debts giving King George and his government so much leverage in the matter, many speculated that it could only be a matter of time. And Sheridan must privately own that he had colluded with that probability. The prince would be forced to marry a princess of Mecklenburg or Brunswick. The lesser of two evils, he assured himself, whilst fervently hoping that the prince would never discover the part which Sheridan had played in scuppering the negotiations with Orléans.

Monsieur Danton had departed for France with his stepfather. Sheridan wondered whether or not Monsieur Recordain had ever managed to purchase a spinning jenny, the purported object of the visit. The work of the National Assembly in Paris was done. The French had their constitution and Louis XVI was henceforth to be known as a constitutional monarch. Georges Danton was predicted to be a snap-in for the new Legislative Assembly. Sheridan would watch his career with interest. He wondered if their paths might ever cross again.

The Duc d'Orléans had also returned to Paris to join the political fray and, with much noisy ebullience, he had expressed his intention to rename himself in the spirit of the Revolution. After toying with Liberté and then Fraternité, he had declared that he would henceforth be known as Philippe Égalité. Sheridan paused to consider whether that was an altogether wise choice. A man that claimed equality — how should that man become a king? People might rightly begin to wonder, *Why Orléans? Why not another man? Why have a king at all?*

There were times over the past two years when Sheridan had thought that to be a Frenchman in these tumultuous days of change would be a thrilling prospect. Now, he felt that for the moment at least he had had enough of Frenchmen and quite enough thrills to last him a lifetime. He was shortly coming to his fortieth birthday, and instead he should keep Eliza safe. They should look forward to the arrival of the infant and the joy that such an event might restore to their lives together.

A NOTE TO THE READER

Dear Reader,

Fact is invariably stranger than fiction. You couldn't make it up, as they say. Richard Brinsley Sheridan lived a colourful and eventful life which often stretched credulity. It was one of the reasons that I was attracted to him as a young student of Hanoverian England and I wrote my undergraduate dissertation about his early years as a Member of Parliament. Following my own writing and teaching career in theatre, TV and film, when I was considering writing historical crime mysteries, Sheridan leapt centre stage.

I was taken with the idea of using a known historical figure as my sleuth, of embedding elements of real history within a fictional landscape, and here was a man with access to all strata of society, who possessed a lively and enquiring mind, seasoned with a social conscience. I will also admit to the temptation to redeem him a little. Sheridan was beset by many flaws to his character, which I hope I do not shy away from. Certainly, he did not always behave well. He was accused by his detractors of idleness and levity, even of having no depth of feeling. But the more I delved into his life, the more I was struck by his abiding qualities of kindness and generosity towards those in need, particularly children. I encountered a man prone to sentimentality and strong emotional feeling, who was capable of betrayal but also unquestionable loyalty.

Amongst the many biographies which I dipped into, I would recommend Fintan O'Toole's *A Traitor's Kiss* for a rounded view of Sheridan. His book also sharpened my sense of the theme which underpins each of the novels in my series, the tightrope which Sheridan walked between Traitor and Patriot.

I hope that readers may have fun identifying the real historical figures amongst the fictional. The plot of *Harlequin is Dead* was partly inspired by discovering that the larger than life French revolutionary, Georges Danton, spent six weeks in London in the summer of 1791 and next to nothing is known about what he got up to at this pivotal point in the French Revolution. Amongst the secondary characters, those I have a soft spot for include Major Hanger (particularly after I discovered what happened to him in later years) and Lady Letitia Lade, whose story really does beggar belief! I discovered that the secret agent, Nathaniel Parker Forth, has a famous direct descendent, a media tycoon — so there's a bit of detective work for you.

I hope you enjoyed reading the novel, and I thank you for taking the time to do so. Reviews are really important to authors, and if you enjoyed the novel, it would be great if you could spare a little time to post a review on **Amazon** and **Goodreads**. Readers can connect with me online, **www.facebook.com/rosiewriter1** on Facebook and **@rosiewriter** on Instagram and you can find out more about my writing via my website: **https://rmcullenauthor.wordpress.com**

Thank you!

Rose M Cullen

Sapere Books is an exciting new publisher of brilliant fiction and popular history.

To find out more about our latest releases and our monthly bargain books visit our website: **saperebooks.com**